LAMAR'S

FOLLY

LAMAR'S FOLLY

FOLLY

JEFFREY STUART KERR

Texas Tech University Press

This book is typeset in Minion Pro. The paper used in this book meets the minimum requirements of ANSI/NISO Z39.48-1992 (R1997). ∞

Library of Congress Cataloging-in-Publication Data

Names: Kerr, Jeffrey Stuart, 1957– author.
Title: Lamar's folly : a novel / Jeffrey Stuart Kerr.
Description: Lubbock : Texas Tech University Press, [2018]
Identifiers: LCCN 2017039118 (print) | LCCN 2017053529 (ebook) | ISBN 9781682830192 (ebook) | ISBN 9781682830185 (softcover : acid-free paper)
Subjects: LCSH: Lamar, Mirabeau B. (Mirabeau Buonaparte), 1798–1859—Fiction. | Texas—History—Republic, 1836–1846—Fiction. | Quests (Expeditions)—Fiction. | GSAFD: Biographical fiction. | HIstorical fiction.
Classification: LCC PS3611.E76347 (ebook) | LCC PS3611.E76347 L36 2017 (print) | DDC 813/.6—dc23
LC record available at https://lccn.loc.gov/2017039118

18 19 20 21 22 23 24 25 26 / 9 8 7 6 5 4 3 2 1

Texas Tech University Press
Box 41037 | Lubbock, Texas 79409-1037 USA
800.832.4042 | ttup@ttu.edu | www.ttupress.org

For my wife and children, who bring me great joy

Preface

In 1841 Mirabeau Lamar, president of the Republic of Texas, dispatched a trade expedition to Santa Fe, New Mexico. Goods from the interior of Mexico had long flowed northward from that city to the United States. Lamar's stated goal was to divert this rich trade to his new Texas capital at Austin, from which goods would be shipped downriver to the Gulf of Mexico, loaded onto fast ships, and sailed to the East Coast of the United States. Avoiding the long, slow trip over the Santa Fe Trail to St. Louis would reputedly cut the cost of reaching the eastern seaboard in half.

President Lamar, though, sought not only to trade with New Mexico but to annex it. Toward that end an American merchant had already delivered a letter from Lamar to Manuel Armijo, governor of New Mexico, in which the Texas president extolled the financial benefits of a union between the two territories. Among the merchants arriving in Santa Fe would be several commissioners charged with facilitating this happy marriage.

Unfortunately for President Lamar, Governor Armijo saw not a peaceful trade expedition arriving in his city but an armed invasion. Texas and Mexico were still technically at war, as no peace treaty had been signed after the Battle of San Jacinto, the decisive 1836 conflict that caused the withdrawal of all Mexican forces south of the Rio Grande and effectively granted Texas its independence. Adding to the Texans' woes were the severe miscalculations made by planners of the expedition with regard to the difficulty of trekking from Austin to Santa Fe. By the time expedition leader Hugh McLeod and his men got anywhere near their destination, they were little more than a band of starving beggars. Governor Armijo's troops easily rounded them up, clapped them in irons, and marched them to Mexico City.

Mirabeau Lamar's failed attempt at territorial expansion cast long shadows on his legacy as president. This novel is a fictional account of how an otherwise intelligent, capable man might have produced such a disaster. The main players—Mirabeau Lamar, Sam Houston,

Edward Fontaine, and Fontaine's slave Jacob—are real. I have taken liberties with their motivations, character, and private thoughts to create a cautionary tale of hubris and its consequences. As for the facts, in 1838 Edward Fontaine did indeed accompany Mirabeau Lamar on his initial trip to Waterloo, the tiny hamlet that became the city of Austin. Evidence suggests that Jacob may have been there as well. Furthermore, Fontaine did briefly serve as Lamar's private secretary, although not for the extended time period portrayed in this book. Beyond that, the personalities, conversations, and motivations of these men as they appear here are total fiction. Poor Lamar catches the worst of this, for there is no reason to think that the real Lamar ever had an illicit affair or schemed as deviously as my fictional version.

Nevertheless, the framework of this story is little altered from actual events. Mirabeau Lamar did suffer the tragic loss of his wife, Tabitha, and his beloved daughter, Rebecca. Lamar and Sam Houston were indeed not only political but personal enemies, each man carrying a hatred of the other until the day he died. Lamar was the man largely responsible for establishing the Texas capital at Waterloo and founding the city of Austin, with Sam Houston fighting him every step of the way. Thus, my imaginary tale, while straying from the facts in many instances, adheres to them in many others. To defend the inventions, I refer to something I once heard a famous Hollywood director say about his history-inspired films: "I get as close as I can to what actually happened, but I never let truth get in the way of a good story." After writing this book, I now understand what he meant.

LAMAR'S FOLLY

1

Some say that if Mirabeau Lamar hadn't shot the buffalo he wouldn't have become president. Others maintain that the incident never happened. Both are nonsense: the one because a man of Lamar's talents requires no parlor tricks to gain high position, the other because I was there and saw the thing for myself.

That day began so many years ago with the usual breakfast of cold beef and hot coffee. We sat crammed together on crude benches around what passed for a table in Jake Harrell's cabin. Jake called it a table, but the rest of us recognized it as a salvaged wagon bed balanced upon a pair of saw horses. We dared not set our coffee mugs upon this weathered relic, so uneven had the numerous dents and gaps in the warped oak boards rendered its surface. "It's a table as fine as any you'll dine on out here in the wilderness," insisted Jake. "Besides, how many woodshops did you pass on your way here?"

The answer to that question was none. Jake's was one of only four or five houses in all of Waterloo, a meager unincorporated village squatting on the muddy north bank of the upper Colorado River. They really weren't houses either, just the usual drab rectangular log pens thrown up by Texas settlers in those days. Jake had constructed two such pens side by side with a dogtrot in between. One pen provided sleeping quarters for him, his wife, Mary, and his passel of children; the other served as living room, dining room, kitchen, and, as Jake described it, "bawdy house." "Me and Mary couldn't hardly touch each other before I added that bedroom," he said proudly. "Now we can squirrel ourselves away over there whenever we want. Yes, sir, the best thing I ever did was add that room."

Nine of us crowded around the table as Mary hurried to keep our coffee fresh.

Jake, Mirabeau, and I occupied one side. Willis Avery, James Rice, and two men whose names I have forgotten sat opposite us. Young Dan Hornsby and his brother Malcolm squeezed in at either end. A scent of sweat mixed with horse dung drifted through the air as we ate. Though the dawn had barely broken, damp warmth already permeated the room.

"Damn, it's hot," said Avery.

"Watch your mouth, Avery," said Rice. "Jake's wife is standing right there."

"If Willis wants to run his damned mouth, it's all right with me," Mary said.

Everybody but Mirabeau laughed. And, since he was the nation's vice president, his silence weighed heavier than the heat; the laughter quickly died.

The door to the cabin suddenly burst open. Several men spilled their coffee, while Dan Hornsby nearly fell off his stool. "God Almighty, son," Jake hollered at the small boy standing in the doorway. "Is the devil on your heels?"

"Pa! Pa!" the boy shouted. "Buffalo! Thousands of 'em!"

We rushed outside to find that the boy spoke truthfully. Beyond the woods enclosing the settlement black splotches dotted the normally verdant grassland stretching toward the horizon. Clouds of dust rose as gray patches into the sky. A low, soft rumbling echoed against the distant hills as tens of thousands of the great beasts lumbered by. They splashed mindlessly across the Colorado, churning that stream into a sea of mud. A sudden breeze carrying their stench had me longing for the less offensive odor of the cabin interior.

"Come on, boys!" Rice said enthusiastically. "Grab your pistols and let's have at 'em!"

"Pistols?" I asked in surprise.

"Yeah, pistols," Dan Hornsby answered. "It's more sporting than rifles."

"I have no pistols," I said. But no one cared about my armaments, so I ran to the pen and hastily readied my horse. I fetched my rifle from the house, checked its load, and leapt into the saddle. "Let's go, Spirit," I cried, and the wind whipped my face.

We raced away from the river up a muddy ravine into the nearest herd. Two or three men fired pistols, for everyone save me seemed to be so armed. A beast twitched but did not fall. Others already lay dead. When I squeezed the trigger on my rifle the blast almost knocked me from the saddle. As I slowed to regain my balance Mirabeau raced past, spraying me with grass and mud. He pulled a pistol from his belt.

Only then did I see the object of his pursuit, a massive bull standing stubbornly between hunter and fleeing herd. Mirabeau fired at point-blank range; he couldn't have missed the animal's skull, but the creature flinched not a bit. Circling around,

Mirabeau fired twice more with similar results. As he reached for his fourth and final pistol, I saw that look of steely determination on his face that set him apart from other men. I knew the beast was doomed, for what pistols might not accomplish, Mirabeau's iron tenacity would.

I didn't see the final ball strike, but as Mirabeau reined his horse his quarry staggered a bit. Bellowing with fury, the animal broke into a brief trot before collapsing. Rhythmic snorting gave way to isolated gasping breaths, which finally ceased altogether. The buffalo was dead.

Once our companions had satisfied their lust to kill they began gravitating back toward Mirabeau and me. Each gazed with wonder upon Mirabeau's trophy. "That's the biggest damned buffalo I ever saw!" I heard more than once.

Thus was Mirabeau's feat remarkable, not because he had killed the largest buffalo that *I* had ever seen, but because he had killed the largest buffalo ever seen by men with years of experience on the buffalo range. The tale spread quickly. By the time we returned to Houston I heard it on every street corner. While he would have prevailed in that fall's presidential election without it, the epic buffalo hunt helped guarantee Mirabeau's landslide victory. I saw no limits on his horizon but, blinded at the time by the brightness of Mirabeau's flame, I overlooked the diminutive stature of his candle.

2

I called him Mirabeau. I preferred the more respectful "Mr. Lamar," but he would not allow it. "Edward, we are the advance guard of democratic man in this wilderness," he told me. "Such formality between equals only binds us to our despotic heritage." By this, of course, he meant our shared European roots, rather than our shallower American stock. I remained unconvinced until he reminded me that the Savior himself had demanded no honorific. Such was his genius at persuasion. He knew that I, an aspiring Christian theologian, must accept a hint from the Lord as iron law. Thereafter, as he wished, I called him Mirabeau.

His stature as a great man is denied only by scoundrels and fools, with which the world and Texas remain amply supplied. Employing slander, innuendo, and blatant falsehood, certain of his rivals labored ceaselessly to diminish his light. One in particular stands out in my memory. Despite being both drunkard and braggart, this man possessed rare political ability. His depravity, however, allowed him free rein in his role of perpetual antagonist. Yet greatness requires such an enemy, for how would we recognize sin in the absence of virtue? And how would a great man reveal himself except by battling a powerful foe?

Be that as it may, one might wonder why I should bother to put all this to paper so many years after the fact. Many of the story's principal characters, including the chief player himself, have passed into the next world. I can therefore neither stoke their pride nor assuage their guilt. Nor do the sensitivities of their families and friends guide my hand, for I care not what they think of me or my tale. For history's sake, then, one might argue, but the events in question have already been so twisted and distorted by the lies of cheap historians that my own feeble efforts are likely to be ignored.

Why, then, torment myself with performing this useless task? I have asked myself that question countless times, so many, in fact, that one motivation is simply to rid myself of the need to ask it again. Another may be to dampen my own remorse at missing so many opportunities to influence events toward a more successful outcome. And finally, I pray that by telling the story I may finally expunge the tortured thoughts of what might have been in order to rejoice more fully in the blessed reality that is my life.

I first met Mirabeau Buonaparte Lamar in the aftermath of the cataclysm at San Jacinto. Perhaps I should first explain *my* presence at that historic conflict. Months earlier, on a beautiful October day in 1835 I stood under a cluster of swaying pines in a Mississippi churchyard. A warm sun blazed in an azure sky. I was chatting with several acquaintances after services when the topic of Texas arose. At that time Texas remained under Mexican rule, although distant rumblings suggested the temporary nature of that arrangement. A man named Robert Ellis commented, "Why all this talk of Texas? I hear it's nothing but disease-infested swamps, Indians, and deserts. Why, the only reason Mexico has let white men settle there at all is because no Mexican is fool enough to do it!"

Disliking the dogmatic tone in Ellis's voice, I spoke up. "Not so, Robert! I recently read a book by Mrs. Holley and she describes a near-paradise. Fertile fields, gentle streams, temperate climate—she has been there herself to *see*!"

"*Mrs.* Holley?" Robert said scornfully. "And what would a woman know about Texas?"

This was typical Ellis bluster, which he employed because he suspected I might be right. "Robert, her cousin is Stephen Austin. He's the man bringing settlers down from the United States."

"Oh, then of course she *must* be an expert," said Robert. "So tell me, if Mrs. Holley is so convincing, why hasn't my good friend Edward Fontaine joined the exodus to that honeyed land? If it's as wonderful as you say, why remain here with us poor Mississippi farmers?"

I had no answer. Everyone laughed, the group drifted apart, and I remained in the churchyard pondering my humiliation. Ellis had a point. Certainly I had accomplished little in Mississippi. My own father thought me a failure. I was finding it more and more difficult to disagree with him. "One dead-end clerkship after another!" he told me during one of our increasingly stormy arguments. "Have I wasted my money paying for your education?"

"Father, what would you have me do?"

"I'd have you stop wasting your time copying other men's letters! I'd have you take some initiative; have a plan, for God's sake. Or do you figure on flitting from one position to another into old age?"

My mother assaulted my self-esteem as well, albeit in subtler fashion. "Well, there must be something wrong with *him* too," she would say after I had left yet another man's employ. "Someday you'll find him, Edward. Someday you'll find a man *worthy* of your assistance."

I had even failed as a suitor. Molly was young, she was beautiful, and she came from a fine family. I thought she enjoyed my company and I pictured a blissful future with her. But my marriage proposal elicited only nervous laughter and condescension. "Edward, no, I don't think so. But thank you very much for asking."

The more I thought about it, the more I believed I *had* to go to Texas. I was a disappointment to my family, my friends laughed at me openly, and the woman I loved had casually spurned me. Perhaps I could redeem myself in Texas. Furthermore, although I had done little about pursuing one, I aspired to a career in the ministry; somehow I determined that journeying to Texas would bring that dream's fulfillment closer. I was a foolish young man, for only after committing myself to Texas did I learn that Mexican law required all Anglo immigrants to convert to the Catholic faith. Implicit therein was the Mexican government's lack of enthusiasm for Protestant ministers.

In such ignorance I left my latest clerkship, bade farewell to friends and family, and sold my few possessions before traveling to Texas. All save one, that is—a servant called Jacob. Why did I keep him? Although loyal and hardworking, Jacob was of little practical use to me. Father had given him to me with the hope that slave ownership would propel me toward industry and self-sufficiency. "Be a master to another and learn to master yourself," he had said. Out of spite I had meant to sell him, but I hadn't found the courage. So now, to avoid the accusation of squandering yet another opportunity, I took him with me.

Jacob was clever for an African. He was also an excellent horseman. Thanks to his skill in the saddle I had won many wagers with friends who thought their horse faster than mine. Jacob also shared my passion for theology, albeit in more primitive fashion. Whereas I preferred spending time in quiet Bible study, Jacob so animatedly pestered local ministers with questions that one even advised me to whip him. But how could I punish him for religious fervor? And I enjoyed Jacob's company. Maybe this is the real reason I took him along to Texas, although I wouldn't have admitted that in those days. Especially to Father. Anyway, no one, not even Jacob, asked me for a reason.

Jacob begged a favor of me before our departure. He asked to visit his mother and sisters living on a farm about nine miles distant. I consented, of course, touched by the emotion in his voice. To those who say that darkies are less than human I will point to their capacity for the same sentimental longings that complicate our own lives as contradiction. So off he went with my written pass, to return a week later in possession of a silver dollar, claiming it had come from one of his sisters. Any African save Jacob I would have instantly charged with theft, for why would a farmhand have a silver dollar to give away? But I trusted my servant and therefore allowed him to keep it.

I never wanted to go to Texas. Why on God's earth would I want to do that? Leave everything I know and everybody I love and go to a place where there's no regular houses, no churches, no nothing except bears and wildcats and Mexicans and Indians and a lot more to kill a man. I had a mama and three sisters to watch after, God rest 'em, and though I could only see 'em on Sundays and then only if their master said so, I figured God knew what he was about and meant for me to be right there in that place.

At first I thought of running away. But then I thought, just where you gonna go? I knew what they did to runaways and it was bad. You was lucky if all you got was a good whupping. I heard of one man who got his foot chopped off and another that was eaten by dogs. And another man—a boy, really—they hung him from a tree to teach him a lesson. Only they left him up there too long so by the time they cut him down he wasn't breathing no more. So I knew I couldn't be so foolish as to try that because nobody ever got away that I heard of. So like I said I had to go to Texas. Lord, I didn't want to but Master Fontaine, he said off we go, so off we went.

I belonged to Master Fontaine and lucky for me he was a good man. Of course, I had a different notion about belonging than he did, but we still got along. I figured belonging meant he had money and some land and the law on his side, so I had to do what he said. He figured like white men did back then. He figured he owned me like he owned his cows and horses and so he could buy me and sell me and even whip me if he wanted. And he could have, too. It's just that I would have seen it as wrong with the Lord and he would have begged to differ. Anyhow, I never gave him reason to whip me, so we didn't have to argue about that.

My name is Jacob. It's from the Bible and I'm proud of that. A man with a biblical name has something powerful on his side right from the start, I always say. The Bible is with that man even if he don't have one with him. Old Mr. Devil don't like that, either.

Friends call me Jake. Only Mama and Master Fontaine called me Jacob. Mama always said, "I named you 'Jacob.' If I'd wanted to call you 'Jake' I would have named you that, fool!" Of course, she was laughing as she said that. She didn't think I was no fool; she was proud of me because I learned to read on the sly when I was little. That's how I know what's in the Bible and what's not. Master Fontaine called me "Jacob" because, well, because he always did so. He was just that way. If a man's name was "Jacob" he called him that and if his name was "Thomas" he didn't call him "Tom" or "Tommy," he used his full name. Even for us.

I could ride in those days. Nowadays I can't hardly climb up onto a horse, but back then I was faster than a rattlesnake. I don't remember a time when I couldn't ride. Mama always said, "If it has four legs then Jacob can make it go." I guess that's about right.

Master Fontaine let me ride his horse now and then, especially if there was a race. He was arguing once with a man about whose horse was the fastest. They were getting nowhere when Master Fontaine told him, "Maybe your horse is as fast as you say it is, but it doesn't matter. My man on my horse can beat anything you put against him." The next thing I know I'm done hoeing weeds for the time being and up on the horse. I whipped that other fellow but good. Master Fontaine was so happy he gave me a dollar.

Mama cried like a baby when I told her where I was going. So many years ago, but I remember those tears like they were yesterday. I was a young man then, not old and gray like I am now. So naturally, I cried too. I knew and she knew she'd never see me no more once I'm gone. And she didn't. My three sisters neither. Two of 'em was older than me and one younger, and they all cried just like Mama. We all sat there weeping and bawling and flooding that cabin with our tears 'til I thought I'd see Noah come floating through on the ark. But there wasn't nothing I could do and they knew it. Finally my oldest sister, Ruthie, she went and got her little bag that she always kept her treasures in. She really didn't have no treasure because where would she get that? Just some especially pretty buttons and a few needles and a cross and some other things I never saw, but they were treasures to her. She got that bag and reached down in there and what do you think she found but a silver dollar. She handed it to me and said, "Jake, you take this here silver dollar with you to Texas. You keep it with you and that way you know we're always thinking about you even though we won't never see you no more." Then she made Mama and the other two kiss it and she did too and I took the dollar and put it in my pocket and it's been there ever since. So that way Mama and my sisters stayed with me.

The day came for leaving, and I don't mind saying I was mighty scared. Master packed his things up and I put 'em on the horse, then I got my own things and put 'em on the mule, who I called Janey. Just as I was about to climb on her, I took out *that dollar and rubbed it for luck. Master said, "Jacob, is that a silver dollar? Let me see that." I handed it over and I thought maybe he'd keep it, but he didn't, he handed it back and said, "Where'd you get that?" I told him and he thought a bit and said, "Well, now that's something," and off he went. I'm mighty glad he gave it back. Yes, sir, I'm mighty glad about that because if he hadn't I'm thinking Mr. Jake would have earned himself his very first whipping. But he did and I didn't, and off we went to Texas.*

3

We rode first to New Orleans, a city I had long yearned to see. The overland journey passed uneventfully. Unencumbered by much baggage, we made excellent time. Cool autumn breezes refreshed us as we rode, I on Spirit and Jacob on the mule. My entire worldly possessions fit comfortably in my saddlebags, amounting to no more than sundry clothing, paper, writing instruments, a few books including my Bible, and a tin cup. Jacob had even less.

With its graceful, elegant buildings and clean-swept brick streets, New Orleans enchanted me. Jacob and I wandered aimlessly about, peering into shop windows, sampling the delicacies proffered by street vendors, and watching people scurry to and fro as if the world depended upon their haste. At St. Louis Cathedral neither one of us knew how to cross ourselves Catholic style. I feared we would be spotted as intruders and evicted, but our clumsy attempts went unnoticed. After leaving the cathedral, I went to the shipping office and secured passage on the steamer *Amelia*, bound for Galveston Bay.

We arrived a week later. A less pleasant week I can scarcely remember, for the waves of the Gulf tossed our craft ceaselessly. Frequent showers kept us to quarters throughout much of the trip and a steamier, less commodious enclosure surely does not exist. Texas beckoned, though, so we endured and arrived safely at Galveston Bay.

To my dismay, as I stepped off the gangplank, I saw not the fertile fields of Mrs. Holley's book, but an impossibly wide, barren strip of sand. Where was the paradise I had been promised? Where were the lush fields of wheat, the sparkling streams, and the verdant prairies? Certainly not in the sand or the foul-swelling swamp that lay beyond it. I felt like a fool.

I lingered only as long as was necessary to rest our mounts before moving inland. The next few days took us over a landscape as flat as the one we had left behind in Mississippi. Sand gave way to tall marsh grasses, which in turn yielded to a level prairie dotted here and there with islands of trees. By the time we arrived at San Felipe de Austin I began to understand Mrs. Holley's enthusiasm for Texas. Now the land appeared fertile and well watered, abundant wildlife provided us plenty of fresh meat, and the fish practically leapt out of the creeks into my frying pan.

The town of San Felipe lay on the banks of a placid and beautiful river known as the Brazos. Primitive but neat buildings lined the streets which, while not yet completely cleared of stumps and rubble, nevertheless provided easy passage for all, mounted or not. Customers entered and exited shops with regularity. Bountiful farms extended out beyond the town in all directions. In fact, San Felipe's prosperity evaporated my initial disillusionment and restored my faith in Texas as a land of great promise.

My first night in San Felipe I passed wrapped in blankets under a live oak tree just outside the town. The following morning I left Jacob in care of our things and went exploring. It seemed I was back in New Orleans, so busy and crowded were the streets. People rushed here and there, knots of animated men clustered around doorways, and no one gave me a second glance. Seeing a man roasting meat under a canvas tent, I approached and asked, "Are you serving breakfast?"

"Come in, friend, come in," he replied, smiling. "Put a dollar in the bowl and eat your fill."

I dropped a coin into a cracked piece of crockery and held out my tin plate, onto which he dropped a chunk of gristly beef. "I suppose you've heard the news by now," he said.

"No, I've just arrived."

"Where from?"

"Mississippi. Through Galveston Bay."

"Oh, you've come from the other direction then," he said, as if that conveyed full understanding.

"The other direction from what?"

"Gonzales. The start of the revolution, by God."

"I'm sorry, I've only been in Texas a few days. Where is Gonzales?"

"Back that way," he said with a vague wave over his shoulder. "A couple days' ride from here. The Mexicans wanted their cannon back, and the boys wouldn't let 'em have it. Whipped 'em good too."

And thus had I arrived in Texas just as the first spark of revolution leapt into flame. A Mexican officer had demanded repossession of an artillery piece given to the town of Gonzales for protection against savages. The Gonzales men refused. And when the Mexicans tried to take it, those brave men thrashed them soundly. The thrilling news had reached San Felipe that very morning. "Those boys licked a whole Mexican army is how I heard it," said the man in the tent. "Now there's another bunch over at Bexar fixing to take San Antone from the Mexicans too. As soon as I sell off this bunch of beef I aim to join them."

"In Bexar?"

"Hell, yes, in Bexar! I don't want this scrap to end before I can shoot a few Mexicans myself. Lord knows, they've had it coming. About time we kicked them out and made this a proper country. You ought to come too."

I had no intention of joining a fight I knew nothing about. As other men entered the tent to distract the proprietor, I slipped away in search of better lodging than the oak tree. I found it at Mrs. Peyton's boardinghouse. In addition to a room for myself, I secured a place in the barn for Jacob. "Don't be late with the rent or you'll find yourself without a roof. And your nigger can sleep out there," said Mrs. Peyton. "Just don't let him wander too near the house, you hear? There's a pickaninny that'll take his meals to him. And there's a pit behind the hog pen for a privy."

And so I settled into my first Texas home. My room contained a cot and rawhide stool and had space for little else. The fare was passable, but barely. Thin soup, fatty meat, dry cornbread, and a few root vegetables were the standard. Deliciously strong coffee almost made up for the blandness of the diet. My fellow boarders typically supplemented their coffee with whiskey, never in short supply in Texas, which proved so pleasant that I began carrying a flask of my own for the purpose. But I partook, and still partake, only at supper and only in moderation.

With lodging secured, I began searching for an income source. I leased Jacob to a local farmer named Thompson, who needed extra hands to clear a field for planting. I made him promise that he would administer no whippings, but would report misbehavior and defer punishment to me. I assured him that the need for disciplinary action would likely never arise. Unlike many of the Africans I saw in Texas, Jacob accepted and thrived in his divinely ordained role.

Finding my own employment proved easy enough. The exodus of young men from San Felipe to join the Texian independence cause created several clerkship vacancies in town. A lawyer named Frederick Morgan engaged me. I thought of Father's admonitions when I accepted the job, but told myself that in Texas I was free of his disapproving countenance. Because of the sudden local manpower shortage, Mr. Morgan offered me the generous weekly salary of twenty-five dollars. When I accepted, he set me immediately to work copying a large stack of letters for his files.

Even now, years after the fact, I am asked why I did not immediately follow others into the Texian army. The answer is simple. Lacking the land hunger motivating many of the new enlistees, I was not stirred by the promised land bounty that sparked their lust for war. Nor did I share their passion for inflicting violence on Mexico. As a newcomer, I had suffered no personal injustice at the hands of the Mexican government and therefore carried no enmity toward it or the Mexican people. Furthermore, my religious convictions produced in me a feeling of horror at the thought of breaking the stoutest of God's commandments: thou shalt not kill. I therefore felt content to settle into a new life in San Felipe rather than respond to the call of a patriotism I did not yet possess.

It was during those quiet days in San Felipe that I first heard the name Mirabeau Lamar. At supper one evening I playfully called across the table, "Mr. Collins, pass the peas, if you please." While handing me the dish Collins said, "Gentlemen, I believe we have another Mirabeau Lamar on our hands."

"Who's Mirabeau Lamar? Somebody quite handsome, I'm sure," I said jokingly.

"Not the fairest face," said Collins, with a seriousness that belied my joke's ineffectiveness, "but the most intelligent man I have ever met."

"Agreed," said another.

"No doubt," said a third.

Seeing the puzzled expression on my face, Collins explained, "Lamar was a boarder here with Mrs. Peyton a few weeks before you arrived. From Georgia, I think. Gone back there now but said he'd return."

"How do I remind you of him?"

"Your rhyme. Mr. Lamar could talk politics, he could talk farming, he could talk religion, philosophy, anything at all. But what he did best was figure out rhymes. Poetry. He wrote some mighty fine poems. Used to read them to us at the table."

"What was that one about the river?" said a man named Taylor.

"Chattahoochee," said Collins. "'At Evening on the Banks of the Chattahoochee.' Now there was a beautiful piece of verse."

I laughed, which seemed to annoy Collins. Not wishing to offend, I quickly said, "I'm sorry. I just didn't expect to come to Texas and discuss poetry. I imagined Texas to be more of a . . . more . . ."

"Primitive?"

"Yes, that's it. When we spoke of Texas back in Mississippi, we didn't imagine men of education reading poetry at supper."

"Well," said Collins, "Texas may seem like a pretty rough place at the moment, but it won't always be like that."

"No, sir," said Taylor. "Sure, we've got our share of louts and ruffians. Maybe more. But there's plenty of men like Mirabeau Lamar too. And it's men like him that'll make this a place for decent folks, folks with children, folks who—"

"Write poetry!" said Collins, laughing. "Jesus, Taylor, what the hell!"

"Mr. Collins, you know how I feel about swearing in my house!"

This was the voice of Mrs. Peyton, who in addition to having a strict law about prompt rent payment, enforced an equally rigorous law against rough language. Which always amused me, given the coarseness of her own language when chastising her servants.

"Boys, I'm done for," said Collins with a smile. "But I must say that Lamar was the one man among us that never ran afoul of Mrs. Peyton on that particular subject." Then, looking at me, he added, "You wait, Mr. Fontaine. You'll hear more from Mr. Mirabeau Lamar."

We got to New Orleans about suppertime and Lord I was hungry. I said to Master Fontaine could we find something to eat that wasn't old cornbread and he said yes, sir, he was hungry too, but instead of eating right off we walked around looking at buildings and such. I'd never seen buildings like that. Some were stacked up three or four floors high and they sat right next to each other without any space between. We saw the biggest church I ever seen or ever will see. It's called St. Louis and I begged Master Fontaine to go inside, but he wasn't sure they'd let me do it. But the man he asked said sure, just go around to the back and there's a door for you. So I did that and Master Fontaine went in the big doors up front, and we met up in the middle. Inside there were goblets and silver candlesticks and a big cross with Jesus nailed to it looking like he was killed just yesterday. I felt the spirit in there, I sure did. If a man can't feel the spirit in a place like that then I don't know if he ever will.

We got on a boat in New Orleans and made for Texas. It had a wheel that turned around to spit the water out back and shove the boat along. Except the ocean was shoving too. So we turned this way and that and seemed to go backwards as much as forwards, but we finally did get to Texas. On the way, though, I spent a lot of my time pitching what I just ate over the side. I had lots of company too. Everybody vomited so much I got to thinking we should just throw the food overboard and save ourselves the trouble of chewing it first. If I never ride on such a boat again I'll not feel deprived.

My mule Janey and Master Fontaine's horse enjoyed the boat ride about as much as I did. We rested them a day or two on the beach and then made for a town called San Felipe. When we got there Master Fontaine found us a place at Mrs. Peyton's, and I got my things off Janey and made for the barn where she told me I could sleep. Master Fontaine of course went in the house for some fine feather pillows, I'm sure. One day I wanted to ask Master Fontaine if I could go fish at the river, so I went around to the back of the house to go in and find him. Mrs. Peyton saw me and said, "Stop right there, boy, where do you think you're going?" I told her and she said, "I'll go find your master. You get back outside until I do." I stayed away from the house after that.

What Master Fontaine figured on doing now that we were in Texas, I had no idea. He took me one day to a farm and said I was to work there. I said I would, and after Master Fontaine left, the farmer said to me, "You better not cross me, boy, or you'll feel my whip." Now, Master Fontaine, he told that farmer not to whip me without talking to him first, so I said, "My master won't like that one bit." But he said, "While you're here I'm your master and don't you forget it." So I knew I should just work hard and leave everything else up to God. Me and two or three other men cleared a field for planting, and I didn't get whipped even once.

4

By the end of 1835 I, like most Texians, believed that Mexico was beaten. In mid-December word arrived that General Cos had surrendered his entire army at Bexar. People ran into the streets of San Felipe to cheer the rider bringing the news. Someone banged the iron bar used to summon Sunday worshippers and the whole town began a celebration lasting throughout the day and night. At supper we toasted the heroes, with the loudest huzzahs reserved for the brave martyr Ben Milam, victim of a sniper's ball. Afterward, too excited to retire, I accompanied my boardinghouse colleagues to a nearby grocer where, for one of the few times in my life, I became quite drunk. Had I remained sober I would have been the only man in San Felipe to do so. As I staggered over to Morgan's law office the next morning, I passed numerous sprawled, sleeping figures on the street. Morgan himself snored on a cot until my loud footsteps jolted him awake.

"Damn, Fontaine, you startled me," he said irritably. "What're you doing here?"

"I came to work on the letters."

"Aw, forget about that for now." He struggled to a sitting position and reached unsuccessfully for his boots. "By God, my head's pounding. Oh, sweet Jesus, have mercy."

Not knowing what else to do I walked as softly as I could over to the desk and sank into the chair. Truthfully, I felt little better than Morgan. I reached for the nearest stack of papers.

"Forget it, I said!" Morgan shouted. "No work today, no goddamned noise! Make it a holiday. Texas Day . . . Texas Independence Day, that's it. To hell with Mexico! Their goose is cooked."

"Do you really think so?" I asked while tossing the letters back onto the table.

"Damn right. They're licked." Morgan began to wake up now, as if the thought of Texas independence had suddenly energized him. "That wasn't an undermanned outpost, you know; that was San Antonio de Bexar and the whole damned Mexican army! Biggest settlement in the territory! Hell, the Mexicans haven't got anything else up here that I know of. And if they did, we'd beat that too. Yes, sir, beat 'em right good. We'll be the United States of Texas . . . or something like that."

"Then this is indeed an historic day! I suppose it's all over."

At that moment, I truly believed it.

Sometimes I slept at Thompson's farm, and sometimes I walked back into town to Mrs. Peyton's barn. Truth is, I didn't exactly trust Thompson and just felt safer around Master Fontaine. By then he had taken on with a lawyer, a man named Morgan, who paid him to write up papers and letters. Morgan was smart, but he spent more time drinking than working. God had some work to do on Morgan, he did. Liquor never did do a body any good and it sure had its way with that lawyer.

At that time the white folks were riled up against the Mexicans. They said Texas should be Texas and Mexico should just go away and let Texas be. Of course, Mexico took a different view of the situation and sent some soldiers up to let that be known. There was some fighting over in Bexar and people said the Mexican soldiers were whupped. Everybody hollered and hollered. A white man even slapped me on the back while I was walking down the street and told me to come on and have a drink. But that way lay only trouble, and I told that man no, thank you, sir and kept on walking. I was on my way back to the farm, but next I saw Thompson. He was coming out of a grocer's and he said, "Come on, boy, take some of this" and he held up a jug of whiskey. I took it because I was afraid not to and then he just ran off. So I went straight to the farm and laid that whiskey on his porch and set to work in the field. And he never said a thing more about it.

It was about that time that I heard a man tell that Mexico aimed to make all the slaves free. There was even talk of the slaves taking matters into their own hands and fighting the white folks. That was hard to figure but I prayed about it and, as good a man as Master Fontaine was, I knew I'd rather be my own boss, so if there was a fight, I'd join in. Then I heard tell that if I was to join the Mexican army they'd give me a thousand dollars and a plot of ground too and I forgot about fighting the white men. One fella said you could live like a king further down in Mexico but you'd have to get out of Texas to do it. I dreamed about that, yes, I did. But I didn't even know where Mexico was or how far it might be. Another fella said he was there once and it wasn't nothing but desert. That gave me pause and I stayed put. Anyway, we never did fight the white folks.

• • •

If life has taught me anything, it is to be most wary when the sun shines brightest. For that is when the norther sweeps in with its sudden fury and freezing rain and killing hail. And so it did in the winter of 1836 in the form of a breathless rider with news of an immense Mexican force on the march. This rider arrived even as delegates assembled at Washington for the purpose of declaring our separation from Mexico. I say "our," for I had now begun to think of myself as a Texian. Our thoughts thus plummeted with dizzying speed from the thrill of freedom to the agonies of war. And, even as we rejoiced at word of the Declaration of Independence, there came two successive hammer blows, the fall of the Alamo and the massacre at Goliad. Where was Morgan's bravado now, as he hastily packed to flee San Felipe? Where was my own naïve belief in his rosy prediction?

"Fontaine, don't worry about ordering the papers, just put them in the trunk," Morgan said as I helped him.

"All right, Mr. Morgan."

"Once this scrape is settled and we're back in San Felipe, I could use you again."

"I appreciate that. I don't know whether I'll be back, though."

"Well . . . you've got to be somewhere. And I'll need a clerk. So if you still want it, the job is yours. In fact, why don't you ride with me in the wagon?"

The offer tempted me. Although I had a little money, I worried that the war might damage its value, no matter the outcome. But I had also tired of Morgan's swearing and drinking sprees. I had not repeated my excess of that December evening, but Morgan had repeated his with regularity. Such consistent vice would end poorly, I had no doubt.

"Thank you, Mr. Morgan, but I'm not ready to leave just yet."

"Suit yourself," he said with a sigh. "But when you see Santa Anna coming up the road, you be sure to light out with everybody else."

I laughed. "I have a fast horse."

"You better, because they're not taking prisoners."

The first Texian soldiers to arrive in San Felipe acted calmly enough. I wouldn't have recognized their military status except for the orders that the officer barked at his men as they dismounted. They wore no uniforms, only filthy buckskin or cotton shirts and trousers. A variety of outer wraps served to warm them, including faded Mexican blankets, tattered wool coats, and buffalo robes. Knives and pistols protruding from their belts gave them a desperate look. All wore hats. None matched.

As onlookers gathered around, the officer drank long from his canteen, re-placed the cork, and announced, "The main body of troops'll be here within a few hours. I'm here to organize provisions. I can pay with government vouchers, but no cash or gold. And you might as well not be too stingy because I suspect you'll get a worse deal from Santa Anna."

After an awkward pause one man in the crowd said, "Them vouchers are no damn good and you know it. Not unless you can chase the Mexicans away."

"And if we can't chase the Mexicans away they'll take your stores without pay-ing a penny!" snapped the officer. "We've a right better chance without a load of half-starved, half-naked men on our hands."

The crowd mumbled among themselves before the same man spoke up. "All right, I reckon that's so. Come with me, and I'll show you what I got."

With no clear objective in mind I returned to Mrs. Peyton's and packed my saddlebags. Finding Jacob in the barn I instructed him to do the same. "We're leaving, Jacob," I told him. "Get the animals ready."

"Yes, sir, Master Fontaine. Where we going?"

"Well . . . " My voice trailed off. I didn't know. At least, I hadn't told myself yet. But I couldn't go home to Mississippi, so there really was only one choice. I just prayed I wouldn't have to kill anybody. "Jacob, let's go find the army."

Mrs. Peyton's grimace as I settled my charges betrayed her exasperation at los-ing yet another lodger. "I suppose you're lighting out so you can go shoot Mexicans like everybody else," she complained.

"Ma'am," I said, "I am truly sorry to leave you on short notice."

Her eyes softened. "You just keep out of the way of those Mexican musket balls, you hear? Now go on and git."

We rode toward the river. Loud hammering and the shouts of tired men reached our ears. A sense of amazement gripped me when I saw that where the day before had been only pasture and sparse timber, there now swarmed a great number of men, with more arriving every moment. All ignored Jacob and me. I approached an officer giving orders to two men holding shovels.

"Sir, I wonder if you could direct me to the commanding general?"

"If you want to join up," said the officer wearily, "I can help you. You don't need a general for that."

"I would indeed like to join up," I said. "I also aim to provide spiritual support to the men."

"A preacher? I'll be damned. We're being chased by a million Mexicans and Providence sends me a Bible thumper."

Embarrassed, I said nothing.

"Well, my name's Baker. Captain Moseley Baker. And maybe you *should* go see the general. *If* he's not too drunk to listen to you."

The venom in his voice as he spat out these last words startled me.

I asked, "Houston's his name, is it not?"

"Yeah, Sam Houston. And he's likely over there somewhere." He gestured farther along the path we had been riding. "Tell him I sent you, and tell him what you told me. Just don't expect Napoleon."

After thanking Captain Baker, Jacob and I spent a frustrating hour searching unsuccessfully for General Houston. When I had just about given up for the day, a rider approached and hailed me before asking, "Are you the preacher?"

"I'm here to be a soldier. But I'm a preacher too," I replied, faking a confidence I did not possess. "I'm looking for General Houston."

"Well, you've found him."

"Sir?"

"Yes."

"You're General Houston?"

"Yes."

"And you're in command of the army?"

"As much as a man can be."

"Sir, I—"

"Son, if you want to spread the Lord's word among my men you have my blessing. God knows they need it. All I require is that you mind camp discipline and that your efforts don't conflict with your duties or anyone else's."

"Yes, sir."

"Baker sent you to me, didn't he? Well, Baker's a good soldier, but I'm afraid he doesn't think much of his commanding officer." He paused momentarily before adding, "You just keep my men right with the Lord and don't believe everything you hear in camp, all right?"

When I nodded, he smiled broadly and said, "Good! Welcome to the Texian army!"

After General Houston had ridden off, Jacob asked, "Master, why do you think he said that? About you not believing everything you hear?"

"No matter, Jacob, our paths aren't likely to cross again."

Thus was I introduced to the *great* man, Sam Houston, falsely described to this day as "the Hero of San Jacinto." Some men laud his courage, but if he was courageous why did he abandon San Felipe to her fate and flee eastward as the enemy approached? Some have praised his boldness, but would a bold man have hesitated to attack at San Jacinto even as the Mexicans were trapped, as did our pretend hero? Many applaud his wisdom, but was it wise to return the tyrant Santa Anna to his lair to continue plotting against us? How do such false idols arise? How is such a flawed man puffed up into the very epitome of heroism? How does the power of reason desert otherwise intelligent men so that they believe the lies?

It is because Sam Houston, for all his venality and incompetence, possessed one masterful skill, an unsurpassed gift of oratory. No man in living memory could match his artful language. His skill at persuasion shielded a shallow mind. His powerful speechmaking overcame the objections of wiser, but meeker men; few could resist his sway in public debate. Even Mirabeau Lamar, possessor of a brilliant political mind, learned to avoid publicly contradicting him; such was Houston's gift at extemporaneous speaking. And Houston labored most strenuously and with great success to convince gullible men of his own grandeur.

He drank. Subsequent to our meeting the reason for his caution regarding camp gossip became clear. During our march to San Jacinto I heard countless tales of Houston's intemperance, his drunken sprees, his earlier liquor-fueled debauchery during his time with the Cherokees, his name among them of "the Big Drunk." How, while governor of Tennessee and heir apparent to General Jackson, he forsook his marriage vows in favor of life in the forest among his dusky friends. He married one of them, if unholy union between a white man and Cherokee woman can be thus sanctioned in God's eyes, only to abandon her on the rueful day that he came to Texas. I heard such stories too often to discount them all. Why did God bestow upon such a man the power of eloquent and persuasive speech?

My insight into the true nature of Sam Houston, of course, developed only slowly over the course of years. One early lesson arrived with his cowardly retreat from our strong position at the Brazos River and the town of San Felipe. With the aid of a steamship, the bulk of the army crossed over safely to assemble on the other side. Here Houston could have formed his line and attacked as the Mexicans attempted their crossing. The men certainly favored this course of action. As one of them told me, "I joined up to fight Santa Anna, not to walk from here to yonder." But, to the chagrin of his officers and the shame of his men, the General ordered the army to resume its march. And, as he fled in disgrace to save his own skin, he ordered San Felipe put to the torch.

I shall not soon forget the gut-wrenching sight of thick, black smoke billowing up from the homes of the innocent people of San Felipe. Cries of distress pierced the air as we slunk away. Refugees streamed from the town, only to find their passage blocked by the very army that had destroyed their lives. Though as blameless as the townspeople, each soldier hung his head in shame at the handiwork of the army's craven leader.

In this state of despair we marched ever eastward. I marched as a soldier, while remaining alert for any man wishing to talk Scripture. Mostly I listened to the men's grumblings and complaints, or their recollections of home or their gossip. In this way I began to form opinions about men who would later rise to prominence in the Texas Republic. Rusk, Burleson, and Burnet were but a few of the personages mentioned to me along the road. I even heard the name Lamar and with it stories of its owner's remarkable learnedness. I wondered, was this the poet from Mrs. Peyton's supper table? I would soon find out.

The Mexicans decided they weren't whupped after all. They sent an army up to Bexar to kill everybody in the Alamo and a different one to catch the soldiers down in Goliad and kill them too. Then we heard they were heading our way. One minute I was in the barn patching a hole in my shoe and the next minute me and Master Fontaine were off to join the army.

The lady of the house was none too pleased when Master Fontaine told her we were leaving. I heard her hollering from out in the yard, but eventually she settled down and even gave us some corn cakes and bacon to take with us. We walked a ways up the river and found the most men I ever saw in one place. It looked like every man and boy in the whole country had gotten himself a gun and come to fight Mexicans. Every white man, that is. The only black faces I saw were busy fetching water or chopping wood.

We walked around a fair piece looking for the head man and finally found him. That was General Sam Houston. Everybody knows who he is now, but back then I never heard of the man before. I liked him right off. He smiled and talked to me like I was somebody and not just another nigger slave. He told Master Fontaine, "We're mighty glad to have you," and then he looked at me and said, "You too, sir." I had never been called sir by no white man before, so I looked around to see who he was talking to. He laughed and said, "Welcome to the army, boys."

Ever since then I've heard men say General Houston was nothing but a show-boat and a drunk. I never saw him drunk, not even once, and I saw him plenty often too. Later on, after he got married, everybody said he quit drinking, but still some folks said bad things about him. As for me, I liked him then and I like him now, even though he's been gone to Heaven for some time.

When they burned the town it was just like Sodom and Gomorrah. We stood there and watched at first but then a man on a horse told us to get moving again. Most everybody said Sam Houston was the one that lit the torch. As we marched away I felt sorry that I hadn't run off to Mexico. Even though I hadn't done it, it gave me peace to think that I could if I wanted. But every step we took after leaving San Felipe only took me farther away from that possibility. One man said, "They lit it on fire so the Mexicans won't get it." Master Fontaine said it was so the Mexicans wouldn't get the food there and they'd stay hungry. Maybe so, but I figured they must have brought some food along and anyway they could probably shoot deer and hogs as good as anybody else. Master Fontaine said he thought so too and that it was an evil deed.

5

Not being privy to the reports of our spies, we common soldiers knew little of the enemy's whereabouts. Camp rumor placed the Mexicans to the south, or to the right of our eastward line of march. We knew that our present course would take us to the Trinity River, beyond which lay the Sabine and Louisiana, but no Mexicans. As we broke camp at McCarley's farm one fine April morning, each man thus knew that our destiny hinged on the direction our column would take. Talk of an upcoming road fork by a man from the area elicited much grumbling.

"If the General wants me in this army, he better not point to the goddamned Trinity River," said one man.

"Officers be damned," said another with a quick gesture south, "me and my musket are going thataway."

Having never before been a soldier, I had little faith in my ability to be useful on horseback. I had therefore lent Spirit to the cavalry and Janey to the quartermaster. Jacob and I thus marched with the infantry, halfway back of the vanguard. A knot of mounted men in the distance conferred amongst themselves. Suddenly a great cheer arose as two of them moved to block the straight roadway. One of the others removed his hat and, with great flair, motioned for the column to veer to the right. A wave of excitement passed over the men to infuse them with an energy they had lacked on the march from the Brazos. When I arrived at the junction, there was Houston seated on his horse. He nodded glumly at the cheering men as they passed. Such a strange sight! A spirited army marching gaily to attack the enemy while their commander sulked as if already beaten! It was at that moment that I began to understand the true nature of Sam Houston.

By April 20 we had arrived at a flat marsh, since called the Plain of San Jacinto. The Mexicans were close at hand. Intermittent artillery fire punctured the morning stillness. A few balls smashed harmlessly through the trees overhead. I had given Jacob over to the labor force, and I prayed he remained safe in the rear.

In the afternoon a minor cavalry charge from our side stirred great excitement among the infantry, many of whom desired to immediately follow their comrades. Only stern threats from the officers prevented a headlong rush at the foe. That evening I heard from one of the mounted participants that the timely intervention of one Private Lamar had saved the lives of two men, the officer Thomas Rusk and a young private named Lane. How odd, I thought, that I hear repeatedly of this man Lamar. By now I had little doubt that the private and the poet were one and the same; our futures seemed destined to collide.

After Mirabeau's brave rescue of Rusk and Lane, General Houston offered him command of the artillery, which he declined. "I had no desire to offend the officer in charge at the time," he explained to me months later. Not long thereafter, however, the men of the cavalry rose as one to demand that he lead *them* in the next day's battle. Ever reluctant to display the sin of pride, Mirabeau demurred, but when Captain Karnes and Captain Smith, the two men then in charge, insisted that he accept the reins of leadership, he acceded to their wishes.

On the eve of the battle I witnessed a scene which haunts me yet. When young Ben Brigham received an order to stand guard that night, he quickly turned to his comrades to plead that one of them take his place. "I've been on duty the last two nights," he said. "If I must do so again, I fear I shall miss the fight tomorrow!"

"Ben, all the men are tired," the officer patiently said, "but we've got to have guards. You must take your turn."

Before Ben could reply, an older man named Cooke spoke up. "Sir, Ben's been dragging since McCarley's. I'll serve picket tonight."

"That suits me," said the officer. Smiling at Brigham, he added, "All right, Ben, find your bedroll."

On the morrow, refreshed from his slumber, Ben Brigham enthusiastically charged into battle, only to fall mortally wounded. It was his twenty-first birthday. Cooke had therefore given Ben one final sleep before eternal rest.

Ben Brigham's eagerness for battle spurred me to take up my Bible and circulate among the men. Most engaged in cards or storytelling, but there were others eager to prepare themselves through prayer and quiet reflection. I sat with those men and read aloud. One verse from Psalms in particular I quoted, for it had long given me comfort in times of distress: "The Lord is on my side; I shall not fear. What can man do to me?"

• • •

We walked til my feet swole up double. I would rather have ridden Janey, but Master Fontaine let some soldiers load her up with about a thousand pounds of I don't know what, so there I was wearing out shoe leather with everyone else. Except I didn't have no shoes. Master Fontaine was gonna get me some in San Felipe but he never got around to it. Every time I stepped on a rock or a sticker bush I got mad but finally all that worrying wore me out and I quit. Even so, I wasn't thinking too kindly about Master Fontaine on that march.

Whenever we stopped, the captains and the generals drilled the men and they'd set me and the other slaves to work fetching wood and cutting grass and toting water. Then we got to a field and Master Fontaine said we wouldn't be walking no more, at least not until after the big fight that was coming. A white man put a shovel in my hand and said to dig a trench. I piled up the dirt for soldiers to hide behind and shoot. That dirt was the worst I ever saw or want to see. It stuck to the shovel like beeswax and no amount of shaking would knock it off. I had to scrape it off with a stick every time I pulled the shovel up.

While I was digging I heard some guns banging way off yonder. I thought maybe somebody was just shooting deer or rabbits but the man I was digging with said, "You dumb nigger, it's the Mexicans killing everybody and they're gonna come kill you too." A white man told him to be quiet and recommence digging. He pointed at me and said, "You too." So I did, but I was saying my prayers at the same time.

The Battle of San Jacinto, when it finally arrived, startled me with its brevity. With the cavalry on its right flank, the main line of the infantry started off silently through thick, tall grass that hid it from the enemy. Expecting fear, I found it. My chest thumped and my legs trembled as I walked between two men I didn't know. Seeing the dread on my face, one of them smiled and said, "They're just Mexicans, friend. Give 'em a Texas yell and they'll run like rabbits." The other man laughed and said, "Let's go kill us some rabbits!"

I broke through a clump of grass when—*pop, pop, pop*—came the sound of shooting from my left. Men ran. One man fired and an officer shouted, "Not yet, damn you!" But the firing only picked up. Soon such a thick cloud of smoke enveloped me that I feared the prairie was on fire. Animal-like cries pierced the air, whether of excitement or anguish I knew not. When men around me paused to fire their rifles, I did the same, the flash from my muzzle disappearing into the dense smoke. Where the balls went I had no idea. Once clear of the smoke I expected to encounter heaps of wounded comrades lying in the grass. Instead our men hurled themselves at the enemy soldiers who, save for small knots of brave men, had already begun to flee. Within minutes the Mexican line simply disappeared. I passed without incident through the deserted camp to arrive at a marsh, at the edge of which our men fired continuously at the writhing mass of Mexican soldiers trapped in the water. I shuddered at the fate of these doomed men, for they found no shelter in the sea. Those that turned toward land found a Texian bullet. Those that fled the bullets drowned. Hundreds perished, but surely God forgives the acts of men fired by the wicked deeds at the Alamo and Goliad massacres. I wept nonetheless.

I turned away from the slaughter and sought wounded men to assist. I encountered none; only Mexican corpses already thick with flies lay beneath the afternoon sun. The emaciated, twisted bodies of these poor souls scattered in the grass evoked pity in some, derision in others. "What was Santa Anna thinking, throwing these scarecrows at us?" cried one exuberant soldier. "Hah!" his companion snorted in reply. "Scarecrows don't bleed!" He plunged an old rusty sword repeatedly into a dead man's back, as if to demonstrate the difference between a man and a sack of straw.

Walking on, I saw so many others, all dead, all sprawled in death's final agony, each bloodied and disfigured by jagged holes, oozing gashes, or crushed skulls. Texian soldiers walked among the bodies looking for signs of life. A Mexican on his back bleeding profusely from a chest wound feebly called out, *"Ayúdame, ayúdame."* One of our "brave" soldiers put a pistol to the man's head and pulled the trigger.

Disgusted, I fled to the shade of one of the few trees in the immediate vicinity, a large, moss-covered live oak with sagging branches. I sat there numbly, head in hands, watching my jubilant comrades plunder the dead and finish the living with a sword thrust or blow to the head. I asked aloud, "Is this glory?"

A voice from behind startled me.

"Son, find your officer and report. There's work to be done."

Turning, I saw a tired but composed man on a fine horse. The concentrated look upon his face belied his relaxed posture. Long black hair hung in strands about his head and shoulders; beads of sweat dripped from his brow. Of medium build, he appeared unimposing, yet majestic. When I tarried too long in answering he spoke again, this time in kindlier fashion.

"Are you hurt? Shall I fetch a surgeon?"

"No, sir," I replied at last. "I'm . . . I was looking for someone to help." I waved my arm at the battlefield. "But there's no one."

Lifting his gaze to survey the carnage the officer said, "Yes, we've won a great victory."

"I know. I just didn't think it would be so terrible."

"God sometimes achieves great good with terrible instruments. Don't you know that? Men serving evil drowned when Moses parted the Red Sea. Men serving evil died today so that a righteous cause could triumph."

I got to my feet and said accusingly, "Have you seen what they're doing? They're killing the wounded and desecrating the dead! Where in the Bible are we told of the righteousness of such acts?"

The horseman regarded me not with contempt but pity. He said, "Son, I'm on my way to stop what I can. But those wounded Mexicans chose their destiny when they agreed to serve a bloody tyrant. Now I can't spend all day debating the issue with you, but if you'll find me later I'd be happy to talk more about it." He spurred his horse into a slow walk. As he passed by he added, "Name's Lamar. Colonel Mirabeau Lamar. Go on now, get back out there. There's men that need you if you keep looking."

Lamar! "Are you the poet?" I shouted at his back.

Laughing, he said over his shoulder, "Poet! My God, man, of course I'm a poet! How could I not be a poet on such a glorious day?"

I don't know how many holes they would have had us dig but I was still at it with a shovel the next day when the big fight started. Me and some other boys were digging under some pine trees when a cannonball tore a tree in half not fifty feet away. A couple of the boys dropped their shovels like they were gonna run off but the overseer said, "You niggers get back to work. Cannonballs ain't gonna waste themselves on you." Once the real shooting started it was so loud we couldn't hardly hear each other talk. Then there was so much smoke I thought the grass had caught fire and we would all burn to death. The white men around us were anxious to know what was going on up ahead. Then a man rode up fast on a horse and hollered, "They're running, boys! We're shooting 'em like turkeys!" Some of the white men around me got real excited. A few of 'em even said, "The hell with this, I'm going up there and get me some Mexicans too." But just then a general came up and wouldn't let 'em.

I didn't see Master Fontaine the rest of that day. Come morning I found him sitting by a fire drinking coffee. I asked him some questions, but he wasn't disposed to have a chat, so I let him be. But I heard other soldiers say they'd about killed the whole Mexican army and won the war. That's how Texas came to be free. Deep down I wasn't too happy about that. You see, I was still thinking about how in Mexico there wasn't no slavery. So when Master Fontaine said that Texas was free I didn't say nothing, but I was thinking, Maybe for you.

6

I found Mirabeau not the night of the battle but the next. Victory's initial flush had ebbed, especially since many of the men passed that first day of Texian freedom staggering about in various stages of drunkenness. Officers organized burial parties to dispose of the hundreds of already stinking corpses littering the landscape. The occasional gun blast proved to be nothing more serious than men sneaking potshots at wolves.

Around midafternoon a great commotion arose in camp when a captured Mexican soldier turned out to be none other than Santa Anna himself. The tyrant was delivered to General Houston, who reposed under a shade tree with an ankle wound. Over subsequent years Mirabeau and I often joked that Houston had shot himself, so great was the political advantage he would derive from his injury. Certainly it helped convince the gullible of a heroism that he did not possess.

A series of inquiries led me to Mirabeau. He sat among five or six men drinking coffee and pulling stew from a central pot. An animated discussion occupied their attention so that no one noticed me when I eased into the edge of the circle. Men expounded at length while Mirabeau listened, nodding or shaking his head from time to time to indicate his point of view. The discussion concerned the fate of Santa Anna. Whether to hang him or shoot him seemed the most salient issue, although at least one man spoke out in favor of sending him in disgrace back to Mexico. That elicited a sharp rebuke from Lamar.

"You would allow a man to live," he began in his low, methodical voice, "who has so recently butchered our comrades at Goliad and Bexar? Who has pillaged and burned his way across our territory, savaging innocent women, making orphans of their children, driving the old and infirm before him as livestock?"

Now that he had the group's attention, he allowed his question to linger a while before speaking again.

"It's more than a question of revenge, though, gentlemen. Our very honor depends upon our response. What nation will fear us if we release Santa Anna? In what esteem will our own citizens hold us if we don't possess the courage to punish the cause of their suffering? Shoot him, hang him, or knock him in the head, I don't care. But do *not* send him away *unharmed*!"

None of the men spoke for a while. Perhaps their awe at his unassailable logic matched my own. For the first time I had seen his mind in action. He had distilled out of a complicated argument an essential truth: that Santa Anna's fate determined our own. He sat there now, his piercing eyes darting back and forth, his hands clasped tightly before him. Finally, the one who had suggested letting the Mexican leader go laughingly offered, "Mirabeau, how about if we hang him, shoot him, and then bash his brains in? Hell, after that we can throw him in the river and drown him too!"

As the laughter died down Mirabeau smiled and said, "Jest if you must, but our actions will be judged by the world. And I shudder to think that the man shouldering most responsibility just now . . ."

His eyes fell upon me. Gesturing for me to sit, he said, "Gentlemen, we're joined by a man of conscience who understandably shudders at the sight of God's terrible justice. My good man, what says the Bible of tyrants and despots? What are we to do with our unwelcome Mexican guest?"

Caught off guard, I froze momentarily before stammering out a response. "W-well, as Thomas Jefferson wrote, 'Resistance to tyrants is obedience to God.'"

"Right you are!" Mirabeau gleefully said. "Righteous men must *punish* the tyrant! There you have it, boys, Santa Anna's fate is sealed!"

Thus I came to know Mirabeau Buonaparte Lamar, intellect, poet, and newly made war hero. Enemies mocked his deliberate speech, mistaking it for dullness of wit, and it is true that his strength lay not in public oration. Yet in small gatherings, such as that around the campfire, his mind displayed an agility that others envied and admired. None could match his analytical powers; none outshone him in private debate. His thoughts consistently outpaced the rate of conversation so that his arguments overcame objections not yet made. In the presence of buffoonery or garrulousness, though, he withdrew, thereby leaving the floor to the man willing to pontificate merely to hear the sound of his own voice.

I watched him with fascination while he shone in his element. As conversation settled on a topic, the men in our circle sputtered and fumed in good-natured debate until one of them would at last ask Mirabeau for his opinion. Then all listened carefully as he outlined each side of the question and patiently explained the strengths and weaknesses therein. Finally he would offer his own analysis, which inevitably drew nods of agreement and shouts of approbation. Viewing that matter settled, the men would then take up another.

Mirabeau's sway over his comrades struck me as remarkable. Taciturn but friendly, disheveled but dignified, he commanded respect with his soft demeanor and focused intensity. Of stocky build, he possessed a rough handsomeness and physical presence that belied his short stature. His eyes bore straight into a man, with creases at their corners to soften the effect. His hands, though thick, cut gracefully as he spoke, while his posture exhibited the self-confidence that sustained him. Here is the type of man, I thought, that will make this a great republic.

As the coffeepot emptied, the men drifted away. Alone with Mirabeau, I asked him why he had come to Texas. A lengthy silence caused me to wonder if I had offended him.

At last he said, "I was a beaten man. I held a seat in the Georgia statehouse but left after a single term. Then I lost a race for Congress. Quite badly too!"

He laughed briefly before becoming serious once again. "*That* I could have endured had I not also lost something most dear to me. I . . . she . . . " He dabbed at his eyes and stared at the ground.

"I'm sorry," I said. "We can talk of other matters."

"You would think," he said, as if I hadn't spoken, "that after so long my eyes could stay dry at the mention of her name."

I remained silent.

"Tabitha," he said softly. "Her name was Tabitha. Such a fair flower of southern womanhood. She had consumption. There were days that I could think of little but her cough. She left me with a child, a daughter. Rebecca is her name. Now in the care of my sister."

I muttered an expression of sympathy. It sounded weak.

"Hardly *your* doing," Mirabeau said. "I used to pray daily, hourly, that she would recover. I came to believe that if I could only offer up the perfect prayer God would grant my wish."

Attempting to sound wise, I said, "God offers strength in times of sorrow."

"Little enough in my case," he said with a snort. "With her passing I lost all desire to live. I retreated into solitude, spending long hours walking in the woods or down by the river. I neglected my work—I had started a newspaper and law practice—and even neglected Rebecca. If not for my sister's attentions I'm afraid the poor girl would have been completely ignored. Then, just as this pain began to ease, just as I began again to see a reason to leave my bed each morning, my brother Lucius took his life."

"Oh, no," I said, feeling foolish.

"What remained for me in Georgia? Love, political office, business success . . . even close family had deserted me. I came to Texas. I would start over. I would leave my pain in Georgia. I fought here," he said, waving his hand airily, "without fear of death, because I truly had no care of my fate. What could be worse than losing so much? What is death compared to that?"

I tried to console him by saying, "You fought bravely, I hear."

"Yes, bravely," he replied dismissively. "And perhaps it wakened within me a spark that I thought extinguished. This is a great land, Edward, or can be. The Mexican race has neither the will nor ability to hold it. Look at what we did to them on this field. Let them send another army—*ten* other armies—and the result will be the same. I want to help build this nation. Her horizon is limitless."

Once again his mind had raced ahead to grasp what eluded me. Whereas my thoughts centered on the recent battle, his penetrated the shrouded mist of an unknown future to point the way. It was my first inkling of his genius. Here was a man capable of fulfilling a nation's destiny. I wanted to witness that. I wanted to help. I wanted to serve. I summoned my courage and said, "Colonel Lamar, no truer words have been spoken. I'm with you."

He smiled. "I'll need such men as you, Edward. There will be important work for both of us."

The next morning, as I nibbled a piece of stale cornbread, I heard a voice call out, "Fontaine!" It was Mirabeau, in the company of several men, all striding purposefully in my direction.

"Good morning," I said.

"Come with us, Fontaine," Mirabeau said. "We're on our way to see General Houston."

"What about?"

"What do you think? About what we were speaking of at the campfire last night. About our friend Santa Anna."

I flinched inwardly at the thought of confronting such a high-ranking officer, but fell in behind Mirabeau. I recognized only one of the other men. "You're Captain Baker," I said to him.

"I am. And you are?"

"Edward Fontaine. You helped me find General Houston the day I joined up at San Felipe."

"Ah, yes, I remember now. Well, I warned you about General Sam, didn't I? Don't worry, we'll set him straight."

We found the general surrounded by a group of officers. He sat propped up against a beautiful saddle decorated with silver studs and intricately tooled designs. Every head turned in our direction as we approached.

"Hello, boys!" Houston called out cheerfully.

"General Houston," Mirabeau and the others said in reply.

"Have a look at this saddle, boys. Have you ever seen such fine work? I haven't. Until yesterday it belonged to our friend Santa Anna. Now, by right of conquest, it's army property. I'm hoping the army won't mind if I use it as a back rest for now. God *damn*, this ankle hurts."

I started at the casual swearing, which I have always felt indicates nothing good about a man.

Baker spoke up. "General Houston, we've come to talk to you about that very subject. Santa Anna, that is. We'd like to know what you have in store for him. We've talked it over and we feel—"

"I *know* what you feel, Moseley. Death to the tyrant. I've heard that argument already from half the men in this army."

"Don't you believe that his actions merit death?"

"God damn it, Moseley, it doesn't matter what I think he deserves. Can't you people see that?" He stopped to brush a fly from his wrapped ankle. "Look, call him a tyrant and a murderer and you'll get no argument from me. But we've got to think beyond revenge. We've got to think *strategy*. To you he's a common criminal who deserves a quick hanging. To me he's a trump card that we've got to play wisely. Besides, string him up today and tomorrow you'll have the rest of the world calling you, calling *us*, murderers and tyrants."

"Any man saying that is a fool." It was Mirabeau.

"It's not *men* I'm worried about, Lamar, it's nations. It's England and France and the United States. Let *them* condemn us and we become the world's pariah. We need their good will."

"We need them to the detriment of our honor?"

"To hell with our honor, you damned fool! Yes, we need them to the detriment of our honor, if that's how you want to phrase it. Will honor put money in our treasury? Will honor gain us recognition as an independent nation? For that matter, will honor protect *you* from the fury of the Mexicans should we hang their president?"

Mirabeau fumed. "Honor, sir, is all that a man has. I'm not afraid to die for my country."

"You'll get that chance sooner than you think, Lamar, if I let you kill Santa

Anna. Now you've spoken your piece, you've *all* spoken your piece, so please, excuse me, gentlemen, I have other matters to attend to."

The officers attending Houston glared at us. Mirabeau started to reply to Houston, thought better of it, and instead told Baker, "Let's go, Moseley. We're wasting our breath."

As we departed, the men around Houston broke out in laughter.

"They've made a jest at our expense," I said.

"We'll make our own jests someday," said Mirabeau.

Once the fighting was through I figured I'd be digging holes from now until the second coming working to bury all those dead bodies. I even had my eyes on the best shovel to go after when the white bosses ordered me to commence to work. But that's not what happened. Instead, they had us gather up only our own soldiers that was killed. There wasn't more than a handful, thank the Lord, and it didn't take no time at all for us to lay them under. I asked a man what's gonna happen with all the dead Mexicans and he said let the wolves have 'em. At first that didn't bother me none but then I saw a boy laying there who couldn't have been more than twelve or thirteen and my heart like to split in two. I prayed hard for that boy's soul. The rest of 'em too.

Toward supper time I was walking over to get some food and I saw Master Fontaine sitting at a fire jawing with a number of men. I heard earlier that some soldiers had caught the Mexican general. His name was Santa Anna and the folks around the fire were trying to decide what they ought to do with him. Of course they didn't get to decide, that was up to General Houston. But they all had notions about it, that's for sure. Seems like most was in favor of hanging him and feeding him to the wolves, but there was one man that felt stronger than the rest. I found out later this was Mirabeau Lamar. I didn't know him at the time but came to know him later once Master Fontaine was working for him. Anyway, I asked Master Fontaine if he wanted me to bring him something to eat and this man Lamar looked at me like I was hog shit. I didn't hear Master Fontaine's answer right off, but before he could tell me again Lamar hollers out, "Use your ears, boy, he said he'll get his own supper." Later on, once he got to know Master Fontaine more, he'd talk more polite, but he always talked down to me like that.

7

Jacob smiled faintly when I told him I was going with Mirabeau. "What's funny?" I asked sharply.

"I'm sorry, Master Fontaine," he said. "It's just . . . why do you wanna work for a man you just met?"

I attempted to explain. "Jacob, this is a new country. It will need men like Mr. Lamar to make it work. I want to be part of that."

"Part of it. Uh-*huh*."

"I can see him running for Congress. After that, why not a higher office? Maybe even the presidency."

"President. *That* would make him important all right."

Jacob seemed unconvinced. So be it. I didn't need his approval; I had left the need for approval in Mississippi. But I did feel I had exaggerated when I mentioned the presidency. And though I expected Mirabeau's star to rise, the rapidity of its ascent surprised me. When word of his battlefield heroics reached ad interim President David Burnet, Burnet offered Mirabeau a Cabinet position as secretary of war. "I'll need a secretary myself, Edward," he said dryly as he told me of the offer. "Am I correct in thinking you'd be interested in the position?"

"Yes, of course. But how did it happen? Why did the president select you?"

A look of feigned shock spread over his features. "Do you think me unqualified?"

"Definitely not. So quickly, though! A few days ago he didn't even know your name. How did you convince him?"

"Convince him?" He laughed. "*He* had to convince *me*! We were discussing the current political landscape when he suddenly offered me the post. When I de-murred—of course I intend to involve myself in politics, but I assumed my first act would be to run for office—he told me he was looking for a man who could resist the destructive forces of self-interest that plague any government. I told him that my sum total of military experience amounts to this one battle we've just fought. 'I'm not asking you to fight with guns,' he said. 'I'm asking you to fight with words and intellect. You have leadership qualities that enable you to run *any* government office. And I've heard from some of your friends of your distaste for the command-ing general, who I fear will soon be elected president.'"

"So he's seeking an ally."

"As am I."

"And his opinion of Houston—"

"Matches mine. We were fortunate to win this war given the ineptitude of our commanding general. Drunkenness, cowardice, indecisiveness—his faults are many. Why, on the day of the battle, as we stood poised to rout the enemy, he turned to me and asked if we dared to attack. 'Dare to attack?' I asked. 'General, how dare we *not* attack!' Do you know what he said to that? 'You're right, I suppose we must.' What kind of generalship is that, Edward? God will not smile long upon such timidity. And Burnet's right, Houston likely will win the election to replace him. Austin will probably run against him and he does have significant support. But some of the men already call Houston 'the Hero of San Jacinto.' Gullible voters have been seduced by less."

"This may be so, Mr. Lamar—"

"Edward, please, call me Mirabeau."

"This may be so . . . Mirabeau, but if Houston wins he'll undoubtedly choose his own war secretary."

"Edward." His face wrinkled a bit, as if he were saddened by my inability to perceive something obvious. "My serving in Burnet's Cabinet, even if only for a short while, elevates me above the mob, which in turn strengthens my ability to influence events on a national level. Houston's term, if he indeed wins, will last two years. By law he can't succeed himself. Who better to replace him than a former Cabinet officer?"

"Aha!" I exclaimed. My earlier statement to Jacob seemed less rash now. "Of course! But you'll have to somehow remain in the public eye over the next two years."

"A challenge, yes, but one easily overcome. I suspect Houston will muddle things up enough that merely pointing out his faults will keep my name in the newspapers. And undoubtedly there will be something more official for me in the interim. Anyway, as Burnet talked, the first rung of the ladder became clear enough. I had to accept his offer." He paused for emphasis. "And so, *you* will now be first secretary to the secretary of war. Congratulations."

"Thank you, Mirabeau. I'm pleased to accept."

What would Father say now?

Master Fontaine told me he planned to work for Mr. Lamar and I asked him how much he'd pay him and he said, "Nothing." So I said, "Well, how are we gonna eat?" And he said, "The Lord will provide, Jacob." Which made sense to me because that's what I tell myself when I'm in need. But at the same time I'm thinking, "Maybe I oughta go shoot up some extra meat for the smokehouse." Because the Lord provides, but maybe just barely. That's the slave's view. We knew the masters would give us enough food to live because they needed us to work, but that didn't mean they cared if we were hungry.

Master Fontaine seemed to think a lot about Mr. Lamar even then. He told me he was an important man and that he might be president someday. I said, "What about Andrew Jackson?" and he said, "No, Jacob, Texas." He was awfully excited about that, but really, I didn't care. Then he said, don't be a fool, I know a good thing when I see it and I don't need you to tell me about it. And I said I reckon that's right. But I was telling myself that being important was something for white folks only. Still is, mostly. Someday, though, maybe the good Lord will see fit to change that.

History has witnessed few political scenes as fluid as that in post-Revolution Texas. Political coalitions formed, dissolved, and formed again at a dizzying pace. Men jockeyed for government posts like children fighting for sweets. Petty jealousies ruled the day. Mirabeau didn't escape their destructiveness.

First, though, we traveled with the government by steamboat from San Jacinto to Galveston Island, the desolate sandbar shielding the bay that had welcomed me to Texas. A more miserable place to conduct business can scarcely be imagined. Mosquitoes tormented us constantly. Gritty sand flavored every meal. Availing ourselves of the soothing sea breezes meant exposing ourselves to a blistering sun; seeking shade meant confining ourselves to the suffocating heat of a dreary cabin. I therefore welcomed President Burnet's order to move government farther down the coast to the town of Velasco.

Alas, Velasco proved little better. True, there was a town, or at least a cluster of buildings masquerading as one. But I was learning through bitter experience that all coastal Texas villages shared two things in those days, sand and blood-sucking mosquitoes. And, whereas in Galveston we could choose between sweltering inside the buildings and baking in the tropical sun, a lack of lamp oil in Velasco removed all choice in the matter. How absurd, I thought at the time, for the members of a national government to conduct its business in the open air. For that matter, I still think so.

My first encounter with David Burnet occurred at Velasco. I had found a rare grassy spot on which to repose when I spied a large man making his way toward me. Bushy whiskers protruding from his chin lent him a comical air as he strode across the sand. Wild hair jutted from his scalp at odd angles. His broad girth promised shade as he approached, but to my disappointment he veered to one side at the last moment, forcing me to rise so as to avoid staring directly into the sun.

"Are you Fontaine?" he abruptly demanded.

"That is my name, sir," I said irritably. "And what is yours?"

He extended a thick hand, which I accepted. "I'm David Burnet. The president. I understand you're Lamar's assistant."

Embarrassed, I became conciliatory. "Yes, sir, Mr. President, I didn't know. Yes, I'm Mr. Lamar's secretary. What can I do for you?"

"Tell your chief I need to see him. It's about Santa Anna. Lamar wants him shot. So does just about every man in the army. I can't say it would disappoint me to see it done. But tell him I've thought it over and can't support it. Too much trouble. The Mexicans would howl, but that's a small enough concern. It's England and France that worry me. They'll see it as barbaric, which is exactly what we don't want. So tell Lamar to come see me."

I nodded mutely. Interpreting my silence as displeasure, the president added, "You want to shoot him too, don't you?"

I blushed. "Sir, it's not my decision. But . . . "

"But *what*?"

"Sir, he's a murderer. The men at the Alamo . . . those men at Goliad."

"Yes, they're all dead because of him. So he deserves to be stood against a wall and shot. Or hanged from the nearest tree. I won't argue that." He paused to gesture at the barren landscape. "But as you can see, there are no trees at hand. Now go fetch Lamar."

He turned and stalked off, mumbling as he went. Marveling at his brusqueness, I reluctantly left my patch of grass to find Mirabeau.

"Why does he want to see me?" Mirabeau asked irritably when I relayed Burnet's message. He sat writing at a makeshift table composed of a saddle set upon pieces of driftwood. "It sounds as if he's already made up his mind."

"I don't know. At first that's all he said. Then he added the part about England and France and said to get you."

Rising, Mirabeau brushed sand off his trousers with one hand and stuffed his unfinished correspondence into a pocket with the other. "Come on, let's go."

We found Burnet seated alone inside one of the huts. To my surprise on such a warm day, a fire burned in the crude hearth. Even as we entered, beads of sweat rolled down my side.

"Mirabeau, come in." He beckoned toward a couple of rawhide chairs and waited for us to settle. His chair and ours, plus a rough pine table, constituted the only furnishings in the room. When I sat, the chair I had chosen sank into the soft earth floor and caused me to spill sideways onto the ground. Mirabeau chuckled, but Burnet remained stone-faced. Without waiting for me to right myself he started an obviously prepared speech.

"Mirabeau, not a word about Santa Anna. I know your position and, frankly, agree with it. But I've concluded that if we allow ourselves the satisfaction of hanging him we'll only invite charges of cruelty. Ironic, isn't it?"

"But we could put him on trial," objected Mirabeau. "He'd have legal counsel. He could summon a lawyer from Mexico. But we've got—"

"*Mirabeau!*" said the President. "I *said* the decision's been made. This isn't what I wanted to talk to you about anyway."

Surprised at Burnet's sharpness, Mirabeau flinched in his chair. His eyes narrowed in suppressed irritation. "Yes, *sir!*"

Burnet looked up quickly. "Your disagreement is noted. So is your impertinence. What I wanted to tell you is that I've decided to put you in command of the army."

Mirabeau opened his mouth but no words came out.

"You want to argue with me about that?" asked Burnet.

"No," said Mirabeau. "But I'm already secretary of war."

"You can be both."

"I see."

"As you know," Burnet explained, "General Houston has left the army to receive medical care."

I winced at these words. General Houston's ankle wound had proved serious and he had asked permission of Burnet to travel to New Orleans for proper treatment. Remarkably, Burnet denied consent; he yielded only when the steamboat captain refused to depart without Houston. Mirabeau entered the dispute when Houston's physician, Surgeon General Ewing, announced that he would accompany his patient on the voyage. As secretary of war, Mirabeau denied Ewing permission to leave the army. When Ewing said he would go anyway, my new chief had me draft a letter stripping Ewing of his commission and charging him with deser-tion. I viewed the action as cruel but naïvely told myself it was necessary for army discipline. Nevertheless, I trembled as I handed the missive to Dr. Ewing. A calm and patient man, he said only, "Please tell Secretary Lamar that I have received his message and accept the consequences of my actions."

Burnet went on with his explanation. "With Houston gone I find myself in need of an army commander. I want somebody I can trust, Mirabeau. I believe I can trust *you*. Will you accept?"

I expected him to say no. After all, he had demurred when offered the post of war secretary by pointing out his lack of military experience. With seemingly little thought, though, he replied quickly in the affirmative.

"Excellent," said Burnet, allowing himself just a hint of a smile. "Your first task will be to keep your men from killing Santa Anna. After that, everything else should be easy."

Mirabeau smiled weakly. He told me later he knew why Burnet gave him the position. "I didn't think he'd be so crude as to state the obvious, but I understood what I was supposed to do." To Burnet, though, he merely nodded and said, "I can handle it."

What Mirabeau was supposed to do, of course, was deflect the common sol-dier's wrath away from President Burnet onto himself. No sooner had his assump-tion of army command been announced than vengeful privates and officers be-sieged him with demands for Santa Anna's execution. Although he merely acted under the orders of his commander-in-chief, Mirabeau paid the political price for the unpopular decision to spare the tyrant's life. On one occasion, he almost paid with his own.

The Texian army encamped along the Brazos River at Velasco was not the same army that had defeated the Mexicans at San Jacinto. Volunteers from the United States continued to stream across the border after the battle, swelling the ranks with men who had not yet tasted the blood of war. Frustrated by inaction, these brave rowdies clamored for revenge against a man who had rendered them no per-sonal harm. Despite his antipathy toward Santa Anna, Mirabeau held little respect for their position. "I'd love to put him on trial, but a lynching would help no one. Are we to be a just or a barbarous nation?" he cried in frustration after sending yet another aspiring executioner from his office.

Early the next day, a mob of drunken soldiers on leave indicated its preference for barbarity. We were just helping ourselves to an excellent breakfast prepared by our landlady when a man rushed in asking for the army commander. "I'm Lamar," Mirabeau said.

Panting heavily, the man said, "You've got to do something. There's a group of soldiers going out to Orozimbo to hang Santa Anna."

"Are you sure?" Mirabeau demanded. "I hear rumors every day about some crack-brain aiming to kill Santa Anna."

"I saw them," said the man. "There's about a dozen, I swear. Most of them drunk and all of them hell-bent on a hanging."

"When did they leave?"

"Maybe half an hour ago. I got here as quick as I could."

Mirabeau turned to me. "Are you coming?"

Outside, we saddled two horses and struck out hard for the northwest. Orozimbo was the plantation home of the Phelps family. It was also Santa Anna's prison. It lay several miles distant. We knew we had to hurry.

We pushed our horses hard. After a few miles, Mirabeau shouted, "Are you armed?"

"No!"

"Neither am I."

Before we saw the house, we heard the mob. We raced toward the sound. A group of men clustered about a large and ancient live oak. As we approached, Mirabeau jumped off his horse without bothering to secure it. I dismounted, tied my animal to a fence, and hurried after his. He ran toward the drunken soldiers.

A large crowd of agitated men blocked Mirabeau's path to the base of the tree. Many brandished weapons; one man excitedly waved a rope over his head.

"Make way," shouted Mirabeau, pushing his way through the men. "Stand aside!"

"What for?" shouted someone in the crowd. "Who the hell are you?" An empty whiskey bottle flew perilously close to Mirabeau's head and sailed into the distance.

"I'm the secretary of war of the Republic of Texas and your commanding general!" yelled Mirabeau.

The mob quieted a little. Once Mirabeau reached its center he turned to face the angry soldiers. He shouted, "What's the meaning of this?"

I maneuvered my way less dramatically to a position where I could see the base of the tree. A small, terrified man crouched beside the trunk, leg irons preventing movement more than a foot or two in any direction, handcuffs pinning his arms to his side. His eyes betrayed fear. Although he wore nonmilitary apparel, I knew this must be Santa Anna. A frightened but determined woman stood beside him.

Mirabeau shouted again for an explanation. Several men hurled angry replies. Mirabeau raised both hands and, at the top of his voice, boomed, "Men, be quiet! I can only listen to one at a time and then only if the rest of you hold your tongue!"

The din died. Mirabeau pointed at the man with the rope and ordered him to speak his mind.

"It's like this, sir," said the man. "We heard that Santa Anna is going back to Mexico. We heard he paid a thousand gold pieces to go. We aim to stop him!"

Men roared in agreement.

"Quiet, men!" commanded Mirabeau. Turning to the soldier, he demanded, "Who told you that piece of nonsense?"

"I don't rightly know," came the reply. "Everybody's saying it, though. Ain't that right, fellas?"

Murmurs of assent rose from the mob. Mirabeau pointed at another man and said, "I'll ask again, who's spreading this false rumor?"

The man said nothing. Mirabeau pointed at several of the soldiers in succession, asking each one, *"You?"* None responded.

"I thought so," sneered Mirabeau. "Not one of you can tell me who's saying this because *no one's* saying it. *It isn't true!* What *is* true is that Santa Anna is our prisoner, *my* prisoner, and I'll not have him lynched today or any other day. Is that understood?"

No one seemed pleased by this, but many of the men at least adopted less threatening postures. Having brandished his authority, Mirabeau offered conciliation. "Men, rest assured that there have been no bribes, there has been no deal; no one has received a single penny. I give you my word of honor on that. I also give you my word that this prisoner will be used only to further the interests of our new republic, the Republic of Texas."

A few weak cheers provided an opportunity to win the crowd over. I shouted, "Cheers for the Single Star! *Huzzah!*"

"Huzzah!" the men shouted back with more enthusiasm.

"Huzzah!" shouted Mirabeau.

"Huzzah!" boomed the reply.

"Men, go back to your units knowing that your country's leaders have your interests at heart. Know that the day a man attempts to betray your trust is the day he encounters my wrath!"

"Cheers for Lamar!" This from the man with the rope.

"Well put," said Mirabeau with a laugh. Then he bowed and added, "Good day, gentlemen."

As the men dispersed and I breathed a sigh of relief, the man chained to the tree said something in Spanish. The lady with him said, "Mr. Lamar, I'm Mrs. Phelps. Santa Anna wishes you to know that he's grateful to you."

Mirabeau grunted and said to me, "Let's get back to our breakfast." To Mrs. Phelps he said, "Tell Santa Anna to go to hell."

Master Fontaine got his horse and mule back from the army and told me to get ready to travel. I loaded up our things, but when I started to climb up on Janey he said, "No, Jacob, we'll lead them down to the water. We're going by steamship." Well, I just about cried. I recollected our trip from New Orleans and how sick I got and I figured I'd be in for that again. But this was nothing. This time the water stayed flat and it didn't take nearly so long to get there. I didn't have to lean over the rail at all. On the way we saw some of the strangest creatures on God's earth or any other. I'd heard of them before but we didn't have them in my part of Mississippi. They're called alligators and they're like lizards, but as long as a man is tall. Maybe more. They float in the water real quiet and sneak up on their food and they say if one catches you up he'll bite you right in two. Whenever anybody saw one everybody grabbed a rifle and started popping away. Old Mr. Alligator was on to 'em, though, because when the boat got near he just slid right down into the water and plumb disappeared. So I don't think they ever killed one.

We stayed on an island a while. It was so big you couldn't see it was an island and there wasn't a single tree that I could see neither. There were mosquitoes as big as birds buzzing around us all day long. Some folks got into the water to get away from 'em, but I can't swim and wouldn't go lest I drown. As far as I know, nobody did drown.

Next we went down the coast a ways and this time we got to ride. Master Fontaine told me we were going to a town called Velasco, but when we got there it wasn't nothing more than some shacks even worse than what I lived in back in Mississippi. Master Fontaine told me it was where the government was and I thought, "Well, this is a rough country all right if the government's got nothing better to live in than what a Mississippi nigger's got."

There was some men that wanted to kill Santa Anna, so Mr. Lamar had to go stop 'em and Master Fontaine went along to help. I didn't have nothing to do, so I went down to the water to have a look at the waves. While I was there, two white men grabbed me and said since I didn't have a white master that they'd just take me for themselves. I told 'em about Master Fontaine and one of them hit me in the mouth. Then he put a rope around my neck and was gonna take me away. Lucky for me a man came by that knew I belonged to Master Fontaine and he made those men let me go. I was powerful glad to see Master Fontaine come back that night.

8

Once it became clear that there would be no lynching of Santa Anna, the troops shifted their focus to their "right" to name their own commanding general. Naturally, they possessed no such right, but that mattered little to the men. One group of mutinous officers organized a committee to "gauge the opinions of the soldiers in the ranks" so as to offer an opinion on the proper course of action. This was a thinly disguised attempt to oust Mirabeau. When Mirabeau sought Burnet's support, the president merely shrugged his shoulders and whined, "What can I do? They're armed. And perhaps a little drunk."

Mirabeau sent me to speak with Felix Huston, chairman of the committee that would decide his fate. Before I located Huston, though, I was intercepted by Thomas Rusk, the officer rescued by Mirabeau at San Jacinto. Rusk had assumed army command with Sam Houston's departure, only to be replaced by Burnet with Mirabeau. I feared an ugly scene. But Rusk, a round-faced, portly man, instantly relieved my anxiety by saying, "Fontaine, I'm as distressed by this insubordination as you are. What does it matter who heads the army just now? After the election everything will change anyway. As far as I'm concerned, this committee ought to be strung up with Santa Anna."

"Colonel Rusk, Colonel Lamar will be happy to hear that. I take it you would obey a presidential order?"

"It's complicated," he said, glancing at the sky. "I *would,* but I'm afraid that wouldn't settle anything. Fact is, the men want to pick their own man. If they're not allowed to, there'll be real trouble."

"I see. So what do you propose?"

"Let them have their blasted way. Most of them will be furloughed soon anyhow. Once they're gone the president can pick a new general if he wants."

"And if the committee decides to recommend Colonel Lamar?"

"Then I suppose we'd have to keep calling him 'General.'"

I immediately passed Rusk's message on to Mirabeau, who seemed little mollified. "It's the Houston men," he said accusingly. "They're out to embarrass me."

"Why?"

"Because they're selfish men serving the most selfish man of all. Because if Sam Houston's puppet can't run the army they'll make sure that no one else can do it either." He paused and paced a while before speaking again. "Edward, I have to decide if this fight would be worth it. Should I stand by what is right at all cost or should I yield to the mob?"

I offered a useless reply. "One should always do what's right."

"Ah, but what if what's right at the moment isn't what's right in the long run?"

"How so?"

"What's the outcome if I successfully fight to keep this job? In a matter of weeks Houston is elected president and removes me from command. I find myself out of a job *after* the elections. And Houston won't appoint me to a post. I'd have to sit idly by for two years while he destroys the country."

"And if you're removed now?"

"I *am* still secretary of war. I'll have given up command of the army for the greater good. When I then announce my bid for office, voters can only say, 'There goes a true patriot!'"

"You'll run for Congress?"

"No, vice president!"

I smiled, at last catching on. Here was a man capable of manipulating events to his advantage.

"And I'll win."

The next few days passed pleasantly enough. Work demands occupied but a few hours a day, so that by early afternoon I was free to explore Velasco's dunes and marshes. The sun beat ceaselessly down upon me, although once I discovered the refreshing breezes sweeping along the waterline I suffered less. I enjoyed shuffling along the damp sand, dodging waves, and searching for colorful shells. I had just returned to our cabin one day with a particularly large whelk when Jacob ran up to me.

"There you are, Master Fontaine," he said with obvious relief. "I've been looking all over for you. Mr. Lamar, he told me to find you quick. He's riled up about something."

"Did he say what?"

"No, sir, he just said to fetch you right away."

I found Mirabeau standing outside one of the decrepit cabins that passed for a government office building. Colonel Rusk and Colonel Huston stood with him, the latter clearly attempting to assuage an animated Lamar. As I approached, Huston said, "Look at the reality, Lamar. The men have clearly indicated who they want as their leader. They consider Burnet's appointment of you as interference."

Mirabeau's face reddened. "I under*stand* that, Huston! It isn't that I question the outcome of this ridiculous election; I question the need for it in the first place." Turning to Rusk, he said, "It seems as if *someone* is attempting to publicly humiliate me!"

"No, no, Mirabeau," pleaded Rusk. "That wasn't my intention at all. I merely—"

"*Save your breath, Rusk!*" Mirabeau practically shouted these words. It was the first time I had seen him erupt in such fashion, the first tiny crack in what I falsely perceived at the time as his perfect character.

Huston, attempting to act the peacemaker once again, said, "Tom, why don't you leave us alone for a few minutes?" Turning to me, he said, "Edward, please stay. Mirabeau's been asking for you."

We watched Rusk stomp off. Mirabeau looked at me and said, "These gentlemen have informed me that the army has voted in favor of Rusk resuming command. I've been trying to tell Huston that I had no intention of thwarting their will; that I fully understood the *reality* of the situation and that Rusk's call for a vote was only a base political maneuver."

"There was a vote?"

"Colonel Rusk thought that a vote by the soldiers would assist the process, Edward," said Huston. "That if the army publicly stated its preference, the government—Burnet—would find it easier to please all sides. Mirabeau, he blundered. But don't compound *his* error with one of your own. Stand aside. Let Burnet know that, for the good of Texas, you've decided to back the army's choice of Rusk as their general. That's no shame. And you still have your Cabinet position."

Mirabeau glared angrily at Huston. Slowly he composed himself, relaxed his face, and stated calmly, "Colonel Huston is correct, Edward. The nation demands obedience and I shall give it." Putting a hand on Huston's shoulder, he added, "Colonel Huston, Rusk can have command. I shall busy myself with my Cabinet position."

"Thank you, Mirabeau."

Once we were alone, Mirabeau sighed deeply. "Edward, I thought I'd seen hypocrites in Georgia, but these Texas boys have them beat."

His failure to calmly adhere to the brilliantly logical plan he had outlined earlier dismayed me. "I thought you intended to give up army command."

"I did. But Rusk's smugness about the whole thing really set me off. What kind of man who loves his country would call for a vote from that drunken mob? And undercut me in the process, I might add."

"I don't know. I thought Rusk was your friend."

"I thought so too."

"I suppose this will give you time to run for office?"

"This will give me time to steer Texas toward her destiny," he said without a smile.

It was hard in those days keeping track of what Lamar was and what he wasn't. Mostly this was because I got news only if I overheard something. Didn't nobody come to me and say, "Jake, let me tell you what we're planning to do about the government." But I was around the big boys a lot, so I heard plenty.

First thing I heard somebody say was that Lamar was to be secretary of war. Well, that's fine, I thought, but ain't the war over? A friend of mine laughed when I said that; he said there was bound to be another war and it might be soon, so they needed Lamar to keep the army going. He'd be sort of like a general, but he wouldn't actually do no fighting. Then I heard that Lamar was in charge of the fighting part too. See, during the battle where they killed all those Mexicans, General Houston got his foot shot up bad and had to go to New Orleans for a doctor. So there wasn't nobody in charge and the president picked Lamar even though he was already secretary of war. But I guess nobody asked the soldiers what they thought because all of a sudden they went off like a hornet's nest. They told anybody that would listen that they wanted their own man and if they didn't get him, there'd be trouble. I saw Lamar stomping around pretty mad talking to Master Fontaine about that. I was going down to the beach to find oysters and he saw me and told me to fetch Master Fontaine. By the time I did that and came back, he was hollering with two white men about something. I heard him say that he's the general, by God, and folks have to do as he says. But Master Fontaine and the other men got him all calmed down and he said, "All right, then, I won't be general." They all seemed pleased with that. I kept waiting for them to tell me to go away, but they didn't even notice I was there. Anyway, that's one way I could tell what was going on. I'd stand by looking busy while really I was listening to the white folks.

Burnet's hold on the reins of government weakened daily. Armed rebellion seemed such a threat that he issued a call for elections to ease the tension. As far as I knew Mirabeau had told no one save me of his plan to stand for office. It therefore came as a pleasant surprise when several of his friends wrote a letter inviting him to run for vice president.

"Gentlemen, I'm overwhelmed by your undeserved faith in me," he replied coyly. "I shall draft a formal response, but my immediate instinct is to answer favorably."

The next day, President Burnet interrupted Mirabeau and me as we conversed with a group of legislators. Tugging at Mirabeau's elbow, the president said, "Mirabeau, may I have a moment?"

After we had stepped away from the crowd, Burnet pumped Mirabeau's hand and said cheerfully, "I am gratified to hear of your plans, Mr. Vice President. Texas is fortunate to have you at her disposal."

"Thank you, Mr. President," Mirabeau replied, smiling. "But you should allow me to win the election before granting me the title!"

"Nonsense! To win you only have to announce your interest, of that I'm sure. No one of prominence has declared his candidacy. Given the influence of your friends and, if I may humbly add, my own support, you're certain to carry the day."

I had to suppress a laugh at that. Burnet's blunt style and refusal to execute Santa Anna had rendered him about as popular with the electorate as the bloody flux. Rather than point out this awkward truth, however, I said, "President Burnet, I've heard a rumor that Rusk will run as well."

Burnet frowned. "Is that so? Hmmm . . . well, he is well known, but my confidence remains with your boss."

"Really, David—" began Mirabeau.

"No cause for alarm, Mirabeau. If Rusk runs it's only because Houston orders it, not because he wants the job. Don't let his name frighten you off."

"I don't intend to."

"Anyway, you're in it now."

Burnet left.

"Can you believe that?" I asked.

"Bluntness is his nature," Mirabeau said.

"I hope he's right about Rusk."

"No matter, he's right about me."

My first summer in Texas taught me that Mississippi is not alone in torturing its residents with a tropical sun. Day after day we awoke to a cloudless sky. Oppressive heat tortured us as early as breakfast; by midafternoon we suspended work or travel to seek shade. Mirabeau nevertheless seemed energized as we laid plans for his political campaign. We began by accepting invitations to visit the hometowns of those who had first urged his candidacy. In each place we attended a public dinner, at which Mirabeau made a speech. Several rounds of drinks and toasts followed until at last Mirabeau would turn to me and whisper, "Let's make an exit." He didn't relish these appearances, for he was retiring by nature, and his orations, while eloquent, lacked vitality. Furthermore, his humility disallowed any notion of enjoying the applause that his speeches elicited. But, after bidding farewell to the dinner crowd, we would slip off to someone's quarters to enjoy the company of a few more intimate acquaintances and talk far into the night. Here the publicly shy candidate shone. Arguments and counterarguments flew about the room while a relaxed Mirabeau moderated and issued judgments in favor of one debate participant or another. In this looser environment his cleverness at conversation revealed itself in a way that I rarely observed in larger gatherings.

Jacob accompanied us on these travels. His primary duty lay with tending our mounts. In addition to our animals there was Mirabeau's fine black mare, Destiny. I laughed when I first heard this name, at which Mirabeau smiled and said, "It's a bit obvious, I concede. But she reminds me that, while we strive ever to control our fate, ultimately there are forces beyond our control. And *no* man is ever completely in control of a beast such as *this*!"

If we remained in a place longer than a day, Jacob had little to do. On such occasions I let him out to one of the locals in exchange for a few dollars. Without this income stream I would have rapidly exhausted my money supply. How glad I was that I had carried him with me to Texas.

One day, in some nameless farming village, Mirabeau and I chatted aimlessly beneath an enormous sycamore tree while Jacob split kindling nearby for an elderly shopkeeper. Mirabeau removed his hat, wiped the sweat from his face with his sleeve, nodded toward Jacob, and said, "See there, Edward, the African works tirelessly in heat that would destroy a white man."

I watched Jacob swing the axe a few times before observing, "He sweats like you or me."

"No, he doesn't," said Mirabeau, warming to my challenge. "Watch. The more he sweats the harder he works. You or I would have passed out by now."

I had to admit that Jacob, though drenched with perspiration, seemed unfazed by his task. His face remained expressionless as he split one stick of wood after another. "He's accustomed to hard work."

Mirabeau smiled triumphantly. "That's precisely my point. He's a hard worker because he's *made* for hard work. We are all created with certain aptitudes and characteristics."

"Characteristics?"

"Oh, come now, you're well enough acquainted with African servants to understand what I mean. Look at Jacob. He's clever enough, but would you argue that he is the intellectual equal of his master? If so, how could you justify his servitude?"

"I've often been of two minds about that."

"You needn't. It's neither you nor I that bind him, but the brutishness of his race. Race defines us, Edward, defines who we are and what we become. This applies not only to the individual, but to populations . . . to nations. Just look at the African continent for proof. What great power in Africa exists to compete with the might of England and France?"

"None."

"And it's the same here in North America. Our ascendancy on these shores is no accident. You've seen yourself how quickly Mexico fell to us."

"Yes, but Mexico was only recently a Spanish colony. It remains in the hands of the sons of Spain."

"Sons of Spain, perhaps," Mirabeau said with a sneer, "but mongrelized sons with savage blood in their veins. Spaniards and Indians have been interbreeding for centuries. The result is that degraded race we call Mexican."

I was unconvinced. I had little experience as yet with Mexicans other than to watch them be slaughtered on the battlefield. "But how are they degraded? What makes them so?"

"Edward!" said Mirabeau in exaggerated surprise. "*How* are they degraded? Could we have so easily defeated a race of equals? Have the Mexicans produced the same caliber of men to be found in America or Texas? *No!* In just a few short months we drove the best army that Mexico could field back across the Rio Grande. That would have been impossible against a comparable European army."

"Perhaps."

"And now we're free to extend our influence westward. What stands in the way of Texas expansion to the west? Only more Mexican territory. Which is occupied by the very people we have just conquered! Plus a few scattered tribes of savages, little more than animals, really, wild men incapable of halting civilization's advance."

His far-reaching mind continued to astound me. The future to me meant the upcoming elections; Mirabeau gazed into a distant age with clarity.

"That will take years," I said.

"Perhaps," he conceded. "Perhaps not. Would you have thought our victory over Mexico would come so soon after independence was declared? I didn't. But Providence seemed to guide us. Despite inferior numbers, despite inferior equipment, despite a drunken demagogue to lead us, we prevailed. We prevailed in the face of logic because we carry the torch of civilization with us. Guided by God we bring light into the wilderness."

"Now you sound like a preacher."

"What's funny is that I used to believe differently. Oh, I was quite young then, but I used to believe that the European settler gained North America only by illegal and immoral conquest."

"Immoral? How so?"

"When I was a schoolboy," he said, "our teacher instructed the class to write an essay answering the question, 'Were the Europeans justified in conquering North America?' Most of the class naturally took the European view and answered 'yes.' As much to be contrary as anything else, I chose to argue the opposite. I naïvely claimed that Indians held North America by right of first possession and that Europeans wrested land from the rightful owners only through force of arms. I decried the bloodshed that resulted, blaming the European for inflicting murderous violence upon an innocent people."

"And did you believe what you wrote?"

"At first, no. But the more I pondered it, the more I did believe it, until at last I was convinced that a great crime had occurred. When the day came to read our essays before the class I awaited my turn impatiently. As each classmate stood to defend our European ancestors I silently sneered inside, knowing that my irrefutable logic would soon humiliate them. But that didn't happen."

"Let's hear the tale!"

"After I finished reading, I looked up at the class to rejoice in the shameful expressions I felt sure I would see. Indeed, there were many bewildered faces in the crowd. But then the teacher, a wise and patient man, destroyed my case with a single question. 'What about civilization?' he asked. 'What do you mean?' I said. 'Mr. Lamar,' he replied, 'do you claim that the wild beast in the forest is as civilized as you?' 'Of course not,' I answered. 'Well, then,' he said, 'how can you compare the lives of this country's savage tribes with our advanced culture?' Naturally, I had no answer. Hurt and angry, I returned to my seat. My classmates laughed. But later, as I thought about his words, I realized how foolish I had been. I realized that God has always favored the advance of civilization. And if this is God's design, who am I to argue? Righteous war is a holy duty, Edward; that was my realization. As we carry civilization's light into the wilderness, anyone or anything barring our way must therefore be standing against God. The red man must yield or perish. That is the only conclusion a logical man can make."

It was cruel logic, but logic nevertheless. Jacob's rhythmic axe blows echoed in the still afternoon heat. Mirabeau glanced over to watch him work, smiled approvingly, and said with finality, "There you have it, Edward, the proof of my words. The nigger knows his place and is content. The savage resists because he is too ignorant to comprehend the Almighty's plan. And thus we must exterminate him. This is unfortunate, but a sad truth is still a truth."

"So that Texas might build an empire?"

"Not an empire, a paradise."

There was gonna be an election and that's when Master Fontaine really went to work. He said Lamar wanted to be vice president and he was gonna help him do it. He told me I'd be helping him and he'd be helping Lamar so that really I'd be helping Lamar too. He never asked me if I wanted that, but what did it matter, they weren't gonna let black folks vote anyway. I liked Sam Houston for president and that's the way it turned out. I liked him for talking to me like a man and not a slave. He did that more than anybody, even Master Fontaine. Lamar was just the opposite. It was "Boy, do this" and "Boy, do that" and be quick about it. He didn't say it mean, but he never smiled, he never laughed, he just pointed and told me to fetch. But if Master Fontaine said to help him then that's what I did.

To get ready for the election they went all around the country telling everybody to vote for Lamar. I went too. We stopped at all the towns. Master Fontaine would find me something to do, then he'd trail after Lamar and I mostly wouldn't see him again until it was time to leave town. I found out later he was going around town telling folks to gather under a big tree or at the biggest house; once they did, here came Lamar to make a big speech. I saw it happen once or twice when I was put to work nearby. I couldn't hardly hear Lamar, he talked so quiet, but I'd hear folks in the crowd hollering out this and that. That might go on all day. Once I chopped up a whole wagonload of kindling and they were still over yonder under the tree listening to Lamar.

At night the white folks would disappear into a house and send me to a shed out back. Sometimes I'd slip over to the stable or somewhere I knew I'd find some company and swap stories and maybe a sip or two from the jug. I always asked Master Fontaine before going but he didn't ever mind. Once a pretty young girl asked me to come over after supper and help her cut up some pumpkins for drying. We sat down next to each other and started slicing but soon she scooted over and I scooted some too and before you know it we weren't cutting squash no more. I did me some praying that night and figured that set me all right again with the Lord. In those days I didn't get very many chances to socialize with a lady and I had to take 'em when I could.

Well, once I was with some friends out by the horses where Master Fontaine and Mr. Lamar were in there talking to a bunch of men. Two of 'em came out, but before they came for their saddles they stood there jawing at each other a while. I heard one of 'em say he wasn't sure Lamar was the man for the job. He said he didn't want a man that was so sure about everything. "Don't you want somebody that knows what he should do?" the other one asked. "Sure," the first one said, "but he seems to know what I should do too." I didn't know it so much then but that was Mr. Lamar all right. Always glad to set you straight about how you was doing something wrong.

I heard bits of what Mr. Lamar believed here and there and it was hogwash through and through. I didn't believe it then and despise the thought of it now. "Africans were made to work," he'd say while watching me and I wished I could say I was born here, not Africa. "Look at them work; they don't get tired like you and me," he said once and let me tell you that ain't true at all. I got plenty tired. I worked hard because I was afraid not to, that's why. I'd seen men beat to death for letting up and didn't want that to happen to me. I didn't have no particular plans for my future—none of us did back then—but I knew I was a man and not a beast. Yes, that man was plain wrong.

10

In the earliest days of the Republic, a candidate for office regarded each man's vote as precious. Not so nowadays, when electoral deficits are overcome merely by having a friend in charge of the ballot box. In 1836, though, we hadn't yet matured enough politically to possess corrupt machines capable of conjuring favorable tallies from distant precincts. There were no far-flung networks of crooked supporters. No well-heeled interest groups had organized to swing an election against the popular will. Mirabeau and I therefore anticipated a close race, especially since his chief opponent, Thomas Rusk, enjoyed fame equal to his own.

I was therefore shocked when Wash Miller found me at a restaurant enjoying a stringy beef stew, plopped down on the bench next to me, and said, "Ten to one."

At first I thought he referred to a horse race. Wash loved horses. More precisely, Wash loved to bet on horses. I first met him on a field outside of town marked out as a track. I was searching for Jacob, as I needed him to ride Spirit against the horse of a particularly cocky army officer. Suddenly, a man raced up to me and said urgently, "Friend, lend me ten dollars and I'll split the winnings with you."

"What winnings?"

"Haven't you heard? Captain Israel is racing his horse against some rube's nag. There's easy money to be made."

"Sir," I said with unfeigned annoyance, "Captain Israel is running his horse against mine. And I dare say she is no nag."

The man cocked his head in amazement. "You're the rube? You don't look like one."

"I'll take that as a compliment. As for my horse, she has taken money from the owners of faster horses than Captain Israel's."

"In that case, lend me ten dollars and I'll bet on you."

I laughed. "What happened to your easy money?"

"Evidently it's riding with you."

I handed him some paper money. "Here. Put this on my animal and bring me my share after the race."

"Thanks."

He started to rush off. "What a minute," I said. "What's your name?"

He stuck out his hand. "Wash Miller. And you better not be lying about your horse."

"Edward Fontaine. And you better pay me back."

Spirit won the race. True to his word, Wash found me immediately afterward and handed over my original loan amount plus another ten dollars. "I think we shall be friends," he said.

"I think we shall."

Now I looked at him in puzzlement and said, "Hello, Wash. Ten to one what?"

"Ten to one," he repeated, "your man wins."

I swallowed so quickly that it hurt going down. "You mean the election results?"

"Yes, the election results," he said while grabbing the piece of cornbread by my bowl. "Lamar won by a ten-to-one margin."

I dropped my spoon. Ten to one! Ten out of every eleven votes for Lamar. What could be more decisive? What clearer indication of God's will could there be?

"Aren't you going to say anything?" Miller asked.

"Yeah, give me back my cornbread."

My elation at the news gave way to disappointment when Miller handed over the bread and said, "All right, I'll get a plate of my own. Houston won as well."

"He did?" I said as he strode to the sideboard for a dish. "Over Austin?"

"Yeah, that surprised me too," he said, returning to the table. "Or at least the margin of victory did. Seven to one. You'd have thought that Austin had more support than that."

"I suppose you're happy about the outcome." Wash was a fervent supporter of Sam Houston.

"I am indeed. Austin's a fine organizer, but he's no leader. Houston inspires men."

"Inspires them to drink."

He turned serious. "Ed, you're wrong. Not about the drinking, everyone has seen Houston in his cups. But you're wrong about everything else. Sam Houston is just what this country needs. He's brave, he's confident, he's—"

I snorted. "Miller, please, spare me the campaign speech. Houston won, and I'll just have to get used to it."

"Yeah," he said, laughing, "because your chief will be working for him."

"Working *with* him, you mean."

He shrugged his shoulders in reply.

The next day's *Telegraph and Texas Register* confirmed Wash's report, at least for Bastrop County. Out of 188 votes for president, Houston garnered 113. Mirabeau's margin topped that as he took 177 to only 18 for Rusk. With a copy of the newspaper in hand, I found Mirabeau in his tiny office just off the main street through town. Really no more than a lean-to shed, the room abutted a dry goods store owned by a political supporter named Beacham. I slogged through a muddy alley to reach it. Two pigs rooted in the muck before the entrance.

"Good morning, Mr. Vice President!" I called out cheerily upon entering the room.

"Good morning, Edward," said Mirabeau without looking up. He sat at a plain pine table just big enough for him to rest his elbows on as he wrote. "What rhymes with 'cherub'?"

"Goodness . . . uh . . . "

"All I can think of is 'scarab.' But why would I mention beetles in a poem to my daughter?"

"You're writing Rebecca?"

"Yes, and I always include a few lines of verse. How about 'Someday, dear, quite like a scarab, I'll scurry home to my sweet little cherub?'"

"It rhymes."

"It'll have to do." He pushed the letter aside. "What have you got there?"

"Take a look," I said, dropping the paper onto the desk. "You not only won, you *demolished* Rusk!"

"Yes," he said, picking up the paper, "and I take no great pleasure in that. Certainly I wanted to win, but I didn't want to humiliate the man." He read silently for a while before adding, "I *do* relish the fact that I outperformed Houston. Look at that. He thinks himself beloved by all, yet fully forty percent are against him in this county." He returned the newspaper to me. "Well, whether he won by one vote or a thousand we're stuck with him for the next two years."

I pulled a chair up to the table and sat down, then pulled a large chunk of cheese from my pocket, broke it in half, and handed a piece to Mirabeau. "Here's some breakfast."

He accepted it silently and without expression. I could tell he was drifting into one of his thoughtful moods. I had learned to leave him to his thoughts in such moments, for they often inspired great insights. At length he mumbled, "I won't help him."

"What?"

"Houston. I won't help him ruin the country. He'll attach my name to various inconsequential projects so that later he'll have me to share the blame with. But I'll have no part of that."

"Are you certain he'll be so ruinous?"

"Yes, and we'll get a taste of what's coming later this morning. We've been summoned to the throne. He wants us there at eleven."

"Me too?"

"Of course. I'll need you to take notes. I want everything between us in writing."

"I'll bring paper and pen."

"Yes, do."

I wouldn't have thought it possible, but Houston occupied a room even more miserable than Mirabeau's. The president-elect of the Republic lived in one side of a double-pen cabin in which much of the mud chinking had fallen out. Lumps of it lay in a line along the walls as if placed there for some purpose. Flies buzzed through the openings. In one corner several wasps worked at building a nest. "What a fine presidential palace," I said in jest as we approached.

"He's not president yet," said Mirabeau.

"Come in, come in!" said Houston in his thunderous voice when he saw us at the doorway. Jumping from his chair, he skirted around a shabby desk before grabbing Mirabeau's arm. "Lamar! Thank you for coming. And if I remember correctly, this is Mr. Fontaine. So glad to see you again."

Mirabeau grimaced as Houston vigorously pumped his hand, an expression I repeated when my turn came. A large man, the president-elect possessed enormous hands, and his grip compared favorably to an iron bear trap. I was surprised that he remembered my name. Except for our initial encounter at San Felipe, I had had little intercourse with him. "Mr. Houston, it's an honor," I said with forced conviction, for I hadn't forgotten the black clouds of smoke that he left over that unfortunate town.

"Ah, the flattery is appreciated!"

Once we all were seated, Houston slapped his enormous hands on the desk and announced, "We must have refreshments!"

But as he reached for the bottle on a small side table, Mirabeau said awkwardly,

"Thank you, Mr. Houston, I cannot partake of strong drink so early in the day."

He turned to me. "Fontaine?"

When I demurred he set the bottle back on the table and faced us. Leaning back casually in his chair he said, "Gentlemen, what a task we have before us. We have been chosen to create order out of chaos. I don't know about you, but I'm a bit daunted by the challenge."

Mirabeau smiled slyly and said, "There have been many daunting challenges so far that brave men have overcome."

I shuddered at the insult, for I was sure that was the intent. Mirabeau had often complained of what he saw as Houston's cowardly hesitation before the attack at San Jacinto. But if Houston perceived injury, he ignored it. With a nod of his head he merely said, "True, true." An uncomfortable silence followed.

I was embarrassed for Mirabeau. True, I held little esteem for Houston, but he seemed to be making a sincere effort at conversation. Mirabeau's chilly response did him no credit.

Houston leaned forward. Adopting a conciliatory tone, he looked Mirabeau in the eye and said, "Look, Lamar, I understand that we have political differences. But I want you to know that I intend for us to serve this Republic as a team. I know of your courage, for I saw that on the battlefield. I've heard tales of your talents but haven't yet been able to witness these for myself. I need your help."

Mirabeau stared back at Houston a moment longer than seemed appropriate before saying, "Mr. Houston, thank you. With your support I can serve this nation well. You can count on me to back any policy that is in the best interest of our country."

A quick tightening of his jaw betrayed Houston's recognition of the implied contingency of Mirabeau's offer. Maintaining his friendly manner, though, he smiled broadly and said, "Well, then, Lamar, the Republic of Texas shall be the winner in this partnership."

They spoke for two hours—although it would be more accurate to say that Houston spoke for two hours while Mirabeau listened and I took notes. A casual observer would have described the exchange as amiable. I knew better. I recognized Mirabeau's long pauses before answering a question as a sign of irritation. There were many such conversation gaps. As usual, Houston spoke eloquently but mostly spouted nonsense. The Republic was broke, he claimed, ignoring the funds sure to flow from the United States and Europe with Texas an independent nation. Consolidate the settled eastern areas before expanding our western borders, he urged, turning his back on the brave pioneers paying for that expansion with sweat and blood. Grant the Cherokee permanent title to their territory, as if savages possessed any rights at all.

This last point particularly enraged Mirabeau. "It's because he's part savage himself," he later scoffed, waving his hand dismissively. "He lived with them for years, what can you expect?"

I had heard this claim before but didn't know how to judge its truthfulness. "Are you certain of that?" I asked.

"Quite certain, he's told me so himself. Once as a boy when he ran away from his family and another time when he abandoned that poor woman in Tennessee."

"What poor woman?"

"You don't know that story?"

I shook my head.

"You do know that he was governor of Tennessee, don't you? Andrew Jackson's handpicked successor?"

"Of course."

"Jackson. There's another fine piece of work. Anyway, while governor, Houston proposed to a woman from a fine family, one of the better families in the state. The very night of their wedding he left her. Never told anyone the reason; just left this poor young woman in shame and humiliation. He just as inexplicably resigned his office and fled to the Indian Territory. He lived there with the Cherokee for several years. Took a wife, who he then abandoned when he came to Texas."

"Remarkable!"

"Yes, remarkable. So when he talks about deeding land to the Cherokee he's really just feathering his own nest. Those people are what pass for his family. He's only looking after his own."

I nodded. "So it would seem."

"He'll one day learn that these people, these illegal squatters, have no rights that the government of Texas is bound to respect. We have good, solid American citizens, *civilized* men, arriving daily. *These* are the people we should accommodate, not savages!"

"He'll be difficult to work with. Look at your policy differences."

Mirabeau snorted. "He doesn't want to work with me. He wants to *manipulate* me. And I won't allow it! The frontier . . . my God, man, he'll leave it to wither on the vine! You've heard me say this before, Edward; the frontier is our ticket to empire. The east will take care of itself. But the frontier, *that's* where we must pour our resources, *that's* where the sprouting tendrils of civilization require our constant care and attention. Otherwise the savage prevails and progress grinds to a halt!"

We shook our heads in disgust. He sighed and said, "Well, Edward, we must bide our time. At the moment, he's on top. But our time will come."

• • •

At first, a lot of folks didn't know that Houston and Lamar didn't like each other. I knew it because I heard Lamar talk to Master Fontaine about it. So after they both won their elections, everybody figured they'd be like a mule team pulling the plow. But it wasn't so. Master Fontaine said Houston pretended that's how he wanted it, but really he didn't. He figured Houston talked nice to try to fool 'em, kind of like you tell your tired mule you're almost done plowing when you ain't. I'm not so sure. Houston never told me no stories. If he said, "Jake, go on and get me some water from the well and there's a nickel in it for you," then you could count on there being a nickel in your pocket when you did it. I can't say that about most white folks and I sure can't say that about Mr. Lamar. He'd tell you to fetch the water and then hold back that nickel because you didn't get enough or you spilled some on the way. I learned to listen real careful to what he said.

11

At Velasco I thought I had experienced the hottest, muddiest, most bug-infested town that Texas had to offer. Then I went to Columbia. Columbia's city fathers somehow convinced Congress that they could offer better accommodations to the government than could be had in Velasco, which merely proves how gullible men can be when they are suffering from foul water, oppressive heat, and gritty food. Mirabeau and I rode together in a wagon to the new government seat. Jacob rode his mule and two or three mounted congressmen came along as well. The road spanned that flat, endless coastal prairie that Texas is known for, intermingled with canebrakes thick enough to deny admittance to a mouse. En route we encountered a bear and two cubs, which Mirabeau and the others dispatched after I amused everyone with a shot that missed badly. The cubs we put in the wagon, but there was no room for the mother, so we left her behind. Ten minutes later a pack of wolves descended on the carcass. We listened to their snarling and barking all the way to Columbia.

At the new capital we expected a wait of several weeks before Mirabeau's inauguration as vice president. We took a room in a boardinghouse near the main square. Jacob spent the first few nights sleeping beneath the canopy of an enormous live oak tree, where he had much company. Then I purchased some planks from a trader at the river, with which Jacob erected a small but serviceable shanty behind our house. Given the increasing workload Mirabeau had assigned to me, I envied his carefree life.

One evening, weary of the repetitious fare prepared by our landlady, I ventured out in search of something other than boiled beef and corn cakes to eat. Finding an elderly man of about fifty roasting wild turkey under a canvas tarp, I asked for a meal and took a seat. Suddenly I was joined by about a dozen soldiers, young men with fuzzy cheeks and great braggadocio. There being insufficient room at the table, several men plopped down around the roasting pit to await their food.

"Sorry to disturb your peacefulness, friend," said the man next to me as he pulled a bottle out of his coat pocket. After offering me a taste, which I declined, he drank greedily before handing the bottle across the table to one of his comrades. Several other bottles appeared. The smell of whiskey overtook the pleasant aroma of the roasting bird.

"You boys having a little off-duty fun?" I asked.

"Yes, sir," answered the soldier at the far end of the table. I started at his overly respectful tone until I realized he looked much younger than my own age of twenty-seven. "Now that we've licked Santa Anna there's nothing for us to do. Right, boys?"

The other men cheered. Those holding bottles took demonstrative swigs. A man by the fire cheering louder than the rest hollered, "That's right, Jimmy! You licked old Santa Anna from all the way back in Tennessee!"

Everyone roared. Jimmy smiled sheepishly and shouted back, "Hey! I can't help it if General Sam was too doggone impatient to wait for me! You'd think he'd have been more polite, seeing as how we're both from Tennessee!"

"Ain't that right?" said another. "If he'd waited for us he could have sent them other fellers home! We'd have licked the Mexicans by ourselves!"

As the men's laughter died down the soldier next to me stood, raised a bottle, and said enthusiastically, "To General Sam Houston, hero of San Jacinto and our next president!"

All cheered as the proprietor set a plate of turkey and boiled greens before me. I dug in while hoping for the soldiers to ignore me.

More toasts elicited more cheers and laughter from the increasingly rowdy crowd. The man across from me said, "To President Houston, by God! Who oughta just go ahead and clear that bastard Burnet out and take the job *now*!" He swayed a bit before dropping back onto the bench. Grinning at me he said, "Whaddya think, friend? Should we tar and feather old Davy Burnet?"

Not wishing to provoke him, I muttered a noncommittal response and stuffed a piece of turkey in my mouth.

"Of course he thinks so!" yelled one of the other soldiers.

"So what are we waiting for?" shouted Jimmy, the one whose boast had triggered this direction of the conversation. "We're *soldiers*, God damn it! *We're* the ones getting killed for the country. Why shouldn't we get to make Houston president instead of that fusspot Burnet?"

A great roar erupted as all the men began shouting at once. The proprietor scurried about with plates of food, hurriedly throwing one down at each place as if suddenly called to urgent business elsewhere. I gulped my supper furiously, eager to quit the scene before the ruckus attracted unpleasant attention. Finally I shoved a turkey leg in my pocket for Jacob, threw a few coins on the table, and fled. As I rounded a corner at the end of the street I could still hear them shouting, *"Cheers for President Houston! Hooray! Hooray!"*

I immediately reported what I had witnessed to Mirabeau. He dropped what he was doing and we set out to locate Burnet. We found him in the common room of his boardinghouse. A fire crackled in the hearth. A large clock on the wall impressed me as one of the few signs of civilization I had encountered in Columbia. I told the president, "I believe those soldiers, while drunk, were quite serious about having their way."

Burnet's face twisted into a snarl. He said, "I thought I left all the fools in this world back in Ohio, but I see a few of them followed me to Texas."

"There's no shortage here," said Mirabeau.

"When does *Houston* get back?" Burnet spat the word "Houston" as if he had just bitten into a lemon.

"A rider came in this morning with word that our great leader has just left the Redlands," said Mirabeau. "He should be here in a day or two. He picked a fine time to go sweet-talk Anna Raguet."

Burnet's bushy eyebrows twitched in surprise. "Anna Raguet? Henry Raguet's daughter? Houston's courting her?"

"That's the one."

"Well, I can't fault him for that. No man wants to be a bachelor forever. And she's a delightful young woman."

I glanced at Mirabeau, for I knew of his intense loneliness since the death of his wife, Tabitha, back in Georgia. He remained stoic, yet his silence betrayed the effect of Burnet's unintentional barb. Wishing to end the awkward moment, I asked, "What does it matter when Houston returns?"

"The sooner he gets here the sooner I can resign."

Mirabeau sprang back to life. "You would resign? But that's yielding to the mob!"

Burnet shook his head and said, "As yet, there is no mob. Only troublemakers in the saloons. There've been no demands, no specific threats. But at the rate things are going, that's bound to change. My resignation would avert a mutiny."

"And that's why you need Houston here in Columbia," I said, deducing his line of thought.

"Exactly," said Burnet. "I can't resign if there's no one here to take my place. Houston's a poor choice, but the people have spoken."

Mirabeau sighed and said, "God save us all."

"He will," said Burnet. "Especially if you win the office next time."

"David, you flatter me," said Mirabeau, smiling. "But the thought has crossed my mind."

"All right," said Burnet. "We'll muddle along until then. But get ready, because when the Big Drunk arrives, the ball begins."

With a wry smile Mirabeau glanced over at me and asked, "Aren't you glad you came to Texas?"

I'd never seen Master Fontaine so worked up. He came back from supper, tossed me a turkey leg, and started in to holler for Mr. Lamar. Once he fetched him, the two of them stomped off to find President Burnet. I sat back down with my turkey leg in one hand and my cleaning knife in the other. I was working on one of the bear carcasses they shot while we were coming over from Velasco. I wished they'd have brought back the mama instead of the babies because I'd rather skin one big bear than two little ones. But they didn't ask me about that.

I was there outside my shed and a group of soldiers came along shouting and singing loud enough to wake the dead. Most of 'em didn't look old enough to wrestle a squirrel, but they sure talked big. One of 'em hollered over at me, "Hey, boy, we're gonna get ourselves a new president, what do you think of that?" I answered that I knew about the election and I heard Sam Houston was to be the man for the job. He said, "Yeah, you dumb nigger, but we're gonna make him president NOW!" Well, I didn't want to rile those boys up, but I knew from Master Fontaine that General Houston was still away up in the Redlands. When I told 'em that, they got real quiet. Then one of 'em said, "Shoot, boys, we might have to wait a day or two, that's all." But another said, "You gonna believe what this darkie tells you? Let's go ask the captain." So off they went and left me with them two dead bears.

When Master Fontaine got back I told him what happened. He said it must have been the same soldiers he saw when he was out eating turkey. But he said it didn't matter none because they had decided to beat those boys to the punch and make Houston president right away. That meant Lamar would be vice president right away too, and then we wouldn't be having time to set around eating turkey and cutting up bear skins. So he said I'd best hurry up with them skins.

• • •

I was coming out of a dry goods store a few days later when I learned of Houston's arrival. Laden with my purchases, which included a box of needles and several spools of thread, I almost knocked Moseley Baker from the porch as I passed through the doorway into the blinding sunlight.

"I'm sorry, Captain Baker, I didn't see you there," I said in apology.

Baker, a friendly but volatile man, merely laughed. "No harm done, Fontaine. I see you're in a hurry to get home to your mending."

Remembering my needles and thread I said, "Yeah, there's a few things to mend and I want to finish them before Houston gets back. Mr. Lamar expects to be rather occupied after that, which means I will be too."

"In that case you're too late. He's already here."

I let out an exasperated sigh. "Are you sure? Have you seen him?"

"No, but I heard it from other folks." He pointed up the street. "And look at that ruckus. I'll bet that's for General Sam."

My eyes followed his finger and saw a crowd of twenty or thirty in front of Hawthorne's hotel. "I'd best go see."

The crowd had indeed gathered for Houston. He faced it from the gallery in front of the hotel as if giving a stump speech. Wash Miller sat in a chair behind him. Robert Irion, Houston's good friend and the newly elected senator from Nacogdoches, was off to one side. Several other government officials stood in the street, including William Wharton and his brother John, Jesse Billingsley of Mina, Branch Archer of Brazoria, and Albert Horton of Matagorda. A festive air continuously attracted new onlookers.

"Are you married yet, Sam?" hollered one man, causing everyone to laugh.

"Now, friend," Houston said with a grin, "you know as well as I do that a gentleman doesn't discuss his lady friends in public."

"If that's so," said the man in playful retort, "go ahead and spill the beans, because *you're* no gentleman!"

Even I smiled at that, although I thought it closer to the mark than was intended. True to his reputation, Houston shrugged his shoulders and laughed along with the crowd. As much as I had grown to dislike him, I had to admit that he possessed an extraordinarily jovial nature.   As the laughter abated, Houston descended the steps and began shaking hands. Wishing to avoid an encounter I turned to go. Suddenly a huge hand snapped on my shoulder like a bear trap.

"Fontaine! Edward! So good to see you!"

I turned, fumbling with my recent purchases so as to free my right hand, which I extended in greeting. "General Houston, how nice to see you back in Columbia."

His gigantic frame towered over mine. I squinted upward into the sun to make out his face, which bore a foolish grin. Several days' worth of stubble had begun to fill in the gap between his side whiskers. He pumped my hand vigorously and asked, "Where's Lamar?"

When I pleaded ignorance he said nonchalantly, "Ah, no matter. We'll see each other soon enough, won't we? Come by for a drink sometime. You and I should become better acquainted."

"General, I will," I said half-heartedly.

He jerked his head backward toward the hotel. "I'm staying right here. Come by any time. Tell Lamar too, won't you?"

Extricating myself from his handshake, I turned again to go. "I will, General. I know he'll be pleased to see you." As I put distance between us, I thought, "May the Lord forgive the polite lie."

Burnet's announced resignation struck the people of Columbia like a thunderbolt, leaving in its wake a moment of absolute quiet followed by a crescendo of excitement. Mirabeau busied himself writing an inaugural speech. He gave me a list of senators and congressmen to acquaint myself with, thus hoping I would sow seeds of political alliance. As I looked over the list I remarked, "I don't see Houston's name."

"You know *him* well enough."

The rushed nature of the inauguration precluded embellishment of the simple ceremony performed in Congress. President Burnet had given notice only a day before he left office. When Congress received his resignation letter, House members voted to effect the transfer of power that same afternoon. The arrival of Senate members in the House chamber filled that room to near capacity. Thus, only a few spectators were able to squeeze in to witness the event. I arrived with Mirabeau, by which time there was not a single available seat. By virtue of my status as the vice president-elect's assistant, though, I found a favorable standing position on one side of Speaker Ira Ingram's chair.

Interested citizens unable to enter the hall flooded the building's veranda and spilled into the street. Calls to the crowd for silence from the sergeant-at-arms proved useless and a steady hum of conversation obligated Speaker Ingram to shout the oath of office. Houston boomed his affirmative response loudly enough that even the most distant spectators heard it plainly. Mirabeau's oath carried throughout the hall but not into the street. Thankfully, his new authority depended not upon the volume of his voice.

The newly installed president and vice president were each invited to address

8

the government. This is the only instance I can recall in which Mirabeau spoke at greater length than Sam Houston. Houston's speech, prepared in haste earlier in the day, sounded uncharacteristically awkward. For once his silver tongue abandoned him; he received only a few rounds of scattered applause as he spoke. His call for seeking peace with the various Indian tribes elicited stony silence. But he ultimately recovered through the cheap trick of grandly handing over his sword to symbolize termination of his army command. Feigning speechlessness, he even wiped nonexistent tears from his cheeks during the act.

By contrast, Mirabeau's address garnered several bursts of cheering and applause. He addressed no specific political issues but confined himself to themes of statecraft, patriotism, and sacrifice. Nevertheless, as members filed out of the hall they spoke only of Houston's dramatic stunt. Such is the price of selflessness!

The fine barbecue that followed the inauguration made up for the ceremony's simplicity and alleviated my annoyance at Houston's demagoguery. Roast pork, beef, turkey, bear, and even some buffalo meat graced the tables set up in the yard behind the Capitol. There was plenty of bread, both corn and wheat, and a greater variety of vegetables than I had so far seen in Texas. Sweet potatoes, white potatoes, green corn, beans, pumpkins, and mustard greens had been prepared to perfection by the cooks. I salvaged enough leftovers to fill a tin plate for Jacob. A little wine would have perfectly complemented the most delicious feast I had enjoyed in months, but, alas, wine in the earliest days of independence was scarce. Liquor flowed readily, as did a particularly strong and excellent coffee. After greedily stuffing myself past satiety I stopped eating with great reluctance, so delicious was the food. That night, as I dropped onto my straw-filled tick mattress, I thought excitedly to myself, "I am secretary to the vice president of the nation!" But in my mind I could hear Father saying dismissively, "Yet another clerkship." Maybe so, I told myself, but many great men have started out as humbly. With this position I believed myself on the road to greatness as well.

General Houston came back and the people of Columbia about jumped out of their skin they were so happy to see him. All except Mirabeau Lamar. And I know Master Fontaine wasn't all that happy either. I never knew why Master Fontaine and Lamar thought so poorly of General Houston. Maybe they were jealous of Houston being president and Lamar was only vice president. But that didn't explain why Lamar still hated him after he got to be president himself. Anyway, I never understood it. I asked Master Fontaine once how come he didn't like Sam Houston and he said he makes folks think he's one thing when really he's something else altogether. I said,

"Lots of folks seem to like him all right," and he said, "Yes, there are plenty of fools in the world." I must have been one of the fools he was talking about because I just couldn't see nothing bad about General Houston. I kept quiet after that.

Anyway, just like Master Fontaine said, President Burnet told everybody he was quitting and that meant they'd need to go on ahead and make Houston president. So Lamar was made vice president at the same time. Of course, I couldn't go inside Congress, so I watched from across the street back where they told us we could stand. I couldn't hear Mr. Lamar, but when Sam Houston got his turn I heard every word. Lord, that man could talk! He'd make a mighty fine preacher, he talked so good, but I heard he wouldn't join no church. Maybe that's one of the things Master Fontaine didn't like about him. So after he was done talking everybody said hey, let's go eat, there's a barbecue out back, but once we got there a white man said, "Where do you niggers think you're going? This food ain't for you." So I went back to my shack to mend some socks. And before long Master Fontaine came home with a plate of food for me. It was so good I could have eaten two more just like it.

12

The inauguration ushered in a long, drab winter. Gray skies settled over the coastal plains. Dense fog obscured many a sunrise, while misting rain kept me indoors most afternoons. I became acquainted with the Texas norther I had heard of back in Mississippi. This peculiar phenomenon begins with a dark streak across an otherwise pleasant horizon seemingly so distant as to require no notice. But the streak enlarges rapidly, soon filling the sky and blotting out the sun. Meanwhile, an icy wind has begun to blow, gently at first, but soon forcibly enough to rattle houses and drive animals to shelter. The unwary are caught in the open by the drenching, freezing rain that follows. Stinging sleet erases all desire to remain outdoors, while hailstones as large as eggs threaten to knock one senseless. I witnessed several of these sudden storms or I would have thought their existence mere fable.

During this dreary season Mirabeau discovered that the vice presidency, while an honor, conveyed little authority. Once he had convened the Senate he, and as a result I, had little to do. Certainly he strove to keep himself informed of state affairs. He made a point of meeting each member of Congress. He knew the committee heads, clerks, and even the porters of each chamber, taking care to note the policy leanings of each man. No detail escaped him; each individual received his attention. All of this kept him busy, yet there was no real *work* for him.

As Mirabeau suspected, Sam Houston's stated desire for the two of them to work in tandem proved false. As vice president, Mirabeau logically assumed that the chief executive would welcome his input regarding the selection of Cabinet officers. But when he approached Houston on this issue, the president listened only briefly before interrupting to say, "Mirabeau, thank you for devoting your energies to this crucial matter. If you'll give your list to Wash, I'll consider it carefully." My friend Wash Miller was now Houston's private secretary. When I sought him out to hand him Mirabeau's list, he said in surprise, "Why, Houston has told me nothing of this. As far as I know, he has already made his selections."

On another occasion, Mirabeau visited Houston to express concern about the presence of the Cherokee in the Redlands. These Indians claimed ownership of their Texas land, a notion that Mirabeau and many others contested. Furthermore, despite professing friendly intentions, they had committed depredations against their white neighbors and were suspected of plotting with Mexican agents against the Republic. Yet in his inaugural address the president had spoken of rewarding their misdeeds with gifts and treaties. When Mirabeau attempted to open a discussion on the matter, the president listened and nodded politely, all the while fiddling with a piece of wood he had been carving when Mirabeau entered the office. At the conclusion of Mirabeau's argument Houston merely thanked him for his views and said, "As you know, my aim has always been to seek peaceful coexistence rather than war." Mirabeau told me this in a voice quivering with anger. "It's quite clear that the president has no use for my advice."

After these and other rebuffs, Mirabeau gave up on establishing a working relationship with Houston. He spent his days in his office reading newspapers or walking about town. Evenings he retired directly to his room after supper, where he wrote long letters home or composed poetry. He accompanied me to the occasional religious service then available in Columbia. There being no organized congregations in the town, we depended upon traveling ministers to satisfy our spiritual needs. I had decided to temporarily lay aside my own aspirations of becoming a minister while I worked for Mirabeau, but nevertheless rose to speak at several of these meetings. I encouraged Mirabeau to follow my example, but he always declined with the excuse, "I'm a politician, not a theologian."

One day, while filing some of Mirabeau's personal letters from Georgia, I teasingly asked him if there were any of a romantic nature. By then we had spoken often enough about his deceased wife that the subject no longer felt so awkward. Several years had passed since Tabitha's unfortunate death. It seemed natural to me that a man of his stature would have attracted more than passing notice from members of the weaker sex. Mirabeau smiled coyly at the question and replied, "There is indeed a lady love in my life, and I am holding one of her letters in my hand." He gave it to me with an invitation to read it. Hesitantly, I unfolded the paper and read aloud the opening line, "Dearest Father, to counter your charge that I never write to you, I offer these inadequate scribblings. . . ."

"Rebecca!" I said with a laugh. "But surely your daughter doesn't count!"

"Ah, but she *does*! More than any other, she is the one who has captured my heart."

"Very clever," I said as I handed the letter back to him. "But surely your heart will extend itself in different fashion one day."

His countenance darkened. "I doubt it; it remains too crippled to exert itself so."

Before I could stop myself I blurted out, "Will you never find love again?"

He shook his head. "It's not that I don't want to. There's a hole in me waiting for a good woman to fill it. More than once have I cried at the thought of it remaining empty."

My brain froze in the awkwardness of the moment and I merely stared at him. At last he broke the spell by asking, "And what of you? You're quite the eligible young man."

I laughed. "I too suffer from a broken heart, although my sorrow pales next to yours. We'll search for love together."

"Then we cannot fail, can we?"

On another occasion the two of us took an after-supper stroll over to the Brazos River. A crisp chill gripped the air as we strode along the path cutting through the marsh grass. Phosphorescent clouds layered the sky up above, while the waning sunlight cast a brilliant glow on the carpet of vegetation below. Birds swooped and circled in all directions. At the riverbank we watched the glassy waters of the Brazos slip silently by. A more romantic scene I had never witnessed. Feeling my spirits soar at the beautiful sights and sounds of nature I said, "Do you not hear the voice of God?"

I expected no answer and certainly not the one that Mirabeau provided. "Not at the moment, but I have."

I turned to look at him. Seeing no jest in his demeanor, I didn't know what to say. He continued.

"I've heard God. Twice. Back in Georgia."

"Really?"

"Both times down by the river. Very similar scenery, except the trees were taller. I used to go down there and sit for hours after she died. Tabitha, I mean. I had prayed and prayed to no avail. Consumption weakened her daily until she at last expired. Why, I wanted to know. Why had I heard nothing, no response, to my entreaties? Why had she been taken from me, from Rebecca? Was I supposed to wither away in similar fashion? I almost came to believe it. There were days when

I barely rose from my bed. Once up, I only stumbled mindlessly about. I sought no comfort in alcohol, yet entire days passed in a blur, after which I would have no recollection of their contents. I wanted to die."

He paused and broke off a piece of cane from a nearby cluster. He looked at it for a moment before speaking again, this time using the cane as a conductor's baton, waving it about and stabbing the air for emphasis. "I thought I *would* die. I used to go down to the river to await the moment. I carried a bit of her hair in a locket, thinking that this would guide me to her in the afterlife. I sat there one evening under the pines listening to the silence, the damnable silence that my prayers had always encountered, when someone said, 'Get up.' I looked around but saw no one. Drifting back to my thoughts, I had almost forgotten the voice when I heard it again. 'Get up!' 'Who's there?' I cried. The voice said, 'Mirabeau, get up. It's not your time.' So I did. I got up. And forgot about dying. The next day I began organizing papers in my office. I had no idea why, I just knew that I should be doing something, *anything*. And as I worked I heard the voice again. This time it said, 'Texas . . . Texas.' 'Texas? What about Texas,' I thought. 'Texas,' the voice repeated, 'Texas . . . Texas . . . Texas.' I could no longer concentrate on the papers. Flinging them aside I rushed out of the house and, without intending to, ended up at my spot by the river. 'Why Texas?' I called out. 'Why?' But the voice only kept repeating that single word, 'Texas.' And *that* was the voice of God."

"Remarkable!"

"So I came to Texas. I came still ignorant of the reason. In fact, I'm still not completely certain of what I'm being called to do, but I know I'm on the right path. I'm only confused by the rather significant obstacle that Sam Houston presents. How can I accomplish anything with him in the way?"

"That *is* a dilemma."

"But maybe I'm not supposed to understand just yet. Maybe the plan will be revealed piecemeal, with the individual elements assembling into their whole only when I am positioned to carry out the assigned task. Anyway, that's what I tell myself. Because the voice has remained silent since I came here."

"But surely, as vice president, you're in position now," I argued.

"Not yet. Especially with Houston's stubbornness. Which can mean only one thing."

"The presidency?"

"Doesn't it seem obvious?"

It did.

• • •

I liked Columbia. Master Fontaine, he found me jobs here and there to make himself some money. If the boss treated me bad, I only had to tell Master Fontaine and he'd say, "All right, Jacob, I'll find something else for you to do." Mostly I'd haul things or chop wood or cut hay, but I didn't pay no mind, I just did what I was told. Then after I was done the white man would give me some money to take back to Master Fontaine. One man, though, he gave me five dollars and then handed me another dollar and said, "That dollar is for you, Jake." I told Master Fontaine what happened because I figured he'd find out soon enough anyway. He just said, "Jacob, if he gave you that dollar then you should keep it because it's yours." I bought a good shirt with it.

We had a lot of rain that winter, but it never did snow. Somebody told me once that it never does snow in Texas, but I know that's a lie because later on I saw it happen. But not that year. I didn't mind the rain because you can't cut hay when it's wet and that's probably the job I disliked the most. You get hay down your britches and in your shirt and then you just can't scratch enough. I cut plenty of hay, but if I had my druthers I'd do something else.

Sometimes a white preacher came through Columbia and all the white folks gathered around to hear him. We couldn't go, of course, but later on he'd hold a service for us and then we could hear him preach. We'd sing the hymns and say the prayers. I knew all the Bible verses, so I'd call 'em out right with the preacher. One time the preacher said, "Boy, you know these Bible verses so good you ought to preach 'em yourself." And he left. So everybody looked at me and I looked at them and I just started preaching. I wasn't sure what I would say, but the Lord put the words in my mouth and I just spit 'em out. All the while people called out, "Amen, brother!" and "Hallelujah!" till I thought angels would come down and scoop me up for Heaven. From then on I was a preacher. I wasn't supposed to hold services, though, unless I could find a white man to be there too. Sometimes I did anyway, but in a place where nobody would see. I preached quieter then too.

The thing I liked most about Columbia was that I always had time to go fishing. Master Fontaine, he liked me to fish because I always brought back plenty for both our plates. He even bought me some hooks once, although mostly I made those myself out of wire or fish bones. One time I was down by the Brazos fixing my line when I heard Master Fontaine and Mr. Lamar a little ways off talking. I was worried they would think I came there on purpose so I could listen in, so I didn't throw my line back in the water. I was hidden by grass so they couldn't see me. Anyway, they got to talking about how pretty it was and then suddenly Mr. Lamar tells Master Fontaine that God Himself told him to come to Texas. He said he didn't know yet why God told him that, but one day he'd figure it out. Best as he could see, God meant for him to be president, which is what Master Fontaine had been telling me all along. Later

I wanted to ask Master Fontaine if God had told him to come to Texas too, but I feared he'd know I was spying on him, so I didn't. That night when I prayed I said, "Almighty God, if you told Mr. Lamar to come here then maybe you told Master Fontaine to come and bring me along. So here I am and I'm your willing servant. You just let me know what I've got to do and I'll do it." I didn't catch no fish that time. When I got home Master Fontaine said, "Well, that's a surprise, Jacob." So we both had a surprise that day.

One afternoon in Columbia I sat in Mirabeau's office copying letters when a loud rap on the door interrupted the tedious chore. Before I could respond, the door burst open and a short, wiry man charged into the room. Of slight build and pale complexion, he sported a mass of tangled black hair atop his head and a determined look on his face. A pair of steel-gray eyes bored into me as he demanded, "Are you Lamar?"

"No, sir, I'm not."

"Then where the hell is he?"

"He rode over to Brazoria this morning with several men. I believe he intends to inspect the town. As you know, most everyone left during the recent war and Mr. Lamar wishes to see about reviving its prospects."

The wild man snorted dismissively. "Hell, I don't care what took him there. I just need to talk to him. When's he getting back?"

"Is there something I can help you with? I'm his secretary."

"No, my business is with him." After an awkward moment, though, he stuck out his hand and said, "Name's Edwin Waller. I live a few miles up the river and I've just had some horses run off my property by a bunch of damned redskins. Again. I wanna know what Lamar is gonna do about it."

"Indians? Was anyone hurt?"

"Naw, they didn't stick around and fight. Just took my horses and disappeared. I tell you, I'm mighty tired of government men sitting on their hands while people are getting robbed blind. I'm out a lot of money!"

"How do you know it was Indians?"

He glared at me as if I had just questioned his intelligence, which I suppose I had. He said, "Son, I've been in these parts long enough to recognize Indian sign when I see it. How many Indian scrapes you been in?"

Abashed, I apologized. "I'm sorry, Mr. Waller. And I'm sorry about your horses. I'm sure the vice president will want to hear of this when he returns."

"No harm done," he said grumpily. "I just hope I'm not wasting my time like I did with that half-breed Houston."

"You saw President Houston?"

"Oh, I saw him all right. I saw him for all of about ten seconds, is all. Fine friend to the white man he is! Thieving Indians in our midst and all he says is, 'Waller, that's a damn shame. I hope you get 'em back.'"

"You'll get a better reply from Mr. Lamar, I'm sure."

"If I do, it'll be the first piece of sense I've heard in this town. Just let him know what I said, all right?"

I promised, but the door slammed shut to drown out my reply. I wouldn't have guessed it from that first encounter, but Edwin Waller would become one of Mirabeau's truest friends.

Mirabeau's claim of heavenly inspiration guiding his decision to come to Texas rang true with me. Nevertheless, certain events in those days led me to ascribe mischievous intent to the Lord that we more commonly associate with denizens of Greek or Roman mythology. In November 1836 our wise men of Congress decided to transfer the seat of government to a new town on Buffalo Bayou. The decision surprised no one, for none were happy with Columbia as a national capital. Nor was I disturbed by the fact that the designated place as yet existed mostly in the minds of its two founders, the brothers John and Augustus Allen. No, what bothered me most, what gave me reason to suspect devilry from above, at least with respect to Mirabeau, was the new capital's name, Houston. Sam Houston, who already loomed as Mirabeau's greatest obstacle, not only occupied the presidency but would now conduct affairs of state from a place bearing his name. What greater trial could God have imposed on the man bearing the cross of political righteousness in the new Republic than to consign him to a city named after his greatest enemy? Perhaps God throws such distractions our way so that we may learn to distinguish between important matters and trivialities.

Mirabeau's response to the town's name was as I expected. "Outrageous! We're to have a seat of government named for a drunk!"

"Don't forget, the designation is only temporary. In 1840 government will move elsewhere."

"Yes, and if you believe that you're a bigger fool than *he* is, Edward. I concede that the act designating the seat of government carries that stipulation, but there's nothing to prevent Congress from extending the deadline indefinitely. Or of failing to act altogether, in which case the capital stays put."

"The city is hardly built yet. People will like it little better than Columbia."

Mirabeau grumbled something incomprehensible before saying, "Houston will see to it that government remains in his city. His vanity is large enough to demand it!"

"Well, *somebody* will have to prevent that."

"Don't you worry, I will."

By now I had accumulated a greater store of possessions than was mine upon my arrival in Texas. Winter and summer clothing, an extra pair of boots, a coffeepot, a few books, a frying pan, eating utensils, several tin cups, and a collection of newspapers and letters proved more than I could comfortably carry in saddlebags. I therefore purchased a small trunk for the journey to Houston. Mirabeau's belongings approximated mine, but since his correspondence filled two wooden crates there was no question of him traveling by horseback alone. We considered buying a wagon but instead opted to risk the waters of the Gulf of Mexico once again. From there we could transfer to a ship for passage up Buffalo Bayou to the city of Houston. The local newspaper editor, Gail Borden, assured us that Buffalo Bayou would be made ready for steamship passage by the time of our arrival at Galveston Bay.

"It's plenty deep enough," he claimed. "A bit narrow in spots, I'm told, but nothing that a boat won't be able to navigate."

"I wouldn't know. I've never seen it," I said.

"Ah, but you have!" contradicted Mirabeau. "It's the same body of water that runs past the battlefield at San Jacinto."

"*What?* Can that be? I saw a lake at San Jacinto. There's room enough there for a whole fleet of ships!"

"The battleground's at the juncture of the bayou with Trinity Bay," Borden explained. "The bayou squeezes down pretty quick. But I've talked to enough men that have run its course to know it's navigable. And, if you'll recall, I had my newspaper in Harrisburg before Santa Anna burned it down and tossed the press into the bayou. Anyway, the Allens are no fools. They've checked that waterway as carefully as a man can. You've likely seen their notice in the *Telegraph*. Houston's at the head of navigation for the bayou. That's what makes it so perfect for them. Ships can make it *to* them but not *past* them. Overland travel starts at Houston. They'll make a fortune."

Mirabeau laughed. "You sound like an investor!"

Chuckling defensively, Borden said, "I suppose I do. I don't have any cash in the venture, but I've sure got a stake in it. I'm moving my press by boat, so if they *can't* get up the bayou I'll be stuck."

"Well," said Mirabeau good-naturedly, "if you've that much faith in it, Gail, I'm sure that Edward and I can trust them with our meager belongings."

We were among the last to leave Columbia. Mirabeau put off the departure several times with the comment, "I'll not hasten to anything named Houston." Finally, we entrusted our baggage to a Brazos River flatboat and rode along a swampy trail to the Gulf. I had neglected to explain our itinerary to poor Jacob, who balked when we began riding south instead of northeast directly toward Houston.

"Master Fontaine," he said with concern, "don't we have to go *that* way?"

When I told him of our plan to travel by ship via Galveston Bay and Buffalo Bayou he rolled his eyes and moaned.

"Now, Jacob," I admonished, "a boat ride is no less comfortable than bumping along on a mule."

"Maybe so," he conceded, "but I've never thrown up on a mule."

Despite Jacob's doubts, our time on the Gulf passed pleasantly enough. Calm seas and a clear blue sky combined to alleviate his dread and draw us to the open deck to enjoy the sunshine. Buffalo Bayou proved a greater obstacle. Once aboard the steamship *Laura* we watched eagerly as we entered the waterway leading to the new capital. We passed quickly from a broad, well-lit estuary into a narrow, jungle-like stream reeking of rotting vegetation. Sharp bends in the bayou demanded hard labor from the boatmen, who stood with poles on either side of the ship to ward off overhanging tree branches and protruding banks. Not infrequently, the ship caught on a shoal or submerged limb. On such occasions a boatman leapt ashore, secured a rope to a stout tree trunk some distance upstream, and signaled the passengers to join him in hauling the boat off the obstacle. This chore we performed cheerfully at first, but repetition soon spoiled our enthusiasm. Once, while straining at the rope, Mirabeau shouted playfully at Gail Borden, "Santa Anna had the right idea by throwing your press into the bayou. It's weighing down the ship."

Borden laughed, readjusted his grip on the rope, and said, "Maybe it's the lead-headed politicians we oughta throw overboard!" Everyone roared. As articulate and well spoken as Mirabeau was, he usually came out second best in quick-witted exchanges.

Buffalo Bayou seemed to stretch endlessly. Each bend in the stream only begat another and our trip from the bay lasted three grueling days. We saw abundant game, mostly deer, but also turkey and even a panther or two. Some of the passengers tried their hand at fishing, with varying success. One day, after toiling for an hour to release the ship from yet another underwater snarl, two exhausted men plunged into the bayou to cool off. Almost as soon as they hit the water another man hollered, "Look, boys, there's alligators over there." Sure enough, sunning on the opposite bank lay several of the fearsome creatures. We watched in amazement as a particularly large beast hauled himself out of the water onto the sand. Our intrepid swimmers quickly transferred their thoughts from refreshing their bodies to saving them. Flailing furiously at the water, they fled to shore with a rapidity that elicited howls of laughter from their fellow passengers.

As I had predicted, the city of Houston proved no more commodious than Columbia. So little was the town built up at that time that our captain unknowingly steamed right past it on first attempt. Only by reversing course and carefully examining the banks for signs of life were we able to locate our destination. Once we scrambled up the muddy embankment we saw only canvas tents and half-built pine huts scattered about in disorganized fashion. Pools of viscous muck lay between the buildings. I was not the only new arrival to express disgust.

To worsen our situation, the following day a drenching rain began that lasted into the next. Already muddy streets became quagmires. Wagons bogged down, animals became stuck, and pedestrians struggled to keep their footwear as they slogged through the mess. Most of the new arrivals, myself and Mirabeau included, spent the first night in the open, as there existed very few boardinghouses and no proper inns. The lodging we eventually found proved little better than the outdoors. Large gaps between the rough wall planks admitted even the weakest draft, while mud oozed up through cracks in the wooden floor. For several nights Jacob made due by stretching a tarp between two wagons and lying underneath. He shared this luxurious bedroom with several other Negroes.

One afternoon, in a mood made foul by our discomfort, Mirabeau and I encountered President Houston on the street. "Good day, gentlemen," he said amiably. "Isn't this a fine place for a seat of government?"

I thought he jested, but Mirabeau reacted in earnest. "Houston, your judgment is affected by the city's name. We are disgraced as a nation by these surroundings."

Houston appeared shocked and hurt by the unexpected barb. "Lamar, my joke has missed its mark. The place is no Paris, or even Washington. But surely it will be improved."

I attempted a diversion. "President Houston, yesterday Rusk pointed out to me your own fine presidential palace." I had indeed seen Houston's abode, which consisted of a one-room shanty with an attached lean-to shed. "Perhaps while living in such luxury you overlook the discomfort of the common man."

"Ah, Fontaine, that's more like it," said the president, beaming. "Yes, you must pay me a visit. But let me know you're coming and I'll have the servants polish the silver."

Later that day we sat under a tree near our boardinghouse playing whist with

Gail Borden and a congressman from the coast whose name I have forgotten. After yet another losing hand Mirabeau reached for the cards and said, "Edward, Borden is invincible today. It's too bad you are burdened with me as a partner."

Borden laughed. "Yes, Edward, bad luck to be stuck with the nation's vice president."

Mirabeau shuffled the deck. "Apparently, you and Houston have that in common."

"Speaking of Houston," said Borden, "how are you holding up in a capital bearing his name?"

Mirabeau sighed. "It's just one more thing to make my job an unpleasant one at the moment. Sometimes I wish I were back in Georgia."

"Why not go there?" asked Borden. "Congress doesn't convene for several weeks."

"Even when it does there will be little for me to do." He looked at me. "What about it, Edward, want to go on a trip? You could see Mississippi again."

Two days later, we left.

I remember the day I saw Mr. Waller for the first time. I was sitting in front of the office in Columbia plucking a chicken when he came storming up like he was gonna kill someone. He looked at me but didn't see me. Just looked right through me the way white folks do. I kept on plucking my chicken and he didn't say nothing, he just charged into the office. I heard him hollering at first and then it got quiet for a spell. Then he came out and nearly busted the door he slammed it so hard. Before he left he finally noticed me and said, "What are you looking at, boy?" I said I was sorry, I didn't mean no harm and he went on his way. And I hoped I'd never see him no more, but I did.

Master Fontaine told me we were moving to Houston and I thought, "Well, here we go again." I was getting worn out by so much moving around and I thought I'd rather just stay put for a while. But Master Fontaine told me we were moving because the government was going up there, so we had no choice about the matter. Once we were set to go I figured we'd follow the river north because I'd been told the town lay that way. But we headed down the other way. That's when Master Fontaine said he forgot to tell me that we were going by boat. "Oh, Lord," I thought, "not another boat!" But, you know, it turned out just fine. No pitching and rocking this time and my food stayed where I put it.

So we went on up the bay and into the bayou. I was standing by the rail when Mr. Lamar came up and stood there too. He pointed to the shore and said, "That's where Texas gained her freedom." He wasn't telling me, but some white folks that were standing there too. I didn't say anything, but I thought, "Texas may be free, but not me." Because after they killed all those Mexicans I didn't see anyone treating black folks any different. And I knew that in Mexico there wasn't any slavery, that they had a law against it there, and I wished maybe the Mexicans had won that fight. But they didn't, so why fret over it? It's in the hands of the Lord, I always say.

Let me tell you, I don't mind if I never see that bayou again. It started out all right, but pretty quick it wasn't no bigger than a crick and the boat we were on was bumping the sides. Or maybe we'd get stuck on something in the water. Then the head white man on the boat would holler for all the slaves to jump off quick. They'd tie a rope to a tree and we'd commence to pulling on it till the boat was free and we could go again. Lord, the smoke that boat made when it tried to unstick itself! And the shore wasn't safe neither. I saw more than one panther and plenty of alligators. Once I saw a panther AND an alligator at the same time. I couldn't say which was worse—to get eaten on shore by the cat or in the water by the gator.

Once we made it to Houston I got to wondering why the government came all that way for that awful place. The houses in Columbia were better and they were none too good. And the mud! Mercy, there was more mud than I'd ever seen before, even back in Mississippi. Once I saw a mule get stuck all the way up to its haunches. Took three of us to haul it out. I never saw mosquitoes like that before neither. At dark they'd come out of the grass and woods in flocks. Pretty soon I was covered with bumps that itched all day and night.

Lo and behold, we weren't in Houston more than a few weeks and Master Fontaine says he's going back to Mississippi. I thought about my mama and my sisters and I asked, "Are we gonna live there again?" He said no, he was just going for a visit and that I'd be staying there in Texas. He found a man that wanted to put me to work helping with some of the buildings they were putting up. That he'd be gone for a while, but be back later in the year. This wouldn't be no different than the other times he hired me out, he said, just a little longer. I was thinking, "Do you wanna tell me who you're leaving me with?" but of course I didn't say that. I just said, "All right, I'll be here when you get back." And the next day, he and Mr. Lamar both left.

The weeks that followed were among the pleasantest of my life. After retracing our route down Buffalo Bayou to Galveston Bay, Mirabeau and I steamed to New Orleans, where we spent several days meeting with local political and business leaders. As vice president of the Republic, Mirabeau received an enthusiastic welcome. Therefore, so did I. We dined, we drank, we toasted each other; I enjoyed myself immensely. Mirabeau seemed pleased with the attention, but as usual his stoic features kept me somewhat in doubt.

After leaving New Orleans we traveled together on the Natchez Trace as far as Jackson, Mississippi. There we parted company, Mirabeau heading east to Georgia, I turning north for my hometown of Pontotoc. A year's absence had not diminished my affection for Mississippi. In Pontotoc I received the same type of hero's welcome that had greeted Mirabeau in New Orleans, albeit on a smaller scale. Even Father seemed proud. Friends and family flocked to me, all eager to hear tales of the "wild" Texas of their imaginations. Many expressed surprise to hear me speak of newspapers, steamships, and Cabinet meetings. Robert Ellis, the wag who had ridiculed Mrs. Holley's book and embarrassed me in the churchyard, said, "Surely you're telling us stories, Edward. Everyone knows that Texas has wild animals and savages behind every bush. Surely you've scalped at least *one* Indian by now!" When I assured him I had not, he snorted derisively and said, "Well, that settles it. What's the use of going there if the place is already civilized?"

Everywhere I went people asked about the Battle of San Jacinto and its purported hero, Sam Houston. Except when among close friends, I withheld the most sanguinary details, such as the slaughter at the swamp and the individual acts of butchery I witnessed. By then I had accepted Mirabeau's explanation of these deeds as punishment of gullible souls lured into wicked service. I thought it unfair to the perpetrators to expose these darker aspects of a righteous crusade.

Mirabeau kept his promise to correspond regularly with me. Given the sporadic nature of mail service in those days, I usually received three or four letters at once. Most contained only news of personal interest, such as a reunion with his brother or a gathering for his daughter Rebecca's birthday. Occasional lines of verse informed me that writing poetry remained a hobby. He must have been happy because, unlike most of the poems he had shown me in Texas, those written during his Georgia interlude radiated optimism. One even touched on his love life. I've since lost the poem but not the letter accompanying it.

"Edward, you'll be pleased to know I have attracted the attention of several lovely damsels in my hometown. If I am not enjoying a dinner at the home of one I am dancing at the home of another. I must say it heartens me to feel this forgotten spark of life; the pleasure of a woman's company has long been denied me. I see no prospect of a permanent arrangement, but am not averse to the right opportunity. Meanwhile, I shall continue with my fun."

One steamy June day in 1837 I opened a letter from Mirabeau that foretold our return to the Republic. "My Dear Fontaine," the note began, "I fear the Cherokee is on the warpath once again." By "the Cherokee" I knew he meant President Houston. "It seems that his tomahawk is capable of leaping forests and rivers to reach the peaceful hearths at which we currently warm ourselves. We prefer our present comfort but—nay!—we are called from on high and must fly! My faithful spy Everitt [this was his friend and Jasper County senator Stephen Everitt] informs me that Houston is fast sinking under the weight of his office. He fears some rash action on the part of our *chief Indian* and is convinced that only my presence will dissuade him. Thus I must beg you to conclude your affairs and journey westward. I'll meet you in New Orleans."

A less whimsical letter arrived from him two days later.

"Edward, the Almighty has beckoned me to Texas. Houston writes that tongues are wagging unkindly at me. He chastises me for quitting the Republic without congressional consent as if he envisions some vital purpose for me at the government seat. I must therefore leave unfinished business in Georgia. I'll neither tarry nor hasten to the capital, wishing to avoid being charged with disobedience or feeding his vanity. I replied to him that I would be *pleased* to return, for I wish only to promote *his* individual happiness! The sting of this barb is likely lost on one so puffed up."

I left Pontotoc in September. Summer heat still permeated the pines as I made my way to New Orleans. I met Mirabeau at the prearranged place in that city without difficulty. We embraced as old friends which, given all that we had experienced together, I suppose we were. True to his word Mirabeau neither hastened nor tarried. After several days of calling on friends and political supporters, we boarded a steamship that took us back to Galveston Bay. On the way up Buffalo Bayou I witnessed a disturbing incident. One evening, just before we reached Houston, a doe cautiously approached the bayou for a drink. When it lowered its head an alligator sprang from the stream, snatched a leg, and dragged the unfortunate creature to a watery death. "I don't believe in omens," I told myself.

I do now.

I worried that Master Fontaine wouldn't come back from Mississippi. I imagined him being with all his friends and family and thinking he'd just as soon stay with them than go back to Texas. There I was in Houston with the mosquitoes and the alligators and the panthers and he was back home with all his kin. Some nights I laid awake thinking about that and about my mama and sisters and the tears wouldn't stop. But then up came the sun and I knew I couldn't think no more about it.

Master Fontaine left me under a man named Ward. Pegleg, they called him, because when he was in the war fighting the Mexicans one of his legs got shot and the doctor had to cut it off. Now, I didn't call him Pegleg, that's for sure. I just called him Mr. Ward, or Boss. At first I felt sorry for him because of his leg, but pretty soon I forgot all about that because he worked harder than most men with two legs. He was a hard man, but fair. He worked us good, but I've got to say he put himself right in there with us. It was me and a few other fellas he set to sawing boards. He had a whole army of white men working for him too. Some of 'em built windows, some of 'em made doors, and some of 'em built furniture, but they all worked hard just like us. See, the government needed a meeting place and Mr. Ward was supposed to build one. He couldn't do it by himself, so he had us. Only we weren't finished by the time the government wanted to commence their meetings, so they met in a room that had no roof. It rained pretty hard one night and the next day the congressmen didn't want to sit on wet chairs, so they lit into Mr. Ward pretty good. He gave it right back to 'em, though. Truth be told, I suspect he was a bit soused that morning because he even took a poke at one of the congressmen. Didn't hit him but didn't have to. That congressmen left pretty quick.

Once we finished the Capitol, that didn't mean there wasn't more work to do. Mr. Ward found us other jobs. Not as big as the Capitol, but still they kept me as busy as the only rooster in the henhouse. I guess everybody in town saw how Mr. Ward put up a big building like the Capitol and figured he could build them a house or a barn or whatever they needed. Houses weren't nice houses like you see nowadays, but little cabins with sheds out back. We could build one in about two days, maybe three. One white man showed me how to use a froe to shave down the logs. After I was done we'd heft the log into place so he could cut the corners. He worked slow because he had to be careful. The corners had to fit together snug and tight or the house would fall down. I didn't have to be so careful with the logs because we left spaces in between that we filled with mud and sand. But I still tried to cut 'em as straight as I could. It wasn't too hard because they were pine logs, not oak or pecan. One day Mr. Ward was watching me work and he said, "Boy, you handle that froe like a white man. Those logs will do just fine." I said, "Thank you, Mr. Ward," and kept on working. It made me feel pretty good.

Summers in Texas were no worse than in Mississippi. I didn't mind how hot it got, it was cold winters I despised. So as long as I was busy during the day I was happy enough. It was nights when I'd feel lonely. Every now and then they'd allow us to have a dance on a Saturday night. There had to be a white man there to watch us, but that didn't stop nobody from sneaking off into the bushes with a pretty girl if he could. And there were some pretty girls. I was a young man then and not disposed to keep up with all the commandments on such occasions. But I didn't see no harm in it and maybe I still don't. I couldn't abide being lonely, that's all.

Along about September Mr. Ward came to me and said, "I'm told you can read, Jake." I was real nervous when he said that because most of the white folks didn't want that a slave should be able to read. I didn't say nothing; I just nodded my head. He laughed and said, "Now don't be scared, boy, because I got a letter here for you. They gave it to me at the post office to give you. I think it's from your master."

After he left I opened it up. It was just a few lines. Mostly telling me to work hard and stay out of trouble and remember the Lord, like I was gonna forget that. Then it said, "I'm coming home soon by way of New Orleans." Mr. Lamar would be coming too. Let me tell you, I wasn't too sad about that! Mr. Ward might be fair but he could cuss a man from here to Sunday, especially when he was drinking, which was a lot. Anyway, I saved that letter and have it yet. Mr. Ward asked me about it later. I told him what it said and he told me, "Yeah, I already know that. I guess we'll see him when he gets here." Then he showed me a stack of logs and said, "Put those logs in the wagon and be quick."

13

I had learned to despise Houston the man and now developed equal feelings for the town. It hadn't rained in weeks when we returned to that dreadful place in October 1837. The streets of mud that we had slogged through in the spring had baked into pottery-like hardness, yielding uneven footing for man or horse. Because of the paucity of springs most of our drinking water came from the bayou or cisterns. That from the bayou tasted of sulfur, while weeks of steeping in cisterns had transformed the collected rainwater into an unpalatable brown tea. Fresh vegetables were scarce. Meal after meal consisted of boiled beef and green corn. Liquor establishments outnumbered all other stores combined so that gangs of idlers and drunken Indians roamed the streets. I ventured out after dark only reluctantly and never alone. Mosquitoes swarmed day and night.

Lodging proved hard to come by. Mirabeau's friend Senator Everitt had managed to save him an office in the Capitol. This cramped space served as our bedroom for a week after our return. We then passed a few unpleasant nights sharing a room with several other men in a decrepit hotel. One snored so loudly that sleep proved impossible. At that point John Allen, one of the town's founders, heard of our plight and rescued us by shaming the occupants of a two-pen dogtrot into vacating in favor of the vice president. Mirabeau and I each took a room, although I shared mine with his desk and papers.

As he had suspected, there was little for Mirabeau to contribute toward running the government. In every meeting with his vice president, Sam Houston offered up blandishments about Mirabeau's importance to this or that project. But when pressed for details, the president would instantly turn evasive. "I must run this past Rusk first," he would say. Or Seguin. Or Jones. Or whatever man's name popped into his head at that moment. Then he would discourse at length on the obstacles being thrown up by that man, obstacles that he would clear away so that Mirabeau could perform the task he had in mind. Somehow, though, the obstacles always proved insurmountable, leaving Mirabeau with nothing to do but complain to me.

One evening I encountered Wash at Gridley's, a greasy tent posing as a restaurant across from a cluster of shops known as the Long Row on Main Street. I was eyeing the stew proffered by the proprietor when Wash called out from a dark recess of the tent, "It's safe to eat, Fontaine, that rat meat is fresh. I saw Gridley kill it myself!" Laughing, I took the bowl from Gridley and joined Wash at the table.

Despite our different political views, Wash and I were good friends. From time to time we ventured into the prairie together to hunt or went to the bayou to land a catfish or two. His affability matched that of his chief, for he now served Sam Houston in the same capacity as I served Mirabeau. He shook my hand as I settled into a chair.

After a minute of small talk about the weather Wash rapped his spoon on the table and said, "Edward, why does Lamar hate the president?"

I stuffed a large piece of bread into my mouth to give me time to formulate an answer. When I could reasonably chew no more I said, "He doesn't *hate* him, Wash. It's political, not personal."

"That's what Houston says too. But I don't know. I've never seen a man turn into ice the way Lamar does when Houston's around."

"Well, why won't Houston give his vice president a chance to do anything?"

"What do you mean?"

I wagged a finger. "Look, Wash, you and I both know that Houston has his circle and Lamar's on the outside. You'd think there'd be plenty of work in running a country for everybody, but if it weren't for his business interests Lamar would have nothing to do!"

"Is that so?"

"*Damn right*, that's so!"

I hadn't meant to be so forceful, but I was angry. Wash looked hurt.

"Wash, I'm sorry."

He waved me into silence. "No, you're right. I've noticed the same thing. Here's what I think. Houston's convinced Lamar intends to run for president next fall."

"He's made no such announcement."

"Don't be coy," he admonished. "The signs are obvious. And Houston's convinced that as president, Lamar will try to undo everything he accomplishes during his tenure."

"I don't see how that explains anything."

Wash slapped his forehead. "He doesn't want Lamar influencing policy *now*. He wants to carry his own programs as far as he can without hindrance. What's the use of giving a head start to the man aiming to tear down what he builds? There'd be no sense in that!"

My food suddenly lost its flavor. "I'm disappointed that our young republic is already soiled with party politics," I said with disgust.

"Not party politics," Wash argued. "One man's politics. Lamar's politics."

"*Houston's* politics. The Houston *Party's* politics."

"And its enemy, the *anti*-Houston Party."

"Just shut up and eat your rat meat."

With Master Fontaine back from Mississippi things settled in about like they were before. He'd rent me out a few days at a time to help build houses or sheds or even a privy or two. Sometimes I'd go over to the colored part of town and help folks there too. Or maybe dig up a garden or just sit around a fire and tell Gospel stories. One night a bunch of us were eating supper and a white woman came up and told us she was looking for her servant. After she left one of the boys said, "Why do they always call us servants when slaves is what we are?"

Another fella stood up and stuck his nose in the air and pranced around fancy like. He sashayed up to the first fella and said, "Well, Blackie, I ain't no slave but if you like I'll serve you up some five-finger pie!" And he stuck his fist up like he was gonna hit him.

We all just about fell into the fire laughing. Then the others started prancing around like they were serving their masters in the big house. Things were pretty rowdy by then with all the laughing and cutting up until nobody but Mirabeau Lamar, Mr. Vice President himself, walked by. He looked none too pleased neither. When he noticed us, he stopped dead in his tracks. Didn't say nothing; just looked at us like we were pigs in his pea patch. Finally he saw me and said, "Jacob, I suspect your master's got better things for you to do than lay idle with this bunch."

"Yes, sir!" I said, and ran off to find Master Fontaine. I never saw Mr. Lamar beat nobody but I swear he always looked like he was about to. He sure did that time.

He called himself *Doctor* Stephen Everitt, but if he ever practiced medicine I am unaware of it. A native New Yorker, he possessed the business acumen found in all Yankees. By 1837 he had parlayed several successful ventures into a sizable

fortune. Land investments, mercantile establishments, even government mail con-
tracts; all turned to gold at his touch. A seat in Congress as the senator from Jasper
County completed his résumé. Mirabeau, whose business dealings met with more
modest success, considered himself fortunate to count Dr. Everitt as a friend and
supporter. "Thank God, he's not my enemy," he once said. "I couldn't afford to have
his fortune working against me."

Dr. Everitt also possessed that same charm common to all Yankees, which is
to say he lacked it altogether. Terse pronouncements greeted any question or observation. To remark that the weather was hot invariably elicited a statement that
it was just the opposite. An inquiry into his health invited a steely glare and a
brusque, "That, friend, is a private matter." His voice carried no malice. Instead,
the admonishment fell with emotionless finality, as if he were merely reciting a fact
known to all reasonable men. I believe this is why Mirabeau found him such amiable company. Both men saw matters as right or wrong, true or untrue, good or evil.
I once heard Dr. Everitt remark, "Mirabeau, the thing is one way or the other. We
need not waste time blathering on about a middle ground that doesn't exist." Mirabeau snapped his fingers and said, "Precisely!" These days such righteous certitude
leaves me uneasy, but back then I lacked the capacity of questioning the judgment
of a man I admired so greatly.

Mirabeau and Dr. Everitt diverged in one very public aspect. Mirabeau cared
little for fashion. He often waited weeks between haircuts and shaved only two or
three times a week. His clothes were clean, but of the old style. He favored loose
shirts tucked into wide, baggy trousers that would have drawn snickers from onlookers were he not vice president. Several of his trousers ended an inch or two
above his boot. He owned coats in two sizes, overly large and overly small. When
he matched a large coat with large trousers, he gave the appearance of one who had
shrunk overnight.

By contrast, Dr. Everitt devoted much time and energy to his appearance. His
wardrobe, while not of the latest styles—that would have been impossible in those
days—was more modern than any other in Texas at that time. His black hair lay in
neat layers upon his head; his mustache never lacked for attention. He was the only
man capable of walking the streets of Houston without collecting mud spatters
on his boots and trousers, a skill I never mastered. Women admired his sense of
fashion; men feigned indifference while secretly envying him.

I devote such attention to describing Dr. Everitt because of the central role he
played in Mirabeau's path to the presidency. In hindsight his victory seems inevi-
table, but at the time Mirabeau and I both saw obstacles at every turn. As the winter of 1837 approached, he even spoke of quitting politics for the life of a farmer.

Usually such talk was triggered by thoughts of his family, especially Rebecca. "She's fast becoming a woman, Edward," he once said with a sigh. "I'm squandering my opportunity of shaping her future." I took him none too seriously but was relieved when Dr. Everitt came along to rekindle his political passion.

A brisk November day found me haggling with a Long Row merchant over the price of some tinware when I heard my name shouted from the doorway of the shop. "Fontaine, there you are!"

I squinted into the bright doorway in an unsuccessful attempt to recognize the voice's owner.

"It's me, Everitt," the man said.

"Ah, Dr. Everitt, good day."

"Edward, settle your account with this good man; you and I have something to discuss."

I disliked his imperious manner, but after paying the merchant I followed Dr. Everitt into the street. There we joined a group that included two other senators, Albert Horton of Matagorda and James Lester of Mina, as well as several men whose names I have forgotten. They clustered around me like hens at feeding time. A round of cursory greetings was cut short by Dr. Everitt.

"To the point, gentlemen, we've interrupted Mr. Fontaine's shopping."

I started to protest, but Everitt ignored me.

"Fontaine," he said, "we've written a letter. You must deliver it to Lamar."

"Of course." I accepted the proffered paper and put it in my pocket.

"You'll want to know what's in it."

"But it's not addressed to me."

"He's waited long enough," said Everitt impatiently. "It's time he made his intentions clear. It's time to publicly acknowledge his interest in standing for the presidency."

"That's right," said Horton. "We all think so. We've talked informally with him about it, but now we want to make it official. He's got our support, and we want him to run."

"I know he'll appreciate that, Senator Horton," I said. "But he hasn't yet made up his mind."

Everyone laughed. Dr. Everitt said, "Of course he has, Edward. He knows he's the best man for the job. Give him the letter and tell him we're coming by this evening after supper. Tell him we'll help draft a reply, if he'd like."

"Yes, sir."

"And tell him to have some decent wine for us." Seeing my puzzled expression, he added, "That's a jest."

Maybe in New York, I thought, but I said, "And a good one, Dr. Everitt!"

That night Mirabeau and I returned from supper to find a house full of company. Dr. Everitt and Senator Horton were there, as were most of the men I had seen with them earlier in the day. One new face stood out, that of the brusque, intense character I had met back in Columbia. Upon spotting me he winked and said, "I know *you!*"

"Mr. Waller!" I said in recognition. "Did you ever recover your horses?"

"Hell, no. By now they're probably up in Comancheria with Injuns on their backs."

"I'm sorry to hear that. Perhaps one day the ranging companies will be able to prevent such thievery."

"Can't come soon enough for me. That's one of the reasons I'm here tonight."

Before I could respond, Dr. Everitt rapped loudly on a small writing table and announced, "Gentlemen, find a seat. Let's get started."

Mirabeau beckoned for Dr. Everitt to sit in one of the two chairs before occupying the other. Several men crowded onto the bed. I leaned against the wall while Waller and another man sat on the floor. The flickering light of a kerosene lamp danced across our faces.

Dr. Everitt spoke first. "Mirabeau, you've read our letter. What's your answer?"

Mirabeau looked slowly around the room before speaking. "I wish only to serve my country as wise men deem best." He smiled. "I see much wisdom in this room."

Laughter temporarily obscured the soft hiss of the kerosene lamp. Mirabeau continued, "There are a few issues that require clarification. What are Rusk's intentions, for example? I fear his candidacy would overshadow mine."

"Nonsense," said Senator Horton. "You killed him last time."

"This is different," argued Mirabeau. "The outcome of a race between us is uncertain."

There followed several minutes of animated discussion about General Rusk's qualifications and his interest, or lack thereof, in running for high office. Several times I heard Waller groan with impatience. Finally, he cleared his throat loudly to interrupt a particularly spirited exchange between two of the men on the bed. "Damn it, boys. Rusk'll run or not, no matter what *we* say. Mirabeau should just ask him."

One of the men on the bed started to say something, but Dr. Everitt cut him off. "Waller's right, Rusk is anything but subtle. Ask him a question, and you'll get a plain answer. Mirabeau?"

"I agree, Stephen," Mirabeau replied. "I'll simply ask him his intentions. If he says yes, I'd likely still run. It's just best to know what we're up against."

Murmurs of assent filled the room. Mirabeau rose, opened his wardrobe, and extracted three large bottles.

"Now, gentlemen," he said cheerily, "I have on hand the wine you ordered."

"Cheers for Mirabeau!" said Senator Horton.

"Cheers for his candidacy!" added another.

"The hell with that!" said Waller. "Cheers for *President Lamar!*"

Mirabeau's three bottles multiplied rapidly as other men pulled out their own. Cigars appeared; a thick, sweet haze soon enveloped us. I drank to lightheadedness, but no more. Mirabeau uncharacteristically imbibed beyond caution. After everyone left, I had to help him to bed. He tumbled onto the mattress, grabbed my arm to detain me, and mumbled, "Ah, Tabitha, I'm sorry."

"Mirabeau, it's me. Edward."

"Edward? Tabitha won't like to see me drunk. God may forgive this indulgence but my dear wife will not."

"Mirabeau, go to sleep. You need it."

"Tabitha . . . Tabitha. God will forgive me, Tabitha. The presidency; is it worth it? Merciful God, is it worth your sacrifice?"

"Mirabeau, you should sleep."

He fumbled under his bed and produced a sheaf of papers. "Listen, Edward, she must forgive me. I wrote this for her." His hands trembled.

"What is it?"

"A poem. To her memory. Listen:"

Take, take my rhyme, O ladies gay,
For you it freely pours;
The minstrel's heart is far away—
It never can be yours.
The music of my song may be
To living beauty shed,
But all the love that warms the strain—
I mean it for the dead.

"Don't you see? 'I mean it for the dead.' For her. Only her."

"It's beautiful."

Tears stained his cheeks. "It's not enough. I failed her. I failed her and she despises me."

"Mirabeau, no—"

"She despises me, Edward." He broke down sobbing. "Lord, take this cup away from me!"

"Mirabeau, it's . . . she . . . "

He waved me away. "Go. Just go. Tabitha, I'm sorry. I'm so sorry."

Not knowing what else to do, I blew out the lamp and left him muttering in the darkness.

Thomas Rusk's lack of interest in becoming president amazed and mystified me. Of all the names that shone brightly in the land of the single star, his ranked among the brightest. No one had surpassed his bravery at San Jacinto; all admired his dedication and service to the cause of independence. Educated, thoughtful, and well spoken, he seemingly possessed all of the necessary qualities of a chief executive. Yet with the prize before him, he turned away.

It would be incorrect to say that he was without ambition. His later successful pursuit of a United States Senate seat belies the charge. Nor could one claim that he declined to run out of friendship to Mirabeau. The two maintained a cordial relationship, but Rusk's politics tilted more toward those of Sam Houston. In fact, those two *were* good friends. Whatever the reason, Rusk's decision to forego a candidacy cleared a major obstacle in Mirabeau's path.

The year 1837 therefore concluded with rosy prospects for Mirabeau's winning the presidency. Dr. Everitt opened his pocketbook so that the campaign never lacked for funds. He penned a supporting editorial that appeared in several newspapers and also sponsored a petition of senators publicly requesting that Mirabeau run. Only three of the senators then in Houston declined to sign, and none wielded much influence.

We attended several dinners given in Mirabeau's honor. He carried himself with renewed energy at these affairs. Political banquets typically conclude with countless toasts and impromptu speeches, many quite tedious. Up until then Mirabeau usually found opportunity to slip away with a few select friends once the toasting began. As featured guest, though, he no longer had that option. I expected him to politely acknowledge the accolades and leave as quickly as tactfulness allowed so as not to prolong the proceedings. Yet there he was, suddenly playing the extrovert, raising his glass after each toast to offer his own ripostes and bon mots. Had I just met him, I would have thought him the gregarious sort. If only such exuberance could be bottled and stored away for more difficult times.

Houston wasn't such a bad place, except maybe for the mosquitoes. Pegleg Ward let me have some logs and boards from his scrap yard and I built a lean-to on one side of the pen that Master Fontaine lived in. I had even saved enough bent nails to hold it all together. I had a flat piece of iron that I used to beat the nails against to straighten them out. One night after supper I sat up pounding nails in my lean-to when I heard Mr. Lamar burst into Master Fontaine's room. I couldn't hear what he said, but pretty soon here came Master Fontaine telling me I should lay off the nail pounding and go to bed. Why Mr. Lamar couldn't tell me that himself I don't know.

More and more folks started coming around to see Mr. Lamar. I asked Master Fontaine why they came to the house and not to the Capitol where he worked. He said it was because of what they had to talk about. Once he started running for president, see, he didn't want everything he said to be heard by just anybody. He had to plan on how to get folks to vote for him and he didn't want them running against him knowing how he'd do it. Master Fontaine was in on those meetings. He'd come out holding papers and books. Then he'd go into his room and shut the door for maybe an hour or two. He told me once he was in there writing letters to all the important men in the country. He was asking them how they felt about Mr. Lamar being president. When I told my people about that, they didn't always believe me. "Why would he tell all that to his nigger, Jake?" they'd ask. I couldn't explain that except to say that Master Fontaine wasn't like other white men. Maybe it was because I could read or maybe because I wanted to be a preacher like him, but sometimes we'd talk together like he wasn't any better than me. He wasn't either; I reckon we're all about the same on the inside. But at the time I thought he was a mighty fine man.

14

By early 1838 Mirabeau was receiving so many letters that the mere act of opening them occupied a good portion of my time. Most were of a political nature. These I read and passed on with a suggested response. Those from prospective immigrants living in the United States I answered myself. Family and business correspondence I did not open but gave directly to Mirabeau. I then slipped from the room to let him read in private.

One cool February day, after I handed Mirabeau a stack of personal mail and made to leave, he snatched the top letter and exclaimed, "Oh ho! This one's from Handy! Let's see what he's got!"

He tore open the paper and spread it on his desk. As was his habit when excited, he bent close to the surface and moved a finger along the words as he read them. "Yes . . . yes . . . this will do. Ah, excellent, only two months. Two months, Edward, what do you think?"

Knowing that Mirabeau referred to his friend Robert Handy, I deduced that two months must be the time estimated for constructing the house on the Brazos River that Mirabeau had commissioned. Mr. Handy, whom Mirabeau had met at San Jacinto, now busied himself with raising a town at the site of old Fort Bend on the Brazos. He had agreed to select river property outside the township for the plantation that Mirabeau planned to establish. Although he no longer spoke of leaving politics, Mirabeau still intended to become a gentleman farmer someday like Washington or Jefferson.

"He's located your land then?"

"He has indeed. It has everything I asked for, save the mountain."

We both laughed. The coastal region of Texas is as level a prairie as exists anywhere.

Mirabeau looked up from the letter, smiled, and asked, "Ready for a trip?"

An easy day's ride to the southwest brought us from the fetid waters of Buffalo Bayou to the serenity of the Brazos River bottom. Two boys throwing rocks at a fence post on the edge of town directed us to Robert Handy's Main Street office. We likely could have found it without assistance, given how few buildings graced the town's streets at that time. Mr. Handy came outside to greet us as we tied our horses.

"Mirabeau! What brings you here? Didn't you trust me with the selection?"

The smile on Handy's face belied the teasing nature of his question.

Mirabeau, often oblivious to such jests, responded this time in kind. "No, Robert, I did not. I had to make sure I wouldn't be living in an alligator-infested swamp."

"Once again you're on to me," Handy said. He glanced at me and loudly whispered, "I told you it wouldn't work."

Mirabeau fixed me with a mock accusatory stare. I shrugged my shoulders. "It was his idea."

A tour of the town occupied mere minutes. The same collection of rough-hewn cabins, tents, and half-finished buildings that I had seen all over Texas dotted the streets, most of which existed only as long, grassy rows marked by stake and string. "Why is it called Richmond, Mr. Handy?" I asked.

"Richmond is a town in England. My partner Lusk has a sentimental attachment to the old country. I wanted to name it 'Lamar' but couldn't overcome a certain party's objection."

"Too close to Houston," said Mirabeau.

Handy saddled a horse and guided us to Mirabeau's property. As we approached the river Mirabeau sighed contentedly and said, "Robert, you've really pulled it off. This is perfect."

Brown, waist-high grass stretched toward the horizon. Green shoots had just begun pushing through the old growth. A thick band of hardwoods lined either side of the river, which twisted sharply away from us in either direction. After dismounting, I reached beneath the blanket of vegetation to grab a handful of the black, claylike earth.

"It sticks to the plow a bit but is quite fertile," said Mr. Handy.

"What makes the best crop?" I asked.

"*Everything!* Oats, wheat, corn, cotton . . . a man down the river made a small fortune on melons last season."

"What will you grow, Mirabeau?"

"I haven't decided. Maybe some of everything," he replied. "It's a wonderful landscape."

"Beautiful."

"She would have liked it."

We wandered toward the Brazos. Mr. Handy spoke in glowing terms of the region's fertility and business prospects, with Mirabeau listening only half-heartedly. We stopped at a large rectangle marked out by rope and wooden stakes.

"This the house?" Mirabeau asked.

"Will be soon," said Handy.

Mirabeau walked carefully around the perimeter to enter the rectangle where the front door would be. Once inside, he giggled like a child and turned to view the river. "Rebecca's coming late June," he said. "Will we have a place to sleep by then?"

"Oh, yes," Handy assured him. "If not here then at my place."

Mirabeau laughed. "No offense, Robert, but I prefer here."

As we turned to go he looked at me said, "Rebecca's all I have left."

Because I was handy with a fishing pole and a frying pan, Master Fontaine took me along on trips if I wasn't busy in town. So while he and Mr. Lamar rode their horses I followed along on Janey and pretty soon we were at the Brazos River. If I heard one white man in Texas talk about the fine home he was gonna build I heard a thousand. Mr. Lamar stood there waving his arms about for the longest time telling Master Fontaine and the man Handy all about how someday his plantation would grow this and that and that his house was gonna be the best in all the land. The other man said wouldn't that be a fine place to bring a wife to and have some children and live like a king. But Mr. Lamar shook his head and said he didn't know if the Good Lord would grant him that pleasure again. Besides, he said, he already had a beautiful daughter and soon they'd see that for themselves. Then he noticed me standing back a ways and said, "Boy, we're gonna be here a while so why don't you go over yonder and catch us some catfish." Off I went.

Whereas a Texas spring delights the senses, a Texas summer assaults them. Each day of sunbaked torment slips monotonously into the next, the clear blue sky dragging meager clouds across its vastness as mocking reminders of the cooling rain it withholds. Moisture hangs heavily in the air, soaking a man with sweat while leaving his throat withered and dry. Heat saps man and beast alike. Brilliant sunlight pains the eyes and an overpowering stillness replaces the normal sounds of life. Only the African toils safely in such a climate, designed by his Creator to withstand equatorial rigors that are dangerous to his master.

Such a day found Mirabeau and me standing on a Houston wharf awaiting the arrival of a steamboat. Thirsty as I was, I didn't dare leave my friend's side for fear of missing the joyful reunion of father and daughter. Suddenly, a whistle blast from the approaching steamer portended imminent arrival.

Even as two burly men threw the heavy gangplank across the gap between ship and shore I spotted Rebecca in the crowd of passengers. A frail-looking girl with milky skin and shimmering auburn hair, she stood next to a well-dressed couple that I soon learned were her uncle and aunt, John and Amelia Randle. Her eyes darted anxiously among the faces on the wharf until locking with those of her father.

"Papa!" she cried. "Papa, I'm *here!*"

Mirabeau beamed. As the girl rushed onto the dock he stooped a bit to receive her forceful embrace.

"Papa! Papa! Papa!" She buried her head in his arms.

"Oh, Rebecca, dear child," said Mirabeau, tears moistening his eyes. The two of them remained locked together like this for quite some time, each occasionally sobbing the name of the other. I stood by awkwardly as Rebecca's escorts approached.

"Are you Mr. Fontaine?" asked the gentleman as he extended his hand.

"Please, sir, call me Edward."

"You may call me John and this is my wife, Amelia." He gestured toward the lady.

"Madam, I'm delighted to meet you." We looked awkwardly at each other. "Well," I said, clearing my throat, "they certainly seem glad to see each other."

"Edward, you have no idea!" said John with a laugh. "Rebecca has spoken of little but her father on this journey. She adores him."

"And he adores her. She is always in his thoughts."

Mirabeau and Rebecca halted their embrace long enough to look up at us. Mirabeau pointed at me. "Rebecca, this is the gentleman I've told you about in my letters. As you can see, his face is even homelier than I have described."

The jest gladdened my heart, for Mirabeau slipped into such playfulness only when completely happy and at ease.

"Oh, *no*, Father," said Rebecca. "I fear you are mistaken. This man is very *handsome!* Perhaps you were looking in a mirror as you wrote your description."

Roaring with laughter, Mirabeau said, "As you can see, Edward, I've met my match in this young girl!"

As we collected the baggage and made our way to a hotel on Franklin Street,

Mirabeau completed the transformation, begun only minutes before, from dignified statesman to doting parent. Holding an umbrella over Rebecca for shade, he marched dutifully beside her while inquiring about her travels. John, Amelia, and I trailed a few steps behind. Father and daughter chatted excitedly with each other all the way to the hotel. Mirabeau clearly loved the girl, which I had expected, but with an intensity that took me by surprise. I wondered if her presence helped fill the void left by his departed wife.

After a night in Houston we traveled by wagon to Oak Grove, as Mirabeau had named his new home on the Brazos. Handy had performed his job well. The house filled the space underneath several large shade trees, with a long curving walkway leading from the veranda down to the river. Decorative trim adorned the gleaming white exterior. Tall, stately glass windows offered sweeping views from within, while light green shutters stood ready for service as shields against sun and storm. Slender chimneys protruded gracefully from either end of the structure.

"It's beautiful, Papa!" Rebecca cried as she caught her first glimpse of her father's house.

"Mirabeau, you've planted civilization in the wilderness," said John.

Smiling, Mirabeau replied, "I know."

I saw the way that little girl pranced off the boat and I thought, "Here comes trouble." I've seen white children boss slaves around like they're owned by them instead of their daddies, and I thought I saw that in her. Thank the Lord I was wrong. Rebecca, poor child, she was just as sweet as any angel in Heaven. She was quick with a smile and treated me like she would any grown man. She even called me "Mr. Jake" until her daddy told her, "No, girl, he's just plain Jake." No, she was no trouble. She was a joy and everybody around her couldn't help but be joyful too.

I'd never seen Mr. Lamar's new house until we rode up in the wagon that day. A fine house it was too. Better than any I'd seen in Houston. Maybe the best I'd seen in Texas so far. But I was only in it once or twice. I carried the bags in and I carried them out but that's about it.

The barn was as new as the house and there were a couple of cabins for the slaves that Mr. Lamar was gonna buy. I heard him talk about it once while he was sitting on the porch. "Yes, sir," he said, "I'm gonna need some hands to work this place, so I guess I'll get some in Houston or maybe New Orleans. I hear prices are better in New Orleans." He said this like he was talking about buying corn or potatoes. But there were no slaves yet, so I got to stay in one of the cabins. It was nice to sleep in a clean, new place.

• • •

Mirabeau told me later that those weeks with Rebecca were the happiest he had enjoyed since Tabitha's death. Most days found him up at dawn going over papers so as to be ready for her when she got up. She was not an early riser, which was to his advantage as it allowed him several hours of uninterrupted work. Once she had breakfasted, the two of them would set out on the day's adventure, often with John and Amelia as company. Most of the trips were short, either into Richmond or to a nearby plantation. Others took them as far as Houston and there was one overnight journey to the coast. Rebecca returned from the latter with tousled, sandy hair and bright red skin. "She looks like a wild Indian!" I said upon seeing her.

"No, that's just someone who didn't wear her bonnet as instructed by her father," said Mirabeau sternly. But when he glanced over at Rebecca he smiled and said, "I must learn to tell you no."

John, Amelia, and I accompanied them on a visit to the battlefield at San Jacinto. After pointing out the locations of the Texian line and Mexican camp, Mirabeau bade us wait in the open while he rode his horse to the edge of the woods. At a distance of about fifty yards he wheeled his mount and shouted, "This is where we started the charge."

He then dismounted, found a long, thin stick, and climbed back into the saddle. Raising the stick over his head like a saber, he put spurs to flesh and issued a piercing "Texas yell." As the horse gained speed Mirabeau lowered his "sword" and leaned forward in the saddle. Thundering hooves raised a thick cloud of dust as he raced past us, shouting all the while. He stopped only when he had reached the point of the Mexican encampment. There he slashed his weapon several times at the imaginary enemy before trotting back toward us. As he approached, Rebecca gushed, "Uncle John, did you imagine that Papa was such a hero?"

John chuckled. "Rebecca, he *did* have an army with him!"

"But he was the leader! He was in charge!"

"Not of the entire army," I said. "Of the cavalry. He was a hero that day but one of many."

Mirabeau arrived on the scene. Noticing the smiles on our faces he asked, "That *was* rather silly, wasn't it?"

"Not at all," I said. "Rebecca is impressed! So am I."

"Me too," added John.

"You should have seen them run, John," said Mirabeau. "Cowards. That won't be the last time we see their backs, I'd wager."

"You mean they might come back to fight? To take back their land?" asked Amelia.

Mirabeau smirked. "More likely we'll be going to get more of theirs."

Just then I spied an unusual rock on the ground and picked it up. As I turned it over in my hands Amelia gasped and John said, "My God, that's part of a backbone." I hurriedly dropped it, but not before Rebecca had seen it too.

"I'm sorry," I said, embarrassed.

Mirabeau said, "Let's go."

On the way back from the battlefield we stopped in Houston to show Rebecca, John, and Amelia the Capitol. Walking through the still unfinished building, John asked in wonder, "Mirabeau, how can a national government function in such humble surroundings?"

"John, the grandeur of a nation stems not from its buildings but from its people. We've only just gained our independence. Give us time and we'll have a capital that rivals those of Europe."

"Oh, Mirabeau," said Amelia teasingly, "I see little promise in these muddy streets!"

"Not here, Amelia! Of course not here. No, the seat of government won't be in this diseased swamp, but somewhere west of here. Out beyond the Brazos."

"But there's nothing beyond the Brazos!"

"Not yet, but there will be."

Back at Oak Grove we enjoyed a pleasant evening of parlor games and poetry readings, after which I stayed up with Mirabeau and John. John had brought a case of Georgia whiskey with him, a bottle of which he opened and poured for us. As we sipped, Mirabeau settled deep into his chair with a dreamy expression on his face.

"This is why we do it," he said with a contented sigh. "We work and struggle to gain these moments of domestic peace."

John said, "Mirabeau, you could do this more often if you'd come back to Georgia when your term is up."

"I wish that were possible, John. I really do. But there's so much yet to accomplish."

"I suppose I'm forgetting your desire to be president."

"It's no desire, John, it's a *duty*!"

"What do you mean?"

I offered an answer. "He means it's his duty to the people of Texas."

"No, that's not it," Mirabeau said quickly. "I mean . . . yes, that's true, but it's more than that. This pursuit of the presidency, this whole political . . . *thing* is a means to an end. Not *my* end, mind you."

"Then whose?" John asked.

The question hung awkwardly in the air for several seconds before Mirabeau spoke. "God's."

"God's?" asked John. "Well, I've got to hear *this*."

Time slowed down. I sipped nervously at my drink as John digested what he had heard.

Mirabeau tried to explain. "God has spoken to me on two occasions. It's why I came to Texas. I didn't know why he brought me here at first—maybe still don't— but God put me here to accomplish something."

"Mirabeau, you've already accomplished so much," John said, eliciting an impatient wave of the hand from Mirabeau.

"Stepping-stones, John. Mere stepping-stones. Think of the things that have happened to me. I've been at the right place at the right time all along the way. I didn't plan any of this. I *couldn't* have. And it certainly hasn't been easy. But every time I think the game is over, something happens to send me further down the road. Now I'm about to become president."

Such talk unsettled me. He was about to *run for* the presidency. A victory seemed possible, but not a certainty.

Mirabeau continued. "And once I'm president, I'll finally be in position to further God's plan for this nation. This isn't a great nation yet, John, but it *will* be. It *must* be. There's only Mexico and a few savages between us and an empire. Why else would God have brought me here?"

"You make it sound so obvious, Mirabeau."

Mirabeau laughed. "It's been anything *but* obvious! I've only come to realize it slowly these past few years. I just wish . . . I only wish I could have figured it out without prodding. Then I wouldn't be here by myself."

I squirmed. I knew where Mirabeau was heading; such talk of Tabitha's death serving as a message made me uncomfortable.

"No, if I hadn't been so *thick-headed* I might have been able to *save* her. Why are divine messages so shrouded in mystery? Why couldn't an angel show up with a written set of instructions? Why did I think my political destiny lay in Georgia? I was *crushed* in my last run for office. Why did I think I could publish a newspaper when there were so many others already in print? Of *course* it failed. But that *still* wasn't enough to steer me toward my fate. No! Only my dear wife's suffering . . . her misery . . . her *death,* was a strong enough message to pry open my eyes. *That's* why I left Georgia. *That's* why I can't go back. At least not until the job is done and her sacrifice is redeemed!"

John cleared his throat and said, "I see."

"Rebecca looks so much like her. It's as if Tabitha's watching to make sure I stay on track."

John jerked forward in his chair. "Now, Mirabeau, that's just preposterous. Of course Rebecca bears a resemblance to Tabitha. She's her daughter, for God's sake. But she's just a child. She's not Tabitha: she's Rebecca. Tabitha's gone."

Mirabeau appeared stunned. His eyes glistened in the dim light.

"Mirabeau, I'm sorry," said John, "I'm—"

"No," interrupted Mirabeau. "It's all right. I don't expect you to agree with me. And I don't *like* the truth of what I see. I've pondered endlessly about it, though, and more rational explanations elude me."

"It's a terrible thought," John said sadly.

"It's a terrible burden."

Looking back through the years I realize that I never saw Mirabeau happier than when he was with Rebecca. As I watched them play at jacks or listened to them tease each other, my heart ached for the motherless child and the still-grieving widower, yet rejoiced at the life-sustaining love between them. One evening Rebecca nestled up against her father on the sofa as he read to her from *The Last of the Mohicans*. He casually draped an arm around her with the deep sigh of contentment known only to proud parents. He caught my eye and said, "Edward, if I died right now I'd die a happy man."

Rebecca snuggled even closer. "Me too, Father," she said. "I'd die happy too."

To which Mirabeau replied, "Let us pray that the good Lord will take an old man before an innocent child, Rebecca, for I would sooner suffer the torments of hell than stay in this world without you."

A week later I stood on the same Houston dock from which I had watched Rebecca's arrival and embraced her to say good-bye. She smiled sweetly, yet wistfully at me, as if she knew we would never see each other again. "I'll miss you, Mr. Fontaine," she said. "I'm happy to know that Father has you to help him."

I returned her smile and replied with sincerity, "I'll miss you too, Rebecca. You're a fine young lady. And your father doesn't need *my* help."

Rebecca and her father hugged tightly throughout my parting conversation with the Randles. She giggled as he whispered something in her ear. As they drew apart, he hung his head, but she gently lifted his chin and said, "Be brave, Father."

Minutes later, as the whistle sounded and the boat withdrew from shore, we watched Rebecca's auburn hair flutter with each frantic wave of her hand. Finally we could see her no more. "Ah, she's an easy one to love, Mirabeau," I said.

"Yes, she is," he said, giving in to tears. "It's God I have trouble with."

• • •

That summer was maybe the quietest, most peaceful time I had in Texas back then. We stayed out at Mr. Lamar's new house. Mr. Lamar carried on so much with his daughter that he mostly let Master Fontaine be. That meant Master Fontaine didn't have much to do, so he let me be too. Oh, there were chores here and there and some fixing up to do, but it wasn't much. I dug up a garden and tended a few hogs and chickens. Built a coop for the hens.

I enjoyed little things like that. I always liked making things. I knew from seeing and talking to some of the other hands on the plantations around there that I had it pretty easy. So I had no cause to complain.

That girl Rebecca, I learned quick that she was just as sweet as she could be. She reminded me a little of one of my sisters back in Mississippi, the youngest one. Not sassy, but ready to speak her mind. Smart too. But always nice and polite. She saw me in the barn one day reading my Bible and asked me what I was doing. I had only just started reading around there because I wasn't sure what Mr. Lamar would say if he saw a slave reading. Then Master Fontaine told me it was all right, that he wouldn't mind. So Rebecca, she asked me what I was doing and I said, "I'm reading my Bible."

And she said, "I didn't ever know a darkie that could read."

I told her not many of us could. That it mostly wasn't allowed. She said that wasn't right, that if she ever had any darkies she'd teach 'em to read herself. Then she asked me to read her a story. I was in the Old Testament, so I read her the story of Samson, the strongest man who ever lived. I told her about how Delilah, a wicked woman, tricked him into cutting his hair off and that took his strength away. So his enemies caught him and gouged out his eyes and locked him up. But over time his hair grew back and he was strong again. Once Samson knew that, he fixed it so he'd be in the temple with all his enemies and before they could stop him he pulled the temple down and killed every one of 'em and him too.

Rebecca said, "I used to think my daddy was strong like that but he couldn't pull down a temple." I told her that the Bible was using that as an example; that you didn't have to pull down a temple with your hands to be strong. I said there's all kinds of strength and that the mightiest of all is the strength that comes from the Lord. "Samson couldn't have done that without the Lord being on his side," I said. "Samson pushed, but it was the Lord that knocked down those walls."

"What does that have to do with my daddy?" she asked.

"Well, it's like this," I said. "Your daddy could be the head man in Texas soon. Then he'd have armies on his side to do what he says. So he'd be the strongest man in the country. Not because he can pick up the biggest rock, but because he could fix it so that the rock does get picked up. Now that's *strong!"*

"But when Samson pulled down the temple, he was killed too!" she said.

"Well, then," I told her, "all your daddy has to do is to not let anybody cut off his hair."

Later Mr. Lamar came looking for me in the barn. "Jacob," he said, "I hear you can read."

Now I was nervous. "That's right, sir," I said, "ever since I was a little boy."

"How'd you learn that?" he asked.

"I don't remember that too well," I said. "I can't really recollect not being able to."

"Hmmm," he said. "And you've been reading Bible stories to my daughter?"

"Yes, sir," I said. "What else am I gonna read but the Good Book?"

"Right," he said. And he started to leave. Then he turned back around and said, "That's good advice, Jacob, about haircuts. I don't expect I'll be letting anybody cut my hair at that." And he laughed and went back in the house.

15

We expected no little challenge from Sam Houston in Mirabeau's quest for the presidency. While the Texas constitution barred him from seeking a second consecutive term of office, no law prevented him from attempting to influence the election's outcome. As winter yielded to spring, it became evident that a Virginian named Peter Grayson had caught Houston's eye. "A tough man to beat," said Mirabeau.

Grayson's lineage certainly seemed to mark him for political distinction. A great-uncle had been president of the Continental Congress and a United States senator, while another relative, James Monroe, was twice elected president. Like Mirabeau, Grayson wrote poetry, but unlike him, he fought against the British in the War of 1812. A Texas resident since 1832, Grayson had established himself on a large and profitable plantation in Matagorda County. Few could match his holdings in land, property, or slaves. In short, every favorable trait of Mirabeau's seemed equaled or surpassed by its counterpart in Peter Grayson.

Except one. Whereas Mirabeau had been able to withstand the tragedies that life can deliver, Peter Grayson apparently could not. Many of his lapses into melancholia were but rumors, but a complete collapse in the 1820s in Kentucky had been witnessed by too many to discount. He was a state legislator at the time. Business and personal setbacks of no greater weight than those borne by the bulk of humanity produced in Grayson a curious effect. Within a matter of days, he withdrew from society and, except while working, kept to his house. At first he continued meeting the duties of his office but eventually absented himself from the halls of Congress as well. Servants said he had taken to his bed as if felled by a terrible disease, yet he suffered from no physical ailment. He remained in this paralyzed state for months, barely able to walk or eat, until his family feared he would perish from starvation. But by slow degrees his health returned. A land grant from Stephen F. Austin in 1830 provided the spark that brought him back to life. All hoped he had left his mental foibles behind him with his emigration to Texas.

Another challenger, Tennessee native James Collinsworth, boasted strong credentials and powerful supporters, but none that could match the influence of Sam Houston or, for that matter, Mirabeau. Only thirty-two years old in 1838, Collinsworth had already held several high offices, including that which he then occupied, chief justice of the Texas Supreme Court. He had been a member of the group that had founded Mirabeau's new hometown of Richmond, although Robert Handy and his partner Lusk had shouldered most of that burden. He had distinguished himself during our revolution as a signer of the Declaration of Independence and a member of Sam Houston's staff at San Jacinto. No less a luminary than Thomas Rusk had commended him for bravery at that decisive struggle.

For all his impressive accomplishments James Collinsworth exhibited one serious flaw, the same affinity for drunkenness that plagued many early Texans. I would have perceived it as precluding his election save for the fact that the incumbent president could outdrink him. Mirabeau, while disapproving, indicated that the chief justice nevertheless managed to fulfill his public obligations quite soberly. "He's never drunk in court," he said, "so he must take his whiskey only when his work is done. Anyway, I fear that in Texas it is sobriety rather than drunkenness that limits a man's horizons."

Mirabeau assigned to me the task of coordinating his political campaign. Mostly this amounted to keeping track of the numerous invitations to public dinners that he received. He couldn't accept them all, of course, but the ones that he did had to occur in logical sequence with regard to geography. It made no sense, for example, to commit to two separate appearances along the coast if there was an event significantly inland in between. "Minimize my time in the saddle, Edward," he commanded.

I was also to coordinate the efforts of his prominent friends. Chief among these was Dr. Everitt, who busied himself writing letters to as many newspapers as would print them. Most of the letters barely mentioned Mirabeau by name. Instead Everitt focused on the shortcomings, and there were many, of the incumbent chief executive. Since everyone knew that Grayson and Collinsworth were Houston men, Dr. Everitt believed that undermining administration support would also weaken their candidacies. Everitt proved invaluable in one other respect, although I strove to keep it from public notice as much as possible. He paid virtually all of Mirabeau's campaign expenses. At least once a week, I delivered an itemized list of campaign expenditures to one of his business associates. Within the hour the same man returned with a small package of money. Usually he brought paper currency, but on occasion he delivered a heavier bundle of gold and silver coins. It seemed a miracle to me, specie being in such short supply in those days, and where Everitt got it I never knew.

Another trusted confidante was the recent immigrant James Webb. The native Virginian had resigned a Florida judgeship before coming to Texas. Not long after his arrival he met and befriended Mirabeau, with whom he shared a reflective nature and a belief in Sam Houston's ineptitude. Webb had a particular knack for sensing a man's true intentions. Mirabeau found him useful when attempting to discern a professed supporter's true motivation. And it was Webb who delivered the news that Mirabeau would indeed become the Republic's next president.

This occurred well before the election. Mirabeau still basked in the afterglow of the idyllic interlude with his daughter. One day around noon I sat at a desk in one of the bedrooms at Oak Grove when I heard a man talking to Mirabeau on the veranda. I couldn't make out his words, but the breathless tone of his voice indicated something of great importance. Dropping a stack of papers, I rushed outside.

It was Webb. He stood hunched over gasping for breath as if he had run and not ridden all the way from Houston. His haste had been so great that he had neglected to secure his horse, which had already wandered a significant distance away. Jacob emerged from the barn and chased after the animal.

"It's true, Mirabeau! Several of the passengers confirmed the story."

"They could have been repeating the same rumor," Mirabeau said.

"Our man was there."

"Bradford?"

"Yes."

Bradford was Terrence Bradford, called Bottle by his friends because he was rarely seen without one, a young and wild Georgian who hoped for political office in a Lamar administration, but who possessed few qualifications for holding one. I had acceded to his request for an introduction to Mirabeau on the strength of a letter of recommendation from a Georgia senator who I subsequently learned did not exist. I incorrectly assumed that Mirabeau had cut ties with Bradford after I informed him of this.

Mirabeau asked Webb, "What did Bradford say?"

"I gave him the money from Everitt. He found Collinsworth near Galveston Bay. The two of them spent several days drinking up Everitt's money and then got on a steamship. Some say that he jumped; others claim he fell in drunken stupor, but the result is that Collinsworth drowned."

"What's Bradford's story?"

"That he was drunk. His exact words were, 'Everitt wanted him to drink and I made sure he did.'"

"And Grayson?" Mirabeau asked. "How is that confirmed?"

"A Tennessee newspaper," said Webb. "Here."

Mirabeau accepted the proffered paper and began reading. Bursting with curiosity, I couldn't help but call out, "What is it? What's happened?"

Webb turned to face me, a huge grin now lighting up his sweaty face. "Grayson and Collinsworth are out of the election! Mirabeau will be president!"

"I can't rejoice in their deaths," said Mirabeau. "Nevertheless, James, I believe you're right."

"Deaths?" I asked.

"Would you believe it, Edward?" said Webb. "First Grayson. Shot himself. Do you remember he was on his way to Washington as minister plenipotentiary to the United States?"

"Yes, a position he accepted with reluctance, I heard."

"Evidently, judging by what happened. He was in Tennessee at a place called Bean's Station. His landlord found him in his room with his brains blown out."

"That's terrible!"

"Perhaps. But it's consistent with his known mental weakness."

"And Collinsworth drowned?"

"Yes. In Galveston Bay. Whether he fell or jumped doesn't really matter; he's no longer a concern."

"They'll say I had something to do with it," said Mirabeau.

Webb snorted. "Ridiculous. What an absurd thing to say."

"Nevertheless, they'll say it. They don't have to prove it, of course. Only get men to thinking about it."

"So we play up the talk of suicide. You can't be blamed for a man taking his own life. And there's a witness in Bradford."

"Maybe you're right, but let's go inside. There's no need to stand in the sun like savages."

"After you, Mr. President," said Webb with a laugh and sweep of his hand.

Mirabeau cut him off. "Two men are dead, James. Laugh not at the hand of God!"

After Miss Rebecca went back to Georgia we stayed at Lamar's house a little while longer. There were so many men coming and going I lost track of them all. I know now they were plotting how to make Mr. Lamar president. Most of them I forget by now. There was one, though, that I can recall for certain, a man named Webb. Mr. Webb came out of Florida, they said, where he was a judge. Why he came to Texas I don't know but there he was just the same. He was always nice to me and might slip me a coin when I took care of his horse. His face was as red as a radish, that's what I recollect the most. That day he forgot to tie up his horse it was even redder than that. I was out in the barn and he rode into the yard like the devil was after him. He jumped off and commenced to waving his arms and shouting at Mr. Lamar. I took off after the horse, hoping for a nickel or two. By the time I caught it and walked it back toward the barn, Master Fontaine was out on the porch too. They were shouting and happy; Mr. Webb kept calling Mr. Lamar the president. This was because the two other men running for president killed themselves. One man blew his brains out up in Tennessee; the other jumped off a boat and drowned himself. Can you beat that? When I'm on a boat I stay away from the rail because I can't swim and here a man goes and jumps off on purpose. He should have known he would drown!

Later I asked Mirabeau about Bradford. He merely shrugged his shoulders and said, "That was Everitt's doing."

"You didn't cut Bradford loose after I told you about the forged letter?"

"Cut him loose from what? I never hired him for anything."

"But you could have told Everitt to stay away from him."

"Everitt's his own man. Nobody tells him what to do."

"But . . . a man's dead because of Bradford!"

Mirabeau shrugged again and said, "Look, Edward, Collinsworth is dead because he drank a gallon of whiskey and jumped into the bay. Bradford was with him. So what?"

"Bradford was with him because Everitt *sent* him." And though I didn't say it, I feared Mirabeau had instructed Everitt to do that.

"Edward, open your eyes. We use the tools that God puts in our hands. This is *His* plan, remember?"

"God wanted Collinsworth dead?"

"I'm not saying that. I only know that God wants me to be president. How he brings that about isn't my concern."

To my discredit, I chose to believe him.

It was Webb who planted the idea of a western tour in Mirabeau's mind. He likely would have gone at some point anyway because he had already conceived the idea of westward expansion by then. But the nudge from Webb made it happen when it did. We were seated at supper one evening when Mirabeau first mentioned the trip. Josephine, a servant girl leased from a neighboring plantation, was clearing away the dishes when Mirabeau said nonchalantly, "Edward, in a few days we'll be making a trip up the Colorado. We could encounter severe weather, so bring warm clothes. Bring Jacob too."

I welcomed the prospect of a change in routine, as the daily grind of secretarial duties at Oak Grove was becoming monotonous. "Where are we going? Columbus? Bastrop?" These were the settlements farthest upriver at the time.

"I'm not sure," Mirabeau answered. "We'll pass through those towns, of course, but I want to see what lies beyond."

"Why? What *does* lie beyond?"

"Beautiful country, I'm told. As for the reason . . . well, the *ostensible* reason is to secure the western vote. Webb suggested it in this letter." He extracted a piece of paper from his shirt pocket. "Listen to this: 'It is the opinion of several of your friends that a trip up the country would be serviceable to you.' Now, I think our friend overestimates the risk of losing western support, especially in light of recent events, but I do agree that a trip would be 'serviceable.' I have long wished to see our frontier, for I'm of a mind to situate the seat of government out that way."

"Really? How? There's nothing there."

"I concede that fact," he said with a chuckle. "But when has wilderness ever stopped the Anglo-Saxon race? What obstacle have we so far not overcome? We won't head into this unprepared, you know. Some very fine men are already there."

"Who?"

"Burleson, for one."

I knew the name, having often heard about the exploits of brothers Joseph, Aaron, Edward, Jacob, and Lord knows how many other members of the clan. "Which Burleson? That's a big family."

"All of them. They've settled near the Guadalupe just a bit south of the Colorado. But the man I'm referring to is Ned. He was at San Jacinto, remember? First man to charge the Mexican line."

"Colonel Burleson? I thought his name was Edward."

"Edward, Ned, same man."

"It will take more than one family to populate a town. Especially a government seat."

Mirabeau grinned and raised an eyebrow. "Edward, I've always taken you for an optimist. Have I been mistaken?"

"No, but I'm also a realist."

"So it's up to us to transform dreams into reality," he said, his steely gaze boring into me. Leaning back in his chair and cocking his head toward the doorway, he shouted, "Josephine, bring us a bottle of wine!"

The young girl promptly appeared, her trembling hands grasping a bottle and two glasses. She set them on the table and fled.

After filling our glasses, Mirabeau sighed and briefly stared out the window before returning to our conversation. "Edward, here is why we must do this. What lies beyond the upper Colorado?"

He's been rehearsing this, I thought. "Savages and wilderness."

"And beyond that?"

"Beyond that is more wilderness. But then you come to Mexican territory."

"Exactly," he said emphatically, pointing a finger at me. "New Mexico, to be precise. Santa Fe, New Mexico. And why is Santa Fe important?"

I didn't know exactly, having not been in Texas long enough to develop much interest in foreign geography. "As far as I know it's a small place populated by common people. Why does it matter?"

"I'll tell you why it matters!" He spoke with the self-satisfied smugness of one who knows a great secret. "Santa Fe is the key to the lock. Turn the key and you've opened the door to empire. A Texan empire."

I laughed. "Mirabeau, what grand scheme have you concocted?"

"Enough, Edward, you sound like Houston!" The smile on his face reassured me that he jested. "This 'grand scheme,' as you call it, is the reason I've been called to Texas. It *has* to be. Now listen. New Mexico Territory, for all its crudeness, contains vast riches. Cattle, hides, wool, Indian blankets, precious metals, salt, even slaves—exportable commodities that must be hauled to market. Santa Fe is the gathering point. The town itself is small, so bringing goods to Santa Fe is only the first step. Once there, goods are traded to American merchants, who then haul them overland to St. Louis. Once again this is only a way station. From St. Louis the goods are transported across the Mississippi and distributed throughout the eastern United States, with most destined for the major cities along the coast. This takes months. Most of the journey is overland, especially between Santa Fe and St. Louis. But what if there were a faster route?"

"The answer is obvious," I reasoned. "A faster route lowers the cost of transport, thereby increasing profit."

"Profit for whom?"

"Well, to the merchants of course. But also to those controlling the route."

Mirabeau slammed his glass down upon the table. "And that will be Texas!"

"And this ties into your trip up the Colorado?"

"Surely you see it, Edward." I did, but I wanted to hear his explanation. He obliged. "I must allow that this idea is not original to me. An American merchant named Dryden has sent me letters describing the desire of the people of Santa Fe to join with Texas. That being the case, the riches of the Santa Fe trade should flow *here*. Instead of trekking thousands of miles to the northeast, merchants will depart Santa Fe on a journey of only a few hundred miles to the metropolis that we will establish on the upper Colorado River. A bit of work on the river will create a shipping lane to the Gulf Coast, at which point goods can be transferred to ships bound for the eastern United States. That will shave weeks, perhaps months, off the current overland trip."

"Mirabeau, that's brilliant!"

"And that's not all. What's between Santa Fe and the Pacific Ocean? Nothing but Indians and Mexicans. We've already demonstrated that the Mexicans are a feeble obstacle."

"And the Indians?"

"The Indians? Well, they'll be civilized or they'll be exterminated. That's up to them."

"Then your empire—"

"Not *my* empire, the *Texas* empire. A Texas empire that will stretch from the Sabine to the Pacific."

Once again Mirabeau had demonstrated to me his amazing powers of prescience. Whereas I could ponder for days or weeks and not formulate a plan beyond my immediate horizon, Mirabeau seemed capable of gazing into the far distant future at will. I dreamed of tomorrow or the next day; he dreamed of later generations. He possessed no knowledge unavailable to me or any other man, but unlike others, he was able to stitch the unrelated bits of information into a quilt that the rest of us could see and admire. This was his power; this was his gift. This was the remarkable genius that God in His inscrutable wisdom chose to waste. But that part of the story lies ahead.

It was about that time that Josephine came around. She'd been working in the kitchen of a big house down the river, but the head lady there didn't like her. So her master sent her on up to Oak Grove. She was a cute thing; young and pretty. At first she wouldn't talk to me much, but after a while we got to be friendly. I'd hang around the yard out back if I didn't have nothing else to do. Pretty soon she started finding me chores to do or errands to run and that's how we'd get to talk. Master Fontaine told me, "Now, Jacob, you treat that girl right," and I said, "Master, you got nothing to worry about from me." And truth is, he didn't, because I pretty quick started thinking about marrying that gal. Nothing came of that, although I did get a kiss here and there. Just about the time she started warming up we set out on that buffalo hunt. That's how it was in those days. A black man couldn't get too attached to a woman because before you know it one of 'em was moving on. Thank the Lord that's different now.

I didn't know we were going out to hunt buffalo. I just knew we were going somewhere that neither one of us had ever been before. Master came to me and said, "Jacob, pack your things because we're heading out in two days."

"Where we going?" I asked.

"Up the Colorado," he said.

"Where's that?" I asked.

"That's one river over to the west," is how he explained it.

"Why we going there?" I told him.

"To help Mr. Lamar become president," he said.

I didn't believe it would help, but he did, so that was that. Then he said that not only were we going up the river, we were gonna get to the very last town and then keep on going. "Lord," I prayed that night, "you must know what you're about but I am in the dark. Please keep me in mind when I'm in that country because I'm not of a mind to get killed by Indians. Please watch over me and keep me in the flock. This poor sheep don't wish to wander."

That prayer must have worked because I'm still here, see? But I couldn't know that's how it would turn out and let me tell you I was afraid setting off. I packed my things like Master Fontaine said. He told me we wouldn't be eating and sleeping in houses all the time, that we might have to find our own food and make our own beds. I didn't worry about the food. I figured as long as we were in range of the river I could get plenty of fish. And Master Fontaine and Mr. Lamar could shoot deer and bear and such. But I didn't much cotton to sleeping in the woods. I slept on the ground plenty in those days, but always near enough to other folks and away from wolves and Indians. So that seemed like the worst part of the proposition to me.

Well, here came the day to depart and wouldn't you know Josephine bawled like a baby. Since we were going away, Mr. Lamar was gonna send her back to her master's house and she didn't want that at all. But she also told me, "I'm gonna miss you terrible, Jake, you're my onliest friend."

"Oh, Josephine," I told her, "dry up your tears. We'll be coming back one day."

We did come back, but it was quite a spell before we done so. And by that time Josephine was bought by a man from the Redlands. That's where she is today, for all I know.

After she was done bawling and I had everything stowed up proper on the horses and Janey, we rode off. All I could think about was the Indians and wolves I was sure would be waiting for us. But Master Fontaine and Mr. Lamar acted like it was no concern of theirs at all. Finally, I told myself, "Jake, you just got to quit worrying about what hasn't happened yet. At least you're not on a boat!"

16

We rode west from Richmond to the Colorado River, which we then followed north to the town of Columbus. Tracing its beginnings to the original American settlers that had arrived with Stephen F. Austin some fifteen or twenty years previously, the town bustled with activity as we rode its dusty streets. At the town center, recognizable by the large empty square of prairie grass surrounded by one- and two-story buildings, we stopped at a trough to water our horses. Several small children played in front of a dry goods store. Nearby, three Negroes worked to dislodge a large tree stump in the road. Mirabeau called out to them, "Boys, where's the boardinghouse?"

The men stopped working and looked up. One of them removed his hat and, pointing to a white frame structure on the opposite side of the square, said, "That one, Boss." He eyed us cautiously as we watered our horses. Once the animals were finished, we led them across the square to the building indicated by the man. Jacob hung back to talk with the laborers.

Robert Handy had accompanied us from Richmond in order to arrange escorts for the journey beyond Columbus. As we entered the house, a large black servant woman cracking pecans on a battered sofa smiled and said, "Mr. Handy, I ain't seen you in a hog's age! How you been?"

Mirabeau leaned toward me and whispered, "Can you believe they let her sit here in the parlor?"

Handy returned the woman's smile and said, "Minerva, I'm well as a man can be." He strode over to the couch, reached into the large bowl of shelled nuts, and popped a handful into his mouth. "Mmmm, these are good. When can I expect a piece of pecan pie?"

Minerva laughed. "Mr. Handy, you ate up all the pie in town last time you were here. I got to shell these pecans before I can make another batch."

"Well, you let me know when you do that! Now go get Mrs. Walton for me."

While we waited for Minerva to return with the landlady, Jacob approached the house. Walking outside, I asked him, "What did those men have to say, Jacob?"

He looked sheepish. "Master Fontaine, I've just been talking to them about what's up yonder."

"What did you learn? Will we keep our scalps?"

"Master Fontaine, you know I'm not complaining."

I nodded.

"Well, they say there's been nobody killed around here for a spell. Last one was before the Mexicans came."

"That's good news."

Mrs. Walton couldn't hide her excitement when she learned she would be hosting the vice president of the Republic. The red flush of her neck and face betrayed her nervousness, as did her overly formal speech. "Mr. Vice President," she cooed, "at what hour would you like to dine?"

Disliking the celebrity inherent to his position, Mirabeau downplayed her deference. "Mrs. Walton, your customary dinnertime will do."

After securing our rooms and giving instructions to Jacob for unloading the baggage, we accompanied Handy as he attempted to round up a party to take us to Bastrop. Away from the main square were several burned-out buildings. Thick weeds poked through the rubble. "From the war?" I asked.

"General Sam," replied Handy. "When he left he burned the town. Some said it was to keep goods from the Mexicans, but that's a load of manure."

"Why do you think he did it?"

"To slow Santa Anna down," said Handy with disgust. "Damn coward wanted to put as much distance between himself and the Mexicans as he could."

"My view exactly," said Mirabeau.

The following morning five well-armed men met us at Mrs. Walton's. "We'll get you to Bastrop in one piece," assured their leader, a man named Jed Carroll. We bade farewell to Handy and struck out for the ferry crossing. From the riverbank we could see a large boom strung across the river a few hundred yards upstream. "What's that for?" Mirabeau asked our companions.

"For the courthouse they aim to build," answered Carroll. "Crews up toward Bastrop cut the pine and float it downriver. That boom catches the logs."

"Hear that, Edward?" Mirabeau said. "Timber enough to spare upriver! That ought to suffice for a seat of government."

Our trip to Bastrop passed uneventfully. As the settlements became sparser, so did the farms, with each successive dwelling appearing cruder than the last. The level coastal prairie yielded to a gently rolling landscape of rich grass interspersed with islands of oak and other hardwoods. Wide strips of dense vegetation crowded the river on either side. Herds of deer browsed peacefully in the distance, completely unconcerned with our presence. Hawks monitored our progress from above.

Ten miles before Bastrop the landscape changed dramatically. Gone were the exposed tracts of grass. In their place arose an immense pine forest, with trees as tall and stout as any I had seen in Mississippi or Alabama. Their appearance excited Mirabeau. "Edward, this is magnificent," he said. "This puts to rest the idea that timber supplies are adequate only in the east!"

"It seems endless."

"Seems that way but it's about twenty or thirty miles wide," said one of our companions, a rough-mannered older man named Will Hooper.

"And what's after that?" I asked.

"More of what we saw back yonder," answered Hooper. "At least for a ways. I haven't been no further than a half-day's ride."

Bastrop looked like every other Texas town I had seen. A few neat frame houses surrounded by far cruder dwellings of hewn logs occupied one side of the river; a large field of pine stumps the other. As we dismounted in front of the largest of the houses, Carroll grinned and said, "Gentlemen, here we are at the edge of civilization. I'll round up a posse to take you from here. After that, watch your scalps!"

What I'll always recollect about Columbus is that's the first time I ever tasted pecans. I was standing out front of the boardinghouse with the horses when a fat colored woman came out of the house grinning from here to tomorrow. "Well, howdy-doo," she said. "Ain't you about the handsomest man I've seen around here lately."

"And aren't those the prettiest eyes of any woman in these parts?" I said. I was joking, just having some fun.

We got to talking about this and that and then she opened her apron and said for me to try some of the pecans she just shelled. I did and said, "Those are mighty good."

"I got lots more in the house," she said.

"You know I can't go in the house," I told her.

"That's not the house I mean," she said. "I got my own house around the back. You come on over after dark and have you some more of these pecans."

"What's your name?" I asked.

"Minerva, honey, what's yours?"

"Jake."

"Well, Jake, I'll be waiting for you after dark."

So I went there and had all the pecans I could eat and I'm not ashamed to say I had just a little bit of Minerva too. No, I'm not ashamed of that. I was lonesome and the Lord provided, is how I saw it then and see it now.

Once we left Columbus we sure hit some pretty country. The grass got taller and after a while came pine trees like the ones back east. The men that were with us talked about the trees like they were something special. I guess they were, because Mr. Lamar got himself all worked up. He commenced to talking about building this and that, which seemed peculiar to me because he had just built a big house. Later on, though, Master Fontaine told me he wasn't planning on building just another house, but a whole new city. That's the way it was back then: white folks putting up houses like there wouldn't ever be enough.

Mirabeau was anxious to move on past Bastrop. He declined an invitation to a public dinner in his honor and afterward told me, "There's time for that sort of thing later." Jed Carroll proved true to his word and found six men from a local ranging company to escort us upriver. I recall the names of four of the men, Jim Rice, Willis Avery, and brothers Dan and Malcolm Hornsby. Avery was one of the men present when I first met Mirabeau at San Jacinto. It had been after talk of Santa Anna had died down that the topic of the Alamo arose. Firelight danced on Avery's face as he related the tale of his father, lost with the other brave men in that fateful encounter. "I'm the one who convinced him to come to Texas," he said. "Mother wanted to stay in Missouri. She reckoned Texas was just too dangerous, that it was all right for young men like me to come down but that he was of an age for staying put. He didn't listen to her, of course. Told her she shouldn't worry, that they'd be moving to an area where there were plenty of other people to guard each other against Indians. I guess he knew what was coming with Mexico, but he didn't tell her. He wasn't planning on getting killed is all. He figured that once the Mexicans were whipped, he'd have the jump on everybody else coming later. God damn the Mexicans, is all I got to say. I shot as many of 'em as I could."

Jim Rice fought in the Revolution too but wasn't at San Jacinto, which he regretted. "I sure wish I'd have been there," he'd say. "But I expect I'll get another crack at 'em. You gotta figure they'll come back." He evidently *had* been able to display his martial prowess in several Indian fights, as the scalps dangling from his saddle horn proved. He procured the grisly artifacts while serving with a ranging company on the upper Brazos. Strangely enough, he refused to talk about it. "I've got no love for those people," was all he would say.

Our first day's ride out of Bastrop brought us to a prosperous farm at a bend in the river. At supper that evening I was surprised when the host, a man named Josiah Wilbarger, failed to remove his cap. He must have seen me staring, for he said, "Mr. Fontaine, please forgive me for wearing this indoors. My mama did teach me manners, but I'm afraid if I remove my hat you might not want to finish your dinner."

Snickering from Avery and Willis increased my discomfort. "I don't understand," I said.

Wilbarger told his story. "It's like this. A few years ago me and some other fellas were showing a group of men the land at the head of Walnut Creek. We were on a hill and I looked over to the next hill and there was an Indian on a horse. I waved him to come over, but he waved me off and pointed to my right a little ways. I saw smoke from a campfire, about a half mile away. That seemed like trouble to me on account of Indians, so me and the boys turned our horses and started back this way. But along about midafternoon Strother says he's hungry.

"'Now look, Strother,' I said, 'there's likely to be a passel of Indians coming along here any minute.' But he was hungry and his friend Christian was too, so against my better judgment we stopped to eat. Not five minutes later they fired from the bushes. Strother and Christian were both hit, which is only right as they were the ones that made us stop. But we were in a jam because those fools had unsaddled and hobbled their horses and they'd wandered off by now. Me, Standifer, and Haynie had the sense to leave our horses saddled and tied to a tree.

"Strother was gut-shot; I knew he was a goner even if we got him home. But Christian took a ball in the hip that didn't look too bad. He couldn't walk, though, so I ran over to help him. I had just handed him his rifle when—*zip*—something stung me in the leg. It was an arrow and now I couldn't run too good neither. I started for my hidey-hole and an arrow hit my *other* leg and a ball struck my hip. I got behind a bush and saw Standifer and Haynie up on their horses about to ride off. I hollered 'Wait for me' and started after 'em. They waited, but before I reached 'em a ball pierced my neck and came out my throat."

"My God!" said Mirabeau, mouth agape.

"Well, that knocked me off my feet and I tried to get up but I couldn't move a lick. Standifer and Haynie thought I must be dead and off they went. From out of the bushes came about five Indians, Comanche I'm thinking. I heard some god-awful noises as they finished off Christian and Strother and then they came for me. My only chance was to play possum and I must have done a fine job of it because they didn't kill me like they did the other two. They wanted my clothes, though, so off they came. All except one sock."

"One sock?" I asked.

"Don't ask me why. Anyway, now this Injun figures he'll help himself to my scalp too. I still couldn't move a lick, but I could feel, and let me tell you I wished I couldn't. I felt the knife cut a circle all around my head and that old boy gave a yank and it sounded like thunder, it did, and off popped my scalp. And then they rode off." He grinned. "And that's why I'm wearing my hat at the supper table."

"But how did you get back?" asked Mirabeau.

Wilbarger's wife, Mary, butted in. I think every other woman I met in those days was named Mary. "Now there's a story," she said. "The boys had left that morning from Hornsby's place about a mile from here and that's where Standifer and Haynie went. 'We got attacked by a thousand Indians!' they said. Reuben Hornsby told them, 'Fellas, Indians aren't in the habit of traveling around in such large packs. How many were there really?' 'Well, it seemed like a thousand,' they said, 'and Josiah and the other two are dead!' Josiah wasn't dead, of course, but he was in bad shape. He made it to the creek and fell asleep against a post oak tree. When he woke up it was the dead of night and standing right in front of him was his sister Margaret. He asked her to help him and she said to stay right there and his friends would come the next day. Then he fell asleep again.

"It was almost dark when Standifer and Haynie made it to Hornsby's, so Reuben figured on waiting until morning to collect the bodies. But that night Reuben's wife, Sarah, woke up and said she'd had a dream. Being the good husband that he is, Reuben said, 'Sarah, that's fascinating and I am unable to sleep again until I have heard the whole story. Spare me no details!'" Here Mary stopped to laugh, Josiah and the Wilbarger children joining in. Once everyone quieted down she said, "Oh, if you only knew Reuben; I'm sure he was violating the thou-shalt-not-cuss commandment. But anyway, Josiah wasn't dead, Sarah said, and Reuben needed to go get him right away. Reuben calculated that Sarah was crazy with grief and got her back to sleep. Later on she woke up again, though, and said, 'I just had that same dream. Josiah's alive! Reuben Hornsby, you get out of this bed and fetch him.' So Reuben got up and he got some other fellas and they rode off. When they got close to Josiah they almost shot him because he was red with blood and looked like an Indian. But he saw them and said 'Don't shoot!' and they didn't and they brought him back. I don't recollect what Sarah said when they got there but I do believe the phrase 'I told you so' was part of the conversation. Sarah fixed Josiah up, my boys went and fetched him to our place a couple days later, and thank the Lord he's still with us."

"With my cap!" added Josiah, reaching for his head.

"Which you are *not* to take off at the supper table," Mary said sternly.

Josiah grinned and lowered his hand. "I'll show you later."

One of the Wilbarger daughters, a girl of about ten or twelve, said, "You're leaving out the best part, Mother! About two months later we got a letter from Missouri, where Aunt Margaret lived. It was from Uncle Jesse and he wrote that Aunt Margaret died and it was on the *very* night Papa saw her in the woods!"

"Is that so?" I asked, glancing over at Josiah.

"Mr. Fontaine, it's the God's truth. I never believed in spirits before, but ask me now and I'll concede I just might."

A nonbeliever in ghosts, I still slept fitfully that night.

The next day's ride took us to the ruins of an old fort. Situated on a bluff overlooking a beautiful creek, this stockade had been home to a local ranging company under a captain named Coleman. Mirabeau told me that he knew of this captain. "At San Jacinto he was one of Houston's aides-de-camp. After the battle he wrote up a pamphlet criticizing the chief. Once Houston got wind of it, he kicked him out of the army. Later on he drowned in the Brazos River."

"I knew him," Rice added. "A bit puffed up, but not a bad sort. His widow lives near here."

Up until then I had witnessed death but had never knowingly had a hand in inflicting it. It pains me to recall my complicity that night. I was asked to stand the second guard shift. The rangers instructed me to keep particular watch over the horses, as these would be the primary focus of any Indian incursion. Being the only man awake on a moonlit night in the wilderness creates an odd sensation of dread. I feared an attack, to be sure, but I also feared the idea of falsely raising the alarm. Naïf that I was, I wanted to prove myself worthy of the trust extended to me by these rugged frontiersmen. And I couldn't bear the thought of embarrassing myself in front of Mirabeau, who seemed more and more like a father to me.

Strangely enough, noises abound after dark. Wind, wild animals, insects, and our own horses combined to lull me into foolish tolerance of sound. Thus, the initial whinnying of the horses failed to arouse my interest. But when the second instance followed immediately upon the first, I strained my eyes toward the rope corral and took a few cautious steps in that direction. Then I saw my first wild Indian.

I thought not of killing him but of surviving. Knees trembling, I stared in horror at this savage who, to my relief, appeared unaware of my presence. He carried a knife in one hand and a noose in the other, which he slowly raised toward the animal's head. When I cocked my rifle he stopped. I didn't move. He peered intently into the darkness. Just as I raised my weapon he saw me and turned to run. I fired. In the second it took for the smoke to clear, he disappeared. By then the other men were up and running toward me.

"What is it?" asked Avery.

"A savage! Over by the horses!"

Several minutes of wary searching turned up no intruder. When the men returned to the campfire, Jim Rice said, "Hell, false alarm."

"No sleep now," complained one of the Hornsbys.

Avery came to my defense. "Boys, we've all done that. Better to shoot at nothing than to be killed by an Indian. Now go on back to your bedrolls."

As the men obeyed, Avery turned toward me. "I did see an Indian," I said plaintively.

"Maybe, maybe not," he replied with a shrug. "Either way, you *thought* you did so you did the right thing. Now get some rest. I'll take a turn at guard."

Naturally, I slept poorly. Even so, Mirabeau awoke before me in the morning. I rose stiffly from my earthen bed and noticed him shuffling slowly around the perimeter of the corral.

"What are you doing?" I called out.

Without looking up, he said, "Edward, I believe you *did* see someone last night. There's blood here. Have a look."

Indeed, several rust-red splotches colored the grass at Mirabeau's feet. Poking at one of them with a twig, I said, "It's sticky."

Avery joined us. After only a brief glance at the blood he roused the other men and ordered them to follow. Grabbing weapons, they obeyed. I trailed behind as they spread out from the campsite.

Five minutes later came a shout from my right. We raced toward it. I arrived to see Rice standing over a wounded man, chest heaving, propped against a tree.

"Look here, boys," Rice said dryly, "that weren't no false alarm at all."

Thick black blood oozed from a jagged hole under the dusky brave's left collarbone. He sprawled against the tree, eyes closed, arms splayed loosely at his side. Gasping respirations rattled noisily in the damp morning stillness.

The dying man began singing. At least that's what Avery told me later. I heard only a strange, atonal caterwauling. Rice shrugged his shoulders and said, "Hell, boys, what do we do with him?"

Mirabeau held out his hands for Rice's rifle. "May I borrow that, Jim?" he asked.

Once he had it in hand he turned to the Indian, reached out the barrel, and rapped it roughly against the man's head.

"Hey!" he shouted. "Open your eyes!"

The young brave did, but continued his unholy racket. Savage orbs stared intently at each of us in turn. He looked so young.

Mirabeau lowered the rifle toward the man's loins. "Where do you want it?" he asked, raising the weapon first to the man's torso, then to his head. Without hesitation the savage defiantly thrust out his chest. Mirabeau fired.

I gasped in shock. Avery said, "Don't feel sorry for him. That Injun would have stuck a knife in your heart if he'd had the chance." Still, I was upset. I had just watched a helpless man, really a young boy, shot and killed. And Mirabeau had pulled the trigger. Mirabeau had murdered a defenseless boy.

Mirabeau noticed my distress and said, "That was the right thing to do, Edward. His wound was severe. He would have died." He spoke as if to a child.

"So you would put a man down, murder him, like a wounded horse."

"That wasn't a man and it *wasn't* murder."

"Then what was it?"

"God's will."

Later I convinced myself that Mirabeau was right. The Indian had been a thief. We *hanged* horse thieves, so how was this different? And the wound had been severe. Fatal, most likely. Finally, was this land not intended for us? Were we not to bring civilization to the wilderness? Yes, I thought, and ignored the fact that shooting a man, even a redskin, in cold blood is anything but civilized.

Though I secretly rejoiced to leave the old fort after that, a surge of anxiety gripped me. Had the Indian been alone? Sitting stiffly erect in my saddle, I maintained a constant vigilance of my immediate environment, expecting the wild shrieks of savages to descend upon my ears at any moment. Dan Hornsby eased his horse beside me and said, "You can relax a bit, mister. You won't see 'em coming anyhow."

"What do you mean?"

"It's like this," he explained. "They'll shoot at us from cover, then take off lickity-split. Those of us not hit will light out after 'em. If we catch 'em, we'll fight 'em. If we don't, we won't."

"But surely it pays to keep a watchful eye," I pleaded.

"As you please."

The trail mostly followed the river, except at the sharpest bends, where it cut straight across the neck of land defined by the waterway. I enjoyed a sense of protection when shielded by the cover of the trees along the waterway until I realized that any attackers would be shielded as well. My unease persisted in the treeless areas away from the river. Grass as tall as a man extended in all directions and limited our ability to see even large objects just a few feet away. Once, a deer sprang across our path without any of us seeing it until its leap. One or a hundred Indians could have been hiding in such thick vegetation.

At length we crested a small rise overlooking the river valley. Several plumes of smoke drifted lazily skyward about a mile distant. "Indians?" I nervously asked, thinking of Wilbarger's story.

Avery said, "No, that's Jake Harrell's place."

"I thought there were no settlements beyond Bastrop."

Avery corrected me. "There's no *towns* past Bastrop. There *are* a few folks living upriver. Harrell was first. He had a tent for a while but then built a cabin and brought his family out. As far as I know there's no one past *them*, though."

"I heard that Ned Burleson was platting a town somewhere out here," said Mirabeau, who had just ridden up to our group.

"Yeah, this is it," said Joe Rice. "Waterloo. But it's not really a town yet. Like Willis said, it's only a few families. There's no stores or nothing."

"Gentlemen," Mirabeau said excitedly, "let's go have a look!"

That Indian was the sorriest sight I've ever seen. He was just a boy, really. The white men said he was trying to steal the horses. Master Fontaine shot him. He told me he didn't know it at the time; he shot to scare him away, he said. Maybe so, but he hit him, sure enough. Next morning that boy lay there bleeding to death. He started raising a ruckus, singing like my people do when the Holy Spirit grabs 'em. That didn't set too well with Mr. Lamar. He took a rifle and he whopped that boy on the side of the head and started cussing at him. Then he shot him. Just shot him dead. Left him laying there in the grass for the wolves. Took his scalp too. I never saw that done before. One of the other white men told him how to do it. He took his knife and quick as you please sliced off the top of his head. Tried to give it to Master Fontaine, but he didn't want nothing to do with it. He said, "You shot him first, so it's yours." But Master Fontaine just shook his head and wouldn't take hold of it. I wouldn't have wanted it either.

I was glad when we saw smoke from some cabins. After what happened I sure didn't want to sleep in the woods no more. One of the white men said, "This ain't no town," but to me it looked like the best town I had ever seen. There may be fancier places, but when you've been sleeping with one eye open watching out for trouble, Waterloo looked mighty fine indeed.

17

Bearing down into the valley we crossed dry grassland before entering the line of trees along the river. Even as we crossed into the welcoming shade there was no sign of civilization. Then we arrived at a small clearing. This was Waterloo, which bore little resemblance to a proper town. Several log houses lined its edge, with more numerous barns and storage sheds arrayed haphazardly around them. Two gray hunting dogs lolled in front of the largest barn. One of them barked at us; the other merely lifted its head and stared.

"Who's there?" shouted a man from within the barn.

"Jake, it's Willis," Avery shouted. "Get your sorry ass out here! There's someone wants to meet you."

A thin, smiling man of medium height emerged from the barn. "Willis, damn you, you like to scared me to Jesus."

"Jake Harrell, if we were Injuns we'd have had your scalp!"

Avery climbed off his horse and shook hands with the man called Harrell. The rest of us followed suit. Avery nodded at the rangers and said, "Jake, you know these fellas." He gestured at me. "And this is Edward Fontaine, and this here," he pointed at Mirabeau, "is the vice president himself, Mr. Mirabeau Lamar."

Harrell gaped. "Well, I'll be. The vice president! It's an honor to meet you, sir."

"Soon to be president, if folks have any sense," Avery added.

"Mr. Lamar, welcome to Waterloo. It's not much, but we're proud of it."

"With good reason, Mr. Harrell. But please, call me Mirabeau."

"How about that, Jake?" one of the rangers said. "Don't call him 'Mister.' Just plain old Mirabeau'll do."

Harrell grinned. "Then 'Jake' is good enough for me. Now come on in the house. Y'all must be hungry."

Jake Harrell's house consisted of two log pens connected by a breezeway, flanked on either side by a door to one of the pens. As we entered the pen on our left, Harrell said, "We cook and eat in this one. The kids sleep here too. Me and Mary sleep on the other side."

"Sleeping's not all you do over there, I bet," Avery said.

"Hush, Willis," said Malcolm Hornsby. "Good God, there's women and children about."

A woman's voice called out. "Malcolm Hornsby, there's a woman right here! And that fella's right as rain, so let it lie."

Stepping into the room I encountered the face behind the voice, which belonged to a small, frail-looking woman with peppery black hair pulled straight back into a bun. Strong creases lined her mouth. She sat at a spinning wheel.

"Mary, I swear, your mother promised I was marrying a lady," said Harrell with a smile.

The woman smiled at him. "And a lady's what you've got, as if you don't notice in the dark. Why, you've brought me some company. Won't you gentlemen sit down?"

Mrs. Harrell's frank talk discomfited me. She arranged us at her table with feminine courtesy, though, and began plying us with food and drink. Perhaps it was her kind manner, but the same cold beef and cornbread I had eaten in so many Texas homes went down like a royal feast in Mary Harrell's kitchen. As we ate, she asked, "Is there anyone outside that might be hungry?"

Before I could respond, James Rice said, "Just Fontaine's nigger. Don't know if he's hungry or not."

"Well, I'll take him a plate of food."

Rice continued. "Hey, Jake, know what that nigger's name is? Take a guess."

Disinterested, Harrell said, "Don't know and don't care, Jim."

"It's *Jake*! How do you like that? Nigger's got the same name as *you*!" He burst out laughing.

Attempting to mollify our host, I said, "He's a good one, Mr. Harrell. Smart too. Hasn't ever given me any trouble."

Rice said, "Well, Edward, then he's a better man than *our* Jake. He don't give us nothing *but* trouble."

To my relief, Harrell laughed with the others and said, "It's all right, Edward, pay no mind to Jim. He's got the brains of a squirrel."

• • •

After a pleasant night sleeping in the loft, Mirabeau and I followed Harrell on a tour of Waterloo. This would have occupied little time, given how few buildings comprised the settlement, save for Mirabeau's constant stream of questions. Each query sparked a discourse from Harrell once he recognized Mirabeau's sincerity. Mirabeau particularly wanted to know every detail about the depth and quality of the water in the Colorado. Finally, Harrell suggested that we go to the river so we could see for ourselves.

Rice and Avery accompanied us. Riding west, we left Waterloo and picked our way along the edge of the tree line bordering the river. After about a half mile we turned south at a deep, flowing stream. "Shoal Creek, it's called," Harrell said. "You'll see why in a bit."

We followed Harrell along a footpath paralleling the creek. Narrow at first, the trail widened as we neared the river. At water's edge were the remains of several campfires scattered about a muddy shore churned by thousands of feet, both animal and human. Here the river was shallow, its broad expanse rippling softly across the rocky bed. "This is the best place to cross," Harrell said. "It's what we always use. Unfortunately, we're not the only ones."

"Comanche?" asked Mirabeau.

"Comanche, Kiowa, Tonkawa, you name it. They all come through at one time or another. What it means is you don't come down here on foot and you don't come alone. There've been a few scares, but no one killed so far."

"A man in Bastrop told me that the Tonkawa are friendly to us," I said.

Rice spat. "Hell, they're all friendly enough once they come in range of my rifle. The Tonkawa give us the least trouble, but you can't trust none of 'em."

"Gentlemen, you won't have to much longer," said Mirabeau. "One day we'll be rid of them."

Rice guffawed. "Now *there's* a man I can vote for!"

What surprised me most about the buffalo hunt the next day was how silently the herd flooded our vicinity in Waterloo. Before Jake Harrell's boy burst in on us at breakfast, I had no idea that thousands of the beasts were already among us. I slept no more soundly than usual the previous night. Jacob slept in the dogtrot and even he heard nothing of their approach. As I bolted from the cabin with the other excited men, I spotted several buffalo ambling slowly in the woods beyond the barn. "Look!" I shouted.

"You ain't seen nothing yet," said the boy.

I've already related how Mirabeau brought down the largest animal that day. I felt vindicated by his feat, given an incident that occurred as we rode toward the herd. Mirabeau's horse stumbled, nearly throwing him, and only a clumsy recovery kept him in the saddle. One of the rangers behind me snickered.

"Hell, he can't ride," the ranger said.

Willis Avery sprang to Mirabeau's defense. "He rode well enough at San Jacinto when he saved a man's life by shooting a Mexican trying to run him through with a lance."

The ranger snorted. "Is that so? He really shot a Mexican?"

"Right twixt the eyeballs, boy."

The ranger looked at me. "Mr. Fontaine, is he telling the truth?"

"He's a brave man," I said, feeling foolish even as the words escaped me. But later, as I stared at the enormous, dangerous creature felled by Mirabeau's hand, a sense of pride replaced my embarrassment, especially when the doubting ranger expressed admiration for the deed.

After the hunt a prearranged bugle blast called us to the top of a nearby hill. The view from its summit included not only Waterloo but also the river and miles of prairie beyond. Smoke puffed from the chimney of the Harrell cabin, as well as from those of the other four or five families of Waterloo. Scores of buffalo still wandered below us, oblivious to the carcasses of their dead comrades. I smelled roasting meat.

"Hey, Fontaine, get over here and taste some of this!" This was Avery, perched on his haunches near a small campfire. He and several others sat round the blaze holding sharpened sticks over the flames. Hunks of sizzling meat hung from each stick. My mouth watered.

"The tongue is the best part," Avery said as I approached the group.

"Don't listen to him, Edward," said one of the other rangers. "The hump meat is the real treat."

After finding my own stick I cut a slab of meat from the huge chunk that one of the men had packed up the hill. As I waited for it to cook, Jim Rice said, "You know what I heard? I heard that Injuns eat the liver first."

"I thought they went for the kidneys," said another man.

"Nothing wrong with that," said a third.

"Maybe," said Rice, "but they don't cook it. They eat it raw. Just cut the belly open, rip out the liver, and take a big bite."

"Well, that's disgusting."

"Sure is. But that's what they do."

Avery said, "I met a man once that traded with the Sioux up on the Missouri. Even went hunting with 'em once. Know what he said?"

"What?"

"He said what they like most is to catch a calf still on its milk. They cut open the stomach and scoop out the curds. Lap it up like candy, he said. I asked him if he tried it and he said he couldn't bring himself to do it."

"Course he couldn't," Rice said. "Cause he's a human being and they ain't."

"Jim, I disagree," I said. "I'll concede their primitive condition, but their humanity can't be questioned." I saw Mirabeau out of the corner of my eye standing just outside the circle of men. "What do you think, Mirabeau?"

"It's not what I think that matters," he replied. "What matters is what God thinks. I believe he intends these lands for us."

"What about the Mexicans?" asked Rice.

"I see no Mexicans about."

"You and the boys at San Jacinto saw to that!" said Malcolm Hornsby.

The other men laughed and whooped, but Mirabeau turned silently to view the river. "Gentlemen," he said, "look at this." He waved his arms at the landscape. "So rich, so lush, so untamed. A blank canvas, upon which we will create a glorious work of art. This is the spot, boys, this is the place."

"For what?"

"A great city! A Texas metropolis. A shining beacon to pierce the darkness of the wilderness and call forth the fruits of civilization."

I thought him overdramatic, but the others sat transfixed. Mirabeau continued.

"Texas needs a government seat and this shall be it. Soon. *This* . . . shall be the seat of *future empire!*"

No one spoke. Jim Rice chuckled and slid from his crouching position by the fire onto a nearby slab of limestone. "And this here rock'll be the seat of my ass!"

Mirabeau laughed and joined our circle. I proffered my stick and said, "Have a taste."

He bit off a piece, smiled, and said, "Delicious!"

I never saw what was so special about a buffalo. They're big, they're mean, and they smell worse than ten dead skunks. The meat tastes like old, dry beef. Now the tongue, sure, that's pretty good. But I didn't get a piece of tongue too very often. The white folks that shot it always seemed to go for that first and not think about old Jake until it was all eaten up. Once they'd sliced off what they wanted they'd let me have a go. I usually could find a pretty good cut around one of the haunches. I liked the liver too.

Now that buffalo Mr. Lamar shot; that was big as creation just like they say.

Even laying dead on its side it was as tall as a man. No, that ain't been exaggerated one bit. Once it was killed we all went up this big hill where we could see the whole country down to the river and then some. The smoke rising from the cabins looked like tiny clouds in the sky. We sat on that hill roasting buffalo meat and they even let me set up by the fire too. I was happy about that because I still thought there were Indians behind every tree. I didn't want to be too far away from the men with the guns.

Well, they were jawing and swapping stories until all of a sudden Mr. Lamar said something that shut 'em up. I didn't hear it exactly, but something about that country being just the right place for what he had in mind. It got real quiet until one of the white men, Mr. Rice I think, made a joke and they all started laughing. But later Master Fontaine told me what Mr. Lamar said just might find its way into the history books. He said, "Think about that, Jacob. That might have been one of the most important things ever said and you were right there!" Well, that sure would beat all, wouldn't it? Too bad I didn't hear it.

18

Ninety-seven. That is the percentage of Mirabeau's fellow Texians that in 1838 believed him to be the best man for the presidency. Only three percent disagreed and this total was split among several candidates. Upon hearing the news, Stephen Everitt quipped, "Three percent? That's Sam Houston and two other drunks!"

By comparison, David Burnet's fifty-five percent majority in the vice presidential race seemed paltry. Mirabeau scoffed at that notion, though. "Most politicians would claim fifty-five percent to be an overwhelming mandate," he said. But, noting the similarities in his and Burnet's political philosophies, he added, "I don't care if it's fifty-five percent or fifty percent plus one. The point is, he's a man I can work with."

The single piece of ill news that arose from the election was Sam Houston's successful bid to represent San Augustine County in the House of Representatives. Mirabeau took it in stride. "Of course he won, there's nobody else in that county of any note."

"I was hoping for a miracle."

"Edward, don't forget, he'll be but one voice among many in the House."

"The loudest and the shrillest."

"He'll try to thwart us, to be sure. But don't worry, I'll be ready for him."

Mirabeau's bravado faltered as the inauguration loomed. One morning, about a month before the event, I found him in his Houston office angrily chastising the newspaper that he held in his hand. "Look at this, Edward," he said in frustration, without bidding me good day. "Slanderous insults even before I assume office!"

"By whom?"

"The . . . uh . . . " He looked again at the paper. "*The Brazos Courier,* that's who. Some fellow named Weir down in Brazoria. Just listen."

I found a seat, knowing from experience that these angry moods did not pass quickly. He read from the paper.

"'No man has ever ruled a community so utterly destitute of the qualifications for their station as this crazy poetaster, whom accident has elevated. The muse of history has bequeathed to us Cromwells and Bonapartes, but Aesop alone has recorded in fable a parallel instance where an ape was made a king.'" He slammed the paper onto his desk. "*I'm the ape!*"

Nothing I could have said would have soothed his bruised feelings. One of the few positive traits I could attribute to Sam Houston was his unflappability, his uncanny knack of allowing the roughest of insults to roll from his back like water from a goose. Mirabeau lacked that ability. Outrage always lay just beneath his skin, ready to gush out in torrents at the slightest pinprick.

He glared at me. "I expect that my *friends* would find those words insulting."

"Mirabeau, *I am* your friend. But there will always be people—fools, really, when you think about it—who spread such manure. To recognize it as such and move on would seem the best policy to me."

He sighed in exasperation and grabbed another newspaper from his desk. "What about this one? 'Mr. Lamar means well, but his poetic, dreamy nature is ill-suited to the task before him. One can only pray that a man wholly unfit by habit or education for the active duties and the everyday realities of the presidency will do no irreparable harm.' Harm! *Talk about harm!* Don't they see how harmful it is to vilify the president even before he's taken office? Am I to ignore that too?"

And so it went.

I prayed for a good inauguration, but only the weather didn't disappoint. December 10, 1838, offered a brilliant blue sky, refreshingly cool air, and bright sunshine. Throughout the morning, men, women, and children gathered in front of the portico of the Capitol in Houston for the historic occasion, the inauguration of the second elected president of the Republic. I was not the only one to view the day as a fresh start for the nation; an abrupt transition from the bankrupt policies of the outgoing president to the promising future of a Lamar administration. By eleven a.m. people thronged Travis Street so thickly that I reached the Capitol only with difficulty. As the noon start time approached, scores of men and boys perched on rooftops and balconies lining the street.

I found Mirabeau pacing nervously in a roped-off area behind the Capitol. I had the final draft of his speech in my hand; when he saw me he thrust out his own hand and said, "Let me see it." After snatching it from me he resumed his pacing.

"By now I expect you have it memorized," I said. "You've been over it so many times."

"Yes, yes," he said without looking up from the sheets of paper. "I expect I do."

If Mirabeau had planned on any further preparation for his speech, his intentions were thwarted by the many well-wishers constantly interrupting him to pump his hand. David Burnet, Stephen Everitt, Ned Burleson, and a host of others hailed him, tried to start a conversation, and turned away once they recognized the far-away look on Mirabeau's face. I feared they would think him arrogant or rude until Burleson grinned at me while walking away and said, "That's our boy. Complete concentration on the task at hand."

Suddenly, a great roar erupted from the street on the other side of the building. Laughter and applause arose in a great crescendo of noise that drowned out conversation in our space out back. "What in God's name?" Burnet asked.

As the noise abated, a writhing knot of excited men moved into view. One man stumbled while trying to stay with the crowd and was thrown onto a boundary rope, which jerked toward the ground and almost snapped in two the sapling to which it was tied. It was Wash Miller. A loud voice boomed, "Careful, Wash, save your drunken capers for *after* the party."

Houston. I should have guessed. Who else but the outgoing president could stage an entrance like that? Who else but the Big Drunk could turn an atmosphere of excited but respectful anticipation into a raucous Fourth of July celebration? Who else but Sam Houston could instantly attract the attention of every man, woman, child, and dog in his vicinity?

With his worst performance, this tower of conceit could employ bombast and a sharp wit to falsely convince men of his self-perceived brilliance. But Inauguration Day 1838 brought forth Sam Houston's best, not worst, performance. As he moved about the enclosure behind the Capitol, he cracked jokes, slapped backs, pumped hands (for he never merely shook one's hand), and distributed outrageous flattery, which seemed to reduce even his political enemies to silly grins and fawning looks. David Burnet, never an admirer of Houston's, stood transfixed and uncharacteristically mute. Ned Burleson, another longtime critic, laughed and swapped jibes with the man he had once accused of treason for denying funds to a frontier defense force. Even Moseley Baker, who had introduced a bill of impeachment against President Houston in the House, joined in the frivolity.

But, desirous of reserving all attention and glory for himself, Sam Houston that day left nothing to chance. Forsaking his usual flashy but contemporary dress, he outfitted himself in a costume that would have better suited George Washington. Blue velvet breeches buckled just below the knee gave way to bright white hosiery, which in turn led to ankle-high black boots topped with silver buckles. Houston's enormous torso sported an overlong purple coat, from which protruded the frills and ruffles of the shirt underneath. He carried an impressively thick walnut cane, which he waved flamboyantly about while entertaining the crowd. And, as if striving to outdo the absurdity of the rest of the outfit, atop his head sat a curious anachronism, a gray, powdered wig.

When Mirabeau spotted Houston he glanced furtively around the yard for an escape route. None offered itself. Seeing he was trapped, he grabbed my arm and pleaded, "Don't go anywhere."

Houston shook off his entourage and strode over to us. "Mirabeau!" he roared. "Mr. Vice President! Today's your big day!"

Tight-lipped, Mirabeau said quietly, "Good day to you, Mr. Houston."

"Oh, come now," Houston protested. "We're way past that. It's 'Sam' to *you*! After all, we've been a team these past two years."

An awkward silence ensued, broken at last by Houston, who turned to me and said, "Edward, it's a big day for you as well. You're about to make your daddy proud. Secretary to the president!"

"I'm looking forward to it, sir."

Mirabeau still said nothing, which to me seemed most ungracious. Finally, Houston bowed effusively and said, "Gentlemen, I take my leave. My congratulations to you both."

After he had gone, Mirabeau resumed his pacing. "Calm down," I said. "You're finally rid of him."

He snorted. "Edward, don't be a fool."

The ceremony began jovially enough. When Speaker of the House John Hansford employed his thick Scottish brogue to call for order, one wag shouted, "Speak English, laddie!" Such an infectious wave of laughter spread through the crowd that even Mirabeau cracked a smile. Hansford next introduced the dignitaries on stage. As Houston's name was announced the crowd gasped in delight at his costume. I caught Wash Miller's eye and said, "Very fashionable."

"I tried to talk him out of it."

"Not very hard, I see."

Wash shrugged. "You might as well tell the wind not to blow," he said with a chuckle.

"That is a lot of wind."

"Good one."

From my position near the front I watched Mirabeau nervously eyeing the spot from which he would deliver his inaugural address. Every now and then he glanced at the speech still in his hand as he recited the words to himself. When Sam Houston rose to begin his valedictory remarks, Mirabeau shifted in his chair as if expecting to be called to the stage momentarily.

He needn't have bothered. When did Sam Houston ever pass up the opportunity of regaling a crowd with tales of his own prowess? After all, he didn't go to the trouble of donning that ridiculous outfit in order to meekly watch Mirabeau's crowning moment. No, as shrewd as he was boastful, the outgoing president seized the opportunity to harangue his fellow citizens for three hours! Clever jokes, grand gesticulations, sham tears, and witty references to those in attendance had the desired effect of riveting the attention of every person in town on the one man Sam Houston deemed worthy of public adulation: himself. Bursts of applause intermittently interrupted him. At such moments he ostentatiously pulled out a handkerchief to wipe his brow. I wanted to wipe the apish grin from his face!

Mirabeau's countenance sagged steadily throughout Houston's performance. For the first hour he continued looking over his own speech. At length he jammed the papers into a pocket, folded his arms, and sat back in his chair. By the third hour he had slumped so far into his seat that I thought him in danger of tumbling to the ground. Finally, he jerked himself upright, stood, and left the stage. I met him as he reached the bottom step.

"Here, Edward, take this," he said gloomily.

"What is it?"

"I'm not feeling well. Read it in my place."

I took the rolled-up papers from him. "But they want to hear *you*."

"They can have me or *that* son of a bitch. Not both."

And he left.

Stunned, I returned to my seat. Wash Miller leaned in my direction to say something, but I waved him off. Sam Houston's voice continued booming from the stage. Suddenly I heard him say, "And now it pleases me to hand over the reins of state to my worthy successor, Mr. Mirabeau Buonaparte Lamar." Mercifully, he had finished.

With great relief I saw Mirabeau return inconspicuously to the stage. Hansford made some forgettable remarks about democracy before presenting David Burnet with a bound copy of the constitution and Mirabeau with a volume of the laws of the Republic. What should have impressed as the highlight of the proceedings, the oaths of office, passed anticlimactically, for all were still too excited by Houston's grand farewell. Once he had received his oath, Mirabeau sat in his chair only briefly before fleeing the stage once again. He left with eyes as sad as those of a child denied a promised treat. I rose to follow him when Hansford called *my* name.

I froze. All was quiet. Everyone looked at me. I realized with horror that I had no choice; *I* would have to deliver the president's inaugural address.

I had to walk past Houston to reach the podium. He grinned knowingly at me. I imagined him thinking, "There you are, boy, try and beat *that!*" Of course I couldn't. No one could. Which is likely the reason that Mirabeau declined the attempt. After all, I had heard more than one Indian fighter say, "Know when you're whipped, boys, and run off to fight another day." Mirabeau was whipped that day, and he knew it. But so was I, and I couldn't run off.

By the end of my recitation most of the crowd had drifted away. Men laughed and carried on from within saloons and gambling houses up and down the street. Only polite applause followed my conclusion. Hansford shook my hand and I crossed the stage to leave. One of Sam Houston's big feet blocked my way. I looked at him coldly. He winked. I recalled telling Mirabeau earlier that day that he was now rid of Houston. He had rightfully called me a fool. I certainly felt like one.

Mr. Lamar sure enough got to be president. Of course, the two men that might have beat him killed themselves, but Master Fontaine said that didn't matter, Mr. Lamar would have won anyway. Probably that's right. Master Fontaine was pretty smart about such things.

That ceremony in Houston was something else. I had never seen so many people in one place except when we were with the army. But instead of killing each other, everybody was slapping backs and laughing and having a good time. A lot of my people were there too. I found some fellas I knew up the street a way off from the Capitol. One of them had a jug he was passing around, and it was the good stuff too. I asked him where he got it, and he said, "Master don't need to know that and you don't either."

Once it was all over, things got pretty much back to normal. The only difference was that I saw even less of Master Fontaine than I ever did before. He bought a little house in town that had a place out back for me. There wasn't a door, so at first I had to share it with any hogs that was wandering by. I made me a door as quick as I could. It was a house I helped build for Mr. Ward when Master Fontaine was back in Mississippi. "If only I'd have known I'd be living here," I thought, "I would have made it real nice." I sure would have put a door on it right off. But it was nice enough for a man used to sleeping under wagons.

It was about that time that the lady that looked like Mr. Lamar's dead wife came to town. I only learned about it later when we lived in Austin, but that's what Master Fontaine told me. She was pretty, I guess, for a white woman, but otherwise you wouldn't look at her twice. Nothing too special as far as I could see. Nice, though. She always had a smile for me when I saw her. Not like most of the white women, who would walk past you without a look. If Mr. Lamar's dead wife was like that, no wonder he missed her is all I can say.

19

By the time Mirabeau became president, anyone who knew him well knew of his intention to push the seat of government westward. He had been coyer, though, with his political enemies, who therefore could only suspect his design. As Congress took up the matter of forming a site selection committee, Sam Houston began loudly denouncing removal from his namesake city. One day as I entered the Capitol he grabbed my elbow and marched me into a side room. "Edward, you're a smart man," he said. "Surely you see the madness of putting government at risk on the frontier." In fact, I saw no such thing. "Furthermore," he continued, "Congress promised the people of Houston that government would be here until 1840. They have responded by spending freely to put up the necessary buildings. If we pull the rug out from under their feet now, they'll be ruined!"

On that point he was correct. The law placing government in Houston stipulated that removal would not occur before 1840. Nevertheless, I resented the fact that the businessmen he expressed such concern for were none other than his own friends and supporters. "Mr. Houston, it's not my decision," I told him.

"Look, I know you think I want to keep things here because the place is named for me, but that has nothing to do with it. Hell, I hate mud and mosquitoes as much as any man. Only the *hogs* are happy here."

That surprised me. I *had* assumed that the city's name influenced his opinion on the matter. But I certainly wanted no debate with *him* about it. "I've got to go," I said.

"Just put a bug in his ear," he called as I escaped into the hall. "He's a fair man. Just get him to think on it."

Mirabeau laughed when I relayed the conversation to him later that day. "He appeals to my *fairness*? That's rich! The man who ruined my inauguration wants me to be *fair*?"

"He said that government promised the people of Houston that it wouldn't move until 1840."

"Yes, the government of President *Houston* promised the people of Houston a special favor. I'm not bound by his cronyism! Moving government out west will benefit everyone, not just Houston's friends."

"Mirabeau, I'm not arguing with you."

"I know, I know. It just irritates me to hear such hypocrisy, even secondhand. But we'll likely hear much more of it for a while. Tonight I'm laying my cards on the table. After that the wolves will howl."

"What do you mean?"

"Come to Mrs. Andrews's tonight and you'll see. I've arranged a supper with a few select men."

"Why?"

He laughed. "Patience is a virtue, Edward. I'll see you at eight."

Mrs. Andrews's boardinghouse was close to the Capitol on one of the least muddy sections of Prairie Street. Several men were eating at the main table when I arrived. One named Stevens winked at me and said, "Don't worry, Fontaine. We'll be done in time for your supper. Mrs. Andrews told us to clear out by eight."

I found Mirabeau alone in the small parlor adjacent to the dining room. A frown creased his face.

"I've seen her, Edward," he said softly.

"Who?"

"Of course, I know it's not actually *her*. But it looked so much like her."

"Mirabeau, who are you talking about?"

"Tabitha. My wife."

"Your wife . . . is gone."

"I know, I know. But this woman . . . God in Heaven, Edward, this woman *is* Tabitha. She looks just like her! What does it mean?"

"It doesn't mean anything. It's just a woman who happens to look a bit like Tabitha."

He stared at me as if I'd just denied the existence of the sky. Shaking his head he rose from his chair and said, "Let's go greet the guests."

Mrs. Andrews shooed the last of the early diners from the room as we entered and said, "Ah, Mr. Lamar, don't you worry, I'll have the tables cleared and new places set in a flash."

Men drifted into the room singly or in small groups until about twenty crowded around the two dining tables. Everitt was there, as was David Burnet and Ned Burleson and several members of Congress that I knew to be political allies of Mirabeau's. But there were others who, if not enemies of the president, had certainly not proven themselves as friends. Chief among these were the senators Juan Seguin and George Barnett as well as Representative Louis P. Cooke. I disliked Cooke for his imperious manner with government clerks, myself included.

Once everyone had a full plate, Mirabeau cleared his throat and said, "Mrs. Andrews, you have outdone yourself. Now if you'll excuse us, we have some rather boring matters to discuss." Mrs. Andrews motioned to her servant, and they both left the room.

Mirabeau seemed to have forgotten the woman who looked like his dead wife. He emphatically speared a piece of beef from a platter and announced, "Gentlemen, tonight we decide the fate of an empire." Not a man stirred. "I've seen the future, boys, and a glittering vision it is. Our destiny lies not on the marshy banks of Buffalo Bayou but on the shimmering waters of the Colorado."

"We heard about the buffalo," George Barnett sardonically said.

Mirabeau uncharacteristically ignored the insult. "It *was* an impressively large animal. And as thrilling as it was to bring down such a beast, we go there not to hunt, but to bring light to the wilderness."

"Our task is to govern, not to settle the frontier," said Barnett.

"Quiet, George," said Louis Cooke. "Let him talk."

Mirabeau said, "Senator, your point is valid. We're tasked with governing. But what are we to govern? Are we to ignore our national destiny by confining ourselves to the east? Or are we to fulfill divine intent and settle *all* of our territory? Surely you see the sin in leaving the west to rot on the vine. Yes, the harvest may prove difficult. Hard work, sacrifice, and perhaps even bloodshed are required. But the reward is national splendor, Senator, nothing less."

"Hear, hear!" said Burleson loudly, as an excited murmur spread around the table.

When it was quiet again, Isaac Burton, the senator from Nacogdoches, asked, "So, Mirabeau, how will a capital city on the edge of civilization bring us an empire?"

Mirabeau's eyes danced with joy as he seized the opportunity to lay out his vision. "Ah, Burton, it's but the first step!" he said. He outlined the details of his plan. A capital city on the Colorado would encourage immigration to the region, which in turn would attract traders from New Mexico. These merchants would quickly realize the advantage of shipping goods to the new city, since whatever didn't sell at the capital could be shipped via the Colorado to the Gulf of Mexico and beyond. The delighted New Mexican merchants would clamor for that territory to abandon the corrupt governance of Mexico for the enlightened democracy of Texas. "After that," Mirabeau asked, "why stop at the Rio Grande? What stands between us and the Pacific Ocean?"

Burnet spoke up. "Only cowardice."

Mirabeau beamed and said, "And I see none of that here!"

No one was interested in the opinions of a secretary and, for a while, I lost myself in the enjoyment of Mrs. Andrews's delicious meat pie. But as I sopped up the last bit of gravy with a scrap of bread, Mirabeau caught my attention by saying, "All right, gentlemen, the first task will be to fix the search area."

"How do you mean?" Seguin asked in his accented English.

"I mean we've got to keep the selection commission focused on the west."

As I listened to the ensuing argument about how to accomplish this, I was struck by the fact that no one had objected to the premise. Mirabeau seemed to have already won these men over to his goal of moving the seat of government to the Colorado. Louis Cooke drove this point home when he said, "Look, gents, suppose we pass a law with a search area that includes the Brazos and maybe even the Trinity. At the same time, though, we word it so that the commission is free to look anywhere within that territory. In other words, it won't be *required* to search the entire area."

"That might keep Sam Houston's crowd happy," said Burleson. "But what if they *want* to go looking back east?"

"Well, that's where it's key to have the right commissioners," said Mirabeau. "And you don't have to give them enough time to search east *and* west."

"You've nailed it," Burleson said. "Get the right men on the job, tell them where the president wants them to look first, then make sure that's all they have time for."

I had attended many strategy sessions by that time, but none that sounded so blatantly manipulative. Nonetheless, a friend in the legal profession once told me that, to win a case, a good lawyer offers up his own version of the truth. "You don't lie," he said. "You mention only the things you want people to hear. It's up to the other side to see what's missing." Thus did Mirabeau and his conspirators design a bill that appeared fair to all, but actually tilted the issue toward their point of view. I disliked such deception. I thought it beneath Mirabeau to resort to a trick to have his way. Maybe if I had voiced my opinion he would have done things differently. More likely the men at the meeting would have mocked me. But I said nothing and now can only lament my timidity.

Louis Cooke brought up the issue of the commission's makeup. "These men have got to be on board," he said. "The moment a bill is passed, Mirabeau loses veto power over the location selected. He can tell them anything, but once they set out they'll go wherever they want."

"You're right, Louis. I don't name the commission under this bill," Mirabeau pointed out. "So here's the plan. I'll tell everybody that what I want most is fairness. I'll suggest that Congress appoint two eastern men, two western men, and a fifth man from what seems like neutral territory, maybe somewhere farther down the coast. No one can argue with that. We can even get up some talk that this neutral party should be the commission head. Then all we've got to do is make sure that he isn't really all that neutral. That he's somebody on our side."

"I could be that man."

Mirabeau squirmed uneasily. I could read his mind. He wanted a tactful man for the position, not a hothead like Cooke. "Actually, Louis," he said politely, "I wonder if your district in Brazoria isn't a little too identified with the east. I'm thinking some of the western men wouldn't go for you."

Burnet eagerly took up that line of reasoning. "You're right, Mirabeau. Louis wouldn't be seen as neutral."

Murmurs of assent filled the room. Cooke scowled. Stephen Everitt rapped his knuckles on the table and said, "Horton." Once all eyes were on him he continued. "Albert Horton. Good man. From Matagorda, which is about as neutral as you can get. Plus, he's looking for work."

Everyone laughed at the jest. Albert Horton had lost the recent vice presidential election to David Burnet.

"Well, I wanted the job for myself," joked Juan Seguin, "but I suppose this man Horton could do it too. What are his feelings about the seat of government?"

"I can speak to that," said Ned Burleson. "Mirabeau, you're not the only one who's been hunting buffalo out at Waterloo. Once I laid out the town who do you think showed up to have a look?"

"Really?" Mirabeau asked in surprise.

"Yep," Burleson replied. "He spent about a week. Didn't say if he planned to buy any land, but he seemed mighty interested. That's all I'm saying."

Mirabeau grabbed his glass and raised it in toast. "Gentlemen, to Albert Horton!"

There was this pretty young girl that worked for a white woman named Mrs. Andrews. Her name was Peggy, but I called her Grits because that's how I met her. I was walking along the alley behind the house one day and she stepped out the back door. She saw me and said, "You want these grits, boy? I was about to give 'em to the hogs but you can have 'em if you want."

I put on a big smile for that pretty face and said, "Well, I ain't no hog now, am I?"

That embarrassed her a little. She held out the bowl and said, "I ain't saying you're a hog, I just thought you might want 'em. There's nothing wrong with 'em. Mistress just ain't hungry right now, is all. Look, I even put butter in 'em."

That's how I got to know her. Lord have mercy, she was a sweet woman. I ate those grits and asked for more and she just laughed and said that's all there was. So we were friends. Truth is, I could have kissed her for a month and not been sad about it, but she had a man that worked on the docks, so I let that be. The worst kind of trouble a man can find comes from messing around with another man's woman. That's in the Bible.

One morning I was walking by that house and Grits hollered at me from the window. She tossed me a biscuit and said, "Where's the Colorado?"

I asked her why did she want to know and she said, "Because last night some white men were talking about it. They said the government be going to the Colorado soon. Your master works for the president, don't he? I reckon you'll be going up there too."

"Well, it's just another big river. I've been there once. It wasn't nothing too special."

Of course, I was just talking big. What seemed special to me about the Colorado is that I especially didn't want to go there again. I felt lucky getting away once with my scalp, so why would I wanna go back there and give the Indians another chance at it?

Soon as I could I mentioned to Master Fontaine that I heard the government might be moving somewhere else. He said, yep, sure enough it was. I asked him where and he said, "You remember that place with all the buffalo?"

I said, "I do. And I remember all that talk about wild Indians too."

Master laughed. He said, "Don't you worry, Jacob, when we go back everything will be different. There won't be just four or five cabins; there'll be a whole city. Just like this one."

I'll believe it when I see it, was what I was thinking.

Mirabeau asked me to sound out Horton on the matter. "Why me? I'm just a secretary," I protested.

"Precisely," he countered. "He won't suspect devious intent of a secretary."

I found Horton at Franklin and Main examining a broken wagon wheel with a man I didn't know. "Can you fix it?" Horton asked as I approached.

The other man, a tall, muscular fellow with a trim beard that matched his straight brown hair, glanced at me before replying, "Sure, I can fix it. I can have it ready tomorrow if you like."

Horton started to say something but was interrupted by the appearance of a beautiful young woman from within the shop next door. Demure and pleasantly shaped, she stood silently for the few moments it took for the two men to notice her. Her smooth skin and auburn hair glistened in the sunlight. "Dennis, I'll be shopping down the street a bit," she said.

"All right, Mother," answered the man with Horton. "Once I've finished with Mr. Horton I'll join you."

When she'd gone the two men turned their attention to me. Seeing the expression on my face, Horton chuckled and said, "Mr. Tucker here has a pretty wife, doesn't he?"

I blushed. "I'm sorry, I didn't mean . . . I mean I didn't know."

"Relax," said Tucker, sticking out his hand. "I'm Dennis Tucker." We shook.

Horton said, "You're Lamar's man Fontaine, aren't you?"

"I am."

"Well, Mr. Tucker and I are about finished. He's gonna rob me blind to fix the rim on this wagon wheel." He winked at Tucker. "I was just riding down the street when—bang—off it came."

Tucker grabbed the wheel and broken rim. "Tomorrow by noon," he said, rolling the wheel away. "Pleasure to meet you, Mr. Fontaine."

"So," said Horton with a grin, "did you come by to see me or to stare at Mrs. Tucker?"

"The president sent me to discuss something with you."

"Well *that* sounds exciting! Come on inside."

Horton's quarters were as sparse as any in Houston. A straw tick mattress on a rope bed occupied one side of the room. A large trunk nearly filled the other. Horton closed the trunk lid and beckoned me to sit on it while he plopped down on the mattress. I explained my mission. He listened intently and with unfeigned surprise. Angular features and coal-black hair lent him an aura of sternness that was belied by his mild-mannered speech. When I had finished, he rubbed his chin and said, "Chairman of the commission, eh? Why me?"

I laughed. "That's exactly what I asked when he sent me on this mission. He said I wouldn't be suspected of anything. I believe he wants you for the same reason."

He laughed. "Oh, there's more to it than that. What else is on his mind?"

"Mr. Horton, I can assure you there's no other reason. He just wants the best man for the job!"

"Mr. Fontaine, with respect I must question the veracity of that statement. I believe *you* believe your statement is true. Nevertheless, no politician is without an agenda. The president's desire to establish a seat of government to the west is an open secret. The question is, why does he think I can play a role in making that happen?"

I hesitated, not knowing how much I was free to divulge. "Well, I was at the meeting when your name came up. One of those in attendance mentioned that you have visited the president's favored location."

"Other than this God-forsaken place I have lately traveled to only two other Texas locations: Matagorda, where I live, and some pissant village on the upper Colorado named Waterloo. Now, nobody, your chief included, is talking up Matagorda as a government seat. So what you're telling me is that President Lamar wants his capital city at Waterloo?"

"Mr. Horton, I don't know how much I should say," I replied uneasily. "All I know for sure is that the president would be pleased to have you chair the selection commission. What he'd like to know is if you would do it."

"Tell him yes," he said curtly. "And tell anyone who asks that I don't own any land up there, because if I did I wouldn't take the job. Understood?"

"Thank you, Mr. Horton, I'll tell the president."

"Waterloo. I'll be damned. That'll boil old Sam's blood, won't it?"

At that time none of us really knew Mrs. Tucker. But Mr. Lamar had seen her and remembered her because she looked just like his dead wife. And Master Fontaine saw her too and remembered her because she was pretty. I don't think I had seen her yet and if I did I forget. After all, it doesn't pay for a black man to notice a white woman.

So one day I'm sitting on a pine stump in the street outside the Capitol and I see Mr. Lamar on the porch. He had a funny look on his face, like he'd seen a spirit maybe. I was doing my best not to be noticed when all of a sudden he came over to me and said, "Boy, you see that woman over there?"

I was scared because the only woman I saw was a white woman in a wagon across the street. I didn't say nothing, I just nodded my head. It's not wise to not answer when a white man asks you a question, but I just couldn't make the words come out.

Mr. Lamar said, "Don't be afraid, boy, you're not in trouble. I just wondered if you know her name, is all."

"No, sir," I said.

He pointed to a group of slaves near the wagon and told me to go over and talk to them and find out if they know who she is. I knew a couple of those fellas, so I ambled over and asked what they knew. One of 'em, a loudmouthed fella named Rufus, said, "Jake, you feeling lonely for the whip? Why you asking about a white woman?"

"I'm not asking for me, you dumb ox," I said. "I'm asking for President Lamar."

That's when he saw Mr. Lamar and he grinned real big like and said, "Now ain't that something. The president's got the hoochies for a married woman."

"Rufus, I don't know about that. He just wants to know her name is all."

"Well," Rufus said and he pointed to a man coming out of a dry goods store, "if you was to ask that big old white boy over yonder he just might tell you himself. But seeing as how he might also take a whip to your hide, maybe I should do it instead. That woman is Mrs. Dennis Tucker and that big old boy is Mr. Dennis. And I expect he'd be none too pleased that you're asking about his missus."

I told Rufus to shut up and went and told Mr. Lamar what I found out. He didn't even say thank you. He just stared at the woman for a spell, then turned around and walked into the Capitol.

Not a week later I was walking through town with Master Fontaine and we ran smack dab into Mr. and Mrs. Tucker on the street. I stepped aside so they could pass, but Master Fontaine tipped his hat and said "Good day" and they all talked for a while. After they left I told him about what I did for Mr. Lamar. He said, "Jacob, I know exactly why he wanted to know that." And he explained about Mr. Lamar's wife dying in Georgia and how Mrs. Tucker looked just like her. "The president thinks it's a sign, Jacob," he said. I could believe that because I know the Good Lord does that sort of thing. That's in the Bible. I didn't know what kind of sign it might be, but it was meant for Mr. Lamar, not me. Signs from the Lord are a personal matter, so only Mr. Lamar would know what it meant. Looking back, I can't help but think he got it wrong.

20

That Mirabeau's inauguration occurred several weeks before the Third Congress adjourned proved fortunate, for it effectively excluded Sam Houston from the debate over the Seat of Government Bill. The ex-president would represent San Augustine in the Fourth Congress, but that body wouldn't convene for several months. Thus, while Congress in January 1839 turned its attention to defining the territory in which to locate the seat of government, which everyone agreed would be called Austin, Houston could only attempt to manipulate events indirectly.

Moseley Baker and David Kaufman supplied the most vocal House opposition to Mirabeau's interests. Neither proved particularly effective as debaters, especially when Kaufman began offering amendments to even the simplest of measures. His favorite trick was to wait until a question seemed settled before presenting yet another trivial amendment. He evidently hoped that fatigue alone would compel his colleagues to go along, but in this he was disappointed. Finally Speaker Hansford, with obvious frustration, ruled Kaufman out of order and the bill passed.

A day spent listening to Kaufman's blathering exhausted me and I looked forward to retiring early. When I entered my room at the boardinghouse, though, there on my bed sat Bottle Bradford. "Hello, Fontaine," he said casually, as if I had been expecting to find him there.

"Terrence," I replied curtly. When he didn't say anything I asked, "What do you want?"

"I was hoping for a friendlier reception."

"It's been a long day. I'm tired."

"Well, I won't keep you." He stood and for a brief moment I thought he would leave, but instead he walked over to lean on my desk while motioning me to sit on the bed. "I've come about my petition for office."

Ever since the inauguration, Bradford had pestered Mirabeau for a position that was not forthcoming. Mirabeau believed Bradford incompetent. "Besides, he drinks too much," he said with finality.

I scowled at Bradford. "I understood that the president had declined to offer you a position."

"That's the problem," answered Bradford sharply. "I think he's forgetting something."

"What's that?"

"You know damn well! Without me, he wouldn't have been elected!"

I laughed. "He won ninety-seven percent of the vote. That's due to you?"

"That's only because he had no opposition. And that *is* thanks to me."

"You got a man drunk. That didn't win the election."

"I'm not going to argue with *you*. *He* knows what I did. He knows he owes me."

"What do you want me to do?" I asked impatiently.

"You have to tell him. There must be *something* he can give me. Tell him that."

"Tell him yourself, why don't you." I motioned to the door. "Now, if you'll excuse me, I'd like to go to bed."

He sneered and said, "He *owes* me, God damn it. If he knows what's good for him he'll remember that."

"I'm sure he will."

But he was already gone.

Senate debate the next day proved entertaining. Senator Robert Wilson, the humiliated runner-up to Mirabeau in the presidential contest, provided the excitement. I didn't know Wilson well but had seen enough of him to realize his capacity for foolishness. Here was a man who seemed to enjoy attention, favorable or not. As the senator from Houston, he rose early in the debate to chastise his colleagues for even considering leaving that city ahead of schedule. As members argued otherwise, Wilson's responses became shriller and more personal. At last, completely exasperated, he leapt to his feet and cried out, "I call upon God in Heaven to strike dead in their tracks those who support this iniquitous piece of legislation!" When called to order, Wilson thundered, "I'll be god*damned* if I'll come to order!" Ordered to sit down, he shouted, "No power but God can seat me!"

By now half of the members strove unsuccessfully to suppress laughter; the other half sat in stunned silence. When George Barnett moved to expel Wilson from the Senate, Wilson must have realized he had overplayed his hand, for he meekly sat down. A quick second preceded a brief discussion and formal vote, and Mr. Wilson suddenly found himself an ex-senator. As the sergeant-at-arms escorted Wilson from the building the disgraced man compounded his sins by bellowing, "The members of this body shall taste the fires of hell!"

With Wilson out of the way the Senate passed the bill quickly. When it was laid before him, Mirabeau uncharacteristically joked, "This kick to the 'seat' ought to get the Republic moving, eh, Edward?" I groaned. He dipped his pen and signed the document.

"Congratulations," I said.

He smiled. "It's only the first step of a long journey."

A few days later, during Senate debate on choosing members of the site selection commission, a loud bugle blast sounded just as Ned Burleson stood to make a point. Wash Miller, seated with me in the gallery, said, "I'll wager this has to do with Wilson. He won his seat back in the special election yesterday."

Sure enough, a number of men burst into the chamber bearing the disgraced man on their shoulders. With the bugler leading the way, the mob paraded up one side of the room and down the other. Wilson grinned idiotically from his perch, waving and blowing kisses at the crowd. I smelled liquor.

After the mob left I expected the Senate to resume its previous business. But, as if striving to outdo Mr. Wilson's time-wasting distraction, several members veered off course by introducing measures to officially censure the ridiculous man. Pettiness prevailed. Other senators took the bait and began arguing in favor of Wilson. Hoping to provoke a reaction I leaned over to Wash and whispered, "Well, at least your side has its champion back," but he only grimaced.

A day or two later, after each chamber had made its selections, I found Mirabeau at his desk and presented him with the names of the five commissioners. "Excellent!" he said gleefully. "Just as I'd hoped!"

"They'll have to pick Horton as chairman," I said.

"Absolutely," Mirabeau said in agreement. "Look at the names. Isaac Burton . . . senator from Nacogdoches, right? He's an easterner. And so is Isaac Campbell."

"Yes, a House member from San Augustine."

"So a Houston man. But then look at the other two. Menefee and Cooke. Cooke from Brazoria and Menefee from . . . uh . . . "

"Colorado County."

"So that's two from the east, two from the west, and Albert Horton sitting right in the middle." Mirabeau leaned back triumphantly in his chair and smiled. "Horton's *got* to be chairman!"

I changed the subject. "By the way, Bottle Bradford came to see me. He still expects you to grant him a post of some kind."

"That day will never come."

"I'm glad to hear it. I as much told him the same thing. But as he left he warned me that if you knew what's good for you, you'd do as he asks. What did he mean by that?"

Mirabeau tightened his jaw in apparent consternation. After a few moments he said, "I'll talk to Everitt."

"Everitt? What can he do?"

"Don't worry about it, Edward. I'll take care of it."

About that time Master Fontaine set me to work building crates. "What are they for?" I asked him and he said they were for the government papers and such that would go to the new seat of government. I asked him if they had picked a place already, and he said not yet but soon.

So I started in to build one crate after the other. I stacked 'em up until there was enough for a wagonload, then I took 'em over to the Capitol and came back to make some more. Mr. Ward walked by one time and said, "So that's where all the wood is in this town, by Jesus! I reckon we'll just have to start making houses out of mud instead of lumber." I could see he was joking, so I laughed and kept on working. He limped by with that wooden peg of a leg on his way to something big, I'm sure. That man did work hard.

Mr. Lamar once came by the house and saw me building crates. "That's mighty fine, boy," he said. "I wish all the darkies worked like you do." I didn't say nothing, just grinned, which was usually enough for a white man to keep on walking. But he pondered a while before asking me how long I had been with Master Fontaine. I couldn't really say, I told him, but a right long time. "Well, boy, he's gonna need you on the trip he's taking soon." A trip, I said, Master Fontaine didn't mention that to me. That's all right, he says, he'll be telling you about it as soon as I fill him in. Of course I didn't know what he was talking about, but that's the way it was with Mr. Lamar. He liked to say something bound to get you wondering, then he'd walk away. Just like that. He told me Master Fontaine would be needing me for a trip I never heard of; then he just went on about his business and left me there scratching my head.

I encountered Everitt on the street the next day while walking to Mirabeau's office. "Good day, Dr. Everitt," I said as our eyes met.

"Good day to you, sir," he replied, not slowing his pace.

"Dr. Everitt, I wanted to ask you something."

He stopped and looked at me with that humorless expression of his. I told him of Bradford's visit to my room. He seemed unconcerned, so I said, "He indicated that Mirabeau would regret not appointing him to office. Mirabeau said not to worry."

"Then you shouldn't."

"He said he would talk to you. Why?"

"That's between me and him. I *will* say that most problems in politics can be solved by money."

"Money?"

He shrugged his shoulders. "I have business down the street. Good day."

I found Mirabeau at his desk. I told him of my encounter with Everitt, including his abrupt departure. Mirabeau merely grunted noncommittally and reached for a nearby bottle of wine. He poured two glasses and said, "Have some wine, Edward." By now I had caught on to his habit of breaking important news to me over a drink. I expected to hear of some House bill or a senator's resignation and was therefore surprised when he said, "This has to do with you."

"Have I displeased you?" I nervously asked.

"Oh, no, quite the contrary," he said reassuringly. "You've been your usual indispensable self. That's why it pains me to send you away."

"Send me away! Why?"

"Because I can trust you. And to a place you're familiar with. I want you to accompany the commission."

"With Horton? But . . . the commission isn't only going to Waterloo. They're going up the Trinity and Brazos as well. Waterloo's the only place *I've* been."

"Yes, I know the extent of the search territory." Mirabeau spoke with precision and patience, as if I were a child. "Above the Old San Antonio Road between the Trinity and Colorado. But you and I both know there's not enough time to properly travel the entire region. They'll have to cut corners here and there. I want you along to make sure that Waterloo isn't one of those corners."

"But they won't have to listen to *me*."

"They don't, but they will. I'm going to ask them to. After all, I *am* president."

I grinned and said, "You're relying once again on your invincible powers of persuasion."

"If only that were true."

Now I laughed out loud. "When have they ever failed you?"

A cloud passed over his face. "I was just thinking about that this morning. I could never win an argument with Lucius."

"Your older brother?"

"Yes. The whole time we were growing up he won every single argument we ever had. If I was a bright student, he was brilliant. Better than me in mathematics . . . grammar . . . history . . . the classics too. He could recite Dante for hours. I once opened a copy of *The Inferno* at random and read aloud a few lines of verse. He picked up right where I left off and only stopped when I threw the book at him."

"Such fights are common among brothers."

"Yes, and this one had the same outcome as always. Be it politics, religion, or even the area I considered myself an expert in, poetry, and the argument always ended with him making the point that destroyed my claim."

"He must have been a remarkable debater."

"He was. And that is the quality that killed him. He was a judge on the Superior Court back in Georgia. He learned that a man he had convicted and sentenced to death for murder was innocent of the crime. The realization devastated him. I tried to comfort him. I argued that he had drawn a logical conclusion from the evidence at hand and followed the law. He remained unconvinced. I tried another tack, claiming that purity of motive shielded him from stain. No, he said, there was blood on his hands. Even if that is true, I said, God will forgive you. But it was no use. Nothing I said had the slightest effect. I left him in that state of despair and went home, intending to return the next day to resume the discussion."

He paused, as if attempting to formulate a different end to the story than the one I already knew. "You never saw him again, did you?" I asked.

"No," he said, stifling a sob. "As I rode up to his house the next morning my young nephew ran out to greet me. 'Uncle!' he cried. 'Father is dead!' I leapt off the horse and embraced him. 'What do you mean?' I said. He said, 'He used a pistol, Uncle, it's terrible. There's so much blood.' I knew immediately that I should never have left him alone. I should have stayed and argued through the night, throughout the next day if necessary. But I didn't."

"You couldn't penetrate his temporary madness."

"And that is the proof that my powers of persuasion are not invincible." He sighed. "So you'll go to Waterloo?"

I was no Lucius as a debater. "I will."

Sure enough, not two days after Mr. Lamar told me I was going on a trip, here came Master Fontaine with the same news. "You'll like this trip," he said. "No boat rides."

"You're going too, aren't you, Master?" I asked him.

"Oh, sure," he said. "You and me and about ten other men. You can catch fish and cook and round up the horses and so on."

I told him I hoped we wouldn't see no wild Indians, and he said don't you worry about that because even if we did there'd be plenty of men and plenty of ammunition, so all I got to worry about is how many fish to fry up. And that's how I knew we were going back to Waterloo.

Soon as I could I went and told Grits what I found out. She said, "I told you so," but then she said, "Honey, I'm gonna miss you terrible." I asked what her man would say if he heard her call me "honey" and she said, "He ain't my man no more. I expect you are." Well, that was a surprise to me and I just wished I'd have known sooner. Still, we had a night or two together before I set off. She sure was a sweet woman. Before I left I asked her if I'd still be her man when I got back. She said she reckoned not, that she didn't want to be without somebody so long and anyway, I might not be coming back. I didn't like hearing that, but it was true. Anyway, I never saw her again.

21

We left Houston early one February morning. There were ten of us in all; the five commissioners, myself, Jacob, a surveyor named Jeremiah Baxter, a draftsman named Will Sandusky, and one of Horton's slaves. Baxter was along to check acreage claims of enthusiastic promoters, while Sandusky's task was to create maps of proposed sites to bring back to Congress. .

I bought a horse and saddle for Jacob before our departure. Without a guarantee of armed escort through Indian country, I wanted him to have a fast mount in the face of danger. I knew he was frightened of the possibility of attack and thought that his trip—and therefore mine—would pass easier if he felt more secure.

As Mirabeau predicted, we completely ignored the Trinity River, making straight for the Brazos instead. I expected a protest from either Burton or Campbell, but neither one complained. Perhaps they had already come to an agreement before our departure.

We followed the San Antonio Road to Nashville, a small hamlet on the east bank of the river. I thought it a fine place for a city and said so. "It's been in the mix before," Albert Horton told me, "along with every other plot of ground in Texas owned by someone looking for easy money."

"Why wasn't it chosen?"

"Not enough in it for the government. Sterling Robertson put it up for consideration. Now *there's* a sharp businessman for sure. Maybe a bit too sharp. He had a map showing all the territory that would go to the government. 'Fine and dandy,' folks said. 'And there's timber and water and fertile bottomland all around,' he said. 'Even better,' everyone said. But then folks learned how much he wanted to be paid for that land and they said, 'Now hold on just a minute.' Of course, Congress will condemn whatever land is chosen and set the price, but here's where Robertson's reputation did him in. See, everyone knows just what a sharp customer he is. They knew that old Sterling wouldn't be happy giving his land away at discount prices, even to the government. They also knew how good he is at politicking, what with all his friends in Congress. So some folks—not all of 'em, mind you, but just enough—figured out they'd be better off finding a site that didn't have Mr. Robertson's name on the deed. And when push came to shove only three or four congressmen voted for Nashville."

I shook my head. "That's a discouraging story. I would think that a patriotic man would base his vote on what's best for the country, not on how a particular individual is affected."

Horton laughed. "Edward, I used to think that myself! And believe me, most of us try to. But if a man is looking at two fine horses and can only buy one, is he gonna pay for the horse owned by his friend or for the horse owned by a man he doesn't know? Or, to look at it another way, suppose a friend says to you, 'You vote as you please, but I sure would be happy if the vote goes this way and not that way.' Why, you'll want to make him happy! You'll tell yourself that there are two good choices, so why not pick the one that keeps your man in good spirits?"

"That's discouraging."

"That's politics."

We rode up the Brazos a fair piece and then turned right around and came back down. I didn't see no point in it. But they didn't bring me along to see a point; just to catch fish. And I caught plenty too. Mostly catfish. Some turtles too.

We went up to a place called the Falls of the Brazos. What a disappointment! In New Orleans once I saw a picture of Niagara Falls and I expected something like that. But these falls were really just a rough patch of water tumbling over some big rocks. The water didn't drop no more than three or four feet in any one place.

Before we left the Brazos we stopped at a town called Washington, which was once the capital of Texas. It's where they signed the Declaration of Independence before the war with the Mexicans started. Wasn't much to the town, just a few buildings made of boards but mostly log pens. Houston, rough as it was, appeared to me a sight better than Washington. But I did sleep indoors that night.

Then we made for the Colorado. On the way the white men got into a fierce argument. Mr. Burton and Mr. Campbell wanted to scout out some more places on the Brazos, but the others said they'd seen enough. Mr. Cooke used some rough lan-

guage and that riled up the others. Mr. Fontaine tried to say something, but then Mr. Cooke, he shoved Mr. Burton and I thought the knives and guns were fixing to come out for sure. But Mr. Horton stepped between everybody and said, "Boys, there's no time for this. We gotta be back in Houston soon and if we don't get over to the Colorado now, we won't get to see the place the president wants us to see. You don't want that, do you?" Then he looked at me and said, "Besides, Jake already caught all the fish in the Brazos and we'll starve if we stay here." That settled everybody's nerves and we kept going. I told Master Fontaine, "That was a close one," and he said, "The president's gonna owe us, Jacob."

There was one other black face on that trip, a fella named Buck. He and I got along all right, I guess, but we weren't best friends. Once while I was off relieving myself in the bushes he took my string of fish back to camp and made like he caught 'em. That was a burr under my saddle, but then one day I fell in the river and he fished me out, so I forgot about the fish. Forgive and forget, that's what the Good Book says.

At Waterloo we stayed with Jake Harrell again. There weren't no buffalo this time, but Master Fontaine still seemed mighty pleased with the visit. So did everybody else. Mr. Sandusky filled up a lot of paper drawing maps while we were there. We went to the top of that big hill for a look and everybody agreed it was the most beautiful place they'd seen since the Garden of Eden. Another time we followed a trail across the river to the biggest spring I've ever seen. Water just gushed out of the rocks. There was a pool so clear I could see the fish at the bottom. I told Master Fontaine I could just get in there and pick 'em up with my hands, but he told me no, that water was maybe twenty feet deep, not just three or four, which is what it looked like.

Then we went back to Houston. I saw no wild Indians on that trip and I did not feel cheated. Lots of times when I was thinking about the possibility I'd rub my sister's dollar in my pocket. I knew that didn't really do anything to keep the Indians away, but it calmed my nerves. The Good Lord had more to do with it, I'm sure. By the time we got back the flowers were out and it was getting warmer. I told Master Fontaine how good it would be to stay in one place for a while now that we were home, but he said, "Don't get too used to that, Jacob, we'll be moving on soon again." It seemed that everybody in Texas was always hopping from one place to the other. Every time some white man had a notion, I'd have to get up and go somewhere else. Then we'd get there and the new place looked the same as the old. Lord, thy ways are mysterious!

22

By the time we got back to Houston, everyone, especially Senator Burton, was in a foul mood. Burton still resented our ignoring the Trinity River for the Brazos and Colorado. An argument with Louis Cooke had led to a shoving match; only a jest from Albert Horton prevented violence. That incident caused Horton to wait a few days after our return before calling a vote. I took the opportunity to report to Mirabeau. "Excellent, Edward," he said over the compulsory glass of wine. "Burton's anger means we've probably won."

Indeed we had. The commission held a secret meeting at the Capitol on April 13. Two days later a brief announcement in the *Houston Morning Star* confirmed Waterloo as the site of the new seat of government. Mirabeau sent me in search of details. "It took all of five minutes," Horton said. "We voted first on the rivers: the Brazos or the Colorado. I made everybody write their choice on a piece of paper so nobody would feel pressured by a show of hands. Especially me. The Colorado won, three to two, with Burton and Campbell voting for the Brazos. I think they hoped I'd see it their way, but there's wisdom in pushing things out west. Once the river was decided, everyone agreed on Waterloo."

As Mirabeau and I discussed the commission's decision he suddenly asked, "What do you think about Waller?"

"He's very decisive."

"That's one of the things I like about him. The man building this city will have to do it in a very short time."

That was Edwin Waller's first observation when Mirabeau offered him the job.

"Jesus Christ, Lamar, Congress convenes in October!"

I blushed at the profanity, but Mirabeau was used to such language from Waller.

Smiling, he poked him a bit more. "Don't forget I'm coming too, Edwin. I'll need a house."

"Well, God damn it, how many ballrooms will this palace need?"

Mirabeau laughed. "Look, I know it's a challenge, but that's why I picked you. You're a dog on a bone and that's what it will take to get the job done."

Waller grumbled, but he said, "Yeah, you're right. One way or the other I'll get it done. Just don't expect anything fancy, is all."

"I don't need fancy," said Mirabeau. "Four walls and a roof on each of the buildings will suffice. On another matter, how will you find your workforce?"

"I know some good mechanics. They'll bring their own tools and I can buy or make whatever they lack. Common laborers aren't hard to find and I can rent plenty of niggers. Wagons might be trickier, but there should be folks willing to rent theirs for cash. I could probably leave in about two weeks. Three tops."

Mirabeau reached out and shook Waller's hand. "I'm sure you'll make us proud."

Once we were back in Houston I commenced to making boxes again. One day I was working in the yard and up came Mr. Waller. I knew him from seeing him with Master Fontaine. This time he came to see me, though. "Hey, boy," he hollered, and I dropped what I was doing and ran over to him. He talked like an army general. "Boy, I was wondering, what would you think about going up to Waterloo with me and the other men?"

I said, "I've been there twice already. It don't matter to me about going back, but I don't know when Master Fontaine wants me to go. He's got me making these boxes."

"I'll talk to your master first," he said. "He tells me you're a good worker and that's what I need. I just wanted to make sure you wouldn't put up a fuss about it. I need men that'll do what I tell 'em without bawling for their mammies. Is that you?"

"Yes, sir," I said. I didn't like the way he was talking, but it doesn't pay to tell a white man something he doesn't wanna hear. I knew Master Fontaine would keep me in Houston if that's what he wanted or send me to Waterloo if that's what he wanted. By then I'd come to figure it wasn't really Master Fontaine making those decisions anyway, but the Good Lord himself. And it seems the Good Lord figured that Heaven wouldn't set right unless I went with Mr. Waller to Waterloo.

• • •

Waller found his wagons and men. He gathered enough tools, packed as much foodstuff as he could, and figured his men could hunt for the rest. Captain Mark Lewis rode at the head of a ranging company guarding the train. I liked Lewis. Everyone did. An easy smile spread across his face at the merest hint of merriment, which he often supplied himself. Furthermore, he carried a reputation of honesty and courage that had earned his men's respect. Some men—Louis Cooke was one of them—grumbled about Lewis being boastful, but few shared that view. As we got under way one bright sunny May morning my horse stopped to relieve itself just as Captain Lewis rode by. He called out cheerfully, "I wish *everybody'd* empty their bladder before we go. We'd make better time!"

I laughed. "This is a fine horse, Captain Lewis. She'll keep pace, just wait and see."

"She'd better," he replied with a grin. "I'd hate to have to shoot such a fastidious animal."

Just then Jacob caught up to me on his mule. Jacob loved all animals and hadn't recognized Lewis's playful tone. "Is he gonna shoot your horse, Master Fontaine? Why?"

Lewis snorted. "Don't worry, I'm not shooting a horse carrying the president's man. I'll leave that to the Houston boys."

Mirabeau asked me to accompany the train to Waterloo and this time I was happy to oblige. Nothing much was happening in the capital with Congress about to adjourn and Mirabeau had made it plain that he intended to rest for a while after Waller was gone. Also, history beckoned. I shared everyone's excitement at the prospect of the Republic's building a seat of government in the wilderness. I wanted to see this process, be a part of it. My only official task, though, was to observe Waller and serve as a liaison with Mirabeau.

Waller thought me a spy. He didn't say so, of course, but his arched eyebrow and skeptical expression at the news of my coming along gave him away. "What's your job exactly?" he asked.

I tried to reassure him. "I'm just an observer. I'm only going to make sure you have what you need."

He scowled. "What I need is for folks to stay out of my way."

"Mr. Waller, I won't be *in* your way. If you think I am, you can tell me to move."

After a few seconds of silence he shrugged his shoulders and softened his scowl. "All right, you do your job and I'll do mine."

• • •

I should have seen trouble coming. I should have recognized the seed of sin in Mirabeau's loneliness and the grief still plaguing him years after his wife's death. I should have wondered about the consequences of a woman bearing such a strong resemblance to Tabitha encountering Mirabeau regularly on the streets of Houston, especially now that her husband would be away with Waller's crews, for Dennis Tucker had been hired by Waller as a blacksmith. I should have seen it, but I didn't. All I saw that morning was a blue sky and a bright, warm sun. I felt only a cool spring breeze. I heard only excited murmurs of hundreds of men saying good-bye to their wives, children, and friends. I smelled nothing but rye grass and spring flowers, tasted only the strong coffee that warmed my stomach. My senses were suffused with pleasure and I ignored the signs of darker days to come. On to Waterloo.

Well, not only did Master Fontaine send me back to Waterloo with Mr. Waller, he came along himself. So after I made my last box I helped load 'em up and then off we went. I was back on Janey this time. Master Fontaine told me, "Jacob, look around you. We've been there twice already with maybe five or six other men. This time there's two, three hundred! And look over there. That's Captain Lewis and he's just about the best Indian fighter in all of Texas. He and his men will keep us safe. You don't need a fast horse this time around, old Janey will do just fine." I was all right with that. Janey rode easy and I agreed that no Indians would attack so many men. So I wasn't worried. At least not about Indians.

What did worry me was what I'd be doing once we got to Waterloo. I didn't mind working hard and I'd worked plenty hard enough already for white bosses. But Master Fontaine told me he was gonna lend me out to Mr. Waller, who had a rough edge to him. Mr. Ward had a rough edge too, but with him you always knew he'd forget about being mad at you five minutes later. It wasn't that way with Mr. Waller. I learned later, though, that Mr. Waller was in charge of so many men he didn't pay no attention to me. Once he put me on a crew it was only the boss of the crew I had to worry about. I knew I could always go to Master Fontaine if things got too rough, but thank the Lord they never did.

Some of the white men wanted to chain us up at night on that trip. They said we'd run off to Mexico first chance we got. By then I knew that Mexico was about a thousand miles to the south and that you had to cross some pretty rough country to get there. I didn't see no point in running because I figured I'd get eaten or scalped long before I made it across the border. Anyway, the white men argued about it for quite a spell until finally Mr. Waller, he said they weren't chaining us up and that was that. After the other men left, though, he turned back to us and said, "First one of you that runs I'll hang myself. Then we'll see about those chains." Nobody talked about running away after that.

We lost two days at Columbus, which was about half the distance to Waterloo. One of the larger wagons broke down beyond repair and it took that long for Waller to scare up another. By then we had been traveling a week. On my earlier trips to the Colorado I had accompanied a small group of well-mounted men. We made fifty miles or more a day if we wanted. But fully loaded ox-drawn wagons travel at an agonizingly slow pace. Every stream or muddy draw means unloading the wagons, hauling everything to the opposite bank, and packing it all up again. Merely hitching up the teams each morning required the better part of an hour. We were fortunate to make ten miles a day and this in level country. Most days we made less.

Beyond Columbus we encountered the gently rolling prairie that I recalled from prior experience. The road was passable, but just so. The last wagons had an easier time than the first, as by the time they reached a particular point, vegetation had been trampled flat and uneven ground had been smoothed. And we were lucky that we had no rain and thus no mud.

There was a boy on the trip—Higgins was his name—whose place in the train was near mine. He walked beside one of the wagons. He fancied himself a skilled mechanic, for he boasted to all within earshot of some window frames he had fashioned for the Capitol in Houston. I learned later he had merely assisted the carpenter by sanding the cuts and mixing glue, but Higgins talked as if he had crafted the frames all by himself. He also bore a hatred of Indians beyond that of most frontiersmen. "Up in Arkansas where I'm from," he said, "we know how to treat those red devils."

"And how is that?" I asked.

"Like this," he replied, while making a slashing motion at his throat.

"What about the women and children? Or the peaceful ones?"

"Ha!" he said derisively. "Devils is devils! Just let 'em cross my path and you'll see."

I thought his words merely a foolish boy's boasts, but I was wrong. Several days out of Columbus, we encountered an elderly Indian man begging at the roadside. He sat on a large stump smoking a pipe. Long gray hair fell in greasy strands about his shoulders, which he had wrapped in a filthy blanket. A toothless grin marked his face and he muttered unintelligibly as we passed. I tossed him a piece of cornbread.

Seconds later I heard a shot from behind me. That fool of a boy Higgins stood triumphantly in front of the old man, who now sprawled on the ground with a hole in his chest. Mark Lewis galloped up shouting, "Who was that? Who fired that shot?"

Before the boy could answer, Lewis nearly rode him down with his horse. "Did you do that?" he shouted. "Did you shoot that man?"

Clearly surprised by Lewis's anger, Higgins meekly nodded and said, "That's a goddamn Indian."

"A goddamn Indian!" shouted Lewis. "*A goddamn Indian!* Yes, that's a goddamn Indian and you're a goddamn fool! You think he's the only Indian around here? You think he lives all by himself and that he doesn't have any friends that might take exception to you shooting him down like he was a rabid dog?"

"I . . . I thought he had a gun," stammered Higgins.

"You *thought* he had a *gun*? So what if he had a gun! He's about nine hundred years old, you jackass! Hell, he just wanted something to eat and you shot him for no good reason."

Lewis got off his horse, walked over to Higgins, and snatched the rifle from his hands. "You can have this back when we get to Waterloo. That is, if I don't feed you to the wolves first." When Higgins tried to speak, Lewis said angrily, "Don't bother, boy. Get back by that wagon and stay there." He gestured to the men around the wagon. "Keep him out of trouble. The next man that fires a shot without reason I'll shoot myself, understand?"

That night about two dozen of the dead man's tribesmen visited our camp. They came unarmed, but their angry faces menaced nonetheless. Captain Lewis and several of his men sat with them at a campfire for about two hours, smoking and talking in low tones. After the Indians left, Lewis came to me with a summary. "They're mighty put out by what happened today. That old man was a worthless bastard all right, but he was one of theirs and they don't see that he deserved to be shot. They're not much of a threat—they're Tonkawas and generally the Tonks are peaceable with us—but they've got a beef and a fair one too. I offered them some horses and a couple of beeves and that calmed them down. They wanted to roast Higgins alive, but I talked them out of it."

"Roast him alive?"

"Yeah, roast him alive. Tie him to a stake, stack some coals around him, and watch him cook."

"That's horrible!"

"Bastard deserves it. But I can't let the Tonkawas—or any Indian for that matter—treat a white man that way."

• • •

For the second time in my life I saw a white man shoot an Indian. Just shoot him dead like it was nothing. And this time the Indian hadn't done anything; didn't steal no horses or nothing. He was just an old man begging for food. That white boy spotted him and easy as you like pulled a rifle off the wagon, walked over, and pulled the trigger. Didn't say nothing either, not like the other time where Mr. Lamar at least asked that Indian where he wanted the bullet. What do you think would have happened if I did that? They'd kill me ten different ways and then feed me to the dogs. But Captain Lewis, mad as he was, just hollered at that boy and snatched his rifle up. Told him to get back in line. And that was it. Anyway, I don't believe that boy opened his mouth for a while.

For a day or two after that none of us talked too much. I mean, me and the other slaves. It reminded us of things we had seen before. Now, I never saw a white man just up and shoot a slave like that, but one boy there said he did. I suppose he was about thirteen or fourteen. Two years before that trip his owner decided to come to Texas from Georgia. Along the way his momma got hurt and couldn't walk good. At first the master kept her going by beating her with a cane, but then she just gave out and said she couldn't go no more. That white man tried everything to get her up again. After a few strokes with the cane didn't work, he poked her with a hot stick, chunked rocks at her, and even hit the boy a few times. That did it. She got up halfway but couldn't make it. By then her hurt leg was all purple and swole up something fierce and she fell back down and commenced to crying. "I'm trying, Master," she said, but he cussed her out and said she never had been good for nothing anyway. So he shot her clean through the heart. Left her laying there too. Told the boy to start walking and not look back or he'd shoot him too. I was crying when he told me that but some of the others didn't shed a tear. I suppose they'd seen awful things too and wanted to forget 'em.

Our bad feelings eventually wore off and as we got close to Waterloo the boys began asking me where we were at. "Jake, are we on the right road?" they'd say and I'd answer what I thought. But soon they started in on me and it took me a while to figure it out. "What about that hill?" somebody would ask and I'd say, "Yeah, I think I've seen that one before." Then somebody said, "Look at this here rock, Jake, what about that?" And somebody else would holler, "Jake, has this tree always been here or did it grow up since you passed by?" So I knew they were funning me, but I didn't mind. It helped pass the time and there was a lot of time to pass. Then one day we came to the top of a ridge. I saw smoke down below. I called out to the boys and said,

"Look here, this rock's been turned over since I was here. And that bush has got more leaves than it used to." Then I pointed down to the smoke and I could just make out Mr. Harrell's cabin and I said, "There it is, boys, that's Waterloo. We have arrived!"

23

Watching God create Heaven and Earth would have impressed me little more than watching Edwin Waller create the city of Austin. We arrived to a wilderness, a sloping prairie broken by a ribbon of trees straddling the river. Only Jake Harrell's cabin and a few others stood in stubborn defiance of the darkness imposed by civilization's absence, small bright lights at last breaking the long night that had ever gripped that fearful land.

Then came an army, God's army if you listened to Mirabeau, a band of two hundred hardy souls wielding shovels and pickaxes, hammers and hoes, with which it broke the prairie sod to plant the seeds of progress. The rectangular house that became the Capitol appeared first, its sturdy walls gazing eastward at the spot where Mirabeau had felled the mighty buffalo scant months before. Next came streets, or at least their outlines, marked by rope and wooden pegs to promise future grandeur. The gully through which Mirabeau and I rode on our way to the buffalo hunt became the main thoroughfare, named Congress Avenue by Waller. Shortly after the last peg had been pounded and the last rope marker laid out, men fanned out from the staging area near the river bearing large wooden signboards. Pecan Street, Cypress, Cedar, and Pine read these planks, for the east-west streets took the names of native Texas trees. Lavaca, Colorado, Trinity, and Brazos read others, for the north-south roads honored the nation's mightiest rivers.

One day I followed Waller to the top of a small hill directly across Congress Avenue from the nearly completed Capitol. "Here's where your boss will live," he said as we ascended.

"Mr. Waller," I said tentatively, "the president instructed me to purchase property for him at the first lot auction and I—"

He cut me off. "Not his permanent home. This is where I'm putting the president's house. For Lamar and whoever comes after him."

"Oh." I felt foolish. "Of course." Looking south toward the river I took in the splendid view. "It's beautiful. He'll be pleased."

"Of course he'll be pleased," said Waller irritably, as if it were an irrefutable fact. "He'll be able to watch the whole damned town from here."

I laughed. "And the whole town will be able to watch him!"

Turning his back and starting down the hill Waller said, "Well, that's democracy!"

I have worked hard all my life but the hardest I ever worked was when we built Austin. The sun wouldn't even be up and the overseer would come around ringing a bell and shouting, "Get up, you lazy niggers, and follow me!" Off we'd set to haul rocks or cut timber or plow a patch of dirt. There were just a few of us at first, so any dirty job naturally came our way. But as time passed there were more dirty jobs than we could accommodate, so the white boys worked hard too. We'd get a water break now and then and meal breaks most days. Food was plentiful but plain, mostly stringy beef and dry corn cakes. Beans now and then too, but no vegetables.

I didn't see Mr. Waller too much after he took me to the white boss. Bartlett was his name, Mr. Bartlett. He liked to be called "Chief." One of the boys said it was because he was part Indian, but I never knew for sure and he didn't look Indian to me. He kept a whip handy, but I only saw him use it once on a fella that ran away. They tied him to a wagon wheel and gave him about ten licks, but I could tell the Chief was laying 'em on light. That boy was back to work in a day or two and didn't run away after that. Besides, where was he gonna go?

Along about that time was the big horse race. There wasn't much for anyone to do in Austin but work, so some of the white men laid out a racetrack east of town near the river. After a while it was all beat down flat and that's when they started holding races for real. For money I mean. I wanted to have a go at it, but the Chief wasn't much for horses and he kept me busy. One day, though, Master Fontaine asked the Chief if he could borrow me for a bit and down to the track we went. Seems some folks were bragging about their horses being the fastest and this time Master Fontaine laid low, but determined to put me in the race. He told me he was low on money and that I could really help him out if I won. First the white men rode their horses, but Master Fontaine just watched that. Then it was my turn.

I was up on Master Fontaine's horse Spirit, which was the same horse I raced back in Mississippi. They shot the gun and off we went. Right away a fella named Jersey Jack fell out of his saddle because he was drunk. I suspect that earned him a whipping. Then another horse went down because of a rabbit hole. There were about six or seven of us left, but me and one other rider started pulling ahead. He was named Elijah, and I didn't know him well. I looked at him, and he was grinning at me. Then he leaned over and tried to poke Spirit's neck with his switch, but I hit his hand with mine and he gave it up. Now we were just riding hard as we could for the finish.

I saw the man ahead with the flag and told Spirit to take over, and she did just that. We got out front of that other fool, and when I reached the flag I had time to look back and see him still coming on. Afterwards he came up to me and said, "Mister, that's some mighty fine riding." I told him I didn't appreciate what he did with the switch and he said, "I was just having some fun. Besides, you whipped me like I never rode a horse before." We both laughed, and after that we were friends.

Contrary to expectations our greatest excitement in those earliest days in Austin came not from Indians but from Mexicans. Soon after our arrival a rumor began circulating of a fight somewhere to the northwest. Many of Waller's workmen laid down their tools, grabbed pistols and rifles, and rode off to investigate. Not long thereafter several members of Captain Andrews's ranging company arrived breathlessly in town. Men gathered around clamoring for news, but Jim Rice, who appeared to be in charge, brushed them off with the words, "Not now, boys, I've got to see Waller." When he spotted me in the crowd he jerked his head as a signal to follow and said, "You should hear this too."

We found Waller in his tent bent over a table holding a pile of surveyor's drawings. The builder Benjamin Noble stood with him. When Waller noticed our entrance he scowled and said, "Can you believe this? The Capitol's footprint doesn't line up with the street plan." He looked at Noble. "God damn it, Ben, I told you we should wait to start until the plats were ready!"

Noble appeared anything but chagrined. "And I told *you* that if I'm to build the Capitol and the president's house *and* all the other goddamn buildings you want by October, there wasn't *time* to wait!"

Waller hung his head in disgust. After an awkward silence he waved a hand airily and said, "All right, just keep on. There sure as hell isn't time to start over." As Noble left he glared at us for a few seconds before demanding, "Well, what in God's name have you fellas come to torture me with?"

Undaunted, Rice said. "We just got through killing a bunch of Mexicans up on the San Gabriel."

Waller's ears perked up. "We heard rumors of some trouble. Hell, half my men jackrabbited out of here looking to join you."

"There must have been fifteen or twenty. Ran into 'em first on Onion Creek south of here. Found some dead surveyors and then we found the Mexicans that done it. Chased 'em that day and all night and finally caught 'em by the river. About half of 'em skedaddled, but the other half charged. Me and the boys made sure they didn't get too far."

"All right," said Waller, after mulling this over for a few seconds. "You killed some Mexicans. Congratulations. Now maybe I can get my men back and commence to building this city."

"That ain't all," Rice added gravely. "There's this." He dumped a large leather saddlebag on Waller's table, knocking several of the drawings to the ground in the process.

"Hell, Jim," protested Waller, "I spent all morning organizing those drawings." He bent as if to pick up the papers, but checked himself, straightened back up, and untied the saddlebag. From within he extracted a large sheaf of papers.

Rice said, "I don't read Mexican, but Crenshaw here does. Ain't that right, Ike?"

A large man next to Rice nodded his head. Waller said, "I read it plenty good enough. These are letters from the Mexican government."

"Yeah, and look who they're for," said Rice excitedly. "Every damn Indian in Texas."

Waller whistled softly. "This one's to that bastard Cordova." I had heard of Cordova. The men in camp referred to him as a spy who led a band of cutthroats constantly stirring up trouble. "But look at this," Waller added. "Big Mush, Bowles . . . all the Cherokee chiefs. The Mexicans want to supply them. They're trying to bring the Cherokee down on us!"

After an excited outburst from Rice, in which he promised to singlehandedly shoot every Indian within a hundred miles of Austin, Waller closed up the saddlebag and announced, "Damn good job, Jim. I'll hang on to these until I can get 'em to Ned Burleson." He glanced at me. "Fontaine, go write your boss."

I took Rice aside and had him relate the entire adventure to me. He told of leaving the ranger camp near Onion Creek to hunt deer when he and another man spied a party of armed Mexican soldiers. The pair raced back to camp and informed Captain Andrews, who immediately ordered pursuit. The Mexicans must have seen Rice as well, for by the time the ranging company returned to the spot pointed out by Rice, their quarry were but specks in the distance. After a few hours of hard riding, several mounts broke down, forcing their riders to drop out of the chase. But Rice and about a dozen others pressed on. The next afternoon the rangers encountered an abandoned Mexican camp. Rice said, "We knew we were close because the coals were still warm. And there were only four fires, so not too many of 'em."

The rangers caught up to the Mexicans at a spot on the North San Gabriel River where the banks are too steep to enable easy crossing. From about two hundred yards away Rice watched the Mexican captain, a man named Flores, order several of his men to his side before directing the remainder to dismount and flee upriver. While the latter group successfully escaped, Flores and his handpicked followers boldly charged our men. Rice said, "They didn't get too far. It was a turkey shoot, really. Ike said it was his shot that took Flores out of the saddle but I'm damned if I didn't hit him with mine. Once they were down we rounded up their horses and mules and I came across that saddlebag. We were hoping to find money—maybe gold coins or some silver—so we weren't too excited about there being only papers. Then Ike read a few of 'em out loud and we knew we were on to something."

"Indeed you are, Mr. Rice," I said. "President Lamar will be quite interested."

There I was worrying about Indians and wouldn't you know the Mexicans decided I should worry about them too. Master Fontaine was bringing me some apples when he told me about it. Seems like some white men came upon some Mexicans and caught 'em up north from us. There was a fight, and all the Mexicans got killed. I told Master Fontaine I thought the Mexican soldiers had left after they got whipped at San Jacinto, and he said there was still some sneaking around. Anyway, after the Mexicans were killed the white men started collecting their things and came across some letters. They were from the Mexican government to all the Indians in Texas. I didn't hear that from Master Fontaine but got it over the next few days by listening here and there as I went about. White men mostly keep talking when I'm about because they don't expect me to understand what they're saying.

Anyway, the way I heard it the Mexicans were promising to give the Indians guns and food and money if they would come on down and kill all the white folks. I'm thinking black folks wouldn't come out of that none too good neither. I asked Master Fontaine what about it and he said don't worry, President Lamar will take care of this. After that my mind rested better, except when I worked outside town. Once they sent me and another boy and a white man up into the mountains to cut some cedar and I couldn't help thinking there was an Indian or a Mexican hiding behind every rock. Finally the white man hollered, "Jake, quit looking over your shoulder every damn second and chop some wood!" I had to forget about it and trust the Lord God above. Which is what I should have done in the first place.

• • •

Had I been paying attention, I would have seen the first signs of Mirabeau's obsession with Mrs. Tucker in his letters to me that summer. But I ignored his references to her, as they were sprinkled in amongst news of greater import. Sometime later, though, when I reread the correspondence, I saw that, with the exception of his daughter, Rebecca, Mirabeau mentioned no other female in any of those letters.

Mirabeau wasted little time in responding to the Cherokee threat. Calling upon Ned Burleson, Thomas Rusk, and Willis Landrum to organize an army of about five hundred men, he ordered them to proceed to the Cherokee lands and evict the tribe from Texas. Much has since been written of Cherokee suffering at the hands of our countrymen, but bloodshed occurred only because of the obstinacy and impertinence of the Cherokee chiefs.

Shortly after his return from the campaign, Ned Burleson filled me in on the details. Our army camped on a creek a few miles from the principal Cherokee village and dispatched a commission to negotiate a removal with Chief Bowles. After a bit of haggling about compensation, Bowles agreed to lead his people out of Texas. Two days later, though, there was still no sign of Cherokee movement. I don't know what Bowles could have been thinking. Perhaps he fantasized that Texian determination would melt in the face of his temporizing. If so, he knew little of the character of Ned Burleson and his men!

Burleson sent in his troops. A brief engagement drove the Cherokee toward the Neches River bottom. The next day our men attacked again and this time completely routed the enemy. Burleson estimated that perhaps a hundred Cherokee were killed or wounded while only a few Texians died. Poor Chief Bowles met an ignominious end. With all hope lost he tried to escape toward the river. A marksman brought him down. Several of our men rushed the chief to tend his wound. One fellow, though, an overexuberant lad still flushed from the excitement of battle, arrived ahead of his comrades and shot Bowles dead. Thus came the ignoble end of a stubborn and shortsighted old man.

A rumor arose that one of our soldiers cut strips of flesh from Bowles's back, which he used to make a belt. I discount such hearsay as fabrication, for what civilized man would commit such an act? I also heard of someone seizing the dead man's trademark hat, given to him years earlier by none other than Sam Houston, and delivering it in mocking tribute to its original owner. This I know to be true, as Wash Miller witnessed the hat's arrival and told me of it later. Houston, who had labored mightily and vainly to secure the Cherokee a permanent Texas home, reportedly took hold of the hat, shook his head sadly, and said, "Ah, my beloved country, what have you done?" Perhaps if he had worked to convince Bowles to leave peacefully instead of making a suicidal stand, he wouldn't have had to ask the question.

> When the soldiers got back from whipping the Cherokee, oh, the ruckus that com-
> menced! I heard so many "Glory hallelujahs" and "Praise the Lords" I thought I
> was in church. It reminded me of that time in San Felipe, but this time there wasn't
> as much liquor to go around. Leastways, none of it made it down to us. Soon Mr.
> Waller, he starts going around telling everybody to shut up and get back to work. "I
> got me a city to build, God damn it!" he hollered. If a white boy seemed a little slow
> Mr. Waller might grab a hold of him and shove him a bit. But when a black man
> named Lester didn't listen close enough, Mr. Waller sure took it out on that boy.
> He made us tie Lester to a post and out came the lash. This time the man that did
> the whipping laid it on hard. We laid Lester under a tree, where one of the women
> cleaned him up as best she could. The rest of us were sorry we'd ever heard about
> the Cherokee.

Autumn's arrival in the south brings with it not the crisp, cold air of the north, but a slight drop in daytime temperature from intolerably hot to mildly uncomfortable. That shift had just begun when Edwin Waller escorted me on a tour of the government buildings erected so far. "Keep in mind they're only meant to be temporary," he cautioned as we began.

In my mind I still oriented myself with respect to the site of Mirabeau's triumph over the buffalo. We stood about a block south of there on the main thoroughfare, which I have already mentioned is called Congress Avenue, in front of several plain log pens lining the west side of the street. "That's the state department," said Waller, pointing to one of the pens. "They're all the same. Nothing fancy. Just four walls, a roof, and a floor. There's partitions inside for private offices. The layout's the same in each one so there shouldn't be any squabbling."

We cut between two of these buildings on our way to a much larger structure that I knew to be the Capitol. A central breezeway connected two large rectangular structures, all sharing the same sloped roof. Unlike the departmental buildings, this one consisted of trimmed boards rather than rough logs. "The painter will slap a coat of whitewash on it, but otherwise it's finished," Waller explained.

"Nice."

Waller ignored me. "As you know, this will only be used until something more substantial is built." He pointed to the hill from which Mirabeau had announced his intention to build an imperial seat. "That's where the next one will go. I wanted to put the Capitol in the center of town, but then I got here and saw that hill. It seemed to me it ought to be at the highest spot. Your boss agreed."

"I do too. I've been up there. You can see for a hundred miles."

"I don't know about a hundred miles, but you can sure see the rest of town. I reckon that once a building is there you'll be able to see it from way off."

A ten-minute walk took us across Congress Avenue to a small eminence. At its top sat a neat, two-story house painted a brilliant white. Knowing this to be the president's house, I had monitored its progress carefully. As we approached the front entrance Waller said, "There's still some trim work to be done inside and the stone mason's still working on one of the fireplaces. Otherwise it's ready for him to move in."

We walked inside. The odor of freshly cut pine greeted us. "It smells like a forest in here," I said.

Waller grunted. "If I'd had time to do a proper job I would have let the lumber age for several months. But seeing as how your boss is in such a hurry I didn't have that luxury. I'm worried about what will happen as it dries out."

"Do you think the boards will warp?"

"I *know* the damned boards will warp! It's just a question of how much."

I admired the spacious rooms, floor-to-ceiling windows, polished floors, and gleaming hearths and said, "It's the finest house in town."

Waller chuckled. "It is for now anyway."

"Mr. Waller, I know the president will be pleased with everything. *I'm* pleased to be able to write him of the wonderful progress that I've seen." When he failed to respond I nervously added, "I do hope I haven't been too obvious a spy."

A smile slowly spread across his face. He laughed out loud. "Only about as obvious as a horny rooster! But that's all right. I'd have done the same thing in his position. Sent someone along to keep an eye on things, I mean. And he'd better like it because, for better or worse, this is what he's got!"

On my way back to Congress Avenue I encountered an older woman eyeing me suspiciously. I nervously tipped my hat. She said, "You don't know who I am, do you?"

Flustered, I said, "Ma'am, I do apologize, but I don't."

"How's that for gratitude?" she asked with a mischievous grin. "I take you in and feed you and now you've forgotten me."

"*Mrs. Peyton!* Of course! Oh, I am sorry, do forgive me."

"I forgive you, young feller, I do. Only it's Eberly now. After San Felipe burned I went down to Columbia and fetched me a husband."

"Congratulations! I'm sorry you lost your place in San Felipe."

"Damn Sam Houston, is all I've got to say. What are you up to now?"

"I'm President Lamar's secretary."

"Lamar? Yeah, I know him too. He boarded with me for a spell."

"I heard that."

"Don't know that I like him any better than Houston. Always fussing about one thing or another. Telling me how to clean the sheets or brew the coffee, as if I don't know my own business."

"Oh, um . . . "

"Of course, he did pay his rent on time, I'll give him that. And now he's president. If this ain't the craziest country. One day a man's nothing and the next he's running the whole show. Well, as long as he don't start no fires I reckon he's all right with me."

A few days later wagons began arriving from Houston. Most carried large crates of government records. Each wagon stopped at one of Waller's staging areas, where an assistant directed the teamster to the appropriate building. Negro servants waited at the buildings to unload the boxes. Government clerks were already on hand to direct this activity.

As wagons bearing personal effects of government workers began arriving, I watched for that sent by Mirabeau. When it came, I smiled at how meager was his wagonload. A trunk of clothes, another trunk filled with pens, kitchen utensils, and other household objects, a bed, a small desk and chair, and a large iron kettle made up the entirety of his earthly possessions. Of course, he owned a house back in Georgia and the one on the Brazos River, but what other head of state in history traveled so lightly? Such was the condition of Texas in those days that her chief executive lived as humbly as any man.

As the arriving freight wagons dwindled in number, hordes of government clerks and civilians descended on Austin. Some of the clerks arrived with families. Soft feminine tones and the shouts of children soon mixed on the streets with the coarse language of mechanics and laborers. The presence of women and children brought an air of normalcy that had been lacking.

I witnessed the Tucker family reunion. Mrs. Tucker and her children arrived on a freight wagon driven by a relative. Bypassing the staging area, the driver made straight for the center of town to inquire after Mr. Tucker. I happened to be chatting nearby with Mr. Bullock, the proprietor of what in those days was the largest hotel in Austin. I recognized Mrs. Tucker straight away. Covered in road dust and bearing the pained look of the weary traveler, she nevertheless radiated a beauty heretofore not seen in Austin.

A man ran off to fetch Mr. Tucker. Mrs. Tucker and the children chattered excitedly with each other while they waited. As he approached, Mr. Tucker called out, "There you are! Finally!" His children jumped off the wagon and ran to their father. He hugged each briefly before reaching up to bring his wife off the wagon. The two embraced tightly for an eternity, their children clinging to them like puppies the whole time. Thinking of my own detached father, I envied their familial bliss.

Later that evening I went to check on Jacob. Jeremy Wilkins, the man then leasing him, told me, "He's a good old boy, Fontaine. Not a lick of trouble and he works harder than any nigger I ever saw."

After thanking Wilkins for the compliment, I told Jacob, "Construction's just about finished. You'll soon be back with me."

"What happens then?" he asked.

"Jacob, why do you think we built this place? Then the excitement begins."

"What's that, Master?"

"The president, Jacob. The president is coming. Don't you know there'll be a fine party then!"

After making all those boxes in Houston I never wanted to see 'em again. But up in Austin, here they came back to me by the wagonload. Only they weren't empty now. They were loaded with all sorts of things, most of 'em as heavy as a mule. By then I was under a man named Wilkins and he sent me all over town to help unload wagons and tote boxes into buildings. There was this one box I remember making out of a busted-up green chifforobe. I reached up into one of the wagons and there it was; it had followed me all the way to Austin. I told the boys, "I made this box," and they said, "Why'd you make it so heavy, Jake?" I just laughed and told 'em, "It wasn't so heavy the last time I saw it. Somebody must have filled it up with rocks."

Wilkins was all right. He kept us busy, sure enough, but he let us rest when we needed it. He'd give us all the water we wanted and once at the end of the day he even slipped us a jug of whiskey. That was a Christian thing to do.

Along about the time the wagons stopped coming, here came Master Fontaine to tell me I'd be going back to him soon. I was ready for that because I figured I'd be able to go fishing some now and maybe even start preaching a spell. He said, "Jacob, this town's just about finished." I said it didn't look too awful finished to me, there were half-built houses and tents and empty streets everywhere I looked. But he said, "No,

I mean the government buildings. They're almost done and soon the government will come. Won't that be something?" I told him I reckoned it would. But I really didn't think so. Why should I, when every white man on the street can tell me what to do? I kept that thought to myself. Then he said, "President Lamar will be coming soon." What could I do but say how nice that would be? I wasn't exactly afraid of Mr. Lamar, but I didn't miss him none either. Later I heard Master Fontaine tell another man that Sam Houston was coming to Austin too. I was glad to hear that and hoped I'd see him. He never said a cross word to anyone that I heard and I still recollect that time he called me "sir" at San Felipe.

24

October 17, 1839. What a glorious day! Sam Houston's lengthy and self-serving farewell address had ruined Mirabeau's presidential inauguration, but as Mirabeau made his grand entrance into the city of his creation there was no Big Drunk on hand to divert attention to himself. At the time I thought it but the first of many such triumphant days to come. But fate, malevolent men, and human weakness conspired against us. Looking back across the years I see that day as the pinnacle of Mirabeau's career. It is also a painful reminder of a glorious Texas destiny denied.

We left Austin at eleven in the morning to meet the presidential party two miles east of town. By "we" I mean just about every man in town and most of the women too. The official greeting committee led the way. At its head rode Ned Burleson and Albert Johnston. Known for his battlefield courage and leadership, Vice President Burleson commanded the respect of every man in the west. He was a popular choice to represent the intrepid pioneers engaged in settling the upper Colorado wilderness. As secretary of war, Albert Johnston's place in the van stirred no controversy either. At the time he still limped from a wound inflicted upon him in a duel fought two years earlier with Felix Huston. Johnston had refused to fire; Huston had not. Huston may have won the duel, but Johnston won his country-men's respect.

Behind Burleson and Johnston rode the flag bearer. The banner he carried con-sisted of a rectangular piece of white cloth with bright blue letters sewn to each side. One side proudly proclaimed, "With this we live—Or die defending," while the other offered the greeting, "Hail to our chief." I took pride in the fact that the women sewing the flag had approached me for slogan suggestions; the latter was my contribution.

Edwin Waller and a bugler followed directly behind the flag bearer. Behind them was a double file of rangers and citizens, each man mounted and wearing his best clothes. I rode near the head of one of these lines. Next was a short but impressive column of carriages; each carriage bore two or three of the fairer sex. Bringing up the rear was an unorganized crowd of common laborers, mechanics, Negro servants, and older boys.

Our route took us east along Pecan Street, across East Avenue, and into the countryside. In May we had entered Waterloo along this same road, now beaten smooth by five months of horse and wagon traffic. We stopped about two miles east of town to await the president. While we waited the bugler blew a few notes of practice before a man to the rear hollered, "Won't somebody *please* stop beating that poor mule?" Everyone laughed. The bugler sheepishly ceased his bleating.

At last the presidential entourage crested a small rise and came into view. Everyone quieted as the party approached. Then a man yelled, "Three cheers, boys! *Huzzah! Huzzah! Huzzah!*" Burleson shouted some orders and his men quickly formed a line on either side of the road. Johnston, Waller, and the flag bearer positioned themselves at the far end of the formation. I caught my first glimpse of Mirabeau. Such a majestic figure! Wearing a new suit of clothes, which uncharacteristically fit him to perfection, and trying unsuccessfully to suppress a joyful grin, he guided his mount in between the two columns. Nodding approvingly to the men on either side of him, he rode solemnly toward his welcoming committee. Burleson and Johnston saluted smartly while the men presented arms. Waller moved to the forefront and delivered a welcoming speech. I recall one line of his address, as it perfectly summed up the selfish opposition Mirabeau had faced in bringing the seat of government to the frontier: "Beauty of scenery, centrality of location, and purity of atmosphere have been nothing in the vision of those whose views were governed by their purses and whose ideas of fitness were entirely subservient to their desire for profit."

I asked Master Fontaine that day would it be all right if I stayed behind instead of traipsing all the way out to the country just to turn around and march right back. He said sure, Jake, you do what you want. So I missed the big parade and all the speeches. I did hear the cannon go off when everybody crossed the creek into town. Lord, I'm sure they heard that all the way back in Mississippi, it was so loud. But I figured on setting myself somewhere along Congress Avenue and watching the doings from there. And that's how I chanced to see Mr. Lamar kiss that white lady.

Of course it scared me half to death to see it. A black man learns early in life to keep his nose out of white folks' business. Once the parade came to town and the hollering stopped, the crowd broke up and Mr. Bullock—the owner of the hotel where the parade stopped—he came out the door and saw me there. "Take this bucket and fetch me some water, boy," he said and he threw me the bucket. He wasn't my master, but that didn't matter. If a white man told you to do something, you better do it. So I went around back to the well behind the main hotel building. There was a big space there and the well was toward the back and then there were a few small cabins around the open yard. I had just dropped the bucket down into the well when Mr. Lamar came out of the cabin closest to the house. Right behind him was that white woman Mrs. Tucker. They didn't see me because I was behind the well and pretty far away. I recognized Mrs. Tucker from finding out her name for Mr. Lamar in Houston. Anyway, it was getting dark and they must have thought nobody else was around. They talked for a spell and then Mr. Lamar leaned in and kissed her. Not a peck on the cheek either; he gave it to her full on the mouth, and she gave it right back. Then off she went and he turned around and went back in the cabin. I took the water back to the street and knocked on the door and gave the bucket to Mr. Bullock. I didn't tell nobody what I saw. Not right away, anyhow.

25

What drives a man to serve an undeserving master? What thought process occurs in which an otherwise reasonable intellect attaches itself to an unworthy cause? Why would a man on the rise assume the role of puppet when the man pulling his strings is a fraudulent demagogue named Sam Houston?

I cannot answer such questions. I can only bear witness to the startling demonstration of self-interest that I saw play out in the Fourth Texas Congress. Hardly had the speaker banged the opening gavel before the representative from Harrisburg rose to introduce a bill that, if it had become law, would have undone all that Mirabeau had accomplished in his presidency thus far. William Lawrence, the legislator in question, could plausibly maintain that he acted only to defend the interests of his constituents. Accepting this argument, though, would yet tar him with the ugly brush of tepid patriotism. For what Texas patriot in 1839 could honestly argue that moving the capital once again would serve the national interest?

Sam Houston's role in the matter became clear early in the debates. His was the first voice to pollute the House chamber with illogical arguments and unsubstantiated accusations. "Fraud!" he bellowed, as if the man who falsely assumed the mantle of "the Hero of San Jacinto" shunned deceit. Certain fools in the House sagely nodded their heads at this nonsense. One could almost see the string connecting each empty noggin to Houston's weaving hands. Houston prattled on like this for an eternity before treasonously concluding, "The day of retribution will come. Easterners will assert their rights; aye, *even if they have to separate from a people who have cheated them out of their rights!*" How shameful, I thought, for a man who had so recently led the country to now call for splitting it asunder.

Not all were fooled. Will Jack of Brazoria offered a stirring rebuttal to the spurious arguments put forth by Houston. When he expressed astonishment at Houston's prediction of rebellion should the bill fail, I was one of many to shout, "Hear, hear!"

Congressman Menefee finally rescued sanity by use of a parliamentary trick unknown to me at the time. Rather than attack the bill as a whole, he introduced a motion to remove the legislation's enacting clause. "What's an enacting clause?" I asked the man seated next to me in the gallery. "It's the introductory clause that gives the bill its authority. You know, by the power of the government of the Republic of Texas et cetera, et cetera. Without it . . .". He made a slicing motion across his neck. In other words, a bill without an enacting clause is a toothless tiger. The vote was close, but Menefee's motion passed and the bill died. I saw Houston grimace and shake his head, but Lawrence slammed his fists so hard upon his desk that the speaker admonished him. To me that signified a sincere but misguided belief in his rectitude, whereas Houston's calm acceptance betrayed cynicism.

I mistakenly thought Mirabeau would express delight at the fate of Lawrence's bill. Instead he shrugged and said, "That bill wouldn't have changed a thing."

"What do you mean? Government might have left Austin."

He laughed. "Not a chance. Have you forgotten who the president is?"

"But it would have been a law! You're bound to uphold the nation's laws."

"Yes, Edward, it would have been a law. And I am indeed bound to uphold the law. But let me ask you this. Suppose you see that a man's house is on fire. He turns to you and tells you to hand him the bucket at your feet. He *thinks* it's a bucket of water but you know it to be full of kindling. You refuse. He's angry, but you grab a different bucket, fill it with water, and douse the flames. Will he now castigate you for not handing him the kindling that would have destroyed his house? Will he not thank you for recognizing and correcting his mistake? Thus it is with a bad law, Edward. Lawrence's bill was a bad one. Some might have been angry had it become law and I subsequently dragged my feet enforcing it. But like the man whose house you saved, they ultimately would have thanked me." Seeing the perplexed look on my face he added, "Don't worry, Edward, God is calling the shots."

I naïvely still believed that. And if a man merely enacts God's will, what blame can be attached to his actions? But Mirabeau's cavalier announcement about ignoring a law with which he disagreed disturbed me greatly. Are not laws the products of men? And are not men capable of making mistakes? It's not as if I disagree even now that the removal law would have been a bad one. But a bad law is still a law and Mirabeau therefore would have had a sworn duty to uphold it. Yet he spoke as if he could ignore that duty without consequence. And therein lies tyranny.

Up until then I had witnessed several small deeds of Mirabeau's that discomfited me. I had been able to rationalize each one as necessary for the greater good. And, while I proved unwilling to mount serious objection to Mirabeau's argument—after all, the law had failed—the first seeds of doubt about his infallibility sprouted within me.

The president's house was surely a fine one. Up on that hill you could see just about everything and everybody. Master Fontaine spent a lot of time hiking up it, which meant I did too. Of course, once we got there I always sat outside with the horses and slaves. We'd jaw at each other about this or that and try to spot folks we knew down below. That's how I saw Mrs. Tucker come walking up the path. She had her children with her, and she was carrying something in her hand. When she got closer I saw it was a book. She smiled at me and I stepped out of the way for her to go by. But she grabbed my arm and said for me to be sure and tell Master Fontaine hello from her. I didn't know she even knew who I was at the time. I said, "Yes, ma'am," and she handed the book to Lilly, the cook for Mr. Lamar, who was out in the yard shelling peas. "Lilly, you take this book to your master and tell him thank you from me," she said. Then she turned and went back down the hill.

Lilly laughed when she was gone and said, "Lord almighty, Jake, who was that? Some friend of Mr. Lamar's?"

I knew, or I thought I did, and I puckered up like I was gonna kiss somebody. Lilly, she made a face and said for me to shut on up, that Mr. Lamar wouldn't go around with another man's wife. "He's the president, fool!" she scolded me. "He ain't allowed!"

I told her I expected she was right and made like I was just funning her. It made no difference what I thought anyway. The Good Lord sorts out that kind of thing.

26

The miracles of the modern age have overcome the dearth of information we suffered from in the old days. Today, if a man tells another a tale of some far-off place, the listener only has to find the nearest telegraph office to verify what he has heard. In 1840, though, Mirabeau could only rely upon the reports of those who had been there. Whether the relayed information was accurate or fanciful he had no way of knowing. Critics charge that Mirabeau heard only what he wanted to hear of Santa Fe and discarded the rest. Nonsense.

By the time William Dryden returned from Santa Fe and came to see Mirabeau in the spring of 1840, the American merchant possessed a reputation as a trustworthy businessman and true friend of the Texas Republic. Why would Mirabeau have doubted his word? I witnessed that meeting and can vouch for the sincerity of Dryden's remarks. He believed every word of his report; therefore, we did too.

Dryden delivered his news enthusiastically. He perched himself on the edge of the fine chair given to Mirabeau by the French chargé de affaires Count Saligny and gushed the news of New Mexico's eagerness to attach herself to Texas. "There's not a man in ten who won't cheer the Texas flag," he claimed. "I heard it everywhere. 'When are the Texans coming?' They're tired of corruption, ineptitude, and the utter rot at the core of the present government. Any Santa Fe man interested in a thriving economy wants no part of Mexico."

"Does that include Governor Armijo?" Mirabeau asked.

"That *especially* includes Governor Armijo! *There's* a man motivated solely by money. Cut him in on the profits and he'll pull down the Mexican flag himself!"

"He won't fight?"

Dryden snorted. "Hell, even if he did, what would it matter? What would he fight *with*? Indians and Mexicans? But no, he won't fight."

After Dryden left, Mirabeau poured two glasses of wine, handed one to me, and sat in the French chair vacated by his departed guest. "Well, Edward, what do you think?" he asked.

"I don't think he'd lie, but it sounds too good to be true."

"I believe him. Besides, even if only half of it is true it's still a golden opportunity."

"So now what?"

"Now we make our move. A trade expedition ought to do the trick. Armed, but only for the purpose of defense against Indians. The best goods we can deliver along with a secret invitation to join our cause. That should win them over."

As long as I had known of Mirabeau's intention, I knew nothing of the logistics of traveling to Santa Fe. Thus I asked, "How far is it?"

"Three, four hundred miles. What do you think, ten to fifteen miles a day? That puts them there no later than a month after they start."

"What of the desert?"

"What of it? The Indians have been crossing it for centuries. There must be watering holes, springs, and the like. We'll find some guides."

"Speaking of Indians, what about that? Suppose they're hostile?"

Mirabeau laughed. "Of *course* they'll be hostile. They're *savages* after all. So we'll bring a bullet for each one of them!"

"You've thought of everything!"

His face darkened. "There *is* one problem."

"What's that?"

"What do you think? *Houston!*"

I thought coming to Austin was about the craziest thing a man could do. Then I heard talk about Santa Fe around town and I asked Master Fontaine about it. He said, "Now, Jacob, you don't need to be worrying about things like that." I told him I just wanted to know what was right so I could tell folks if they was wrong. So he said, "Well, the president plans on sending a mission there to ask the folks in Santa Fe if they'd like to be part of Texas." Now I'm thinking, why would they? Weren't the folks in Santa Fe the same Mexicans that got whipped before? Why would they join up with Texas now? But I didn't really care nothing about that. I was mostly worried about just one thing and that was, would we go there too? When Master Fontaine said no, we'd be staying in Austin, I threw up my hands and said, "Thank the Good Lord!" I shouldn't have said it the way I did because Master Fontaine, that didn't seem to make him none too happy. He didn't scold me, though. In fact, he tried to explain. "Jacob, think about Moses in the desert leading his people to the Promised Land. That's what the president aims to do."

I was feeling foolish, so I just told him yessir, but he told me, now look, this is something that's got to be done and don't you think God means for us to build this nation? Well, how would I know about that? I never heard God say one thing about Santa Fe. But in the Bible God didn't tell the Israelites everything he told Moses, so maybe he did tell that to Mr. Lamar. Because that's what Master Fontaine said next. And when the Lord tells a man to do something, I reckon he better do it and fast. He just better make sure he heard right.

Mirabeau spent the summer and early fall of 1840 lining up support for the mission to Santa Fe. It proved an easy sell. Newspaper editors around the country wrote glowing reports of its benefits. Every public gathering in Austin buzzed with the talk of men anxious to volunteer. One day, as I sauntered past Loafer's Logs, a jumble of uncut pine left over from the construction of Bullock's hotel at Pecan and Congress, a man named Thomas Bell hailed me from a group seated on the timber. "Hey, Fontaine, come here!"

I declined his proffered whiskey jug and asked, "What is it, Thomas?"

"Well, now, Fontaine," said Bell, slurring his words, "me and the boys was just having a friendly wager and thought you could help settle it."

"If I can. What's the bet?"

Jerking a thumb at the man next to him, Bell said, "Richards here says the *señoritas* in Santa Fe are prettier than the ones in Austin, and I say they're not. What about it?"

I laughed. "Thomas, I've never been to Santa Fe and can't vouch for its women, but I will say that the ladies of Austin seem to me as fair as any in the world."

Richards snorted at this. "Hell, there's no women *in* Austin!"

"Watch your language, Richards," another man said. "Fontaine's a church man."

"A church man knows about hell, don't he?" Richards asked. Turning to me he said, "We'll know about them *señoritas* soon enough, won't we? Once we get to Santa Fe, I mean."

"I suppose, but I won't be going. My job keeps me here."

"That's too bad," he said in a consoling tone. "*We're* all going. Aren't we boys?" Everyone nodded.

"We're gonna get rich! But don't you worry, Fontaine, we'll bring you back a doubloon or two."

"Maybe even a *señorita*," said Bell.

When I told Mirabeau of the encounter, he pointed a finger at me and crowed, "See, Edward, I told you there wouldn't be a problem with recruitment. The difficulty will be turning away the men there's no room for!"

"You don't need to lecture *me*," I said. "I believe you. Manpower won't be a problem."

"By the way, I've drawn up a list of men I'm considering appointing to the mission. What do you think?"

He thrust a piece of paper at me, which I sat down to read. "Burleson's an excellent choice to lead it," I said. "There's no one trusted more by his men. And Cazneau is the man to organize the supplies, I agree." Looking down the rest of the list I saw nothing objectionable, although one name puzzled me. "Dennis Tucker? The blacksmith? Do you need to concern yourself with blacksmith appointments?"

He chuckled nervously and said, "The blacksmith? Oh, I'd forgotten I wrote that on there. No, I suppose Burleson or whoever's in charge can figure that out."

I handed the paper back to him.

"But I do hear that Tucker is a good man," he said.

Later that day I was walking along the Avenue when a woman's voice hailed me. "Sir? Could you help us?"

The voice belonged to a petite young woman sitting in the bed of a wagon stuffed with trunks and furniture. A light blue dress graced her trim figure. Golden hair flowed past her shoulders and shimmering red lips adorned a face as fair as Helen's. Despite the road dust clinging to her features, she struck me as a true beauty.

"Haven't you ever seen a woman before?" The question came from the wagon's driver, a scrawny young man with a scraggly black beard and wide-brimmed felt hat. Next to him was another man who looked so much like the first that I took them for brothers. They both scowled at me.

"I'm sorry. I didn't mean to stare."

A different woman's voice asked, "Are we there yet?" The speaker's head popped up from between two of the trunks.

"Not yet," snapped one of the men. The woman glanced quickly at me and disappeared again.

The golden-haired beauty spoke. "Sir, we've just arrived and are looking for lodging. Could you direct us?"

I pointed down the street. "That white building is Bullock's. Around the corner are two more boardinghouses."

Without a word, the driver snapped his whip and the team stirred. The woman said, "Thank you."

"My pleasure, Miss . . ."

"Lee. I'm Julia Lee. These are my brothers and Sleeping Beauty there is my sister. What's your name?"

"I'm Mr.— I'm Edward. Edward Fontaine."

"Pleased to meet you, Mr. Fontaine. I suppose we'll be seeing each other."

I fervently hoped so.

Ever since I beat Elijah in the horse race me and him were good friends. We'd get together when we could and go have some fun, which wasn't often because there was always a white man around with something for us to do. Lord, I don't know how many rocks I toted or fields I cleared or logs I split, but a city doesn't just build itself, I suppose. Anyway, me and Elijah liked each other's company, so we spent a lot of time together fishing at the river. I always caught more than him, which got under his skin sometimes. But like I said, we were friends.

One day we were down on the riverbank, and Elijah says he's decided to go to Santa Fe. What do you mean, I asked, a black man can't just decide to get up and leave. He said, yeah, that's right, but his master is going, so he's got to go too. He'd been thinking about it and decided he'd like to go anyhow, so that's why he said he's decided to go. Because if he wanted to do it, then it didn't really matter that his master told him he's got to.

Why do you wanna go, I asked, and he said it's because Mexico's a free land and he'd never been in such a place before. I told him it may be a free land but you're not free and going there won't make you so. Besides, you know how you're gonna get there, don't you, I told him. Walking, that's how. Through the desert past about a thousand Indians that would just love to tie a black scalp to their saddle. You ever think about that, I asked him.

He said, yeah, he did, but he wanted to go anyhow.

I don't know why you'd wanna do that, I said. I don't know why you'd wanna go get yourself scalped by Indians.

He thought a while on that and finally said he figured he had to go. That's what his master told him, so that was that.

Now that was the God's truth.

In 1840 Wash Miller won election to the House as representative from Gonzales, which meant he was in Austin with the government. Despite his alignment with Houston, we remained friends. A favorite excursion of ours was to cross the river and ride to Barton's spring, the largest natural spring I have ever seen. There we passed many pleasant hours fishing and bathing in the clear pools formed by the spring's flow. Occasionally Mr. Barton, or "Uncle Billy" as he preferred to be called, would join us, although never to swim. "Water's for fish, boys," he'd say. "I got no gills."

One day the three of us lolled on the bank of the largest pool when Uncle Billy said, "Edward, what's all this talk about Santa Fe? The way I hear it we're sending an army over there to chase out the Mexicans."

Suspecting that Wash opposed the expedition I groaned inside, but answered, "Not an army, Uncle Billy, a group of merchants. A peaceful expedition aimed at widening our trade network."

"That's not what I heard," he said. "Hell, Dick Brenham said there'd be at least a hundred soldiers going along."

"For protection. There are a lot of Indians between here and Santa Fe."

"That's true. Still, I wonder what the Mexicans will say when all those Texas rifles come marching into town."

Wash laughed. "They'll say, 'Howdy, boys, come on in and make yourselves comfortable.' And the women will spread rose petals on the streets for our boys to walk on."

"Not a chance," said Uncle Billy. "I reckon they're still sore about San Jacinto."

"Oh, no," said Wash. "They're over that. They figure we've done such a fine job with Texas since then that they're ready to give us New Mexico too."

Uncle Billy smiled. "Edward, I think he's having some fun with you."

I attempted to keep the conversation light. "Uncle Billy, Wash is just pulling your leg. The Santa Fe trade is lucrative. Diverting it through Texas will benefit everyone."

"Not everyone believes that," said Wash.

Wash was beginning to annoy me. "Not everyone believes that trading with Santa Fe will benefit people in Austin?"

"Not everyone believes that sending men to die in the desert benefits *anyone*. You'll be lucky if one man in ten reaches Santa Fe alive."

"Wash, you know that's not true. You've been listening to your boss too much."

"I don't have a boss anymore. And what does *your* boss know of the desert? Has he been there? Is there a road through it? Are there inns and watering holes along the way? *Ha!* Maybe the Comanche will invite us into their tipis!"

"There will be experienced guides leading the way."

"There *are* no experienced guides. *Nobody's* made that trip before. Except the Comanche, and they're not volunteering to show us the way."

"They'll get there just fine."

"And what if they do? How long do you suppose they'll last? Do you honestly believe that the Mexicans will let us just waltz into town? No, sir! It'll be Goliad and the Alamo all over again."

"Texas boys can take care of themselves," said Uncle Billy.

"Maybe so," said Wash. "But Houston and other right-minded folks are gonna make sure they don't have to."

My face felt warm and the hair rose on the back of my neck. Just as I was about to lay into Wash, though, Uncle Billy cackled and said gleefully, "Hold on, boys, I think I got me a big fish on the line."

I held my tongue and looked at the water.

Uncle Billy yanked on his pole until something flew out of the pond. "Nope, it's just a stick," he said with disappointment. He threw down his pole, stood up, and said, "Hey, boys, have I ever shown you my two buffalo calves? Come on up to the house and have a look."

As we walked up the bank Uncle Billy said ruefully, "Dang it, I sure thought I had me a fish."

As the Fifth Congress convened in the fall of 1840, Mirabeau confidently expected to gain congressional approval to send a mission to Santa Fe. The western men stood ready to support a bill, while the expected opposition from the eastern bloc seemed less than formidable. No one, though, expected the bill's passage in the House to come as easily as it did. Oh, Sam Houston and his lackeys made some noise during the debates, but even Houston was uncharacteristically subdued. In fact, he could offer no better argument than to compare the expedition to Napoleon's fateful march to Moscow. Whatever dramatic effect he intended foundered when John Caldwell of Bastrop called out, "Christ, are the Russians in Santa Fe?" I didn't appreciate his blasphemy but had to laugh at the prick to Houston. Even *he* smiled.

Human frailty now intervened. Why God allowed it is a mystery to me. As the House debated the Santa Fe bill, Mirabeau lapsed into a sickly state with hacking cough, labored breathing, and fatigue. I thought it a small thing at first, but when a week passed without improvement I became concerned. The problem in Austin at the time lay not with a dearth of excellent physicians but in the difficulty of procuring medication. Mirabeau therefore determined to seek treatment in the

United States. In early December he set out for New Orleans.

Neither of us anticipated difficulty with the Santa Fe bill after his departure. Vice President Burnet was a supporter. Unfortunately, his elevation to the position of acting president resulted in the election of Anson Jones, a member of the Houston party, as president pro tem of the Senate. Mirabeau had predicted that Jones's patriotism would override his Houston leanings and that he would therefore shepherd a bill representing the will of the people through the upper chamber. Alas, this proved false; Jones threw up obstacles at every turn. Stacked public hearings, secret negotiations, and blatant falsehoods resulted in one delay after another until the bill lost momentum and died for lack of action. The reason for Sam Houston's tepid performance in the House became clear with his frequent visits to the committee rooms behind the Senate chamber. Knowing that he was unlikely to overcome the bill's supporters in the House, Houston concentrated his efforts on weaker members of the Senate, Anson Jones foremost among them. When Mirabeau returned to Austin—blessedly recovered from his illness—he found congressional approval for a Santa Fe expedition a dead issue.

A few days after Mirabeau's return, David Burnet and several others gathered at the president's house for dinner. Edwin Waller was there, as was Ned Burleson, Albert Sydney Johnston, General Felix Huston, and the corpulent Hugh McLeod. General Huston still basked in the glory of his recent victory over the Comanche at Plum Creek, a small waterway thirty or forty miles south of the city. He and his troops had intercepted several hundred savages returning from a raid on the coast and thrashed them soundly. Some said that the attack commenced only when Burleson and Matthew Caldwell pressed Huston to give the order. When I asked Burleson, though, he scoffed and said, "Any good commander listens to the advice of his officers. Felix was in charge."

That evening brought my first encounter with Hugh McLeod, although I had certainly heard of him because of his position at the time as adjutant general of the army. He shook my hand with an enthusiasm that matched his reputation for joviality. "Edward Fontaine, I have wanted to meet you!" he said, his large belly rocking and his thick chin quivering with delight.

"General McLeod, it's a pleasure. I've heard so many good things about you."

He laughed heartily at the compliment and said, "You must have been talking to my mother!"

Even as the first course arrived at the table, talk turned to Santa Fe. "What now?" asked Vice President Burnet with his usual brusqueness. "That idiot Jones killed the bill."

"Reintroduce it," said Burleson. "Tweak it a bit and give it another chance."

"They're not stupid," said Johnston. "Jones and his boys in the Senate killed it once and they'll do it again."

"It wasn't Jones," argued Burleson. "We both know who was really pulling the strings."

"Houston."

"Right."

"Would that he would drink himself to an early grave," said Mirabeau.

Johnston chuckled and said, "Unfortunately, the Big Drunk appears to have stopped imbibing. I hear his new wife is to blame."

"Margaret?" asked Felix Huston. Despite the fact that Huston had almost killed Johnston in the duel years previously, the two appeared cordial with each other. "She's a delightful lady. Why on earth she'd marry a man like Houston is beyond comprehension."

"She's lovely indeed," agreed Burleson. "But we'll see how long this conversion lasts. Meanwhile, we've got to figure out a way to win this thing in Congress."

"What's Congress got to do with it?" Edwin Waller spoke this forcefully enough that everyone quieted and turned in his direction. "Mirabeau, are you in charge or not? Why do you need a goddamn bill to send traders to Santa Fe? Hell, just do it!"

Hugh McLeod laughed nervously and the others began talking all at once. Mirabeau waved them to silence. "Waller's right," he said calmly. "We don't need Congress to do what's right. I'll organize a private trading mission and send it on its way with my blessing. That's something any private citizen can do."

"But how will you pay for it?" asked McLeod.

"How will *I* pay for it?" Mirabeau asked in return. "*I* won't. I won't have to. Anyone with common sense knows of the profit that awaits him at the end of this trip. Merchants will put up their own goods. And they'll reap their own rewards. That's their right."

"And for protection?" Huston asked. "How can you send the army without congressional approval?"

Mirabeau smiled. "Relax, Felix. What's to prevent a man from organizing a private militia and marching his company to Santa Fe? That sort of thing happens all the time."

"The men would expect compensation."

"And they'll get it. But that's chicken feed. I'll find the money." He looked at me. "We'll find the money, won't we, Edward?"

Caught off guard, I merely nodded. I knew of no secret piles of cash, though, and did not share his confidence. What I failed to grasp at the time was that there were still aspects of his determination unknown to me. I also believed that what God inspires can only be righteous.

• • •

Try as I might, I couldn't get Lamar and that white lady out of my mind. Why did God let me see such a thing? He would have known I wanted no part of it, but there I was lookin' at it just the same. And when a black man sees something that a white man wants to keep secret, then that means trouble for him.

I didn't have to ask if Mr. Lamar wanted that kept secret. Any fool could see that. I was just fetching water like I was told and there he was. If only I hadn't been standing by that door at Bullock's, if only Bullock hadn't come outside just then, if only he didn't need water, if only this, if only that. But I was by the door, Bullock did come outside, he did want some water, and I went to the well and, yes, Lord, I do love trouble, so thank you very much. And I told myself, "Jake, you got to be quiet about that, ain't nobody gonna believe you, not even Master Fontaine." And I wish I could have done that, I really do.

27

And so we ignored Congress. This disturbed me. Mirabeau, however, was unfazed. "The people want this," he said.

"But the people's representatives in the Senate failed to approve it," I countered.

He scoffed. "The House passed it and it only stalled in the Senate because of Jones. In a year even he will be running around town telling everyone that the mission was *his* idea."

He began the task of implementing his plan by approaching William Cazneau. As commissary general, Cazneau was the man to arrange the practical necessities of the expedition. When he asked how to pay for supplies, Mirabeau replied, "Promissory notes. Same as a commander in the field. The merchants won't mind because most of them will have a stake in the expedition's success. Once this thing pays off we'll be able to honor those notes ten times over. And tell anyone that refuses your note that their trade goods aren't welcome on the wagons."

After Cazneau left I asked Mirabeau about the notes. "Even if the expedition is successful Congress will still have to authorize payment."

Mirabeau laughed. "Edward, when this mission succeeds, congressmen will trip over themselves paying the merchants so they can get in on the next expedition! Public servants are as greedy as anyone else. We'll take advantage of that."

Edward Burleson agreed to lead the military arm of the mission. Mirabeau believed there was no better soldier in Texas. I agreed. In addition to his exploits in the late revolution, Burleson possessed years of experience battling savages along the frontier. According to the men who served under him, there was no cooler head or steadier hand than that of the general. Burleson's choice of Hugh McLeod as second-in-command inspired further confidence. The two immediately put out a nationwide call for volunteers that quickly swelled the ranks.

Newspaper editors Samuel Whiting and Jacob Cruger proved to be important allies to the cause. Although their politics differed—Whiting supported the Houston party while Cruger was a firm anti-Houston man—both expressed enthusiasm for Mirabeau's plan. Their supportive editorials triggered similar expressions throughout the country.

One rainy day in April 1841 Mirabeau asked me to invite four men, Dick Brenham, William Cooke, Jose Navarro, and George Van Ness, to a dinner at his house. The makeup of this foursome puzzled me. A physician, Brenham had served in the army during the revolution but done little to distinguish himself. I knew him as a respected member of the community but saw nothing else that would have attracted Mirabeau's attention. Van Ness seemed an even greater mystery. He had a successful law practice but had not involved himself in government or military matters. William Cooke's stature loomed larger in that he had recently been nominated to run for vice president. He had declined the honor, however. A signer of the Texas Declaration of Independence, Navarro had represented Bexar County in the House of Representatives, where he was one of Mirabeau's most ardent supporters.

Mirabeau had not shared with me the reason for holding this dinner and I could see no common interest among the invitees. Each man accepted his invitation. Brenham even seemed to understand the purpose of the gathering, commenting, "Ah, good. I'm anxious to hear more about it."

The small talk throughout dinner that evening frustrated me. Finally, after servants had cleared the table and passed out cigars, Mirabeau cleared his throat and said, "All right, gentlemen, let's get down to business. You know why you're here. Will you go?"

"Hell, yes, I'll go," Brenham said. "Why wouldn't I?"

Van Ness and Cooke offered similar statements.

When Navarro said nothing, Mirabeau turned to him and asked, "As a native Mexican, Jose, your risk is the greatest. What do you say?"

Navarro puffed several times on his cigar before answering. "Yes, Mirabeau, I'll go to Santa Fe. But what shall I do there? Surely you don't need me to go merely to translate."

"No, but it will be nice to have a native speaker along. Many of the men speak Spanish, of course, but it's not their native tongue. Yours will be the most influential voice there."

"Of course. What do you wish me to say?"

Mirabeau smiled. "Don't be coy, Jose, you know very well what you'll say. You'll tell Armijo that a golden opportunity has fallen into his lap. You'll tell him that he'll become a rich man once he throws in his lot with Texas. You'll tell him that history will remember him as a *great* man."

"And how will he know that I'm speaking the truth?"

"I'll put it all in a letter. Then we'll get Whiting or Cruger to print up some official-looking documents, stamp them with the seal of Texas, and awe Señor Armijo with our magnificence."

"So this trade expedition is merely camouflage?"

"No," said Mirabeau. "I doubt that the merchants coming along see themselves as camouflage; they wish to make a profit. But it is their successful interaction with the New Mexican traders that will sway any doubters on the other side. As you present the offer to Armijo, you'll be able to point to the jingle of coins on the plaza as reason enough for him to accept."

"And the offer will be what precisely?"

"Join us!" said Mirabeau. "Take down that hideous Mexican flag and raise the single star of Texas! Be free of the shackles of tyranny! Join the cause of liberty, justice, and equality!"

"And become rich in the process."

"Exactly!"

Navarro grinned and stubbed out his cigar. "I think that will work."

"It will indeed!"

"To Texas!" Brenham cried.

"Lilly!" shouted Mirabeau to the kitchen girl. "Bring us some wine!"

I did see more of Julia Lee. A few questions around town informed me that she was staying with her siblings at Mrs. Sawyer's boardinghouse on West Pecan. I began detouring to Pecan Street on my way to and from the Capitol. On the third day, fortune had her exiting the house as I passed by. "Good day, Miss Lee," I called out.

She turned and smiled, stirring butterflies in my chest. "Mr. Fontaine! How nice to see you again." She nodded toward the house. "As you can see, we followed your directions."

"Mrs. Sawyer keeps an excellent house. I trust that you're comfortable?"

"I am." She gave me a knowing look. "You know, you needn't call me Miss Lee. My name is Julia."

"And I am Edward."

I didn't want the moment to end but could think of nothing else to say. She took a step toward me and said, "I've been wanting the see the Capitol. Do you know anyone who could show it to me?"

I did.

• • •

I tried not to say anything. But Master Fontaine, he's a pretty smart man and he could tell that something wasn't right. "What's gotten into you, Jacob?" he asked me. "You been acting like a sick puppy and now you better tell me what's eating your insides."

"Master Fontaine, it's nothing," I lied. "Just some trouble with one of the boys on the job."

He wasn't fooled. "I don't believe you," he said.

Of course it wasn't true, and I knew it and so did he, so I had to search in my head and come up with something that came close to the truth that he'd believe. I couldn't do it, though. I told him I saw something I wasn't meant to see, and he said, well, what is it then? So I explained about fetching water and seeing two people come into the yard and hug and kiss. And I left it at that.

"Well, who were they?" he wanted to know, and I said I thought it was Mr. Lamar but maybe not because I was clear across the yard. But really I knew it was him. Anyway, he laughed and said there's nothing wrong with a man kissing a lady, but then I guess he saw there was more to the story because he told me to go on. So I told him that the woman with Mr. Lamar wasn't just any woman, but Mrs. Tucker. Now he got serious and asked me what did I really see and I told him again. Well, he walked around the yard a little and finally said I must be mistaken and sure I saw some people kissing, but it wasn't Mr. Lamar and Mrs. Tucker. I told him no, it was Mr. Lamar all right and Mrs. Tucker too. He got mad and told me he already caught me in one lie and I best not give the Lord another one to hold against me. I got riled up too and told him I'm a God-fearin' man just like him and I've got no reason to make up stories about Mr. Lamar. He stared at me a while and finally said he was disappointed in me, that he didn't know why I'd make it up either but I sure enough did. Then he said I better think twice before lying to him again; that maybe his pap back in Mississippi was right after all and that sometimes a nigger's just gotta be whipped. Then he walked off leavin' me feelin' like I just got kicked by a mule. I waited for a whippin' but it never happened. But for him to call me a liar felt almost as bad.

Why would Jacob lie to me? He had never done so before. He was clearly nervous when he told me the lie about a quarrel among the slaves. His eyes darted about and he searched for words as he spoke. When he told about Mirabeau and Mrs. Tucker kissing, though, he looked straight at me and spoke without hemming and hawing. No, I had to conclude that Jacob *was* telling the truth, or at least the truth as he saw it. That left only one possibility: that he was mistaken. Yes, he saw a man and woman kissing in the yard, but how could he be sure it was Mirabeau and Mrs. Tucker? Certainly he didn't run up for a closer look. By his own admission he was a good distance away. Why, then, couldn't he have mistaken the identities? The answer, I decided at the time, was that he could have and did. I felt bad about accusing him of lying, so I gave him a nice ham. He didn't say much, just nodded and mumbled his thanks. But he remained rather glum for a day or two.

A few days later, a seed of doubt about the incident took root in my mind when I encountered William Cazneau on the street. "I'll wager that *you're* a busy man these days," I told him.

"I am at that. Organizing this Santa Fe business would tax the devil."

"So how's it going? Are you having any trouble with the supplies?"

"No, there's plenty of beef to be had, although vegetables are a different matter. Water casks, blankets, medical supplies, and such are trickier too. Still, I think the men will have what they need."

"Well, if I can be of any assistance, let me know."

As I started to leave he said, "You know, I *am* looking for a particular fellow." "Who?"

"Blacksmith by the name of Tucker. Do you know him?"

"Yes, but why are you looking for him?"

"Name's on the list. It seemed a little odd to me at first because I assumed the company captains would recruit their own blacksmiths. But Lamar said he wanted some non-military men to look after the merchant wagons. Makes sense, I guess."

I told him where I thought he might find Tucker.

"Much obliged," he said cheerfully before walking away.

I couldn't share his sunny disposition.

I didn't ever want to see that woman again but how was that gonna happen in such a small town? Understand, I didn't have nothing against her, but I was scared she might have seen me at the well. Then along she came one day while I was brushing Janey. It wasn't an accident either; she came right to my shack behind Master Fontaine's house on Brazos Street.

"Your name is Jacob, isn't it?" she asked me. I told her it was. "Well, Jacob, I brought this for you and your master." She held out a basket. I didn't take it right away, but I did stop brushing the mule. "Go on, take it," she said and I did. "Well, look inside." When I did she said, "I made 'em myself. They're pecan biscuits. It's hard

to get pecans right now, but I found some in a store over on Pecan Street. Isn't that funny?" And she laughed. It was a gentle laugh like a lady would make; I wondered what she was doing married to a blacksmith.

I told her thank you, and she said for me to give some to Master Fontaine but be sure and keep the biggest ones for myself. I took a bite of one and told her how good it tasted. Then I started to give a piece to Janey like I always do when I have something to eat, but I caught myself and she said it was all right, that mules got to eat too. So I gave it to her and I took another bite of what was left and she said she guessed she'd be going along but maybe she'd be back one day with a cake or blackberry pie. Later on when Master Fontaine came home I gave him the whole basket. He frowned a little and told me to keep half of 'em, which I did. I ate one of the biscuits later and remembered how much I like pecans. That reminded me of the pecans that Minerva gave me back in Columbus, which reminded me of Minerva, and I thought of Mrs. Tucker and Mr. Lamar and I just couldn't eat no more of those biscuits after that. But Janey was not so particular.

Sam Houston had indeed stopped drinking. Although I had never seen him drunk in Austin, I simply assumed our paths had not crossed when he was in his cups. But when I asked Wash about it he said, "It's true. Now, some of the rumors about his drinking are exaggerated. Nevertheless, I have known him to go a sip or two past sobriety. But ever since his marriage—his engagement, really—not a drop of liquor has passed his lips. He'll even turn down a glass of wine or beer."

"Remarkable."

"Not so remarkable when you consider the reason. Have you seen his fiancée?"

"I haven't had the pleasure."

"She's a beauty. *I'd* give up drinking for her. Shoot, I'd give up eating and breathing, for that matter."

I gave a red-faced chuckle.

"What a man won't do for a nice ass, eh, Fontaine?"

"Don't be crude, Wash."

Mirabeau hadn't been avoiding Houston, but he had ignored him since assuming the presidency. Thus, it surprised me to have Houston call on him. Mirabeau winced as he stood to shake Houston's hand, an act that did not pass unnoticed. "My dear Lamar, are you in pain?" his visitor asked.

"No, no. Not for at least two years," said Mirabeau with a smirk.

"Excellent," said Houston, with false enthusiasm. He gestured to a chair and said, "May I?"

The two of them sat. I reached for paper and pen to take notes. Houston cast me a quick glance of dissatisfaction, but didn't object. He said, "Mirabeau, you seem determined to send this mission to Santa Fe."

Mirabeau nodded.

"Congress hasn't approved."

Several seconds passed before Mirabeau replied. "The House *has* approved. In fact, it voted overwhelmingly in favor of the expedition. It died in the Senate only because Jones took advantage of my temporary absence."

"Which means that Congress as a body failed to give approval."

"The people are behind it."

Houston snorted. "Did I miss the plebiscite?"

"The people are behind *me*," Mirabeau insisted. "So is Congress. And if that isn't true they have it in their power to remove me from office."

"You'll be leaving office at the end of this year anyway. Your term will be up."

"How does that matter?"

"How does that matter? You send these men to Santa Fe, and the next president will have to clean up your mess!"

Mirabeau smiled. "What mess is that, Houston? I don't see a mess. I see a great success that the next president—you perhaps—will gladly take credit for."

"I haven't announced my candidacy."

Mirabeau said nothing. Houston continued.

"Mirabeau, my point is this. Yes, the House gave you the vote you wanted. But, for whatever reason, the Senate didn't. And in a democracy the president is bound to act within the laws passed by Congress."

"I know how a democracy works," said Mirabeau irritably. "And if the *people* think I am exceeding presidential authority, there is a constitutional solution."

"God *damn it*, Lamar. That's the refuge of a scoundrel! Act like a tyrant and dare the people to throw you out? Have you no respect for the nation?"

"I have *great* respect for the nation," said Mirabeau through clenched teeth. "What I do *not* respect are the men intent on ruining it."

"*Lamar!*" I had never seen Houston so emotional. "This expedition will *fail*! Men will *die*! Are you willing to have that on your conscience? Are you? And there's no money to pay for this insanity. There's not a dollar in the treasury; have you thought of that? Your term ends *this year*, man! If you persist in this madness, the next president will inherit a disaster!"

Mirabeau's eyes narrowed and his expression hardened. With lilting sarcasm he said, "What's that to you? You haven't announced your candidacy."

A heavy silence enveloped the room. Houston stood and turned to leave. As he reached the door, he paused and said without looking back, "You think this will be your legacy. And it will. Just not the legacy you want."

The door slammed. I straightened my notes. Mirabeau leaned back sharply in his chair, exhaled, and asked rhetorically, "How is it that I'm always right and he's always wrong, yet *he's* 'the Hero of San Jacinto'?"

By then Julia and I were seeing each other several times a week. After supper I'd bring fruit or nuts to Mrs. Sawyer's, which we enjoyed out back under a cedar elm in the company of her siblings or other lodgers. Once I arrived with a small pot of honey and we dipped bread and nibbled until well after dark. When she stood to say good night we realized we were alone in the yard. We kissed, and I forgot the sweetness of the honey.

I had never met a woman like Julia. The girls in Mississippi, while pretty, were vacuous and preoccupied with their place in society. In addition to being beautiful, though, Julia possessed intelligence and a sharp wit. And there was no society in Austin for her to fixate over. She was educated; she was self-confident; she flirted mercilessly. I was helpless. I was in love.

I was on a crew with Elijah one day and while we were taking a water break he asked what that white lady wanted with me. I knew he was talking about Mrs. Tucker, but I said for him to shut up because he was just talking nonsense. He said I shouldn't tell stories. He knew she was looking for me because she asked him where I lived. She knew his master, see, and his master must have said me and him were friends and that's why she asked him that. Well, I said, you must be talking about the lady that brought Master Fontaine some biscuits, and he said, yeah, she was carrying a basket of something, but she didn't ask for Master Fontaine, she asked for you. I told him I didn't know nothing about that, and what would a white lady want with me anyway? He kept pestering me but I didn't talk any more about it.

28

If Mirabeau hadn't been at his desk as I copied the roster of those going on the expedition we wouldn't have quarreled. There he was, though, in the high, stuffed leather chair that seemed to swallow his short frame. He snatched the top copy from the stack I had accumulated, glanced at it, and said, "Ah, yes, very good."

"That reminds me," I said, "why do you care so much about Tucker going along?"

His eyes flitted around the room. "What are you talking about?"

"I saw Cazneau on the street. He was looking for Tucker."

"Cazneau was looking for Tucker?"

I nodded.

"Well, maybe you should ask Cazneau then."

"But he said you sent him to find Tucker. Why would you do that?"

"Look, Edward, what are you getting at? Is there something wrong with asking the man? We need blacksmiths. Tucker is a blacksmith."

If not for the sincere look on Jacob's face when he told me what he saw behind Bullock's, I would have stopped there. But I had concluded that Jacob believed what he said. "Is it because of his wife?" I asked.

Mirabeau looked stunned. He glared at me for several seconds before asking, "What are you implying?"

"I'm not implying anything. I'm merely asking if Dennis Tucker's wife has anything to do with you wanting him to go on the expedition."

"Why would she?"

I couldn't hold back any longer; the look on Mirabeau's face told me that he understood exactly why I persisted. "Because Jacob saw the two of you kissing behind Bullock's."

His face slowly contorted in anger as his mind absorbed my words. "Jacob!" he shouted. "*Jacob?* Jacob said he saw me with another man's wife? Is this Jacob your *slave* that we're talking about?"

His fury intimidated me, but I couldn't stop now. "Yes, we're talking about my man Jacob. He's never lied to me. I don't think he's lying now."

"Well, *of course* he's lying," said Mirabeau. "He made it up! Somebody gave him a dollar or a bottle of whiskey and said, 'Here, go tell your master that you saw the president kissing Mrs. Tucker.'"

"Jacob wouldn't do that. You don't know him."

"By God, I *do* know him! I know all I need to know. He's lying because he can't help it. He's lying because he's colored. He's lying because he's a *goddamn nigger!*"

"A darkie can't tell the truth?"

"Of course not! It's their nature. They *all* lie."

"So there's nothing between you and Mrs. Tucker?"

"I swear I hardly know the woman, Edward. I greet her on the street as I would anyone. As for her husband, I know him to be an excellent blacksmith and he is therefore useful to the expedition. And he *wants* to go, believe me. You won't hear him complaining when he's paid."

"*If* he's paid."

"What does that mean?"

"There's no money, Mirabeau. Government is broke, you know that."

He shook his head disapprovingly. "Edward, there's money enough. If I didn't know better I'd think you a Houston man."

"I might be if I thought you were lying."

He slammed a fist onto his desk. "A word of caution, *son!* Men have dueled over lesser accusations!"

Ordinarily, an outburst like that from Mirabeau would have silenced me. I sensed something false about his outrage, though, so said, "I don't want a duel, I want the truth! Jacob told me he saw something and he's never lied to me and so I'm wondering, *what did he see?*"

"*He didn't see a damn thing!*"

His ferocity had the desired effect. I thought I might faint. But Jacob saw something. He said he saw Mirabeau and a married woman kissing. Maybe there was an innocent explanation. Unlikely, but maybe so. And now, in Mirabeau's flushed, trembling, self-righteous fury I saw the panic of Adam holding the apple core. If he had come up with some story to explain the two of them together I would have believed it, flimsy or not. But I couldn't believe an outright denial and therefore could only assume the worst. Mirabeau wanted Dennis Tucker to go with the expedition so that he and the man's wife could carry on an affair. And if that were true, what else about Mirabeau might be false?

I heard 'em yelling. Master Fontaine had me go with him to the president's house to help plow up a garden for Mr. Lamar. All of a sudden I heard Mr. Lamar shouting all sorts of terrible things, but what I remember most is Mr. Lamar saying, "Of course he lied, he's a nigger." I thought, "Oh, Lord, leave me out of this," and then Master Fontaine came charging out of the house. He didn't even look at me, but I knew I should follow, so I set down my shovel and took off after him. He didn't say nothing to me until we got to the bottom of the hill, and I asked if everything was all right and he looked at me like I was crazy. When we got to his house he said, "Damn your hide, Jacob, damn your ugly hide." I asked him to tell me what I had done so I could make it right, and he said he thought I'd made everything up about Mr. Lamar and Mrs. Tucker, but now maybe I didn't and he asked why I had to go poking around behind Bullock's anyhow. I said I was sorry and he told me to be quiet and go find a gun and shoot him. I must have looked funny then because he quick said never mind, he didn't mean that, but leave him alone and from now on mind your own business.

I got to thinking about that later on. He believed me now about what I saw and he and Mr. Lamar must have had words about it. If that's so, then why didn't he say he was sorry for making me out to be a liar? I know most white folks wouldn't tell a colored man sorry if it kept them from the eternal fire, but up until then I didn't think Master Fontaine was like most white folks. After that, things never were the same between me and him.

For several days Mirabeau and I avoided each other. I busied myself organizing papers in the executive office on Congress Avenue but refrained from my usual jaunts up President's Hill. He evidently stayed in his house; if he ventured into town I knew nothing about it. Then one day I looked up from my desk and there he was, smiling nervously as he entered the room with several sheets of paper. "Here, Edward," he said, "I want you to make six copies of this for me."

I took the papers. "I can have them by this evening."

"No, tomorrow is fine. But please return the original with the copies, as well as any scratch sheets you'd otherwise throw away."

"Of course." I began clearing a space on my desk in order to begin the task, but he didn't leave. "Is there something else?" I asked.

"Edward . . . about the other day . . . I didn't mean to come off so strongly."

"No, of course not. I shouldn't have brought that up."

"No, you were right . . . I mean, you were right if you had a concern to bring it to my attention. But there's really nothing to it—just lies and rumors—and I should have let it go at that. After all, the office attracts the attentions of petty people."

I grunted noncommittally.

"It doesn't matter that there's no money in the treasury, you know," he went on. "What matters is that this is the right course for Texas."

"Yes, of course."

"They'll see. They'll all see. This expedition will be the crowning achievement of my administration. *Our* administration. And it's just a first step. Burnet believes in this as well. If he can win the next presidential election he'll carry us all the way to the Pacific."

"That will be a glorious day, indeed."

He found a chair. "Edward, you know why I'm doing this, don't you?"

"Because it's what's best for the country?"

"Yes, but why am *I* doing it? Why does it have to be Mirabeau Lamar? Why not someone else?"

"I don't know"

"Tabitha."

"Your dead wife."

"Yes. Tabitha died in Georgia, you know. She died to free me up to fulfill a divine plan. If she had lived—and I wish daily that she had—I would still be in Georgia. We had a fine house and a beautiful daughter. I had family and political connections that would have gotten my career back on track. I loved my wife and wanted nothing more than to please her. She wasn't an adventurer, you know. She wasn't a pioneer. No rope beds and rawhide chairs for her! No, she was an elegant woman, a proper lady. More fit for a European court than Texas. I wouldn't—*couldn't* have brought her here."

"I'd like to have known her."

"But God needed an instrument. He needed me. And he knew I'd be of no use in the Georgia pines. So he . . . took away any excuse not to go to Texas."

He turned his head away as a tear rushed down his cheek. I shifted uncomfortably in my chair.

"I've been so lonely . . . so lonely. Mrs. Tucker and I struck up a friendship in

Houston. But it's been completely proper, I assure you. I do wish Tabitha were with me. But it's all right. It was necessary and I accept that. But now . . . now I know. I can't fail. This expedition is right. It has to be. It *must* succeed. Because if it doesn't . . ."

"It will."

"If it doesn't, then it will be my fault. I'll have failed her. I'll have failed Texas. I'll have failed God. And you're a theologian. You know. What awaits the man who fails God?"

"Mirabeau, I don't think—"

"But it won't, so we won't worry about that." He smiled thinly. "Of course it won't. But now you see why there can be no discussion about money or who wants to go and who doesn't. It will all work out because this is God's plan, not mine."

"And God has given you a free hand in devising the means of success."

He looked at me as if I were a child. "Whatever I do, I do for God and Texas. And you know what else?" His smiled broadened. "Dennis Tucker is going to make a fortune. He'll come back to Austin as rich as all the rest of them and he'll thank me for allowing him to go. Who wouldn't want *that*?"

When I was alone again I undertook the task of copying Mirabeau's letter. Now I understood his request that I return not only the original but any waste paper as well. The letter was addressed to Santa Fe Governor Manuel Armijo. In it Mirabeau extolled the virtues of the governor's rule, as well as the good fortune that placed his territory adjacent to our own. He introduced the leaders of the Texan expedition, while taking pains to describe Navarro's role. The trade expedition would be the first of many aimed at cementing the friendship of Texas and New Mexico. Imagine the prosperity of the two territories, he urged. Imagine the even greater prosperity of his people without the corrupt influence of faraway Mexico City! Why not follow our example and throw off the reins of the tyrant Santa Anna? The name Armijo would shine through the ages as a beacon of democratic enlightenment! His people would love him in his new role as governor of the Texan state of Santa Fe. Who knows, perhaps his well-known talents would one day make him president!

This was hypocrisy. At the time, we knew very little about Governor Armijo. What we had heard from American traders had certainly not been complimentary. Dryden called him "ignorant and venal" and I had heard Mirabeau repeat that phrase numerous times. Clearly Mirabeau hoped to exploit Armijo's vanity and greed. Until then, I had thought Mirabeau incapable of practicing the blatant deceit so common in other politicians. Now my eyes were opening to a talent for manipulation that rattled me.

Perhaps I shouldn't have worried. After all, politicians since Julius Caesar have shaded the truth to their advantage. Yet, I had always viewed Mirabeau as avoiding the slimy gutter wallowed in so cheerfully by others. He had so often accused Sam Houston of wielding lies as weapons. Was this any different?

I swallowed my discomfort and copied the lies. I gathered up the original, the finished letters, and the sheets of discarded paper and carried the bundle over to President's Hill. Dusk descended as I climbed the hill. I heard Mirabeau's familiar voice as I neared the house. Near the front door was a small carriage. The driver was receiving last-minute instructions from Mirabeau. "Keep quiet after leaving the hill," he said.

"Yes, sir, boss," said the driver, an African unknown to me.

I called out, "Good evening."

Mirabeau jerked back from the wagon. Addressing the driver again, he said, "Go on, what are you waiting for?" But by now I blocked the wagon's path. The driver relaxed the reins and tipped his hat to me.

"Edward!" said Mirabeau with alacrity. "I didn't expect you until morning."

"I finished and thought you might like the evening to look these over." Now I was close enough to see the passenger. It was Mrs. Tucker. My startled reaction eliminated any chance of pretending I hadn't recognized her.

Mirabeau acted nonchalant. "Mrs. Tucker, may I introduce you to my secretary, Mr. Fontaine?"

"Oh, but I know Mr. Fontaine already," she said. "We met in Houston."

"Well, Mrs. Tucker must get home before dark," said Mirabeau. He gestured at the driver. "Off you go, Clarence." The wagon left.

Mirabeau and I stared awkwardly at each other. Finally, he said, "Will you come in for a glass of wine?"

I made up an excuse.

He said, "Mrs. Tucker had some questions about the expedition. Since her husband will be going along I felt obliged to answer them."

I could have pointed out that ordinarily people with questions about the government sought Mirabeau at his office during the daytime. I also could have said that citizens with private concerns actually approached *me* first to secure an appointment. Instead, I merely nodded and said, "I'm sure it was all very harmless." I didn't believe that, though. I believed I had caught him in a lie.

I was afraid to talk to Master Fontaine after that lest he get angry with me. I thought if I just laid low things would eventually settle back to normal. I felt lonely and sorry for myself because talking to Master Fontaine, or really him talking to me, made me feel more important than I know I was. Most white men didn't talk to their slaves except to boss 'em into doing something, but with me it had always been different. Sometimes we'd sit down with a plate of fried bread or a pot of beans and talk about any old thing. Mostly God and Bible verses. Sometimes the government. Old Mr. Somebody showed up for a meeting drunk on corn whiskey or maybe that fella who wears the fancy clothes split his britches. It wasn't much, but I liked it because I knew the other slaves never sat around jawing with their masters. And I reckon I missed being treated equal, even if it was only when nobody else was around.

So when he told me I was going to Santa Fe I was struck dumb. "Master, Santa Fe?" was all I could say and he told me not to worry because practically a whole army would be going along and I had nothing to fear. But I was afraid. Up until then he had said nothing at all about sending me out there. I asked him if he was going too and he said no, he was needed in Austin, but a man named Horn had offered a lot of money for me to go along and help him with his team and supplies and he couldn't turn it down. Besides, he said, from what he'd heard this would be no more trouble than the trips we'd taken together so far. "Why, Santa Fe's no farther away than Mississippi and you didn't worry about coming here," he said. Well, I did worry about that, I just hadn't told him. I worried a lot.

When I told Elijah he smiled from here to Sunday. "Jake, you and me are gonna have a fine time," he said. I told him I didn't know about that and he said, "Don't forget there's no slaves in Mexico. Why, we just might be free out there." I said I'd believe that when it happened and not before. The way I really saw it was I'd be dead before I got there and I wondered why the Good Lord wanted me dead. He didn't, I suppose, because I'm still here, but Elijah is long gone.

29

We failed to recognize the disaster foretold by the numerous minor and seemingly surmountable misfortunes plaguing the Santa Fe Expedition before its departure. Had the cumulative burden of these troubles struck all at once, Mirabeau would have had the good sense to delay things until the following spring. But the ill omens appeared piecemeal, so that each had seemingly been overcome before the arrival of its successor.

Illness forced Ned Burleson out of the expedition. Hugh McLeod cheerfully stepped into the breach, but not before several weeks of fine spring weather were wasted vainly awaiting Burleson's recovery. More time was lost when fever laid McLeod low too, although he recovered quickly. These delays meant that the hundred-man militia ate up much of their food supply even before starting out. In particular, the men went through several of Cazneau's beeves. The herd was already meager because of the larger than expected number of recruits. Cazneau purchased more, but not enough to compensate for what the men ate prior to departure.

During the delay, several merchants dropped out of the expedition. Charlie Horn cited the perishable nature of his goods, mostly dried fruit and flour brought up from Houston. Having already held his stock so long, he didn't believe the caravan would reach Santa Fe before spoilage set in. Buck Reynolds and Willie Cressman each claimed to have received offers on their merchandise too lucrative to refuse. Ike Clayton got homesick and went back to Brazoria. Appeals to patriotism failed to sway these men.

I particularly lamented Charlie Horn's departure because of the large sum of money he had offered to rent Jacob for the trip. I jumped to accept his proposal, for I was grievously short of funds when he made it. Jacob complained, but I remained firm and reassured him he would be all right. Now I would never see that revenue. As events unfolded, though, I realized what a stroke of luck that had been.

True tragedy struck when a young recruit named Andrew Jackson Davis accidentally shot himself. Davis was demonstrating the manual of arms to his comrades when his rifle's trigger caught on a flour sack. The gun discharged, sending a ball into his brain and killing him instantly. Mirabeau said that the letter he sent to the boy's family was the most difficult he had ever written.

Despite the setbacks, mid-June 1841 found the expedition ready to go. One sunny morning the soldiers marched from their various camps to the head of Congress Avenue. They organized by companies into two columns, the artillery bringing up the rear. A bugle blast sounded and Hugh McLeod led the men in a parade down the Avenue. Banners snapped in the breeze as onlookers cheered. Larger than all the rest was a deep blue flag bearing a white Texas star below the words "Santa Fe Pioneers." Made by the ladies of Austin, this banner was presented to McLeod by Mrs. Cazneau.

Mirabeau and Secretary of War Branch Archer waited at the end of the Avenue. People crowded under the shade of the live oaks to watch Mirabeau review the troops. The broad smile on his face sabotaged his attempts at solemnity. He delivered only a brief message of encouragement, but Archer rose to the occasion with a rousing and lengthy speech. As the soldiers returned to their camps, people pressed food and trinkets upon them. We expected an even more joyous parade with the expedition's triumphant return.

The Lord decided he didn't want me dead after all. Not two days after telling me I was going to Santa Fe Master Fontaine said I wasn't. Master Fontaine told me I could stop acting so childish now that I'd be staying in Austin. I thought this a hard thing to say since he wasn't going, so how did he know how it felt? When I told Elijah he just shook his head.

After that I wasn't too disposed to talk to Master Fontaine, and I didn't know if he'd come talk to me, so I thought I might miss that parade. I couldn't just walk over their without asking to go. But that morning I was out by my shack throwing a stick for a dog that was hanging around when here came Master Fontaine. "Well, aren't you going?" he asked and I threw the stick one more time and set in behind him. When we got there he went off to look for Mr. Lamar, and I joined up with some friends gathered around Jake Harrell's house down by the river where the parade would end. Just as the soldiers came near I saw Elijah come walking up from the river. "Soon you'll be marching with those boys," I said.

He didn't say nothing at first but just started snapping a twig he was carrying into tiny pieces. Then he said, "Jake, I gotta tell you, I don't wanna go."

"What are you talking about?" I asked him. "Just the other day you were strutting around like the only cock in the barnyard."

"I know," he said, "but I've been thinking about it since then. I was born over on the Brazos near Groce's and coming here to Austin's the farthest I've ever been. How are we gonna get all the way to Mexico from here?"

"That's no problem," I told him. "You just put one foot in front of the other like when you came here."

"I don't think I'm coming back, Jake. I had a dream where I was with some soldiers and all at once they were gone, leaving me alone in the desert with nothing to eat or drink. Suddenly, Indians were shooting arrows at me, so I took off running. I saw a man and hollered for him to help, but when he turned around he had an arrow in his eye."

"Then what?"

"Then nothing. I woke up. But I can't go on this trip, Jake. Somebody's gonna shoot me for sure. Else I'll starve to death or get eaten by a bear or Lord knows what else."

Right about then the soldiers reached us and everybody started cheering. I told Elijah he didn't have a thing to worry about because look at all those men with rifles that were going with him. He didn't say nothing. He looked sadder than an orphaned pup, and I thought he might cry. People started crowding around me so I had to move some, and when I looked for Elijah he was gone.

About a week later I accompanied Mirabeau, Branch Archer, and a few others up to Brushy Creek to see the expedition off. Mirabeau mingled with the men, chatting and smiling. Just before supper he gave a speech that was the best I ever heard from him. Gone was his usual nervousness in front of a crowd. He spoke with a confidence I had rarely seen him exhibit in public. When he finished, the men mobbed him to slap his back and shake his hand.

When the excitement abated he opened his pack and began preparing our meal. His polite refusals of assistance impressed everyone. "There's a man of the people!" they said. As darkness fell he reinforced this image by spreading out a bedroll to sleep in the open with the men. He told one, "Don't forget, not so long ago I was a soldier myself."

The expedition's departure was anticlimactic. Drab, gray clouds hung low overhead as McLeod gave the order for the wagons to move out. An hour passed before the last wagon lurched forward to lumber on its way. By then the head of the caravan had passed from view. The creaking of wagon wheels and shuffling feet of the oxen produced a dull, steady drone broken occasionally by shouting teamsters. The gay sound of men singing "Not a Drum Was Heard" drifted back to us as we watched the last wagons disappear over the horizon.

As I prepared my saddlebags for the ride back to Austin, Mirabeau approached and handed me the reins of his horse. "Will you take her back for me?" he asked. "I'm escorting some of the women back to town."

"Shall I ride with you?"

"No, go ahead. It will be a while before their wagons are ready."

"I'll wait. I'd like the company."

Mirabeau scowled but said nothing and walked off. I paid little attention to the dozen or so nearby wagons being prepared for the journey until I saw a particularly striking woman step into one of them. Mrs. Tucker. Her children bounded into the wagon bed, while Mirabeau climbed into the seat beside her. I caught Mirabeau's eye and gave a small wave that he ignored. My mind eased a bit when I saw Branch Archer take the reins of Mrs. Howard's wagon and several other government men do the same for other wives left behind by expedition participants. "Why wouldn't he help take the women back?" I asked myself. But he didn't escort just any woman. He escorted Mrs. Tucker.

How many times in my life did I get to liking somebody only to have 'em up and go somewhere else. I did the same thing to my momma and sisters, but I didn't have no say in that. Elijah didn't have no say either. I told myself he'd be back, but that was just wishing. Santa Fe's a long, long way from Austin. Even if they met no trouble I figured it'd take a year for them to get there and back. And there's always trouble. At least for a black man. That's why I try to stay in good with the Lord.

I thought once the men left there wouldn't be much for Master Fontaine to do, but there was. The town was all fired up about picking another president now that Mr. Lamar's time was almost through. A man couldn't be president twice in a row, so Mr. Lamar couldn't run. Vice President Burnet figured he was the man. I steered clear of him. He wasn't too hard with me, but he wasn't nice either. He always looked like he just spit out a lemon.

Sam Houston ran against him. Mr. Houston was about the nicest white man in Texas in my opinion. I heard a story about him where he bought a young boy just so he'd stop crying. Seems this boy had been split up from his momma a few days before and was bawling at the market like a lost calf. Mr. Houston laid down his money, put his arm around that boy, and told him he didn't need to cry no more because he was gonna take him home and take care of him. He did too, the way I heard it. That's the way he treated me and all the other slaves too, like he was no better than us. Even so, I couldn't say anything when Master Fontaine and Mr. Lamar talked bad about Houston. They hated that man. Burnet did too.

Anyway, Master Fontaine got real busy trying to help Burnet win the election. He'd sit down with Lamar and Burnet once or twice a week and they'd jaw all day and most of the night. Then Master Fontaine would be writing letters all the next day and maybe the next too. If letters could get a man elected president I reckoned Burnet had to win. I was happy to see all that letter writing because it meant more time for me to do what I wanted. Oh, I had chores like chopping wood and taking care of the animals, but there wasn't any extra work and I was happy. More time to fish and I caught plenty of 'em. The creeks were full, and one time I pulled a catfish out of the river that must have weighed a hundred pounds. Can't say he tasted good, but that was some big fish!

30

I honestly thought Burnet would win the 1841 presidential election. After all, Mirabeau had been swept into office to pursue his policy of westward expansion, a goal shared by virtually every voter in the country. David Burnet vigorously supported this policy. I saw no reason for voters to reject the man who would carry on the work Mirabeau had begun.

I believed this despite Sam Houston's entry into the race. What had Sam Houston accomplished since leaving the presidency? Nothing. He opposed Mirabeau's expulsion of the Cherokee, which made him less popular, not more. He fought against moving the seat of government to Waterloo, a move that the city of Austin's vitality and future prospects already justified. And he schemed against the recently departed Santa Fe Expedition, which at the time of the election seemed destined to bring glory and riches to the nation.

Burnet concocted a simple plan to achieve victory. "Just tell them the truth," he said. "Sam Houston is a lying drunkard who nearly ruined us once. Don't give him a second chance."

Mirabeau agreed, but with a note of caution. "The devil is notorious for fooling men over and over again. Houston is capable of that as well."

At Mirabeau's direction I helped Burnet draft a series of anonymous letters for publication in newspapers across Texas. Burnet signed them *Publius*; in them we laid out Sam Houston's character for public examination. "Where to begin?" one letter asked. "With the drunkenness that earned him the sobriquet among the Cherokee, The Big Drunk? With the cowardice that caused his hesitation at San

Jacinto? With the timidity that caused him to ignore multiple insults to Texas from south of the Rio Grande? Or the casual vindictiveness with which he has promised to 'desolate' the city of Austin that thrives despite his opposition?"

This latter charge stemmed from the testimony of several men who approached Burnet with the claim that Houston had bragged of removing government from Austin once he returned to the presidency. "I won't be satisfied until grass again grows in the streets!" he had reportedly proclaimed. Houston denied having said it—no surprise there—but his antipathy toward Mirabeau's frontier capital was well known. Mirabeau more than once expressed concern about the fate of the town should Houston win.

Houston countered with his own anonymous letters. He signed them *Truth*, but they were devoid of that commodity. He brazenly pointed with pride to his actions as president, as if defending savages and tolerating Mexican insults were proud accomplishments. He also leveled charges of drunkenness of his own against Burnet.

About two weeks before the election I decided to treat myself to a meal of buffalo steak at a restaurant on Congress Avenue. Log cabins and small framed structures had by then replaced the tents of early days. I had just entered one such establishment, pausing to allow my eyes to adjust to the dim light, when I heard that unmistakable voice. "Fontaine! Just the man I was hoping to see. Come join me."

There was no escape. The only other men in the place were playing cards at a small table cluttered with dirty dishes. I cursed my bad luck and joined Houston.

"Edward, I've just ordered up a rather hefty meal, but I believe Hoffman is well supplied today. How are you?"

"I'm doing well, Mr. Houston."

"Sam, call me Sam."

He gave me that ridiculous, broad grin that he used on Mirabeau when trying to pass himself off as a friend. When I said nothing, he launched into a tedious account of his predictions for the weather, followed by a more interesting tale concerning a horse race earlier in the day on the track outside of town. I murmured agreement here and there, striving to confine conversation to harmless topics. In vain, as it turned out.

"Edward, tell me something, what's going on in Burnet's mind?"

"What do you mean?"

"Those letters. Publius. What utter rot! Does he think to advance his cause with such nonsense?"

I suppressed a grimace. There was no avoiding a response. "Burnet is an honorable man. He believes what he writes to be true. And his letters do not go un-answered."

"Yes," he agreed. "They're answered by a more accurately named correspon-dent."

He must have seen my disgust at that remark for he asked, "Edward, what do you have against me? Why don't you like me?"

"Mr. Houston . . . Sam, I don't dislike you. We simply find ourselves on opposite sides of a political divide."

He thought about this a while before responding. "No. Lamar hates me, you can't deny that. I think some of that has rubbed off on you."

Remember the commandments, I thought, and tell the truth, hard as it may be. "Well, I don't hate you. But I've heard some disreputable things."

"Go on."

"Your marriage in Tennessee, for instance. You humiliated that poor woman."

"There's more to that tale than is generally known," he said with resignation. "As a gentleman, I've foresworn airing that dirty laundry."

"Then you lived with a Cherokee woman. You left her too."

He started to talk, but choked on his words as if he might cry. Finally, he said, "I still miss her."

"I shouldn't say anything more."

"I've heard worse. Don't stop now."

"Well, there's the drinking. And San Felipe being burned on your order. Then you wouldn't fight the Mexicans until you were forced."

"Ah, yes, the usual litany of charges. Maybe you haven't heard, but I've given up drink." Wash had told me that but I hadn't believed it. "It's true. I had to do it for Margaret. She's a beautiful thing, Edward, and I don't intend to lose her. Someday you'll meet such a woman and you'll understand."

I thought of Julia and took another bite of steak.

"As for San Felipe, have you ever seen proof that I ordered the town burned? You won't, because I gave no such order. And the retreat? Good God, Edward, if we had turned and fought Santa Anna with that pitiful excuse of an army before we reached San Jacinto we'd all be speaking Spanish and blessing the Pope! You saw those men. You were there."

"I saw men who wanted to fight."

"Wanting to fight and being able to fight are two different things. Hell, my dog wants to fight every bear and javelina that comes along, but if I let him, he'd have been torn to pieces long ago! Those men needed training. They needed time. And the only way to buy that time was to head east. You think I was *forced* to fight? Do you think I'm *afraid* to fight?"

He said this with rising voice and reddening face. I held my tongue for fear of provoking him further.

He grinned and said, "Like I told you, I've heard all of this before. Let me tell you something, Edward, if a man is going to be in public life he's got to learn to shrug off a lot of shit. That's Lamar's problem, too thin-skinned. With him, you're either a supporter or a traitor. Everything is black or white, good or evil. I know I can't convince you otherwise, but everything you've heard about me is false. Talk to Wash sometime, he'll tell you."

"I will, Mr. Houston."

"Call me Sam."

Mrs. Tucker kept on being friendly to me. Austin was a small place in those days, so if a man was out working on the street most everybody in town would see him at least once during the day. Mrs. Tucker always made sure to cross over and say good day to me, which set everybody to laughing and cutting up once she was gone. Once, though, she saw me by myself as I was taking Master Fontaine's money to Seiders Grocery and she said to me like she was asking about the weather, "Does your master ever talk about me, Jacob?"

I said, no, ma'am, not as I recollect, and she said, "Well, if he ever does you tell him I know the Bible as well as he does." I promised her I would and she looked at me kind of sad and said, "I'm a God-fearing woman, Jacob, you remember that." I was struck dumb. After a while she smiled and told me I'd best be on about my business.

Not two days later I was out in front of Master Fontaine's shack and up rode Lamar on a big horse. Instead of ignoring me like usual he got off his horse and reached in his saddlebag. He said, "Here, Jacob, I have a little corn whiskey that needs drinking and you might as well be the one to do it." He handed me the bottle and I thanked him and he said, "Be good, boy, and there's plenty more of that." To my way of thinking, that proved I hadn't made no mistake out behind Bullock's.

Somewhere along in there Mr. Houston came to town for a fancy dinner. I was cleaning fish for Mrs. Bullock and I could hear him and Mrs. Bullock in the house. Mrs. Bullock was telling him about the food she was gonna serve up at dinner the next day and he asked what she had planned for the colored folk. She didn't have nothing planned, she said. He told her that wouldn't do, that servants gotta eat too, and why don't you kill an extra hog and I'll pay for it. She said she would, but it seemed peculiar to her because coloreds can't vote so why would you wanna feed them? Maybe they can't vote, he told her, but they got stomachs the same as you and me. Things like that is why I didn't believe all the things I heard Mr. Lamar and Master Fontaine say about Sam Houston.

I did talk to Wash about Houston's drinking. We were at Loafer's Logs and he was reading a copy of *The Austin Spy*, a humorous bulletin left sporadically at the logs by an anonymous publisher. "Another congressman drunk at the faro table!" he cried out with glee. "Take a look."

Without glancing at the article I asked, "The Big Drunk?"

He turned serious. "No. And that's not funny."

"Publius thinks it is."

"Then Publius is a fool. I've told you before, Edward, Houston doesn't drink anymore."

"Oh, come now," I protested. "His alleged temperance is just a campaign ploy."

"Honest, it's not. You can believe it; it's absolutely true. His wife has worked a miracle."

"I believe that you believe it, Wash. I just have trouble believing it myself."

His face flushed with anger. "He's reformed, damn you. Besides, your boss is no saint himself."

My ire rose. "What do you mean?"

"Please, Edward, everyone knows the true purpose of this Santa Fe foolishness. It isn't a trade expedition at all; it's a plot to conquer New Mexico!"

Had the letter leaked out? "You don't know what you're talking about."

"I damn well do! And Lamar has lied about it from the beginning."

I squirmed, knowing this to be true. I tried to recall Mirabeau's justifications. "Every politician withholds information until its proper time," I said.

"But not every politician courts a married woman!"

I gasped with unconcealed horror. "That's a serious accusation, Wash!"

"I'm not accusing anyone of anything. I'm just telling you what's in this paper." He shook the copy of the *Spy* in his hand. "Is our gallant president sparking another man's wife?"

I couldn't believe what I was hearing. I jumped up and snatched the paper from his hand, crumpled it, and threw it at his feet. I turned and stomped away. But I didn't argue. I couldn't. I feared it was true.

That evening I attended a meeting of the Austin Lyceum in the Senate chamber at which an undercurrent of anti-Lamar sentiment previously unknown to me boiled over. The Lyceum existed to promote the intellectual development of the town. A typical program involved a speaker on either side of a topical issue addressing the audience, after which a general discussion ensued. The question posed at that night's meeting was "What is the destiny of Texas?"

Government clerk George Sinks addressed the crowd. His view mirrored that of Mirabeau's: a Texas empire would one day stretch from the Sabine to the Pacific. "The plum is ripe on the tree," he said. "It is the duty of the Anglo race to reach out and pluck it."

Silas Hendricks, a congressman from one of the eastern counties, immediately rose to challenge Sinks. "That fruit is rotten; pluck it at your peril!" he warned.

When Sinks protested that he hadn't finished, one audience member called out, "Don't want to hear it, George," whereupon several others chimed in to support Sinks.

Hendricks suddenly stood, grabbed his chair, and banged it forcefully to the ground. "It's the same old claptrap!" he cried. "It's what Lamar has been pushing on us all along. Send a trade mission to Santa Fe, he says, when what he's really doing is invading another country. There'll be *war* soon enough!"

Everyone shouted at once.

"By rights it's *our* country!"

"Our lands will be burned and our families killed!"

"Only cowards fear a fight!"

"Lamar is a tyrant!"

"Lamar is a despot!"

"Impeach Lamar!"

"Impeach, hell, let's tar and feather the bastard!"

Others tried to shout down this call to violence, only to be overwhelmed by a growing chant: *"Impeach! Impeach! Impeach!"* George Sinks stood helpless at the podium, waving his hands and vainly calling out, "Gentlemen, gentlemen!" When a scuffle broke out on one side of the room, two or three men began herding ladies out of the building. Fearing that someone in the impeachment crowd would see me as an appropriate target for anti-Lamar sentiment, I hurried outside as well. Even as I reached my house two blocks away the uproar continued.

I expected Mirabeau to dismiss that evening's events with the same facility that he had dismissed all prior criticism of his Santa Fe plans. Instead, though, as I told him what had happened, his brow furrowed and he began pacing the sitting room of his house. "Impeach me? For what? For taking what is ours? For leading this country to greatness? For bringing civilization's light to a *benighted land*?"

His ferocity surprised me.

"By God, Edward, they're a cowardly lot. They'll have their comeuppance, I promise you that! By the hand of God the righteous shall triumph and the wicked shall burn in hell!"

"Mirabeau, calm down," I said nervously.

He turned on me. "You as well? A coward? A fool? A . . . *a Houston man*?"

"Mirabeau, no! I'm with *you*!"

"You had supper with Houston just the other night! He's seduced you! Don't think I don't know. Did you believe I wouldn't find out?"

"That's not true! Yes, I had supper with him, but not by choice. He practically accosted me in the restaurant. I'm not a Houston man. I . . . I *hate* him as you do!"

This stilled his trembling, though his eyes flashed anger. "All right, Edward, I'll choose to believe you. But damn that man and damn those fools at the Lyceum last night. Impeach me. *Impeach me?* Is this what I've sacrificed so much for? To be handled so roughly?" He grabbed at his head and shook his hands so violently I thought it a wonder that he didn't cry out in pain. Turning his back on me, he strode forcefully from the room with a primal shriek. As he ascended the stairs he shouted, "They'll see, Tabitha, they'll see!"

That ruckus in the Capitol sure riled up the town. The next day white folks were saying they'd whip anybody that so much as looked at 'em cross-eyed. I was fetching water at the colored well on East Pine when Lilly walked by toting a load of sweet potatoes and hollered, "Jake, what did your master tell the president this morning?"

"What do you mean, woman?"

"Your master came up the hill this morning. He wasn't in the house more than five minutes before I heard Lamar hollering like he was fighting the devil. Then here comes your master out of the house. He's usually got a kind word for me or at least a 'Good day to you, Lilly,' but today he walked on by like I wasn't nothing but a cow."

Trying to make her laugh I told her don't be so hard on yourself, you ain't all that big, but she told me to shut up, she was serious. "That hollering went on a good long time. I heard things thumping in the house like he was throwing furniture down the stairs. I was scared, but I thought he might have hurt himself, so I went to the bottom of the stairs and hollered up is he all right. It got real quiet and then he said, 'I'm fine, Lilly, just fine, thank you,' like nothing was going on and he was just getting ready to go to church on Sunday. I went outside to finish hanging the clothes and soon here comes a bottle flying out the window to smash into a million pieces. So I wanna know, Jake, what did your master tell Lamar that boiled him up so much?"

I didn't know what Master Fontaine might have told Mr. Lamar, but I reckoned it had to do with what all the other white folks were so riled up about. I couldn't explain so I just said, "Lilly, I expect he told the president they're running out of silk sheets to give to the niggers," and this time she did laugh. She told me if I was to find out to come tell her, and I said I would. I never did find out, though. Later on I asked Master Fontaine how his day was going, and he told me fine like he was really telling me to mind my own business. That's what I was trying to do all along! Then he said, "It must be nice to live such a simple life." I asked him what he meant and he said, "You've no more worries than a child. I feed you and clothe you and take care of all your needs. If only I had it so easy!" What could I say to that? I'd heard such things before, how white folks was always calling us children and saying we were lucky to be taken care of so well. I never heard a black man say it, though, and I expect I never will. Even now. Yes, sir, I'd have changed places with him quicker than hot molasses, but don't you think he would have declined to make the swap?

31

I preferred to remain ignorant of the details of the relationship between Mirabeau and Mrs. Tucker, but it had become impossible to ignore the fact that they spent much time in each other's company. On the day of the election in September 1841 I encountered the two of them talking in front of the voting station at the treasury office. Three of the Tucker children played chase in the street while the youngest clung to his mother's skirt. Mirabeau and Mrs. Tucker chatted comfortably as I watched from across Congress Avenue. In contrast to his usual manner when conducting business about town, Mirabeau seemed in no hurry. I walked toward the voting station intending to pass them without comment. But as I approached, Mirabeau called out, "Going to vote, Edward? I've just done so myself."

"Yes, I'm about to."

Mrs. Tucker blushed beneath her bonnet and said, "Good day, Mr. Fontaine. We've just been discussing the election."

Mirabeau grinned uneasily. I said, "A popular topic today."

"Well, I must go," said Mirabeau. He bowed to Mrs. Tucker. "Good day to you, Madam. I'm afraid I must now attend to duty."

"Of course," she said. She gathered her children and left.

I moved toward the building, but Mirabeau stopped me by saying, "Edward, I was just being polite."

"I know. You've already told me she's just a friend."

"That's right, a friend. I have many friends about town."

"But only one that draws the attention of *The Austin Spy*."

I knew he had seen that paper; I had made sure of it. Instead of pursuing the subject, though, he said, "Take the rest of the day off, Edward. There's no work today."

I started to walk past him.

"And try to remember to vote for Burnet."

I did vote for Burnet. How could I not? But for every man who agreed with me there were three who bought Sam Houston's lies. Judging from that result, Burnet never really had a chance. Mirabeau had deluded himself. I had too. Even the city of Austin, which owed its existence to Lamar and the anti-Houston crowd, voted heavily in favor of the man intent on its destruction. Why, God, why?

I expected Houston's triumph to throw Mirabeau into melancholia. It didn't. He received the news with an equanimity that seemed out of character, especially after his recent explosion over the incident at the Lyceum. "The nation survived him once and will do so again," he said dismissively while perusing the official tally.

"But he opposes everything you've accomplished," I said in dismay.

He shrugged. "He can't bring the Cherokee back. People won't let him. The city of Austin has a secure foundation. It would be madness to destroy it, and I think him duplicitous, not mad. And the expedition is well on its way."

"There's been no word of its progress."

"All in good time, Edward. McLeod left three months ago. He must be in the vicinity of Santa Fe by now. The next communication we receive will undoubtedly be a gracious note from Governor Armijo thanking us for the invitation to come under our protection. Houston may prattle on about this or that, but no one will listen. Instead, they'll be busy passing resolutions in our honor and making plans for governing our new territory. Even Houston won't be able to stem the tide of expansion after that. No, there will be work to do. We'll clear the Colorado, expand coastal shipping, and construct warehouses here. A great metropolis will rise to take its place in the sun. The road to the Pacific will open before us as a beckoning paradise. No one can stop the stampede once it starts."

I thrilled at his optimism. "Then let's celebrate. I'll find Waller and a few others and we can discuss our bright future over drinks and cigars in your parlor."

"Nothing would please me more," he said a bit nervously. "But, uh, well, the thing of it is, I've promised Mrs. Tucker I would escort her on a ride to Barton's spring."

"Mrs. Tucker?"

"Yes, she desires to take her children to swim and fish in the spring. Also, I'm told Barton has two buffalo calves as pets that she wishes to see. She can't very well ride over there by herself."

"Of course not. She needs an escort and none will do but the president of the

Republic."

"I'm a simple citizen, Edward, who happens to be president at the moment. That's the nature of a democracy."

"And Mrs. Tucker is a married woman whose husband happens to be hundreds of miles away in Santa Fe on an expedition arranged by you."

"Edward, I am offended by your aspersions."

"What aspersions are those?"

"Don't be coy!" he said angrily. "You seem to find it inappropriate for a woman, excuse me, a *married* woman, to have the protection of an escort on her way across the river. You're implying that I purposefully sent her husband away so that I could spend time with her. You are, in effect, accusing me of adultery. *That* I will not abide!"

"I don't find it inappropriate for a member of the weaker sex to have protection. I find it . . . *convenient*."

"Then you slander and insult me! Must I demand satisfaction?"

Against the prospect of a duel with a man I admired, I collapsed. "Mirabeau, there's no need for that. I meant nothing and I retract what I said. I wish you a pleasant afternoon."

I left him there in his office looking as if he expected all to turn out well. Only moments before, I had felt that way myself. Now I wondered what was to become of him.

I called on Julia that evening feeling irritable and melancholy. She noticed right away. She asked, "Is it the election results? Are you sad to give up your job?"

"I'm worried about the future, but not my own. I'm worried what will happen now that Houston will be president."

She gave me a surprised look. "What's wrong with Sam Houston?"

"Don't you know that Houston and Lamar are enemies? He'll ruin everything we've tried to do."

"Oh, are you the co-president?" she asked with a laugh.

"You know what I mean," I snapped. "He's a corrupt, venal man."

She frowned. God, even her frown radiated beauty. "How can you say that? Do you know something the rest of us don't? I've heard nothing about Sam Houston being corrupt."

"Why would you? Are you the president's secretary? Do you attend Cabinet meetings? He'll be a ruinous president and that's a fact."

Her face darkened further. "Edward, I don't like your dogmatic tone. I can have opinions without attending Cabinet meetings. In my opinion, Sam Houston is a gracious man with sincere beliefs and many talents."

"You don't know him then. You'll see."

"You talk as if he's the devil. President Lamar is no saint, you know." I snorted derisively and she delivered a hammer blow. "He evidently cares little for a certain woman's reputation."

"That's . . . *hogwash!*"

"What's hogwash?"

"It's hogwash that he doesn't care for a woman's reputation."

She pounded her fists on the arms of her chair. I had never seen her so angry.

"I'm not talking about any woman's reputation; I'm talking about *one* woman's reputation. Mrs. Tucker's reputation, to be precise."

My stomach churned. I wanted to erase this whole conversation and start the evening over. "I . . . Mrs. Tucker . . . my God, Julia, are you deranged?"

"Edward Fontaine, don't you dare insult me in such fashion! This is a small town. Women talk. They know things that men don't. And the women I talk to say that Mirabeau Lamar and Mrs. Tucker are more than friends." She stood up. "I'm going inside. Good night!"

Rising quickly, I took her arm, but she shook me off. I tried to kiss her. She turned and my lips brushed her cheek. It was a poor kiss, and the last I ever had from Julia Lee.

Why did I care who was president? What difference would it make to me? Sam Houston or David Burnet, neither one would change my life. You could wake me up in the morning and tell me the devil himself was president and you know what? I'd still be a slave. Just another colored man bound to serve his white master. So why should I get all worked up about who the white folks chose to run things? Except I wanted Sam Houston to win. I liked him. Sure, he owned some slaves too, but I heard him say once that God was gonna figure out a way to put an end to all that. Slavery, I mean. And besides, I never forgot the story of him putting his arm around that boy and trying to get him to stop bawling. I don't believe I ever saw another white man touch one of us that way.

I never told nobody. Nobody white, that is. Not even Master Fontaine, though I suspect he would have said nothing about it. He wasn't the kind of man to pitch a fit when you don't agree with him. No, he usually just frowned some and bit his lip like he might say something but then he wouldn't. But I didn't tell him anyhow.

I told plenty of my own people. We talked about it a lot, even though none of us thought it made a redback's worth of difference. Most of us were for Houston, all but one or two field hands I knew. And they couldn't say just why they were for Burnet. Even Lilly said she'd vote for Houston if she could. But who would let a woman vote?

So when word reached Austin that Sam Houston had won, colored folks acted like the jubilee had come. Not in front of the white folks but out back behind the barn or when we were out chopping cedar. Here's how it was in those days. If you were colored and you saw a white man, you put on a face like you didn't know nothing about nothing, especially when it came to politics. See, if he was standing there talking to somebody about politics and he saw you, you didn't say nothing. And if he asked you something you'd tell him real polite that why would you know about that, all you're thinking about is what's for supper. I saw a man whipped once that forgot that.

Did God intend for me to open that letter from Rebecca? Or am I merely attempting to blame the Almighty for my own transgression? As he had done so many times before, mail carrier Jackson Peavey entered the executive office bearing a large pouch, which he deposited unceremoniously upon my desk. "There you go, Fontaine, all the news for the president from parts beyond," he said with a smile.

"Anything good in there, Jack?"

"How should I know? I just haul 'em; I don't read 'em."

"What's the news from down Houston way?"

"Well, let me see. Some jackass of a preacher informed the gamblers that they're on the road to eternal damnation, but the faro tables are just as crowded as ever. Enos Tadlock pulled a two-headed fish out of Buffalo Bayou. And Harvey Cooper lost a bet and had to ride a donkey down Main Street wearing nothing but his skivvies."

"What was the bet?"

Peavey laughed. "Son of a bitch said he could piss from one side of the bayou to the other. Once his pals took the bet he said he could only do it after drinking a bottle of whiskey. They ponied up for the booze, which old Harvey poured down his gullet."

"And?"

"We all marched down to the bayou for Harvey to make good. Well, he unbuttons his fly—we checked first to make sure there were no women around—and Harvey whips out the trouser snake and starts pissing."

"How far did he make it?"

"About as far as I can spit. Then Bob Pennock starts laughing; Harvey gets mad and turns on him and sprays piss on half a dozen men in the process! Well, that set loose the wildcats! Once everybody calmed down, though, Harvey said he coulda done it if Pennock hadn't laughed. Nobody believed him, especially the ones that got pissed on, and they had the donkey right there too. After a full bottle of whiskey Harvey was in no shape to put up much of a fight, so off came his britches and before he knows it he's riding down the street in his long johns!"

"That ought to teach him not to make foolish bets."

"Who's foolish? Harvey got himself a free bottle of whiskey."

Jack Peavey left, but his story had me laughing as I began going through the letters he brought. Distracted, I opened one and began reading:

> Dear Father, how delighted I am to hear that you have made such a wonderful friend as Mrs. Tucker.

Stupidly, I wondered who would address me as "Father" and kept reading.

> That she bears such resemblance to my dear mother fills me with a desire to lay eyes upon her myself. How fortunate for her that she has you to sustain her while her husband is away on the grand expedition to New Mexico.

Now I knew the letter was for Mirabeau from his daughter. I'm ashamed to say I couldn't force my eyes from the page.

> Your description of her fair countenance and kind nature renders her an angel in my imagination. I thank God that He has blessed you with a friend to combat your loneliness.

I refolded the letter, applied a new wax seal to it, and placed it in a pile of papers set aside for Mirabeau. What was I to do? What more proof did I need that Mirabeau had transgressed the bounds of decent behavior? Yet how could I act upon knowledge gained so disgracefully?

My eyes drifted to the letter. Surely Mirabeau wouldn't have confided full details of an illicit relationship with Mrs. Tucker to his daughter. Even so, for Rebecca to refer to the woman in such glowing terms indicated that Mirabeau had at least done *that* in his letters. And if he had possessed feelings for Mrs. Tucker as he organized the expedition, had he indeed singled out her husband as an expedition member solely for the purpose of removing a rival from the scene? Furthermore, just where *had* he come up with the money to pay for the men to go to Santa Fe? Why didn't he publicly reveal the true purpose of the mission, to bring the New Mexico territory into our fold? Had he sent three hundred men to risk the wrath of the Mexicans without telling them of the risk? He had no proof that Governor Armijo would receive the men favorably. Only the word of an American merchant supported this claim. Was Mirabeau secretly hoping for the mission's failure so that Dennis Tucker would never return?

Such thoughts tortured me as I struggled against the temptation to read the rest of Rebecca's letter. The opportunity slipped away when the door to the office again banged open. "Good Lord, Fontaine, you look as if you just ate a piece of rotten meat."

It was Wash Miller.

"Oh, hello, Wash. What do you want?"

"Well, *that's* a friendly greeting!"

"Sorry, I was just thinking about something."

He pulled up a chair. "I'm here for you, friend. Tell me all about it."

He had approached at just the right moment, by which I mean precisely the wrong moment, I suppose, for me to ignore common sense and unburden myself. I told him everything. Mirabeau's infatuation with Mrs. Tucker. His targeting of Dennis Tucker as an expedition member. His flippant attitude about the lack of congressional funding for the expedition. The secret letter to Governor Armijo. When I had finished, I sat back in my chair and breathed a heavy sigh.

Wash said, "You didn't mention Bradford."

"Bradford? Bottle Bradford? Why should I have mentioned him?"

Wash shook his head. "Poor you. So many of your ideals exploded, and now I'm about to blow up another one."

"What are you talking about?"

"I'm talking about Bradford and James Collinsworth. I'm talking about the time that Bradford took Collinsworth on a weeklong, all-expenses-paid bender. Poor Collinsworth got so drunk that he fell off a boat into the water. Or jumped, depending on who's telling the story. Only now if you're lucky enough to be a fly on the wall when Bradford is in his *own* cups you hear a different tale. You hear Bradford boasting about Stephen Everitt pressing a large load of cash onto him with instructions to take Collinsworth drinking. You hear him say that Mirabeau Lamar was there when Everitt did it. And when Bradford took his leave, Everitt remarked that if something happened to Collinsworth while he was drunk, no one would say it was anything but his own fault. And if you're there just before Bradford passes out blind drunk you might hear him sob and say that Collinsworth didn't fall or jump off that boat. No, Bradford pushed him. He pushed him into the bay and watched the poor bastard sink like a rock, may God forgive his sorry soul. And that, my friend, means that our self-righteous president had such an easy time of it in the election not through accident but because a chief rival was murdered. And while the Honorable Mr. Lamar didn't commit the deed, he was indirectly responsible for it and has known about it all along."

"That's . . . impossible."

"Is it? Come now, Edward, everyone knows that Peter Grayson was mentally unstable, but James Collinsworth? He was the happiest man you've ever met. He did *not* kill himself!"

"He fell," I said with waning conviction.

"No, he didn't. I can't prove it was murder, of course, but I was one of three people in Dolson's one night a month ago. There was me, Bradford, and Bradford's cousin from Tennessee. Dolson had gone out back to take a piss and Bradford was drunk enough to think there was no one left in the building but him and his cousin. I was that fly on the wall, Edward. I heard Bradford tell his cousin that he pushed Collinsworth. I heard his cousin whistle and say, 'By God, Terrence, I didn't know you had it in you.' That was the last thing either one of them said before passing out. I got up and left and haven't told anyone about it. Until now."

"Why tell me?"

"Because you're so goddamned infatuated with Mirabeau Lamar and his saintliness. Your news doesn't shock me or even surprise me. In fact, it pales against this."

I suddenly recalled Bradford's visit to my room in Houston and his warning of what would happen if Mirabeau didn't find him a position. Unfazed, Mirabeau had merely indicated he would talk to Everitt. And Everitt's only comment was that money could solve almost any problem in politics. Everitt obviously had bought Bradford's silence. "Oh, my God."

"My God, indeed. The tragedy is that because he seems convinced he has Heaven's blessing he allows himself any action which furthers his goals. Santa Fe, for instance. Have you heard anything good from Hugh McLeod lately? Of course not. You won't either. Mirabeau Lamar sent three hundred men on a fool's errand that will kill them all."

"He truly believes in the value of the mission," I said in protest.

Wash laughed. "Spare me! The things you've told me today prove that what he truly believes is not half as important as what he actually does."

"Wash, please," I pleaded. "I'd like to be alone."

As he stood to leave he took a parting shot. "James Collinsworth was murdered. Think about *that* the next time you complain of 'the Big Drunk' to me!"

Master Fontaine was a different person after that election. At first I thought he was mad about Sam Houston winning, but why would he take that out on me? One morning he saw me taking off for the river with my fishing pole and he hollered that he had things for me to do instead. I made a joke about fishing being more important than any chore and he said, "Don't sass me, Jake!" Another time I dropped some dishes I was carrying out of his place to wash and they broke. He came over and pushed me down and cursed and called me a "stupid nigger." Now, white folks treated their slaves like that all the time but not Master Fontaine. I knew that something was bothering him, but still I didn't think he should be laying hands on me and talking to me like that. I just wished I knew what was wrong so I could try and set it right.

I was waiting for him to change back to his old self and maybe tell me I did a good job grooming his horse or talk Bible stories with me like he used to. But he got worse and worse until I thought he was no different than any other slave-owning white man. And maybe he wasn't. But it wasn't like Master Fontaine to be that way. I prayed and prayed for the devil to let him be.

I couldn't bear to attend Sam Houston's inauguration. I heard later that someone had rigged up a telegraph wire from the Capitol to the armory on Water Street. The instant that Houston took his oath of office a signal flashed across the wire for the men at the armory to fire a cannon blast, which I heard at my house several blocks from the Capitol. As the crowd's cheers reached my ears I morosely put on my hat and headed toward the president's office. Julia's certainty about Mirabeau and Mrs. Tucker weighed heavily upon me as I walked.

I intended only to retrieve the last of my personal effects before Sam Houston took possession of the office. Remembering that I had lent Mirabeau several pens and a bottle of ink I opened his desk drawers one by one until I found them. They sat on a stack of papers neatly assembled at the bottom of the drawer. At the top of the first page I saw the words "To Martha."

Martha was Mrs. Tucker's first name. I gingerly picked up the page and began reading. It was a poem, written in Mirabeau's stylish hand. Many of the words had been scratched out with other words scribbled in tiny letters underneath. One whole section of the page had a large "X" marked over it.

After all this time I can't recall the entire poem, but I do remember specific words and phrases, and they were damning. "Fair, beautiful Martha" appeared several times. The words "your fair breast" were used to rhyme with "my pounding chest." Another line included the phrase "our hearts beat as one." But the phrase that appeared over and over to burn a hole in my own heart was "our love so blessed and cursed."

I carefully placed the piece of paper back in the drawer. Gathering my ink and pens, I walked outside and paused on the porch. I felt hot. My hands shook as I withdrew a kerchief from a pocket to wipe my face. "Oh, Mirabeau," I said softly as cheers resounded from the Capitol. As I walked back to my house someone hailed me and said happily, "Hey, let's go to the barbecue!" I walked on in silence.

This time I didn't ask Master Fontaine about going to the inauguration, I just went. I figured he couldn't hardly be any madder at me than he was, so I didn't care what he might do. I looked for him to be hanging around Mr. Lamar but never saw him.

After all the fine speeches, I wandered over to the barbecue. Lilly was one of the women serving up the food. I slipped up behind her when there wasn't anybody near and said, "Hey, Lilly, how about a little taste?" She smiled at me, threw some beans and pork onto a plate, and handed it over. Then she told me to leave before the white woman in charge saw me.

I found a tree to sit under where some of the other slaves had gathered. A boy named Thaddeus asked me where I got the food and when I told him he said, "Aw, she won't give me none. I tried to kiss her once, and she slapped me." After I was finished I snuck the plate back to Lilly and started walking home.

From up the street I saw Master Fontaine sitting on the steps of his house. He had his head down and his hat in his hands. When I got closer I could hear him talking to himself.

"Master Fontaine," I told him, "I'm back from the inauguration. Is there anything you need me for?"

"The inauguration," he said. "Oh, yeah, that." He looked up at me. His face was red and shiny, like he was crying. "I don't suppose so, Jacob. You go on."

As bad as he'd treated me lately I felt bad for him. "Master Fontaine, are you all right?" I asked.

His eyes turned mean when I said that. He plopped his hat on his head and stood up. "Just get out of here," he said. "Go on, leave me alone." As I left I wondered if I'd ever hear another nice word from him.

32

As Sam Houston assumed the presidency we still awaited word from Hugh Mc-Leod and the Santa Fe Expedition. The braggadocio of the town folk had waned; one rarely heard the expedition mentioned on the street any longer. There was occasional newspaper speculation, but only about when a letter would arrive and not about the expedition's outcome, which was still expected to be favorable. Mirabeau remained confident. "A thousand things can delay a letter," he told anyone asking. "Everything will be fine."

I hadn't confronted Mirabeau about the poem I found in his desk. Part of me was afraid of revealing that I had been snooping. The rest of me, I'm ashamed to admit, was simply afraid. And I was preoccupied with the possibility of losing Julia, which, in fact, was already reality.

I ran all sorts of scenarios through my head about how such a confrontation with Mirabeau would play out. All of them ended horribly. And it wasn't hard to find excuses to delay. I had to pack. Mirabeau was busy. I should be looking for future employment. The result was complete inactivity on my part.

Ultimately, a notice in *The Daily Bulletin* rendered anything I might do pointless.

GOVERNMENT PROPERTY TAKEN

The person who has taken away without leave, from the late president's dwelling, one mattress, one pillow, one bolster, and two linen sheets marked "Lamar," will return the same without delay, otherwise a prosecution will be instituted—the present executive not being disposed to encourage such practices.

I saw this as a harmless, if unfunny joke, but Mirabeau felt he had been publicly accused of thievery. He charged into my room waving the paper about so violently as to drive any thoughts of his relationship with Mrs. Tucker from my head.

"Look at this, Edward! Just look! He's calling me a thief!" he shouted indignantly.

"Who's calling you a thief?" I asked as I took the paper from his hand. He had circled the offending passage with a red pencil and underlined "such practices" with several bold strokes.

"Oh, I saw that already. I thought it merely a joke," I told him.

"A joke? This is public slander! He's questioned my honor!"

"Whiting wouldn't do that. Sure, he's a Houston man, but he's just poking fun." Whiting was Samuel Whiting, the newspaper's editor and a Houston supporter, but also a fair man.

"Not Whiting. *Houston!* This is Sam Houston's work! How else would Whiting even know that I removed anything? Anything I took was *mine*, Edward. Why would I stoop to taking a few pillows? He knows that! He's intentionally slandering me!"

I disagreed but was smart enough not to say so at that moment. He raged a few more minutes before saying, "He won't get away with it, by God. I'll make him pay!" And he left.

I didn't witness what happened next but heard it from Wash. Houston was behind Bullock's with Wash and several others, mostly members of the new government, when Mirabeau found him. He charged into the middle of the group, held the paper out, and said angrily, "You're behind these words, aren't you, *Mr. President*?" He spat the words "Mr. President" as if they were poison.

"You mean that trifle in the *Bulletin*? I had nothing to do with it. I'll admit, I laughed a bit when I read it, but I think that was the point."

Mirabeau was unfazed. "I expected you to deny it. As usual, the truth is foreign to you. But you won't get by with it this time."

"Get by with it?" According to Wash, Houston seemed genuinely surprised. "Trust me, Mirabeau, Whiting wrote those words, not me."

"Trust *you*? I don't trust a word out of your mouth! You're a liar, Houston. A goddamned liar."

"Now hold on there, friend, those are heavy words."

"I'm not your friend. And now, *you're* president. That's what tears me up. *You*, such a despicable man, are now in charge of our nation. You'll ruin everything. Tear it all down just to spite me."

Ned Burleson tried to intervene. "Mirabeau, you need to reconsider. Do you realize what you're saying?"

"God damn it, Ned, yes! This man will ruin us all. He's a liar, a drunk, and a cheat!"

No one spoke. Mirabeau stared venomously at Houston, who remained calm and finally said, "Tear what down, you jackass? This?" He waved his arms in the air. "Austin? Why would I tear it down? Sure, you were an utter fool to build it, but you frittered away what little money was in the treasury to do so. Even if I wanted to dismantle this place I couldn't, because *you* have bankrupted us."

"There'll be money soon enough."

Houston laughed. "From Santa Fe? From those poor bastards you sent off into the wilderness? From the expedition we haven't heard from in months? We'll be lucky if the worst that happens is everyone involved ends up broke. Anyone with the sense of a mule knows that. I just hope those men aren't already dead."

"Sir, you are beneath contempt to wish those men dead."

"I didn't wish them dead, you idiot, I said I hoped they *aren't* dead."

They stared at each other a long while. Mirabeau broke the silence. "What did I expect from such a man as you? Truth? Honor? From a man who abandoned not one wife, but two? Who fled his duty in Tennessee to go live with Indians? *Indians!* And even *they* called you 'The Big Drunk.'"

"I don't know if you've heard, Lamar, but I've given up drink."

"So *you* say. But judging from your aversion to truth I'd guess you're still no stranger to the whiskey jug. You're an evil man, Houston. The fires of hell await you."

"Lamar, you've taken leave of your senses. You dare threaten me with hell even as you carry on an illicit affair with another man's wife?"

Wash said that Houston might as well have struck Mirabeau with an iron rod, so stunned did he appear. Two of the men broke away from the group and left the yard. The rest maintained a shocked silence.

"Don't act so surprised, Lamar. Did you really think it could go unnoticed in such a small place as this? People notice. People talk."

Mirabeau regained enough composure to speak. "You're impugning the reputation of an innocent woman."

"Tell me this, Lamar. Why did you seek out Dennis Tucker for the expedition?"

"He . . . he's an excellent blacksmith."

"I'm sure he is. And there are about fifty other 'excellent blacksmiths' in town. Why Tucker? I'm not aware of any other blacksmiths being approached by the president of the nation. What was so special about that one?"

An innocent man would have had an explanation. An innocent man would have defended a woman's honor to the point of exhaustion. An innocent man would have demanded satisfaction through a duel. But an innocent man would *not* have fled the scene. Which is precisely what Mirabeau did.

I was digging a drainage ditch over at the Capitol when I heard a man shout, "Jacob, you're just the man I wanted to see." It was Sam Houston, walking toward me with his hand out like he was gonna shake mine. No white man had ever shook my hand before, not even Master Fontaine, so at first I just stood there. Then I saw he wasn't fooling, so I put my hand out too. I just hoped nobody saw it that might give me trouble later on, but everybody was rushing this way and that so they didn't notice, I suppose. Mr. Houston asked me if I knew how to drive a wagon and I said I sure did, I used to drive back in Mississippi, and I reckoned I hadn't forgot. He said, well, that's fine, and then talked about the weather a bit and started to go on his way. Then he said he wasn't talking about no farm wagon but a carriage that a lady and her children could ride in. I told him if it had four wheels and was pulled by a critter with four legs then I could drive it. He said how fine that was again and off he went. That made no sense until later.

33

Mirabeau said he was planning on going back to Oak Grove as soon as he could wrap up his affairs in Austin. I had planned on confronting him about the poem but couldn't muster the courage to tell him I had been snooping in his desk drawers. Then Wash told me about the scene with Houston and I dropped the idea. I figured that if everybody in town already knew of the affair, there was no point in my bringing it up. That was probably true, but I'm not proud of how quickly I accepted this as an excuse for inactivity.

Mirabeau continued telling everyone within earshot that the mission to Santa Fe would result in a great triumph. The longer we went without word from McLeod, though, the more people lost faith. Sure, they smiled and nodded politely as Mirabeau spoke of Santa Fe, but I could see the doubt in their eyes. Or maybe it was fear for friends and loved ones. Mirabeau remained oblivious. He saw only the smiles.

Rumors drifted into town. A man just arrived from Galveston said he heard from a ship's captain that a great battle had been fought on the outskirts of Santa Fe. The Texans had prevailed and were in the process of forming a new government for the territory. Another man from St. Louis had met an American trader in that city who swore that the Texans had stormed Santa Fe, captured Governor Armijo, and clapped him in irons. Yet another said there had been no battle. Instead, Governor Armijo himself had ridden out to greet the Texans and invite them into the city for a great feast, during which he proclaimed his love for the Texas republic.

Then a mail pouch brought a copy of the *Colorado Gazette and Advertiser* to town, in which we saw this:

There is a rumor in town that the Santa Fe Expedition has been captured. It is said to have been derived from a Mexican journal which purports to give the particulars of the capture, and says that they were taken without the firing of a gun.

Of course, no one believed this. "McLeod surrender without a fight?" people asked incredulously. Some conceded the possibility of defeat but insisted it would have required an army of three or four thousand Mexican soldiers. And everyone insisted that no Texian would surrender until his ammunition ran out.

One early morning I answered a knock at my bedroom door to find Ned Burleson standing before me. I was about to go to breakfast, but when I invited him to join me he said, "I think I should tell you this privately." I offered him the single chair in my room and sat on the bed.

"Edward, we received a letter yesterday through Colonel Flood." Colonel Flood was the American envoy. He roomed at Bullock's. I had often seen him rushing up and down Congress Avenue from one government department building to the next. "By the time we read it and talked it over it was after midnight, so we decided to wait until this morning to come to you."

"Why me?"

"Because you're Mirabeau's closest friend."

I flinched at that, given that I wondered whether we remained friends at all, much less close friends.

"Flood has a letter from the American Secretary of State Daniel Webster that verifies McLeod's surrender."

Despite the doubts about the expedition that had been creeping into my thoughts, this news surprised and horrified me. "Why?" I asked.

"Why? Who knows? All we know for sure is that the whole force was captured by the Mexicans. They're being marched to Mexico City as we speak."

"The whole force?"

"Everyone that didn't die in the desert. About a dozen men did. There's a list."

"A list," I said. My brain felt sluggish, refusing to process what I was hearing. "Who's on it?"

"I don't know. Houston's got it."

"Why are you telling *me*?"

"I already said, because you're Mirabeau's friend. This will devastate him. You know how important this was to him."

"I do." I did. It was everything. It was the second step toward his Texian empire, the construction of Austin being the first. The expedition and the subsequent acquisition of New Mexico were to be his legacy. The expedition still would, but only as a mark of failure.

We sat there in silence. I wished for Burleson to speak, because I didn't know what to say. But he only stared at the floor, watching a spider run to and fro between us. Finally, he reached out a foot to squash the bug and said, "I'd best be getting back. You'll tell him, won't you?"

I nodded glumly and watched him go.

I dreamed about Santa Fe. I'd never been there and didn't know what it looked like, but when I'd wake up I'd feel like I'd been there a hundred times. There was a big white church building on one side of a square. All around the square were smaller brown buildings made of smooth rock walls, some of them with poles sticking out in a line along the top. There were people everywhere, some walking around; some sitting on the ground selling blankets and jewelry and other such things. My dream was always the same. I'd be walking along with Elijah looking at the blankets and jewelry when suddenly I couldn't see him no more. I'd ask everybody where he was, but they wouldn't answer. Then they'd all go into the church. I'd go too, and when I'd get inside there was Elijah laid out on the altar. Some of the people would be crying, but most would be laughing and pointing at him. I'd cry too but someone would say, "It's just a nigger," and when I'd go up closer to the body there'd be wolves all around it chewing the bones. I'd look up where Jesus was nailed to the cross and he'd say, "He's with me now, Jake." I never got no further than that.

One time I told Master Fontaine about that dream. He said dreams don't mean anything and I should pay it no mind. "But Jesus talked to me," I said, and he said for all I know it could have been the devil acting like he was Jesus. I told him it had to be one or the other; either dreams don't mean anything or it was the devil or Jesus or somebody trying to tell me something. He got a bit riled and said, "Enough of your African superstitions, Jacob!" That ended that. I wanted to tell him I've never been to Africa, I lived my whole life in Mississippi and now Texas, but I thought better of it.

After Burleson left, my head was swimming. I couldn't think of a way to break the news to Mirabeau, so I went to breakfast. Everyone at the table was talking and joking as usual, but I could only look down at my plate and eat. Someone finally said, "Edward, if I didn't know better I'd say you were working off a mean drunk, but I've never seen you with a bottle. Is something wrong?"

"No, everything's fine," I lied and kept eating. Once conversation moved on I pushed back from the table and left.

Mirabeau had moved out of the president's house and taken a room at Mrs. Eberly's on West Pecan. I found him in his room sorting clothes into stacks for packing. "Good morning, Edward," he said tersely, with barely a glance in my direction.

"Good morning. May I sit down?"

As there were no chairs in the room he motioned to a large, closed trunk, upon which I took a seat.

"I'm sorry about what happened with Houston," I said.

He glared at me for several seconds before replying. "I suppose you want another explanation."

"No, I'm not here about that." I struggled to find the right words. "Ned Burleson came to see me this morning. He says they've received a letter from the American secretary of state through Colonel Flood. The letter says that the Santa Fe men have all been captured."

He stopped sorting clothes and sat on the bed. A wasp buzzed at the single open window and Mirabeau reached up to push the shutter closed. "More rumor, Edward," he said.

"Burleson doesn't think so. Neither does Houston or anyone else who's seen the letter."

"I didn't think Ned so gullible."

"Mirabeau, it's true. This isn't a rumor. Some men have even died. . . . There's a list."

He paused to think this over. He began going through the clothes again. "A list, eh? Well, then, that makes it official," he said sarcastically. When I remained silent he added, "Do you really believe it?"

"I'm sorry to say that I do. We should have heard something from McLeod weeks ago. Now I think we know why we didn't."

He stared at the bed. Picking up a shirt, he wound it into a rope and twisted it upon itself. He gripped it so tight that his face turned red. Then he relaxed, straightened out the shirt, and folded it neatly before placing it on one of the piles. I stood to go.

"Tell Ned . . . tell Ned . . . oh, *hell.*"

"Mirabeau, I'm sorry."

"And what good is that?" The loud volume of his voice startled me. I moved toward the door.

"Don't leave. Tell them . . . I didn't do anything wrong."

"All right." I left the room

"Nothing, damn it. *Not a thing!*"

• • •

I can still see those boys marching down Congress Avenue. Oh, they had some kick in their step, let me tell you. People laughing and cheering like they were going on a picnic and instead they were heading off to the dungeon or worse. Once I heard the news that they weren't coming back, at least not any time soon, I started praying for Elijah. I prayed for all the others too, but I prayed hardest for my friend. There'd been all sorts of rumors about the mission, but most of it sounded like just that, rumors. I didn't pay it no mind. But then I heard there was a letter from somebody in the American government. I didn't believe somebody like that would write a letter about rumors and most nobody else did neither. So it had to be true. There was a list of those who got killed, but they didn't put that up for me to see. I believe they just went around telling their kinfolk. I wasn't kin to Elijah, so nobody would have come to me or anyone else in Austin that I knew of. His master had gone too, so there was nobody who cared. Except me. And I never found out for sure, I just know that I never saw Elijah again, not even to this day. Maybe when the Mexicans captured everybody they saw that Elijah was a slave and set him free. I tell myself that's what happened, but I can't really believe it. My dream was too powerful. I just hope the wolves didn't really get his bones. And I don't believe that was the devil in my dream neither. I believe it was sweet Jesus himself telling me that Elijah was safe with him up in Heaven. Thank you, Lord Jesus, is all I've got to say.

I didn't know whether Mirabeau believed what I had told him but, frankly, I didn't care. Time proved it true, and that's all that matters. Most everyone else in Austin believed it, as I found out that morning after I left Mrs. Eberly's. A larger crowd than usual surrounded Loafer's Logs, and the men spoke of nothing but Santa Fe. Their grim faces told me that few believed the report to be anything but the truth. Even David Burnet, the staunchest of Mirabeau's allies, shook his head when he saw me and said, "It's a sad day, Edward."

From Loafer's Logs I walked all the way to the river—what else was there to do?—where I sat under the same live oaks that had shaded the men of the Santa Fe Expedition at the end of their parade down Congress Avenue. Some men carrying fishing poles walked past me on their way to the river. One of them was Dan Hornsby, whom I hadn't seen since my first visit to Waterloo. He recognized me and, after chatting with me a bit, invited me to tag along. "No, thanks," I told him, and returned to my melancholy. Then I saw some young boys throwing rocks at a group of cattle grazing a block or so up Water Street, so I walked over and made them stop.

Now that I was back on my feet I headed back up the Avenue. As I neared Pecan Street I noticed Mirabeau standing on the edge of the group gathered at Loafer's Logs. I hung back a bit, as I had no wish to speak to him at that moment. Suddenly, a woman screamed from across the street, "Mirabeau!"

All eyes turned toward the source of the scream, which was none other than Martha Tucker. Her two youngest children were at her side. She took them in hand and dragged them across the street, stopping when she reached Mirabeau. She was crying.

"Oh, God, Mirabeau. What have you done? What have you done?"

I'm quite certain that people blocks away could hear Mrs. Tucker clearly, so loud was her voice and so quiet had the crowd become. Mirabeau gaped in surprise, looked around at the crowd, and said, "Mrs. Tucker. What can I do for you?"

Mrs. Tucker let go of her children and raised trembling arms. Tears streamed down her face. "Oh, God, Mirabeau, he's dead. *He's dead!* He's on the list, and he's *dead!*"

"Mrs. Tucker, please, can we speak about this privately?" Mirabeau pleaded. She ignored him.

"You killed him. He wasn't going to go, I told him *not* to go, but then *you* asked him. He said if the president asks you to do something, you have to do it. So he went. And now he's dead."

"Mrs. Tucker, I'm sorry."

"Stop calling me 'Mrs. Tucker.' You never call me that. Call me 'Martha,' like you do when you come by the house. 'Martha, Martha, he'll be fine,' that's what you said. You *promised* he'd come back safe. You promised we'd have a better life because of it, and now he's dead. Now my children don't have a father, and I don't have a husband. Who's going to take care of us now?" Her words were difficult to understand, given the barely controlled sobs that punctuated each phrase.

Mirabeau blushed ferociously but said nothing. Everyone stared, first at him, then at her, then back at him again. Heads poked out of windows and doorways. Passersby stopped in their tracks; men no longer worked at loading wagons; even children stopped their games to watch. Mirabeau took a step back but otherwise remained stiff as a tree. Then another step, then a half-turn, and a few more steps, and then he was briskly striding away from the scene. Mrs. Tucker whimpered as he left. The crowd maintained a shocked silence. Finally, Mrs. Cazneau broke away from the crowd at the logs and approached Mrs. Tucker, who buried her face against Mrs. Cazneau's chest. Mrs. Cazneau beckoned to her husband for assistance, and the two of them took Mrs. Tucker and her children home.

• • •

Once we heard about Santa Fe, everything got real quiet. Used to be you'd walk up the Avenue and hear men laughing and carrying on up and down the street. The news put a stop to all that. If I heard anything it was ladies weeping and wailing and folks talking sorrowful. Even them that didn't have no kin taken prisoner walked around like their best hunting dog just died. And everybody had a bad word for Mr. Lamar. Mr. Fontaine told me it wasn't all his fault, but he must have been the only man in town to think so.

You'd think that a man that everybody was saying bad things about would lay low, but not Mr. Lamar. He went out walking the town like usual. Then Mrs. Tucker found him and lit into him pretty good. I was mending a fence for Mrs. Eberly about a block off the Avenue, and I could hear her plain as day from way over there. Her husband was killed by the Mexicans, and she blamed Mr. Lamar. But more than that, she talked like she and Mr. Lamar was more than just friends. I already knew that, but I hadn't told anybody except Master Fontaine, and I'm pretty sure he kept that to himself. Now the whole town knew. After that Mr. Lamar just sort of disappeared.

34

After the scene with Mrs. Tucker, Mirabeau couldn't stay in Austin and he knew it. Still, he had several loose ends to tie up, so he was still with us when yet another letter bearing terrible news arrived. I learned of it after receiving an urgent summons from Mrs. Eberly, who greeted me at the entrance to her boardinghouse.

"Mr. Fontaine, I'm glad you could come," she said grimly. "I didn't know who else to tell. I think Mr. Lamar is sick. He's been in his room since yesterday morning and he's only come out to use the privy. I asked him if he wanted something to eat, and he walked past me like I wasn't there. This afternoon I knocked on his door to see if he was all right and he told me to go away. That's not like him; he's usually so polite."

I was beginning to think Mirabeau had no other friends in town, so often were people asking me to intervene on his behalf. "I'll talk to him."

I walked down the hall to his room, paused briefly at the door, and knocked.

"*Thank you*, Mrs. Eberly, I'll not need supper tonight," Mirabeau called from within.

"Mirabeau, it's me. Edward. Mrs. Eberly asked me to check on you."

I heard the creak of the bed as he rose. He opened the door. His forlorn, disheveled appearance startled and frightened me. He stared at me for several seconds before saying, "Come in."

I sat on the same trunk from which I had given him the news of Santa Fe. He collapsed on the bed.

"Mirabeau, is this about what happened on the street with Mrs. Tucker? Everyone could tell she had taken leave of her senses."

Without speaking he reached under the bed and grabbed a sheet of paper, which he handed wordlessly to me. It was a letter from his sister Amelia.

Dearest Mirabeau,

It pains me grievously to convey the terrible news of your darling Rebecca. Last week she contracted a sudden fever. At first we thought little of it and Dr. Hamilton was confident that it would quickly pass. Within two days, though, she became delirious. Her condition steadily worsened until she lapsed into a sleep from which she never awoke. If there is any solace to be taken it is that she suffered little. Dr. Hamilton assured me that once a fever-induced sleep takes hold there is no pain. Rebecca is with her mother now in a land of eternal joy. The sorrow her passing brings is but temporary, as we will someday join her in Heaven. We cannot yet know why; we must accept that this is but part of God's plan.

There was more, but I felt no need to read further. I set the letter on the bed and said, "Mirabeau, I'm so terribly sorry."

"A part of God's plan, she said. Can you believe it? What kind of god plans a child's death?"

What to say? He continued, tears in his eyes. "He already took Tabitha. *That* was His plan, wasn't it? To take Tabitha and force me to Texas? Well, I came and looked what happened. Oh, God, look what happened!"

Sobs overtook him.

"Mirabeau, I—"

"For nothing. *Nothing!* Oh, God, Tabitha! Rebecca! Rebecca!"

"It's not your fault," I said weakly.

"I failed you, Tabitha. I'm so sorry. I failed. And now I'm being punished . . . for killing you."

"Mirabeau, you killed no one. God's will is hard to understand, but you've only tried to please him."

"God's will be damned!"

Long seconds ticked by on the clock in Mrs. Eberly's hallway. I stared at Mirabeau, who lay on his back with an arm drooped over either side of the narrow bed. He gazed at the ceiling. Someone began talking, and at first I couldn't tell who, even though there were only the two of us in the room. It was Mirabeau, in a voice so childlike, so pitiful, that I struggled to withhold tears. "Rebecca . . . Rebecca . . . dear child. Oh, Tabitha, I'm sorry. I tried. I tried. God took you . . . He had a plan. Why? Why you, Tabitha, why you? And why Rebecca? She was just a child. Tabitha . . . why would He take you if He would allow me to fail? Oh, damn this place, this land. Damn this vile land and its people. They're not worthy of you. I shouldn't have come. Oh, God, what have I done?"

"You've done your best, Mirabeau."

He bolted upright in the bed. "No! I didn't! That's what killed Rebecca! I should have done *more*, but *Houston* stopped me! Damn that man. He's been against me from the start. They all have. They'll be sorry now, though, won't they? The country is finished. Houston. He'll ruin it all, every last bit. It's his fault they're dead. He killed Rebecca! He killed Tabitha, not me! This was God's plan, not mine, and Houston stopped it! It's his fault, Edward, *his fault!*"

He slumped back onto the mattress and sobbed piteously. I left the trunk to kneel by his side.

"Mirabeau, I'm so sorry. May I pray?"

He whimpered a bit, which I took as an indication to proceed. I held his hand and prayed aloud. I prayed for Rebecca, I prayed for Tabitha, I prayed for Mirabeau, and I prayed for Texas. Then I even prayed for myself, albeit silently. I squeezed his hand. He stopped sobbing and lay still for several minutes. I thought he had fallen asleep when suddenly he rolled toward me, wiped his face, and said, "I'll make him pay, Edward. I'll make him pay. It's his fault. He killed my family. He killed my dream. He killed Texas. But he won't kill me."

I let go of his hand and stood. In no way did I think that Sam Houston had played a role in the death of Mirabeau's wife and daughter, but it served no purpose to contradict him. "I'm just so sorry," I said again.

"I know. Thank you. Now go. I'll finish packing. I'm going back to Georgia. I'm going back home."

I still wasn't talking much with Master Fontaine but I did have to take care of his horse and my mule. She wasn't really my mule, but after all we'd been through together it seemed like she was. Anyway, I went into the stable behind Master Fontaine's house to comb and brush the animals and there sat Master Fontaine on an overturned pail. His head was down, and it sounded like maybe he was crying, so I wasn't surprised by how red his face was when he looked up at me. "Rebecca's dead," he said.

"Rebecca?"

"Lamar's daughter. You met her when she came to visit from Georgia. You read Bible verses together."

"Oh, dear child." All I could think was how pretty and how bright that little girl was and how nice too. Why would the Good Lord strike her down? Life is such a

mystery, but I tell myself you just got to keep the faith. Because once you stop believing in the goodness of the Lord you might as well roll over and die. I preach that to my people and that's what keeps them going, even the ones that are treated the worst. Even them with the deepest scars on their backs.

"I'm going back to Georgia with him, Jacob. We leave in the morning."

"All right, Master Fontaine, I'll have everything ready. We'll be passing through Mississippi, won't we?" I hoped I might see my mama and sisters.

"Jacob, I'm sorry, but you're staying here. I was going to tell you but didn't get the chance."

I thought he meant he was loaning me out again and I wondered if it would be to Mr. Ward, who ran one of the government departments now. "All right, Master, how long will you be gone."

"Jacob, I have no plans to return."

"What do you mean?"

"After I get Mr. Lamar to his family I'll be going back to mine. I may come back to Texas someday, but maybe not."

A woodpecker pounded in my chest. "What about me?"

"You'll be fine. I've sold you. Mr. Houston has agreed to have you. He wants someone to drive his family around town."

"You sold me?"

"Yes, Jacob, but only for a very good price. And to someone who should treat you well."

"To Mr. Houston. For a good price."

"Yes, to Mr. Houston."

"You don't like Mr. Houston."

He thought on this a spell. "Maybe I don't. But Mrs. Houston is a good woman; I hear she's made Mr. Houston stop drinking."

"And I'll be driving her around."

"That's right."

So there it was. He sold me. The man who brought me to this God-forsaken land was leaving me here to go back home. And another man put some money in his hand and now, according to a law made in hell, I belonged to that man. So Master Fontaine was no different than the rest of them. That's what I thought. It hurt me bad that he wasn't taking me with him. I thought he was like a friend, but how would a man's friend just sell him to another man? Right about then I was wishing I'd gone with Elijah, even if the wolves chewed his bones. Because nobody was gonna buy or sell Elijah no more. And that was more freedom than I had ever known.

35

After packing my things the next morning I went over to Mrs. Eberly's to help Mirabeau. "He's over at the springs," Mrs. Eberly said as she let me into his room.

"The springs?"

"Barton's place. He said he needed some peace and quiet, so he rode on over there. Of course, if Uncle Billy's there he won't get much quiet because, lordy, that man can talk a blue streak."

I thanked Mrs. Eberly and settled in to wait for Mirabeau. When I heard someone entering the building several minutes later I stepped out of the room expecting to see him. But instead it was Sam Houston towering over me in the hallway. "Hello, Edward, is Lamar about?"

I explained about the ride to Barton's. Houston said, "Well, I'm sorry I missed him. I heard about his daughter and I wanted to express my condolences." He must have seen the surprise on my face, for he added, "No one deserves to lose a child, Edward. That's a terrible pain."

"I'm touched that you came by to tell him that."

"I do mean it. As you know, the two of us haven't always been on the best of terms, but as far as I was concerned it was just politics. I think we might be friends if we were in some other line of business."

I laughed. "Mr. Houston, I'm having a hard time imagining you being anything but a politician!"

"Maybe you're right," he replied with a chuckle. "But, the fact is I am deeply sorry for his loss. You'll tell him that, won't you?"

"I will."

"How old was the little girl?"

"Fourteen, I think."

"Fourteen," he repeated sadly. "What a tragedy." He started to say something else but stopped to choke back a small sob.

"Mr. Houston, I'm . . . thank you for coming by."

He sniffled a bit more before smiling at me and saying, "You're supposed to call me Sam."

I didn't know how to say good-bye to Master Fontaine. It was hard to say good-bye to my folks in Mississippi, but at least we all felt free to bawl and hug each other and so on. It wasn't like that now. Master Fontaine seemed to feel the same way. He hemmed and hawed and finally told me he knew how proud I would make him and he said a prayer and then he shook my hand. That was the first time he ever did that. Maybe I should have been flattered, but really I was still hurt that he was leaving me behind. Then he joked about all the fish I'd catch without him giving me chores and that was that. He left.

He had already brought me to Mr. Houston's, so there I was with a new master. Mr. Houston grinned at me and said how glad he was I'd be staying with him now and he hoped I'd come to like it as much as I liked being with Master Fontaine. How about that? No white man had ever told me he hoped I'd be happy about anything before. There wasn't much to do at first because Mrs. Houston wasn't in Austin; she and her children were back in east Texas where Mr. Houston had a nice big house, he said. So he showed me the wagon I'd be driving and there wasn't anything to it. I just hitched up the horse and we rode all over town. I saw some of my friends pulling stumps or chopping kindling and they stared at me going by like I was the king of France. I had fun with that. Once when we were riding by some boys I knew, Mr. Houston said let's play a joke and he took the reins so it looked like he was driving me around. Don't you know their eyes got as big as turkey eggs? When we got home and I was settling the horse he told me something I've never forgotten. He said, "Jacob, I suppose I own you because that's what the law says, but I want you to know you're a man just like me, and I aim to treat you that way. If you think me or anybody else is treating you like less than what a man deserves, then you come tell me." I was surprised and embarrassed, but I told him I would. I never had cause to do it.

36

I accompanied Mirabeau to his Georgia hometown. On the way we talked mostly of trivial things, avoiding anything connected with politics and his time as president. In New Orleans I bought a copy of the *Picayune,* which I intended to share with him. But inside was a long story about Mirabeau's presidency with a headline that said, "Did Lamar Ruin Texas?" I dropped the paper in the gutter.

John and Amelia welcomed us warmly in Georgia. I felt out of place, but they insisted I stay with them until I left for Mississippi. Rebecca had already been buried, so they organized a memorial service that was attended by well over a hundred people. John told me later that the preacher simply repeated most of what he had said at the funeral. I found his sermon comforting, so perhaps it bore repeating.

I stayed two weeks beyond the service. Mirabeau's spirits improved daily, so that by the time I left he was back to himself. I told John I had been concerned that his initial despair seemed strong enough to spur him to self-destruction. He said, "Maybe, Edward, but I've known Mirabeau twenty years now, and I'm confident any danger has passed."

The night before I left I found myself alone with Mirabeau in the Randle family parlor. A fire crackled in the hearth; Mirabeau relaxed in a rocker with a glass of wine. It felt like old times back in Austin. We reminisced about our initial meeting at San Jacinto for a while, and then he said, "Edward, I suppose I've disappointed you."

Back in Austin I would have agreed with him. I had softened, though, and come to see him as a victim of the pain that had driven him to Texas. Nevertheless, his actions toward Mrs. Tucker had been shameful. But I was not blameless.

Why hadn't I picked up on the clues of the illicit relationship sooner? Why was I so quick to disregard Jacob's report of them kissing behind Bullock's? Why didn't I object more strenuously when the truth of the situation could no longer be denied? Why, why, why? For if the Santa Fe Expedition damaged his political career, his infatuation with Mrs. Tucker destroyed it, and mine as well. How different might Texas be today if I had been a wiser and better friend? Instead of dwelling on unhappy events, though, I said, "Far from it, Mirabeau. I admire you as one of the greatest men I have ever known."

He blushed. "Not so great, Edward. I was supposed to build an empire, and I failed."

And he had. Whatever chance there had been of an empire died in the New Mexico desert. So instead of arguing the point, I simply said, "It doesn't matter about the empire. You came to Texas as humble as any man and rose to the presidency. No one can change that."

He mulled that over before draining his wine glass. Then he changed the subject. We passed the rest of the evening speaking only of pleasant things.

A newspaper man once tracked me down and said he heard I was there with Mr. Lamar on his first trip to Waterloo. I said I sure was, and he said that really must have been something to see. I said no, it didn't seem like all that much to brag about. Mr. Lamar shot a buffalo but so did all the other white men. "But it was the biggest buffalo anyone ever saw!" the man said. I told him maybe so, but buffalo are easy to kill because they're the dumbest creatures on God's earth. I also told him what happened after, when the men gathered around to look at it. Somebody cut out the tongue for cooking and another man asked Mr. Lamar if he wanted to cut off some of the meat for his trip back to Houston. He shook his head and said no, that would be too much trouble. Everybody laughed and they left it for the flies and wolves.

The man kept asking questions and wanted to know what Mr. Lamar was really like. I didn't want to say because, even though this was after we got our freedom, I was afraid some white man would read what I said and come looking for me. But the newspaperman swore that he wouldn't write my name in his article. I made him put his hand on the Bible, and once he swore again I told him what I knew.

I said, "You want to know what Mr. Lamar was really like? Well, I'll tell you. He was a hateful man. The Bible says 'Love thine enemy' but Mr. Lamar seemed to hate just about everybody. At least he hated anybody who didn't agree exactly with what he said."

"What do you mean?" the man asked.

I said, "I'd hear him tell Master Fontaine how some congressman was against a law, and he'd say that man would go to hell. How can that be? I don't recall seeing anything in the Bible about somebody going to hell because they voted against a law in Congress."

"What else?"

"He was self-righteous, always spouting off about how God told him this and God told him that. I've heard the Lord in my prayers, but if God really told half the things to Mr. Lamar that he said he did I don't see how He'd have time for anybody else. And bull-headed, I declare! Sometimes I'd hear him and Master Fontaine arguing about something, and Mr. Lamar never would give an inch. What it always came down to was Mr. Lamar saying how he knew he was right and Master Fontaine was wrong so there was no point in talking about it anymore."

"I hear he didn't get along too well with Sam Houston."

"That is a true statement, mister. He hated Sam Houston worst of all. Why, I don't know, because him and Master Fontaine were the two nicest, friendliest white men I knew back then. Then again, Master Fontaine didn't like Sam Houston none too much either. But I knew Sam Houston and I knew Mirabeau Lamar, and I'll take Sam Houston any day."

"What else can you tell me?"

I started to tell about Mrs. Tucker but didn't do it. Even though the newspaperman swore he wouldn't put my name in the paper I was afraid somebody would find out I was talking about a white woman and come after me with a rope. I've known that to happen. So I just told him I supposed that was all I knew, and he took his leave. I never saw his article.

After leaving Mirabeau in Georgia, I never saw him again. He remained a public figure, though, and I kept up with his career in the newspapers. After returning to his Texas plantation he underwent a remarkable transformation from a man devoted to the cause of Texas independence to one equally passionate about annexation to the United States. He came to see the state as a bulwark against the growing abolition movement that he felt threatened the South's prosperity.

When in the late 1840s Texas was again threatened by its old adversary to the south, Mirabeau unsheathed his sword to fight with distinction for the United States in her war with Mexico. When his service had ended, he returned to Texas to represent Nueces and San Patricio counties in the Texas legislature. Subsequently he was named US minister to Nicaragua and Costa Rica. That same year he published a well-received poetry collection, *Verse Memorials*, a copy of which resides on my shelf as I write. The curious reader should know that the poem to Mrs. Tucker did not appear in the book.

Mirabeau even married again, to Henrietta Maffitt, daughter of a Methodist minister. I often wonder if the marriage at last drove the guilt over his first wife's death from his mind. God blessed the union with a daughter. Upon learning of the happy arrival, I prayed that her presence would bring him a measure of peace in his final years.

When I think of him now my mind strays to one of the poems in his book. He called it *On the Death of My Daughter,* and its rhyming verse eloquently portrays the joy and anguish that Rebecca's brief life conveyed. The final stanza, though, seems to stray from that theme.

> *The only boon, O God, I crave,*
> *Is soon, thy face to see;*
> *I long to pass the dull, cold grave,*
> *And wing my way to thee—*
> *To thee, O God, and all my friends*
> *In thine eternal sphere,*
> *Where I may make some poor amends*
> *For all my errors here.*

It is only speculation, of course, but I believe the last line refers to the errors that I witnessed.

He died at his desk in Richmond, pen in hand, blank paper laid out before him. I like to imagine that his mind had just conceived a great poem. There he sat, ready to feel the words flow from hand to page, when a heart attack claimed him at age sixty-one. In my old age I soothe myself with the expectation of hearing him recite the unwritten masterpiece in the afterlife.

A lot of years have passed since then. I feel lucky to have seen it all, lucky for a black man for sure. And my luck held even beyond that. Some years after Master Fontaine left Austin, he came back to set up a church. He asked Mr. Houston if I could be the church sexton, and he said yes. Mr. Houston asked me if I wanted that, and I said I did. He asked if I'd rather he sell me back to Master Fontaine, and I said I supposed I would. I was sad to leave Mr. Houston but felt like the Lord was calling me to be in that church. I worked there right through the war and then some. It is called St. David's, and it's still there.

Once the war was over I took up preaching full time. I'd been preaching a lot before that and had even started doing it on the sly when no white man was around. That was dangerous, but I figured the Lord would watch out for me and He did. Anyway, I started setting up my own churches in Austin. Master Fontaine went back to Mississippi again, and this time I didn't feel bad about staying in Austin because now I was free and got to decide for myself. He became a famous preacher back there, so I suppose he found what he was looking for. I know I did.

My wife asked me once what I remember most about the early days. I had never thought about it before, but the answer came to me right away. "The parade," I told her. Everybody singing and happy and having a party, and before you know it all those men were gone. Everybody said there'd be an even bigger celebration when they got back, but you know that's not what happened. Master Fontaine told me Mr. Lamar believed God had told him to send those men. I don't believe it. Lamar may have thought that, but he was wrong. Only he figured he was right and everybody else was wrong just like he always did. A lot of men died so he'd see that wasn't so. He's dead now too, but I wonder if he ever felt sorry. Well, God forgives him. That's in the Bible.

About the Author

Jeffrey Stuart Kerr is the author of several books, including *Seat of Empire: The Embattled Birth of Austin, Texas*, winner of the Summerfield G. Roberts Award and a True West Best Western Book.